$\mathcal{H}$EIRESS

HEIRESS

Susan May Warren

summerside
PRESS™

Summerside Press™
Minneapolis 55337
www.summersidepress.com
Heiress
© 2011 by Susan May Warren

ISBN 978-1-60936-218-8

Scripture references are from the following source: The Holy
Bible, King James Version (κjv).

All characters are fictional. Any resemblances to actual people
are purely coincidental.

Cover design by Peter Gloege/Lookout Design, Inc.
www.Lookoutdesign.com

Interior design by Müllerhaus Publishing Group
www.mullerhaus.net

*Summerside Press™ is an inspirational publisher offering fresh,
irresistible books to uplift the heart and engage the mind.*

Printed in USA.

For your glory, Lord.

SISTERS

NEW YORK CITY
1896

Chapter 1

With the wrong smile, her sister could destroy Jinx's world.

"Loosen your breath, Esme, and the lacing will go easier." Jinx sat on the ottoman, watching Bette pull the stays of Esme's new corset as her sister hung onto the lacing bar.

The corset, a silk damask with embroidered tea roses, pale pink ribbons along the heart-shaped bustline, and a polished brass busk, had arrived only yesterday in a shipment from Worth's of Paris.

Esme didn't deserve the beautiful undergarment, not with her gigantic twenty-one-inch waist, the way she fought the corsetiere during the fitting, and now held her breath instead of exhaling to lose yet another half-inch.

Jinx, still in her training corset, had long ago shaved her torso down to eighteen inches. She deserved a damask corset, in the new S-shaped style, the way it erected the posture, protruded her hips, and forced her body into the elegant shape of a society woman. But her own corset wouldn't arrive until her mother ordered her debut trousseau, hopefully after the end of this year's society season. After all, she'd already turned seventeen, would be eighteen when the season started next November.

She should have been born first.

Esme closed her eyes, as if in pain. "Mother, I can't breathe. I will faint during the quadrille."

"Perhaps you will be recovered by someone of significance." Their mother Phoebe sat on a gold-foiled Marie Antoinette chair, the red plush velvet like a throne as she perched upon it, surveying her eldest daughter's preparations. "It wouldn't hurt you to be found swooning during a waltz, into the arms of the Astor heir."

Esme frowned. "More likely, I'll find myself discarded in the sitting room, one of the Astors' maids fanning me to consciousness." She released the lacing bar. "Please, Bette, that is enough." Letting her arms fall, Esme cast a look at their mother, who hesitated briefly before assenting with a flick of her hand.

Jinx bit back a huff of disgust. It simply wasn't fair that, despite Esme's almost militant repulsion to securing a husband, men lined up to call on her during her at-home days, appeared after church to walk her home, vied to be seated beside her at dinner parties, and begged her to partner with them in golf and tennis. Most of all, they bedecked her with bouquets of dark red Jacqueminot roses or deep pink Boneselline rosebuds before every ball.

Jinx blamed Esme's exquisite beauty—her straw-blond hair, too-blue eyes, a form that, frankly, needed no corset to enhance—because Esme had interest in none of her suitors, despite their pedigrees. Worse, her sister almost purposely confused the etiquette of dinner, refused the language of the fan to signal suitors, and occasionally wandered out onto some dark balcony to view the stars while the after-dinner German dance was called, leaving her suitors with no one to present their flowers or party gifts to. Jinx had no doubt her sister wouldn't hesitate to attend Caroline Astor's January ball wearing a tea dress, uncorseted, while she pressed her nose into some dime novel.

God had been so unfair.

As if Esme could read Jinx's thoughts, she turned to her mother, even as Bette followed her to fasten her stays. "Really, Mother, are you sure I must attend tonight's ball? I'm exhausted. Tea today at the Wilsons', and last night dinner at the Fishes', and the opera the night before? I am simply wasted to the bone—"

"That's enough, Esme." Phoebe's clipped tone could draw even Esme up straight, silence her. "You are a 'bud,' as you well know, which means you have responsibilities. We have confirmed our attendance to Mrs. Astor's ball, and she expects us. Imagine, for a Price to cut one of Caroline's parties—we might as well move to Philadelphia, or perhaps Baltimore, for all the invitations we'd receive. I am sure Mrs. Astor would see to it that all of society turned their backs on us."

"It's one ball, Mother."

Esme's sardonic attitude about society would be the ruin of them. Jinx wanted to cheer when her mother scoured her with a look that—at least for now—silenced Esme and her whining.

"It's Mrs. Astor's annual ball. The most lavish, elite society event of the season, and the first in Caroline's new chateau. Do you know what social favors your father and I had to promise to acquire this invitation? And, do I have to remind you that this is your second season without a match—not that there weren't plenty of suitors last year. It's time you married. I'll not tolerate one more word of complaint from you. Bette, help her into her knickers."

The former chambermaid had turned into a first-class lady's maid. She was quiet, efficient, and discreet.

Jinx smoothed her simple skirt, her tucked shirtwaist with the high neck and mutton-chop sleeves, and tried not to watch as Bette attached the stocking suspenders to Esme's corset then assisted her sister into her silk and lace knickers.

Indeed, if her sister didn't accept an offer of marriage soon, they'd have to travel overseas to find a mate—some homely duke or a widowed baron. Then Jinx's debutante year would be further delayed. If only her father weren't so old-fashioned, determined to marry off his eldest daughter before presenting his second daughter into society.

"You will wear the white tulle tonight," Phoebe said. Bette had already retrieved the dress from the cedar closset, bound in muslin and stuffed to retain its shape. The perfume of the lavender sachets used to preserve it scented the chamber, along with the rose-scented lotions and talc powder from Esme's bath and preparations. "You have yet to wear this costume, and you need a dress never before seen for this evening." Phoebe glanced at Jinx, a smile tweaking her lips before she dismissed it. "I believe it may be a special one, for many reasons."

Esme met Jinx's eyes in the mirror. Jinx raised a shoulder, but her mother's words, the way she glanced down at her hand then worried her sapphire wedding ring, sparked hope.

Perhaps her parents had already arranged a match for Esme. Perhaps, by this time next year, Jinx would have her own satin gown and be bedazzled with diamonds from head to toe. Maybe even a cadre of society's bachelors gifting her with bouquets, requesting appointments on her dance card. Vying for her hand in marriage.

Please, Esme, cooperate.

Esme settled herself on an ottoman as Bette helped her into her ivory satin slippers, tying the bows. Then she stepped into her new crinoline, something even the newest buds had discarded from their trousseau, according to the gossip at Mrs. Graham's Seminary for Young Ladies. But Phoebe Price wasn't taking any chances on society's disdain.

Bette tied the tapes then went to retrieve the gown.

Phoebe rose, graceful despite her portly curves. "I need to attend to my own toilette. I will meet you in the front hall for our carriage. Do not keep me waiting."

"I feel as if I am already ill," Esme said as Bette attended to the dress. "I heard that Mrs. Astor is serving duck croquettes. It's bad enough that I must taste everything, but to know its origin! I swear I cannot eat another serving of creamed oysters and terrapin or I will lose my supper into one of Mrs. Astor's potted ferns. Not that I have any room for food." Her hands brushed over her corseted stomach. "Still, I have no doubt that tomorrow I will only be able to survive tea and toast."

Jinx couldn't hold herself back. "Please be on your best behavior, Esme. The season is at its height and you have the power to usher us into the inner chambers of society, if you choose."

Esme seemed not to hear her as Bette gathered up the tulle, opened the bodice, and helped her dive into the finery. Oh, to have such a lovely dress, the way the gold thread shimmered under the bright gas-lit chandelier in Esme's boudoir. Esme stood like a statue as Bette secured her dress. It draped over her, fitted to her body, cascading off the shoulders with seemingly only pearled straps to secure it. A teardrop trio of pearls fell from the apex of the tulle bodice, stitched with white glass beads and paillettes to make it shimmer. A white satin band secured her waist, then the garment fell into trained ruffles at the hem, fanning out behind her.

The dress and Esme's demi-parure of jewels for tonight's ball probably cost as much as Father's new yacht.

"I love that dress," Jinx said, mostly to herself.

Esme scowled into the full-length mirror, gilded at the edges. "I hate tulle. It scratches my skin, and I believe I must be allergic to it."

The mirror captured the immense room—the red velvet divan and gold-edged chairs, the polished oak dressing tables, Esme's writing desk, and beyond that, the windows that overlooked the city.

When the Price family built their mansion on Fifth Avenue, only blocks from the Vanderbilt's 660 Fifth Avenue palace, Esme had asked for the room with a view of Central Park. Never mind the walnut wainscoting, the green, floral damask wallpaper, the seventeenth-century tapestries, or the Marie Antoinette gilded canopied bed built on a platform like a throne. August Price hadn't spared a penny on his eldest daughter.

Jinx's room, however, overlooked the private garden. She would have enjoyed seeing the street instead, with its parade of traffic—the landaus, motorbuses, delivery wagons, automobiles, and bicycles. She loved watching the mounted policemen directing in the middle of the street, the drivers attired in livery colors and seated on the high boxes. The clanging trolley bells, shouts from the cabmen, clatter of horses' hooves on the cobblestone, the growl of motorcars, and the shriek of railways made the city sound alive.

And, at night, sometimes Jinx retired with her mother in Phoebe's third-story room, watching the stars sparkle over the park, a thousand diamonds almost within her grasp.

As soon as Esme was married, Jinx planned on moving into her boudoir.

"I hope the ball doesn't last all night. I'm in the middle of Jules Verne's *Around the World in Eighty Days,* although journalist Nellie Bly's true-life account is vastly more exciting," Esme said as Bette straightened the dress on her frame.

"You can't be serious. You have an invitation to the most exclusive ball of the season, and you are pining for a book?" Jinx turned away, staring at the lacing of frost creeping up the sill. Despite the central heating and the fire in Esme's marble fireplace, the winter crept through the windowpane, chilling the room. By the end of winter, the frost could choke out the view entirely, except for a breath blown into the middle. "You shouldn't spend so much time reading. You know it's simply fantasy. I don't know why Father allows it."

"He fancies that I might be like him, a newspaper man. That's why he allows me to visit him at his offices. He knows I like the smell of the ink, the hum of the presses, the clicking of the typewriters. I would love to be a journalist like Nellie Bly, to see the world, to research asylums and sweatshops. To see my name in print on the front page of Father's *Chronicle.*"

Jinx rounded on her. "Are you mad? You are not Nellie Bly. She is a working woman! You are a debutante, destined to marry William Astor, or perhaps a Fish, a Morgan, or a Rothschild. What a shame society doesn't yet have a Vanderbilt within marrying age. But you will have a fashionable seaside estate in Newport, a home on Fifth Avenue, a life in the social court. You will live a life of prominence and influence. A life of blessing."

Esme's mouth opened.

Jinx stood and walked to the dressing table. "Don't appear so offended, it doesn't become you." She ran her fingers over her sister's jewels—a dog collar strung with a cascade of diamonds and pearls on silken threads that would cover Esme's décolletage, a cluster of diamond and pearl earrings, and a filigreed rosebud tiara, encrusted with diamonds, pearls, and shimmering emeralds.

Drawing in a breath, Jinx schooled her voice. "Nellie Bly is a disgrace. She travels unchaperoned around the world, often lunches with men, and pretends to be insane to secure a berth in a psychiatric hospital. Some might call that living a life of deceit. She will marry poorly, if at all, and die without acknowledgment."

"She's made her own way. And spoken the truth. Perhaps she doesn't need to marry."

Jinx met Esme's blue eyes in the mirror, so naive for all her bookish ways, her fluency in French and German, her ability to dance the quadrille. "Father would never let you write for the newspaper."

Esme stiffened as Bette touched up her hair. The maid had parted Esme's hair in the center, heated the front into the shape of water-waves, padded the rest of it with matching blond rats, then swept the loose tresses up into tight curls atop her head, secured finally with diamond-encrusted barrettes.

Jinx had already required her maid, Amelia, to begin experimenting with her own—sadly unremarkable—dark hair, and collecting and washing the loose strands that would create her hair rats.

"Perhaps he doesn't have to know," Esme said quietly.

Jinx froze. "What are you talking about?"

Esme lifted her creamy shoulder, mischief flashing through her eyes. She blinked it away. "I am simply suggesting that there are other ways for a woman to have her voice heard."

"The way to be heard is to influence your husband, give him a voice in society," Jinx said. Oh, she knew it. Her sister had always been out of hand, too vocal. Now she'd even begun to believe the things she read in *Godey's Lady's Book*.

"For now. But soon, perhaps, we'll have a real voice. One in politics and the workplace."

Jinx walked to Esme's desk, picked up a copy of the magazine, and opened to where a piece of writing paper marked the Employment for Women section. She could have guessed. "I thought mother cancelled our subscription."

"I'm twenty years old, with my own allowance. I ordered it myself."

Jinx closed the magazine, tempted to throw it in the trash receptacle. It only filled her sister with rebellious, untoward thinking. Someday she would be forced to reveal to their parents where Esme hid her stash of dime novels, everything from *Maleaska, the Indian Wife of the White Hunter* to a stack of DeWitt's Ten Cent Romances. It was time her sister started behaving as her status demanded.

Jinx easily found her mother's tone. "You have fooled yourself into the world of your dime novels, where women decide their own futures, choose their own husbands, and pursue careers. Continue this, and you will disgrace us, cause us to be ostracized from society, and ruin any chance of either of us marrying someone with the proper name."

"I don't think that's fair. I don't want to marry. I'm a journalist—"

Jinx rounded on her. "You're the *daughter* of a journalist, born to wed, not become some stringer, rooting around dark alleys for a story. You have been trained to be a wife, to run a household, to keep your husband's name in the conversation of good society. Father and Mother are—*we* are—expecting you to make a match this season, to marry well. To usher the Price family into society's elite, to behave in a manner befitting the heiress of the Price family." She drew a breath, cut her voice low, glanced at Bette. It mattered not that the servants were handpicked for their discretion. Of their thirty-five house staff, not everyone could be trusted.

"We must marry up if we want to continue our ascent in society. Father has bought us that opportunity, and you owe it to him to honor his wishes. If Father—or any eligible men—caught you writing something, even anonymously…" She closed her eyes, her frustration huffing out of her. "I should have been the firstborn."

Yes. Then Esme could have done as she wished, the requirements of the firstborn—acquiring a man with a pedigree—happily borne on Jinx's shoulders. She opened her eyes, held up her hand, as Esme made to speak. "It doesn't matter. I suspect Mother has already found you a match."

Esme drew in a breath then rose from her chair. She stared at herself in the mirror, submitting to Bette's adornment of the dog collar, the earrings. Finally, she bowed her head for the tiara. Certainly she appeared regal as the jewels captured the light. A Price, waiting to be won.

Esme turned to Jinx, her blue eyes cool, glittering. "It doesn't matter. I will not submit to their arrangements and marry for the sake of society, for the sake of privileged invitations to teas filled with gossip and insufferable dinners where I must choose my fork correctly or be cut from a Vanderbilt matinee. Or balls where the incorrect flutter of my fan condemns me to a dance, or even more. I loathe this life and all it requires, and *if* I marry, it will be for love."

"Love? Please. How will you tell the difference? You're a Price, not some scullery maid. You will never know whether you are loved for your money, or your beautiful mind."

The words seemed to slither out, and Jinx tasted in them the poison she intended.

Indeed, Esme flinched, as if afflicted. "I will know because my husband will respect me, hear my mind, allow my freedom." Her words emerged stiff, with an edge.

Even as Esme said it, her maid had begun to sheath her fingers into her kid gloves, ordered a size smaller so as to curve the hand into a delicate pose. Jinx had tried on the gloves and lost the feeling in her fingers within an hour.

Jinx picked up Esme's vellum dance card and pencil. She handed it to Bette, who slid it onto Esme's gloved wrist. "Power, wealth, prestige—that's what gives us freedom. You're blind not to see *that*," Jinx snapped.

"That is prison. And you are blind not to see that." Esme allowed Bette to drape upon her shoulders her silk brocade evening cape, trimmed in mink. Her lady's maid tied it in front then moved behind her to valet her charge downstairs.

Esme stood for a moment, towering over Jinx. "And you weren't born first, I was. You must wait until I marry."

"Only until you are shipped off to Europe and married to some titled, decrepit baron in need of an heir and a spare. Don't forget your fan."

Esme's face knotted and she scooped up the fan from her dressing table. She found her retort, however, by the time she reached the door. She turned, smiled, her voice sweet. "If I tarry in marriage, perhaps father will delay your debut yet another year. Sadly, by then, Mrs. Astor will most likely be too senile to host her annual soirees. Shame. Have a lovely evening."

Jinx wanted to throw one of Esme's dime novels at her, or perhaps the array of gifts on her bureau—fans and cigarette cases and even a pearl-inlaid brooch, received from too many adoring suitors who hadn't a clue they were courting a budding suffragette.

But her throat tightened, her chest burning. Esme just might refuse a match. Turn down the hand of a blue-blood. Then she'd see her name in print, all right, right on the front page of *Town Topics,* or on Page Six of their father's *New York Chronicle.*

Jinx might as well begin packing for their trip abroad to escape the scandal.

She walked to the window, watching as Esme and her mother exited the front doors of their home, across the carpet rolled out by the footmen, liveried for the evening in eighteenth-century style with knee breeches, silk stockings, and shirts, their royal blue waistcoats and tailcoats rich with golden embroidery.

Her mother knew how to make a Price entrance. Tonight, she'd even required the footmen to powder their hair.

The group waddled out to the street where first her mother, then Esme, and finally their father, regal in his top hat, his ermine-trimmed greatcoat, white silk scarf, and gloves, disappeared into the closed carriage, their lady's maids and Father's valet following in the carriage behind them to attend them at the ball.

Across the street, electric lights from Central Park twinkled through the trees, winking. Snow began to drift from the sky, like flakes in a globe, bedazzling the wonderland of New York.

Jinx pressed her palm to the window, letting the chill seep into her skin. When she pulled it away, her handprint remained.

She watched it fade slowly into the night.

*****

Esme might be playing a game, but she intended to play by her own rules.

She was like Nellie Bly, undercover journalist.

She stood at the edge of the ballroom, filing away every detail. For tonight's article, she'd start with overstuffed and snobby Mrs. Astor greeting her four hundred ball guests, affecting the air of a royal in her black velvet dress with lace appliqués and tulle, bedazzled in a diamond tiara and an armada of diamonds. Then she'd catalog the ostentatious bevy of flowers and decorations, from the holly and ivy dripping from the standing chandeliers, the snowballs of white carnations eclipsing the candelabras, to the thirty-six red satin stockings stretched across the white marble fireplace, filled with toys and bonbons. A giant bough of mistletoe centered on the balcony, tempting would-be dancers while the orchestra warmed up for the after-dinner cotillion.

Esme wouldn't soon forget the buffet dinner, either, the way her stomach now gurgled. She tasted the sweetbread climbing back up her throat, although it might not have made it all the way down to begin with, what with the competition with the consommé, the pâté de foie gras, and the bonbons. She pressed her hand against her stomach, although it would hardly move, given the way Bette had strapped her into her corset.

She had even managed a glimpse of the fellow dancers, from J. J. Astor Jr., to Mr. and Mrs. F. W. Vanderbilt, to Mr. and Mrs. Stuyvesant Fish, names among names in society.

She'd catch it all, just like Nellie Bly, in a tell-all article, betraying the dalliances and follies of society.

She hoped Oliver caught their pictures. She spied him, assisting Joseph Byron and his son, Percy, as they posed society's finest, capturing their images for *Town Topics* and their own prideful posterity. Oliver had taken her picture at her debut ball, and perhaps the truth had hit her at that moment, when she'd seen herself reflected upside down.

She didn't fit in this world.

But she wasn't sure, exactly, where else she might belong, who indeed she was supposed to be.

She heard Jinx's voice, an echo chasing her to the party. *Behave in a manner befitting the heiress of the Price family.* What, exactly, might that be? She certainly didn't feel like an heiress.

And, if Mrs. Astor's high society knew who penned the articles featured on her father's Page Six, highlighting their escapades, they wouldn't treat her like one either. They would feel betrayed and stamp her an interloper.

"There you are, Esme. Were you hiding from me?" Her mother appeared, her skin flushed, the sour hint of wine upon her breath.

"Of course not, Mother. I'm simply blistering. And tired. And, like I said, I believe I am allergic to tulle. Please, must we remain?" After all, she'd already seen enough to detail this night in her anonymous submission to her father's paper.

"Bite your tongue. We are staying until Caroline Astor turns out breakfast." Phoebe lowered herself to the settee beside her, her gown less cumbersome than Esme's, a simple yellow satin edged in French lace with diamonds stitched into the bodice.

Across the two-story ballroom, in an alcove opening off the second story, the musicians in the gallery began to warm up for their opening number. They played under the view of the gods and goddesses sculpted into the coved ceiling. Guests from all corners of the house returned to the dance floor.

"Truly, I feel unwell. My stomach is churning. Every time I dance, it threatens to betray me. I must escape this corset." She wasn't *exactly* lying. And the longer they stayed, the more her mother's words about the night burned into her thoughts. *I believe it may be a special one, for many reasons.*

She needed to leave before her parents decided that tonight would be the night to sell her into marriage. She'd been playing the debutante's game in order to secret herself into this world, uncover the excesses, the scandals. She wanted to reveal to the starving world stories about Christmas cards encrusted with diamonds, dogs eating from silver bowls, and the millions of diamonds on Mrs. Astor's tiara, all while her servants netted less than five hundred dollars a year.

Someday, she might reveal her name. And then she'd be among the ranks of Jacob Riis, chronicler of the slums and tenements, and Nellie Bly, crusader for women. She'd be her father's star reporter. Be commended by the president of the United States, have supper at the White House. Prove to the world that, although she'd been born into wealth, she hadn't been born without a soul.

"Your upset stomach is simply nerves. I noticed you were inviting with your fan the attention of a suitor. To whom were you directing your invitation?" Her mother smiled, anticipation in her eyes.

"I was using the fan to cool myself, Mother, nothing more."

Phoebe's countenance fell. "That is not its purpose—you should know better." She rearranged the smile on her face. "Did you see Harry Lehr dance with Elizabeth Drexel Dahlgren? She seems quite smitten with him."

"He only wants her money."

"Esme! Sometimes your tongue!"

"She's a widow with a fortune. And he's a flirt."

"He's the best social coordinator in the city. He plans all Mrs. Astor's and Mrs. Vanderbilt's parties. Please, stop talking."

Laughter trickled in from doors open to the grand entrance off the ballroom, and with it the crisp allure of fresh air. Esme leaned into it, closed her eyes. With over four hundred dancers packed into Mrs. Astor's ballroom, the place swam with the odors and humidity of exertion. That and...oh, never again, sweetbreads.

"Let me see your dance card."

Esme handed it to her and Phoebe perused it. "Yes, good. I am glad to see Foster Worth's name for the waltz, and the lancer. Very good. But no one for the Mazurka?"

"The speed upsets my stomach. Why must they schedule that dance first?"

"You mean to tell me that you turned down a partner's request?"

"I will sit it out. It will not be a snub."

"Esme, the sooner you are married and your rebellious ways corralled, the better."

No, the sooner she figured out how to turn her anonymous articles unwittingly published by her father into a full-time job, just like Nellie Bly, the better.

Her father had no idea that by publishing her anonymous social commentary, he had begun to set her free. Yes, she still had to rely on Oliver to submit her opinions of society high life along with his photographs of their soirées. Sometimes, he'd also described for her the photographs he captured as he patrolled the streets looking for crime. His heartbreaking shots of orphans sleeping under doorsteps or the illegal five-cent beds in the tenement house or the pictorials of the misery of life in Hell's Kitchen moved her so that she'd taken his impressions, put words and opinions to them, then he'd submitted those pieces with his photographs.

They'd even made money. Stringers, he called the two of them.

The paper had published those shots, those opinions, and named her byline simply...Anonymous Witness.

Indeed, she might never get married. Simply travel the world, writing stories about foreign places. Europe. China. The American West.

And, someday soon, no longer anonymous.

Once her father discovered her pen, the articles she'd published, he would welcome her into his world with her own editor's desk. She would wrest herself out of her corset stays and into a life with her own byline. Maybe someday she might even run the paper.

"At least you will dance two with Foster," her mother was saying, still perusing Esme's dance card.

"Only because he is an old friend of the family, Mother. I have no interest in him."

"He is the son of Frederic Worth, and he's just returned from Europe. Of all the bachelors in this season, Foster is the most eligible. He would be a suitable match and you would be fortunate to receive a proposal from him."

"I am not going to accept a proposal from anyone, Mother, especially not Foster. Yes, he's handsome, in a way that good breeding begets, with his dark hair slicked back, his broad shoulders. But he has clammy hands, and there is something rather…unsettling about the way he looks at me, as if I might be something edible. And, worse, he has cold eyes. I mentioned to him once the plight of the newsies—the orphans sleeping below the steps of Father's paper, pandering the daily for a nickel, and he actually said, 'Where do you expect them to live?' Like that kind of life might be acceptable."

"For their class of people, it is to be expected."

Esme's mouth opened. Closed. "Have you not read Jacob Riis's book? The plight of the poor? He asks, 'How shall the love of God be understood by those who have been nurtured in sight only of the greed of man?' We need to take care of the poor—"

"Henry Riis is not appropriate reading for someone of your stature."

"Mother, it is our Christian duty to care for the underprivileged— it's not just the *noblesse oblige*, Jesus commands it. Did you hear nothing of D. L. Moody's speech last year?"

"I did. He said to obey your parents. Which is to be married. Have a family."

"I love children, but Mother, I have other plans. I want a career, something besides hosting parties and raising children and running my husband's household. That's Jinx's ambition, not mine."

Phoebe stared at her, a spark of warning in her eyes that should have silenced Esme. A year ago, before she had heard Mr. Moody speak, before she'd heard him say, "We can stand affliction better than we can prosperity, for in prosperity we forget God," it would have.

She had forgotten God, until that night when she'd stared at her upsidedown figure reflected in Oliver's lens. Had forgotten that she had a duty to love justice and be merciful. That day of her debutante ball, a light turned on in her head as bright as Oliver's flash, and she realized that she could use her debutante season to be like Nellie, go undercover, tell the truth.

Perhaps shame would wake up high society.

"A career? You will stop that thinking immediately. I don't know where you get it from."

"I get it from Father."

"Hardly. You get it from those books you bring home."

"Father respects my ideas."

"Your father laughs at your ideas." Her mother turned to her, her dark eyes sharp. "He puts up with your whimsy because you have always been his favorite. But mind my words, Esme, he wants you matched well. It wouldn't hurt your father's resources to have you married to a shipping magnate, one who owns department stores around the world. Imagine the advertising they would buy. Foster Worth has shown an interest in you, and you will reciprocate."

"He could have anyone, Mother. Didn't you hear the other buds in the dressing room tonight? His name was on everyone's lips, including Carrie Astor's. He doesn't want the girl who beat him in tennis when she was twelve."

"I daresay he let you win." Her mother reached out, took Esme's hand. "The Worth boys have always had a special eye out for my daughters. I'm just thankful that one of them turned out with marriageable qualities. With all Bennett's womanizing in Europe, Mamie needs her eldest to restore the family name, pick up the reins during her husband's decline. Yes, you will be kind to Foster Worth. It's time to let him win." She squeezed her hand. "There's your father."

Esme glanced at her, but Phoebe had already risen, taken August Price's hand. In public, they appeared the adoring couple.

He placed a kiss on her mother's cheek. What it cost him, he didn't betray. He nodded to Phoebe, and then Phoebe glanced at Esme, a smile tugging at her mouth.

August pressed his wife's hand to his arm as the music began for the Mazurka. Debutantes took the floor on the arm of their partners, began the triple-meter polka dance to a Chopin piece.

Heat rose to Esme's neck. Especially when her mother caught her eye from the dance floor, her words raking up to fill her mind. *I believe it may be a special one, for many reasons.*

Oh, Mother, you didn't… Her stomach roiled, now coating her throat.

She pressed herself to her feet, wove through the crowd, and exited the ballroom. Already the air seemed lighter, and she crossed the corridor toward the front doors.

No, she shouldn't be unchaperoned, but perhaps a few moments of brisk air would settle her stomach, keep her from pitching to the parquet floor during the waltz.

She could simply refuse the marriage request, right? She didn't have to marry…

She wasn't really a debutante. No.

The footman at the door must have read her mind, for he opened the massive gilded bronze-and-glass doors. "Miss, may I get your cloak?"

She shook her head, not slowing her pace until she reached the front step.

The brisk January air swept her breath from her lungs, prickled her bare arms, shoulders. But she closed her eyes, losing herself to the cool lick of fresh air. Along Fifth Avenue, the chateaus lit up the street, turning the soft-falling snow ablaze, puddling light into snowdrifts along the cobbled, almost magical street. Landaus and motorcars lined up to retrieve the guests at their leisure, yet across the street, a man bundled in rags chipped ice from the sidewalk with a spade. She wrapped her hands around her upper arms as a chill stole through her.

"Esme?" Her name emerged on whispered sibilants and she glanced up.

Oliver. He must have seen her exit the house. He stood away from her, tall, broad-shouldered in the glow of the house lights, the snow like diamonds on his coal-black hair, catching in his long, almost mesmerizing eyelashes. His shaven whiskers had begun to scuff his chin. He shucked off his tailcoat. "What are you doing out here?"

She glanced at the footmen nearby, some of them smoking, others stamping their feet to keep warm. Others had sought refuge inside the carriage room, to the back, where most of the livery waited. Still, no one should see her talking so freely to her former footman, the butler's son.

Even if they had grown up together.

Even if he now worked for Joseph Byron, society photographer.

Even if her father had arranged for his job.

Especially because Oliver was her partner in crime.

"I don't feel well. My head hurts, and my stomach is woozy."

"Let me take you home." He draped his jacket around her shoulders. His smell—husky, yet bearing an exotic sweetness, probably from the chemicals he used for his plate development—lifted, and she pulled the warmth around her.

"I—I can't. Mother would be furious."

He tightened his mouth, as if biting back something more.

"Actually, I—I think my mother is trying to betroth me to someone."

Oliver stared at her, his face stony. For some reason she searched his eyes, not sure what she might be hoping. He looked away, blew out a long breath. "I see."

"What does that mean?"

"It means I should have expected that. Congratulations."

"You know that turning him down would mean scandal for my family."

"When has scandal stopped you?"

Her mouth opened.

"I'm sorry. I shouldn't have said that. But…" He stared at her, hard. "Do you love him?"

"I don't even know him, really. We were childhood acquaintances."

"*We* were childhood acquaintances, and you're not marrying me."

She sucked in a breath. "That's different."

"Is it, Esme?"

He looked away, and she knew him well enough to see hurt on his face. Why… "What are you getting at, Oliver?"

A muscle tensed in his jaw. "You can't have both worlds, Esme. Choose one."

She flinched. "Maybe the air out here isn't as fresh as I thought."

"You stay, I'll go."

"No." But she winced at the need in her tone as she said it. "I—I don't want to stand alone."

He considered her a moment. "I'm sorry, Esme. But I never thought this was a game to you. Perhaps that was my mistake."

She looked down, at the snow soft upon her gown. "Do you ever dream of leaving New York? Of going out West or traveling the world?"

He let her words dissolve in the frosty air before he answered. "I used to. I wondered what it might be like to travel back to Ireland, the home of my mother. And yes, I read the dime novels you smuggled me. I would like to see Oklahoma, become a cowboy, maybe."

She pulled his jacket around her tighter. "I want to go to Montana."

"You would make a fabulous Annie Oakley."

She glanced at him, trying to hide her smile. "Did you deliver this week's article?"

He didn't look at her, matched her lowered volume. "Yes. Yesterday, to the op-ed desk when I turned in my photos."

"Maybe it'll go into tomorrow's paper."

He sighed. "Have you considered what might happen if you get caught?" He hazarded her a look, and the concern in it tugged at her.

"Maybe—maybe I should tell him. Maybe he should know that his daughter is—"

"Anonymous Witness."

"Just like him. A journalist."

"Indeed." His eyes twinkled, and for the first time this night she saw his dimple emerge. She loved that little indentation that so matched the sparkle, the way Oliver looked at her.

A ripple of heat went through her.

"Miss Price, what are you doing out here in the cold?"

She stiffened, and she watched as Oliver turned away, becoming invisible as Foster Worth stepped out onto the stoop. Too many years as the Prices' footman, perhaps.

Foster peered down at her, without a smile, seemingly irritated. "I was looking for you for our waltz, but you had disappeared."

"Did it begin?"

"I'm afraid it is over." Foster reached out, slid Oliver's coat from her shoulders. Without looking at him, Foster handed the coat back to Oliver. Like he might be a coat rack.

Foster slipped off his own jacket, draped it upon her. Into her settled the odor of his many dances, the cigar smoke from the after-dinner gathering with the men in the library. And a line of sweat from his collar.

"I'm sorry," she managed without shivering, "I needed some fresh air."

Foster stuck out his elbow, and she took it, glancing at Oliver. He didn't meet her eyes.

Foster escorted her inside, the humidity of the hallway dense against her skin. "I need to talk to you."

From the ballroom, the lively romp of Tchaikovsky suggested she'd also missed her polka with Colin Rutherford.

Oh, Mother would be incensed. Perhaps Jinx had been correct— she should have been born first. Then Mother would have her debutante, her escort into high society. Jinx could speak French with a Belgian count, dance the quadrille or the Muzant with a German duke, and counsel an English butler on correct table-setting placement. She could probably even make Foster Worth crack a smile with her witty banter.

And Esme? She'd be free to write for her father. He'd always said that he expected great things from her.

Any forthcoming engagement was all her mother's doing, Esme knew it in her bones. She'd simply explain—

"Let's go in the drawing room." Foster had her by the elbow, directing her toward Mrs. Astor's white-paneled salon, with the gilded boiseries and mirrored doors. As they entered, she stifled the urge to hide amidst the clutter of bowers of roses and towering apple blossoms in gold-etched pots, the Victorian staging of busts of Shakespeare and Wagner, stuffed birds in glass domes, Louis XIV-style gilded divans and chairs. But how could she escape the eyes of the immense portrait of Mrs. Astor, the mistress of the manor, peering down on her?

Suddenly, she felt it, everything Jinx had been trying to tell her. The dictum of society and its import to their future. From the next room, the music ended, and a lancer began. Everyone turning in step, schooled for their role in society.

Foster escorted her to an ottoman. She sat, her heart lodged in her throat.

Oh. Wait…

He took her hand as her brain scurried to keep up.

He lowered himself onto one knee. She stared at her curved hand in his, unable to meet his eyes, tasting her heartbeat.

"Esme, your parents have agreed to allow me to ask for your hand in marriage. I believe we would make a winning match. I know we haven't yet had the opportunity to deepen our friendship since our youth, but I am confident that in time we will come to care deeply for each other."

She glanced up at him, caught his eye. He gave her a quick smile. "Will you do me the honor of becoming my wife?"

Perhaps he could be labeled handsome. Brown wavy hair, a stern brow, deep gray eyes, a confidence about him that said he would work hard, provide. Perhaps even remain faithful.

She hadn't expected the rush of emotions, the heat in her chest, her eyes. Hadn't expected the unfamiliar thrill that cascaded through her. Wife. Someone's wife.

She looked up at him, words netted in her chest.

She saw herself in a moment, hearing Foster's proposal then turning him down to the din of Chopin.

Or not. What if she said yes? What if she became Mrs. Foster Worth, the world at her fingertips?

Couldn't she change it that way also?

Over Foster's shoulder, she spied Oliver, entering the room to gather his equipment. Invisible. Anonymous.

Oliver looked up then and, for a blinding moment, met her eyes. *You would make a fabulous Annie Oakley.*

"Esme?" Foster said.

She drew a breath. No. She could say it. No. Simply explain to him that she wasn't ready, that she wanted more out of life, that she wanted a man who loved her, who believed in—

"Yes."

She looked over at the voice. Her father stepped into the room, regal in his coattails, cigarette smoke curling over his head, a smile on his face as if he'd just scooped Pulitzer. He settled his hand on her bare, cold shoulder, hot, heavy. "Of course, her answer is yes."

Foster slipped a ring on her numb, gloved finger as Oliver shouldered his tripod and walked from the room.

Chapter 2

"What are you doing still in bed? You're engaged! You should be dressed and out shopping, or planning a tea to host your engagement. Get up!" Jinx had opened the doors to Esme's chamber and stood in the soft press of darkness, the only light in the room sliding out from the edges of the drawn velvet drapes.

Esme lay in her massive bed, huddled in the middle. She snatched the blanket over her head as Jinx flung open the curtains. Light spilled into the room, across Esme's form.

"Go away, Jinx."

"No. It's a beautiful day—the snow is like a blanket of diamonds on Central Park. We should go ice skating." Indeed, the fresh-fallen snow enchanted the park, trees glistening with icy jewels, horses' breath caught in the air like a cloud. They would go skating and she'd hear the gossip from others, instead of her mother, taste the envy in their voices, and revel in the glow of conquest.

Her sister would marry Foster Worth. Jinx had seen him from afar since his return from England, at church twice, and at the onset of the social season at the New York Horse Show. Handsome, with his dark wavy hair, regal nose, high cheekbones, assessing eyes. Then, his name began to curl off debutantes' lips more often than "prism"—the word intoned for the correct placement of one's lips into a perfect pucker. Foster Worth. He'd graduated from West Point, and for the last two years had run his father's shipping business in London. He'd probably even been to court. She'd heard that he had impeccable manners.

"I don't want to go skating. In fact, I'm never leaving my bed."

"Did he kiss you?" Jinx sat on the edge of the bed. "Let me see the ring."

"It's on the bureau. Next to my gloves. And no, he didn't kiss me."

"Did you want him to?"

"I'd rather kiss Mother's pet chow. No, of course not. I hardly know the man."

"He's going to be your husband."

"Go away."

Jinx found the ring, held it up to the light. Platinum, with a center-cut diamond and a floral motif of diamonds surrounding it, it caught the morning sun, turned the ceiling to kaleidoscope. "It's gorgeous. Why aren't you wearing it?"

"It's too loose. It'll fall off me, then how will I give it back?"

"That's not funny."

Jinx glanced at Esme then slipped it on her own finger. It fit her perfectly, but then again, she hadn't been born with elegant piano fingers like Esme.

"Tell me how he proposed. Was it terribly romantic?"

Esme still hadn't emerged from the covers. "No. And don't get attached, because really, I'm not marrying him."

Jinx stilled. Something in Esme's voice—she couldn't be serious. "What?"

Esme finally flung the covers off, sat up. Her hair hung in ratted tangles around her head, still in the form of her party coif. "I'm not marrying him, and I would have told him that if Father had given me a chance to answer."

Jinx stared at her. "Have you lost your mind? Of course you are marrying him. He's Foster Worth. He's proposed. Your life is set—you will marry him, he will build you a glorious Fifth Avenue chateau, a home in Newport, and you will enter society already included on the register."

Esme pressed her hands to her face. "No, my life is over. Foster Worth will want a wife who births out an heir then plans his parties and runs his household." She looked at Jinx, shaking her head. "I don't want that life. Besides, I don't love him."

"You'll grow to love him. No marriage is perfect, but you adapt, and you accept. He'll be a wonderful husband."

"He has sweaty, tight hands." Esme slid out of bed, reached for her robe. "We danced afterwards and I wanted to bathe."

"You're overreacting." Jinx kept her voice schooled, just in case Esme might be serious. Not marry Foster Worth? Jinx had no illusions about love—look at her parents' marriage. But such a union would mean a life of worth, of success. Happiness.

If Esme returned his ring, they would all have to board a steamer and hope they could find some bankrupt count in Europe who hadn't heard of the family's social disgrace.

"Esme, with time, I am sure that Foster would allow you to write in your journals, perhaps pen something for a ladies' paper—"

A knock came at the door. Bette stood with Esme's breakfast tray.

Esme waved her in as she sat at her table. Bette set down the tray, and Esme took the newspaper while Bette poured the tea.

She opened to the last page, and a smile spread over her face. "Indeed."

"What are you reading?"

"A piece by A.W.—Anonymous Witness. She wrote an opinion piece about the state of tenement buildings in Hell's Kitchen." She put the paper down. "Ten families live in a room this size. Their children live without fresh air, fresh water."

"They're immigrants. It's what they can afford."

"And some landlords charge five cents per bed per night. These houses are a cesspool for tuberculosis and diphtheria. For crime."

"She?"

Esme frowned at her.

Jinx pulled out a chair. "You said 'she.'"

"She who?"

"Anonymous Witness. You think the author is a woman?"

Esme picked up a piece of buttered toast. "Why not?"

"A woman writing for the newspaper? Father would be the laughing-stock of the journalistic community. Women should write dime novels and society columns, not news." She picked up the paper, glanced at the headline. "'Tenements' Dwelling a Disgrace to New York.' I've read the articles, and yes, they do have an emotional slant to them."

"They're powerful."

"They're whiny, bloodletting pieces, meant to stir the guilt of the wealthy."

"They sell papers, don't they? And father even said that he would love to know who writes them. Last week he put an editor's note at the bottom of the article, asking for the name of the writer." She nibbled at her bread. "What if it is a woman?" She stared out the window, her eyes shifting to Jinx and back.

No. Jinx froze. "Esme—you haven't—you..."

Esme's mouth tightened.

"You're Anonymous Witness?"

A smile edged up Esme's mouth, and Jinx wanted to wipe it away even as a chill rippled through her, touching her bones. "But how? Please tell me that you haven't visited a tenement?"

Esme cut her voice low. "I have, what we call in the journalist's world, a source."

"Someone is feeding you stories."

"Someone is doing my research. But..." She turned to Jinx, a smile on her face Jinx didn't recognize. "Yes, I'm A.W. And...see, that's why I can't—why I won't marry Foster Worth. I have the right to my own life."

"No, you don't! You have a responsibility—"

"I'll reveal myself to Father and he'll realize that I don't have to marry to make my way. He'll give me a job at the *Chronicle*. I'll be like Nellie Bly—"

"Stop. Stop talking." Jinx stood up. "You can't do this." She grabbed the paper and stared at the headline, at the article.

Then she tore the paper in half.

"What are you doing?" Esme rose, grabbed for the paper, but Jinx tore it again, and again, shaking.

"Stop, Jinx, please—"

Jinx rounded on her, flung the pieces like shards at Esme. "You make me sick. You're engaged to the catch of the season, and you sit here and talk about immigrants and tuberculosis and other disgusting topics that a lady doesn't speak of—and—making it on your own? Being a journalist? Mother was right—you don't deserve to be a Price!"

Esme stared at her. Jinx heard her words echo back at her, but she couldn't stop them. "You don't even look like a Price. If you haven't noticed, you're the only one with blond hair in this family."

"What are you talking about?"

"Father cheats on Mother. He's had other children. You're probably the illegitimate daughter of some scullery maid—"

"Have you gone mad?" Esme knelt and began picking up the shreds of newspaper.

"No—it suddenly all makes sense! I heard Mother and Father arguing last year, right after the social season and—"

Just how many bastard children do you intend to have, August?

Jinx had stood outside her father's study, paralyzed by her mother's tone, not sure she recognized the raised voice, the shrill tone.

The hurt in her mother's voice.

Isn't it enough that I had to take one into our own home? Care for the child?

You hardly care for her, Phoebe. You barely tolerate her.

Her?

All I can imagine is that she is carrying the product of your adultery. Again.

You're one to talk. Like you haven't had a slew of indiscretions.

The silence tore through Jinx like a dagger. She'd longed to flee, her heart already outside her chest, but horror affixed her to the parquet floor. Indiscretions? Her mother?

No. With certainty, the truth slid through her, solidified, turned her heart to marble. Father was the cheater. The betrayer. An adulterer who would say anything to defame her mother. Indeed, Phoebe confirmed it with her clipped tone. *"Your lies and accusations won't absolve you, August. Not this time. Get rid of her, and her child. Or I swear, this time, I will divorce you."*

"I can't throw her onto the street. The scandal would make headlines— 'Chambermaid Claims to be Mistress of August Worth.' You'd never let that happen."

Jinx had heard a quick, horrible intake of breath.

"Besides, you can't divorce me, Phoebe. Your father deeded everything to me, and I'll make sure you're penniless."

"I'll prove my fidelity. And my constant devotion. I've given you children. I've run your home."

"Perhaps if you were a real wife, I might not have to look elsewhere."

Something crashed and Jinx jerked.

"Four miscarriages, August. Four. Is that real enough for you?" Footsteps across the floor. They stopped at the door, just as Jinx came back to herself. She slipped into the salon, hiding behind a bust of Shakespeare as her mother flung open the door to the study. *"Be glad I haven't printed the truth in your beloved newspaper! Send her far away, I don't care where, or she's not the only scandal you'll have to endure—"*

Jinx heard a sharp crack.

"Oh!"

A second later, Phoebe emerged into the hall, slamming the door behind her. August's voice followed her out. *"I'm not done with you—"*

Phoebe had stood for a moment, gathering her breath.

Jinx gritted her teeth when her mother swiped her hand across her reddened cheek, a handprint pressed into the flesh, her eyes glistening

She'd watched as her mother gathered her composure, her neck stiff as she climbed the marble stairs, probably returning to her rooms on the third floor. Jinx longed to run after her.

Her mother had taken her father's illegitimate child into her home?
Was Esme the illegitimate daughter?

Or...was she?

The thought pressed into her, grew blades. She'd simply have to prove her Price bloodline.

"And?" Now, Esme stood before her, holding the ripped layers of the paper, her eyes sharp, waiting for Jinx to complete her sentence.

"And...maybe there's a reason you don't want to marry. Maybe you don't deserve to marry Foster Worth. Maybe you don't deserve any of this."

"You're babbling."

"I'm telling you the truth. Father cheated on Mother. He had children—illegitimate children. And one of them lives right here in this house." She let the rest linger, simply raised an eyebrow. Took a breath as something acrid burned her throat.

Esme appeared as Jinx must have, stone-faced, pale. "You're a liar."

She swallowed away the heat in her throat. "Ask Mother, if you dare. But be prepared for the truth."

"Father would never cheat on Mother." But her voice held a tremor.

Jinx smiled. Looked out the window. A few skaters had found the pond, women in dark dresses and cloaks, etching the ice with their crisp blades. "You might want to consider why he is so eager to marry you off."

Esme stared at the paper.

"If you don't start behaving like a Price, you just might end up in one of those tenements, right beside your whore mother."

Esme hand went back to slap her. Jinx jerked, caught her arm a second before Esme's hand would have hit her face.

"I should have expected that from someone of your breeding."

"Get out!"

Jinx let her go. "Marry Foster Worth and I'll keep your little secret about your extracurricular writing activities. Go to Father, and the rumors of your parentage will hit the front page of *Town Topics* by tomorrow."

"You wouldn't."

"Betray us and you will discover yourself betrayed. That's a Price promise."

She walked out, closing Esme's door behind her. It wasn't until she reached her own chamber, closed the door, and collapsed, shaking, on her satin ottoman, that she realized she still wore Esme's engagement ring.

The eastern sun reached into the room, turning the floor to fire, and Jinx examined the ring on her hand, the filigree, the diamonds. The ring belonged there.

If you don't start behaving like a Price, you just might end up in one of those tenements, right beside your whore mother.

Her words rang in her ears. How could she have said that, spoken so crudely to her sister? But Esme only saw the world from the position of a savior. She didn't have Jinx's view. Jinx's room looked out over their tiny garden and beyond, into the slum neighborhoods of the Upper East Side. Coal smoke from the hovels stretching to the river darkened the sky, their filthy sewage-strewn streets seeping toward the homes along Fifth Avenue.

She turned away from the window, considered herself in the mirror, seeing herself tear Esme's article, hearing her words. *You don't even look like a Price!* She pressed her hand to her face, searching in her reflection for something of her mother. Her nose, perhaps, but Jinx had the wide nose of her father, nothing petite and delicate of Phoebe's features. Jinx also had her father's wide, manly hands, but none of his tall frame. In fact, if Jinx had inherited anything from her mother, she could claim her mother's dark hair and over-endowed bosom.

Esme, however, had their mother's blue eyes. Jinx had ended up with August's green ones.

She shouldn't have flung those words at Esme. Not when Jinx harbored the sick niggle of truth that perhaps they rightly belonged to her.

What if Jinx was the product of her father's indiscretions? No wonder he despised her. Why he decreed that Esme would marry before Jinx could be presented. He didn't want to reveal Jinx into a society that nourished itself on gossip. On speculation.

His sins would be discovered, and although he had made his millions, their new money wouldn't protect them from the shunning of the Knicker-bockers, the keepers of society.

Indeed, if the truth were discovered, the entire Price family might find themselves taking up residence among the slums.

But not if Esme—or someone else?—married into the Worth family. Their lineage, their pedigree—no one would dare scuttle the Worth family name.

Jinx twisted the engagement ring on her finger, round and round and round.

If Esme didn't marry Foster Worth, then Jinx would.

She'd be the heiress the Price family needed.

* * * * *

Esme didn't have to look in the mirror, examine her features, to know that Jinx spewed out lies.

August Price lived an honorable life. He worshipped every Sunday from the Price family pew at Grace Church. He gave to the poor, and wasn't it her father who pushed to establish the Newsboys' Lodging House with the Children's Society?

Yes, he had answered for her last night, but only because her acquiescence into debutante life conspired to make him believe she wanted to marry.

"That's tight enough, Bette," Esme said, and let Bette fix her stays while she could still breathe. A corset should hug a woman's body, give it shape, not deform it. At least, that's what Alice Stone Blackwell said in *Women's Journal*.

She kept that tucked in the drawer of her bureau, under her *Godey's Lady's Book*.

But if women could write for the *Journal* and for the *Lady's Book*, couldn't they write for the *New York Chronicle*?

She stepped into her skirt then held up her arms as Bette tucked in her shirtwaist and tied the floppy bow at her neck.

After Jinx's words, Esme had dismissed Bette, not wanting her maid to witness the effect of Jinx's cruelty. She hadn't believed her sister could be so wretched, although she'd long suspected that Jinx would lower herself to nearly any behavior that might accomplish her goals.

Namely, marrying a man of noble name, if not birth.

But to accuse their father of adultery…

Good thing Esme had only taken tea and toast for breakfast.

She finally washed her face and summoned her maid back, a plan fixed in her mind.

Bette finished tying her boots then fetched Esme's day hat, a narrow-brimmed hat with a rich purple plumage and a wide satin bow. She affixed it on Esme's head with pins.

"Ow—Bette, watch your hands. They're shaking."

"My apologies, Miss Esme."

"It's forgiven. Are you well? You seem upset."

Bette raised her gaze, ever so briefly, and met Esme's in the mirror. Funny, Esme had never noticed how green her eyes were. She never considered Bette pretty, but she had a petite delicacy about her that suddenly seemed fragile. "I'm fine, ma'am."

"You would confide in me if you weren't, wouldn't you? I do care for you."

"Yes, ma'am."

Bette finished attaching the hat then helped her into her kid gloves, the larger ones that didn't constrict feeling in her hands.

"It's rather brisk outside, ma'am. Shall I fetch your mink cape?"

"And my muff, please."

She gave a thought to wearing Foster's ring and decided against it. She didn't want her father to believe that she'd truly accepted his proposal.

He'd simply assumed her response last night. Thought, perhaps, she had no other prospects.

But, like Teddy Roosevelt had said, that day she'd lunched at Delmonico's with her father, the apple hadn't fallen far from the tree.

Her sixteenth birthday. Instead of a gala bash, she'd asked her father for a tour of the *Chronicle*.

Anything for my Esme. Those words she'd tucked away into her heart. He'd taken her on his arm on a grand tour through the arched gateways of the Chronicle Building, into the circular counting room, then through the second floor, stopping off first in his office to view Chronicle Square, the trolleys and buses and courtyard below where the newsies gathered beneath his statue. Then, past the council room, down the hall of editors' offices, where he'd ducked in and introduced her, then into the gallery of city reporters, clicking at their typewriters. They'd stopped in the library, then downstairs to the linotype room, and finally the press room where his four-cylinder presses cranked out and cut the paper. She drank in the acrid odor of ink and deliberately ran her fingers across a fresh page to imprint it onto her ungloved hands. Her father had laughed.

Then, to the delivery room, where they bound the papers. She'd waved to the newsies lined up outside the door to peddle them on the streets.

She could have stayed for years, but they had taken lunch at Delmonico's on Fifth Avenue, and her father made her laugh with stories of his editors, of his early days as a student at West Point, and at the end of the meal, stood to shake hands with the police commissioner, Theodore Roosevelt.

Roosevelt had beefy, powerful hands, the kind that could crush a man to his knees. He smiled at her, more with his eyes than his mouth, hidden as it was by his moustache.

Then, he shook her hand. His hand encased hers and caused her mouth to bubble out the first thing she could conjure, "Thank you for all you did during the heat wave this summer." She'd read about the blistering temperatures in the *Chronicle* while summering in Newport, how over 1,500 people perished. "You brought ice into the precincts of the poor, saved the lives of so many children."

He'd stared at her then, as if caught by her words, his hand warm around hers. "We all must do what we can."

"Indeed," she may have replied, but Mr. Roosevelt had turned to her father.

"The apple doesn't fall far from the tree, does it, August?"

"Not with this one. I expect great things from my Esme."

Great things.

She stood still while Bette helped her on with her cape then fitted her hands into the muff.

Jinx hadn't lied about the crisp blue day, the way the fresh snow turned to jewels under the glittering sun. Esme's breath caught in the air as the footman helped her into the closed carriage. "Not a word to my mother, Bette, until I return."

Not that Bette would betray her, but her mother might inquire after her, especially with her leaving unchaperoned.

Coal smoke bit into the fresh air, but she reveled in the glorious day. If it weren't so chilly outside, she'd walk to the Chronicle Building; but then she'd need a maid for company.

This conversation she needed to have in private.

Father, I have something to tell you. You know those opinion pieces that have sparked such recent popularity?

She knotted her hands together in her muff, watching the traffic— motorcars belching out black smoke, an elderly couple seated in the back of their Victoria, an omnibus with top-loaded passengers, a horse-drawn delivery truck filled with casks of milk.

She was grateful her driver would cut through the park, a scenic route out of the clutter of traffic on his way to the *Chronicle* office at Sixth and Broadway.

They eased into the carriage entrance and lost the city behind them, dark eyes that watched them disappear into the meandering drive. She leaned back and drank in the refuge. *Father, you always told me that a man needed to work for what he had. Would that apply to a woman too?*

They passed the pond, a handful of skaters. To the west, the Dakota Building rose like a castle overlooking feudal land.

Father, you told me you expected great things, what if I told you I was…

In the summer, before they left for Newport, she strolled the park with her writing paper in hand, the ever-present Bette at her side, camping out at the rustic waterfalls, the ornamental ponds. She composed best next to water.

Perhaps her father would give her an office.

They exited the park and the driver added her carriage to the congestion. A street trolley clanged past her. Someday, perhaps she'd ride one. Awnings over entry doors fluttered in the window, snow lifting off them as if they'd sneezed. Street sweepers dusted the last of the snow from sidewalks with their brooms. They passed St. Patrick's Cathedral and, across the street, the twin ornate palaces of William Vanderbilt.

At Lord & Taylor, she watched two women step out of their carriage and drift into the store, followed by a boy in a stiff livery assigned to carry their packages.

Someday, that might be Jinx, a trail of young boys shuffling behind her.

Once upon a time, one of those boys had been Oliver. She closed her eyes, trying to escape his words.

We were childhood acquaintances, and you're not marrying me.

The strange tone in his voice nagged at her, dug into her chest.

They finally pulled into Chronicle Square, freshly mopped of snow. As Esme climbed down to the curb, the bronze statuettes of the angel Minerva, the bell ringers, and owls tolled the hour from the apex of the two-story triangular Chronicle Building. The chime resounded through her, shook her, and for a moment, she stilled. Swallowed.

I expect great things from my Esme.

She entered the arched doors, inside to the circular lobby, and climbed the stairs to the second floor. The ticking of the typewriters from the nearby city department echoed through the marble hallways, matching the staccato of her heartbeat.

Pressing her hand against her stomach, she entered the reception hall. She considered simply brushing by the reception desk, but she'd changed in four years, and certainly the young man at the desk wouldn't recognize her. Besides, she should wait to be announced, although she could hardly bear to wait for her father's reaction.

"I'm here to see my father," she said without introduction.

She'd place the man in his early twenties, eager and spare. Perhaps he'd been a newsie once, for he had a sharp look about him.

"He is in his office. I will announce you."

"Please." She smiled at him but didn't sit as he knocked on her father's door, peeked inside.

In fact, she pushed right past him as her father, seated at his desk, his back to the paladin windows overlooking Chronicle Square, replied, "Who?"

"Me, Father. I need to talk to you."

He'd always been larger to her than his actual stature, tall and wiry, with deep green eyes that could bore through a man and discover the truth. He'd put the *Chronicle* on the New York landscape by covering the sensational murder of a showgirl and had the audacity to point the finger at the son of a Tammany Hall politician while the police department named a young doorman for the crime. The jury found the doorman not guilty, and the true culprit escaped with impunity, a departure the *Chronicle* decried as a travesty for all of New York.

August Price could reduce a reporter to garble, but she didn't know a woman in town who didn't look up with a smile when her father entered the room.

Including her.

"What are you doing here?" He wore a smile, but she didn't hear it in his tone. He came around his desk, took her hands, kissed her cheek. "Is everything okay?"

He helped her into a chair then leaned against the desk. Folded his arms.

She could feel her words turning to glue in her chest. "I—I need to talk to you."

"If it's about last night, I know you were surprised. But Foster Worth is quite smitten with you. You will learn to love each other. It's a good match, Esme."

She opened her mouth. Licked her lips. Blew out a breath.

"What is it?"

Perhaps she only imagined the compassion in his tone, the way it softened, as if he might mean his words. Still, "Father, I don't want to marry him."

He drew in a breath, his shoulders rising. "Why not?"

"It's not Foster, Father. He's...suitable. But I don't want to marry anyone."

Her father raised an eyebrow. "Do you intend to live your life as a spinster? As a companion?"

"I want to work."

He made a tight knot with his lips. Glanced at the door, perhaps to see if it was closed. "Where is your mother?"

"I don't know."

"You came here alone?"

"I needed to tell you something. I already know what I want to do. And actually, you do too."

She heard her voice begin to rise, fought it as the words tumbled out. "I want to write, Father. I want to be a journalist, like Nellie Bly."

For a beat, her father didn't move, didn't breathe, as if still waiting for her words. Then, he laughed. A short burst that stripped from her the coiled breath inside. "Oh, Esme. What ideas you entertain."

Ideas. "No, Father, you don't understand. I...am writing. I have been writing."

"I'm sure you have. I know how you enjoy your walks through the park."

"Father, I'm Anonymous Witness!"

She didn't mean to shout, but, oh—she pressed her hand to her mouth as her father stared at her, his face pinching.

"What?"

"I'm A.W. I'm the one writing the opinion pieces. Selling your paper."

His smile had vanished. His jaw closed, he breathed out through his nose. "Go home, Esme."

He leaned up from his perch on the edge of the desk.

"Father, don't you understand? I can write! You even said last week that you wanted to know the identity of the journalist."

"Not anymore."

His tone cut out her breath. "I don't understand. I thought you liked the articles."

He sat down at his desk, looked at her. "Who is your source?"

"My source?"

"The person who's been feeding you this information. I can find out—I'll ask my editor who's been delivering your letters to his desk."

No. She shook her head. "No, I…Father, listen. Don't you see? I could work for you. I could be a reporter, or a…I'd even work the society pages. You liked my reports on the balls and the matinees."

"And turn us into the laughingstock, or worse, the Benedict Arnold of Mrs. Astor's society? It's one thing for them to believe the words are the jealous tirade of some society outsider. If they knew it was a debutante, they would turn their backs on our family. It's bad enough that I know. Now get out. Go home, now."

"But I thought you said…" She hung onto her voice before it deserted her. "You said that you expected big things from me."

He narrowed his eyes. "You will marry Foster Worth, and you will represent the Price family in society. That is big enough."

His words burned into her, churned her stomach. She stood up, her breath webbed in her chest. "No."

He too had risen, come around the desk. "What?"

"No, I won't marry him. I won't marry anyone. I don't need you or your job—I'll go work for Pulitzer! He already has Nellie Bly—"

The blow came fast, an open palm, landing on the side of her cheek. Flame exploded on her face, and she fell back, landed in the chair behind her. Her breath caught and she cried out.

Her father stared down upon her, unmoved. "You will marry Foster Worth. This summer, in Newport. And tonight, you will take every last book in your room, including the *Women's Journal* that I know you've been hiding, and you will burn them."

She pressed her hand to her hot cheek, feeling as if it might be split open. Tears slurred her vision.

"Go home, Esme. Don't make me escort you out like a stray puppy."

Somehow she pushed to her feet, gripping the back of the chair for balance. Her father returned to his chair, turned, and stared out the window overlooking the street.

She found her reticule, the one with a new story inside.

"By the way, I won't publish anything written by A.W. again. Nor will any other paper in this town, I can promise you that."

She wiped her soggy face. "Yes, Father."

He stopped her just as she began to close the door. "Esme?"

She paused in the crack between his office and reception, her eyes closed.

"I'm only trying to protect you. You have no idea what kind of world is out there. Trust me, I only want the best for you."

She wanted his words to balm her, but they only burned inside. "Yes, Father."

He said nothing more as she let herself out. She didn't look at the receptionist. The clack of the typewriters turned to bullets in the corridor. She gripped the railing as she descended the stairs, her legs numb. She couldn't breathe, couldn't think—

"Esme?"

The voice stopped her as she hit the landing, but she couldn't turn toward it. He'd see her failures.

"Esme, what is it?"

Oliver cupped his hand beneath her elbow. She shook her head but he came around her, lifted her chin with his hand.

"Your face—did someone strike you?"

She put her hand to her mouth, but it trembled.

"Come with me."

She let him lead her toward the cloakroom, into the vestibule off the main entrance. He turned on the overhead light, shut the door, and motioned her to sit on a stool. Coats hung from a rack, smelling of grease and the street, the cold. In the feeble glow of the electric light, Oliver seemed tired, his collar turned up, his dark hair tousled. He knelt before her and peered at her with those devastating brown eyes that always seemed to see more than she intended.

"Have you been up all night?"

"Byron wanted to develop his shots. I just turned in the ones he selected for the society page."

He still wore his dress shirt, open now at the neck, and smelled faintly of chemicals. His hands as they took hers felt soft, freshly washed. "What happened?"

"I told my father."

Oliver froze, but he didn't take his hands from hers. "About A.W.?"

She nodded, her throat again tightening, and looked away. Would she ever erase her father's face, the sharp laugh, the sting of his hand? "I thought that perhaps he'd see that—"

"That you don't want to marry Foster Worth?"

Something in Oliver's tone made her meet his gaze. She nodded, and for a second a smile nipped at his face. Then, "What did he say?"

She slipped her hand to her face. His expression darkened. "He struck you." He climbed to his feet.

"Oliver."

"He struck you. A man never hits a woman, Esme. Ever."

"He's my father."

"I'll kill him."

"He's your boss."

"Not anymore. Not—"

She grabbed his arm. "No. Leave it, Oliver. I—I do entertain too many ideas. I'm full of fancy. I thought I could be like…well, be a journalist. I thought that's why I was born into this family—to help people. By writing."

He knelt before her again. "You can. You could write for the *Globe*. Or the *Sun*, or *Town Topics*."

"No. I was a fool to think I could be someone else."

"You're an amazing writer, Esme. I believe in you. Prove to him that you can write—better than any man in his city department."

"He won't care."

"Make him care. Do something that will make him realize that he—"

"No." She stared at him, the earnestness of his expression. An hour ago, she thought she possessed that also.

Instead, with her father's words, his hand upon her face, she'd realized she'd simply been playing a game. She couldn't make the world a better place. Couldn't stand up to the forces of poverty and evil.

She couldn't even stand up to her own father.

She stared at Oliver, and as if something else possessed her, she reached out and touched his neck, tracing her finger into a scarred groove just below his collarbone. "I still remember when you got this."

He seemed stripped, his eyes in hers.

"It was when you were twelve. You were running toward me, then suddenly you went down and landed right in the hedgerow. Came up with a stick in your chest."

"I thought—I thought I heard someone calling for me." He let his words hang there and she stilled. "I thought you were calling for me."

She made to move her hand, but he caught it against his cheek. His voice dropped to a whisper. "Please don't marry Foster Worth."

Oh.

Then he leaned forward, stopping a breath away. He…did he want to kiss her? His breath was so close, she could taste it, feel the touch of his lips on hers. She met his eyes and saw in them something she hadn't noticed before.

You can't have both worlds, Esme. Choose one.

He searched her face, his gaze settling on her lips, and it ignited something unfamiliar clear through her. "Esme, I—"

"Esme?"

Her father's voice echoed down the marble steps, into the corridor, the effect of a jolt upon her skin. She jerked back, away from Oliver. "I have to go. He was probably watching and saw that I didn't go out the front door. He ordered me home."

He took her hands, his gaze in hers. "Leave with me. Today, right now."

"Oliver, what are you saying? I can't—"

"Esme?" Footsteps now on the staircase above.

"I love you, Esme." His words turned soft, urgent. "I have for years. And I'll take care of you—I don't know if I'll ever be rich, but I promise you'll never be hungry, and I swear no one will ever hurt you—"

"Esme?" Her father sounded as if he might be on the landing.

Oliver loved her? She stared at him, the way his hair fell into his eyes, his immense shoulders, so much history behind them. *You can't have both worlds, Esme. Choose one.*

"I can't, Oliver. I—"

"Do you love me? Because I think you do."

"Esme? Are you still here?" The voice came past the coatroom and she stilled, her eyes caught in Oliver's.

"I have to go."

He closed his eyes.

"You don't understand."

"I think I do."

"Please, Oliver. I—I don't have a choice. What else can I do?"

"You can be the woman you were meant to be."

She swallowed, his words stirring, tugging. And then she saw her life.

Living on the street, in those tenements, perhaps sharing a room portioned by a cloth, scrubbing her undergarments in a tub, fighting the rats for stale bread. Or perhaps they'd have a room, one sparsely furnished, with a rough-hewn table, a straw mattress on the floor, all the while scrabbling for stories together on the streets.

By the way, I won't publish anything written by A.W. again. Nor will any other paper in this town, I can promise you that.

Her father would destroy her.

And Oliver.

"I am that woman I was meant to be." She got up, and he drew in a breath. She blinked back the burn in her eyes, her throat.

Finally, he nodded, his face hard in the dim light. Footsteps returned, passed by. She listened to them move across the circular entryway.

Oliver took her hand. "Quickly now."

He pulled her out of the room, across the corridor, and to the employee entrance. "Go out, take a right. Your carriage will be just down the street."

"Oliver."

He turned and caught her eyes. His smile seemed pressed out of a dark place inside, despite his gentle tone. "I will never forget how you pulled the stick out of my chest. Then bandaged it every day until it healed." He pressed a kiss to her forehead. "Any lower and it would have been fatal."

He pushed her out the door. "Be well, Miss Price."

Chapter 3

Jinx could taste spring in the breeze that stirred through the elms, hemlock, cedars, blue spruce, and empress trees that lined the winding pathways of Central Park. Winter's bite had lost its edge, despite the fresh dusting of snow, the below-freezing temperatures. Two more weeks and the season would turn toward new life, red and orange buds on the trees, and not long after that, the arrival of her debutante trousseau from Paris.

She drank in the blue skies, the snap of the air, the euphoria of flying as she glided over the Central Park pond.

"Jinx! Are you coming into the warming house?"

Alistair Whitney skated up beside her, turning backwards to grin at her. He wore a Russian shopka, his greatcoat collar turned up, a white silk scarf blowing in the breeze. A boy poised at the edge of manhood. After his graduation from prep school, he would attend West Point or Harvard, but like Jinx, he had surrendered to the pull of a Saturday afternoon with his chums.

"I'm not cold yet. I'll be in presently."

Her maid, Amelia, waited in the warming house with hot tea and a warming blanket, along with Delphine Wilson and Elizabeth Fish. They'd conspired the outing during dance class yesterday, while in the arms of the boys from Dodsworth's Dancing Academy. Lizzie and Del had already ordered their trousseaus, and the jaunt to the skating rink served more as a way to compare notes. In six months, they might not be talking to each other as they competed in the social arena for the right catch.

Alistair skated off, and Jinx closed her eyes, spreading out her arms, letting the wind caress her face, drinking in the fresh air. Finally, she would step into her life, the one she'd whittled herself to fit. With Esme's marriage to Foster Worth, doors would open to Jinx. She would be included in the parties of the Vanderbilts and the rest of high society.

Even if Esme despised her role. Thankfully, she hadn't fought her engagement, but retreated instead into her chamber or spending endless hours at the piano, filling the music salon with Chopin or Mozart. Mother had to drag her to her fittings for her gown, and Jinx had taken over the planning of Esme's wedding in Newport, an activity she seemed born to.

Jinx helped Mother plan the transformation of the ballroom of Seacrest, their Newport cottage, into a lush and exotic garden—from palm fronds to lilies to roses that would hang in cascades from the chandeliers. She convinced her mother to employ a sixty-piece orchestra and had already begun working with the chef on the perfect menu of terrapin and squid.

It ignited in her the resolution that someday, she would be the doyenne who watched the "buds" through her lorgnette and determined their suitability. She would be the one to set society's standards. She would create the perfect world and never again wonder where she belonged.

"Look out!"

Jinx opened her eyes a second too late to stop herself from plowing into the tall bulk of a skater, his hands open to catch her. She slammed into him and then, in an inglorious moment, tumbled them onto the ice. "Oh!"

She landed hard on her knee, her hands slamming into his chest.

His arms curled around her to cushion her, but she collapsed onto him, gray dots before her eyes as the confines of her corset sealed off her breath.

"Are you okay?" He pushed her off him, setting her on the ice.

She fought to catch her breath. "I...think so." Or, perhaps she wasn't, because as she looked up... "Foster?"

He smiled, and in that moment, something curled inside her. Warmth, perhaps—she felt her face heat as he climbed to his feet then reached down and hooked his arm under her body.

She held onto his arms as he swooped her to her feet. "Thank you."

"Are you sure you're okay?"

She still had a grip on his greatcoat and fought for her composure. But he had amazing eyes—gray, yet flecked with green and the ability to whisk the words from her chest. And her legs hadn't recovered, it seemed, as he smiled down at her. "Hello, Jinx. It's been awhile."

She smiled. So, he remembered the days when his family would visit hers, at Newport. But then, she'd been about ten years old to his sixteen.

"I never did know, why do they call you Jinx?"

"My real name is Jacqueline, but my father started calling me Jinx when I was young. It stuck." Lately, though, she'd begun to wonder if he hadn't meant it as a term of endearment, but rather an epitaph to her unfortunate birth.

"I like Jacqueline better."

Oh.

He held out his arm. "Just until you get your feet under you."

She slipped hers through and he pushed off.

"I know I should have been by to see Esme, and of course renew my acquaintance with you and your family earlier. After the engagement, I had to return to London and then Paris to secure the spring line of clothing for our stores."

"I've never been to Paris, although my father did suggest a trip there for Esme's trousseau."

"I didn't know she was going to Paris. Then again, she doesn't talk to me." He had his hand on hers, over her glove, warming it. "I fear I have offended her."

Why did Esme have to trouble everyone with her moods? "She is fine. Simply busy with the wedding. And, she can be rather…bookish."

"I remember her sitting beneath the oaks on your estate, lost in a book while we played croquet."

"You remember our croquet game?"

"I remember you cheating for the win."

"I didn't cheat!" She glanced up at him and found his smile. "You are simply a miserable croquet player. You stole my ball and flung it into the surf!"

"That was my brother, Benny, if I recall." He winked at her. "He was always the sore loser. You remember him—he's just about your age."

"Of course." She remembered him as the boy who mocked her for her freckles. "Is he still at West Point?"

Foster laughed. "No, sadly, he couldn't quite manage the military. Father sent him to Paris before he fell ill. Bennett is managing our shipping there, if that's what you want to call his position."

"Oh." She didn't know what to say as he continued to skate with her, cupping his hand over hers.

"I'm afraid Father extended too long a leash to Bennett. He'll be back before the season at Newport, most likely, looking for a fresh advance on his allowance. Oh, I shouldn't have said that." He winced, shook his head, found her eyes again. "Family."

"Indeed."

"I hope that after Esme and I are wed, such a term will be met with endearment between our people."

He had long strides, but she suspected he shortened them for her as he directed her around the pond. She spotted Amelia standing outside, her cloak blowing around her, waiting for Jinx's arrival. She ignored her.

To be seen on the arm of Foster Worth, her future brother-in-law, couldn't hurt her prospects for next season.

Although, for a moment, she'd forgotten about her debut and simply hung onto Foster. He hadn't exactly let her go, either.

"We're not going to Paris, by the way."

"Oh. Very good. After the social season ends, I would like to call on your family more often, and it would be ever so pleasant to have someone there with whom I could have a conversation, and who, perhaps, enjoys mine?"

He glanced at her, and for a second, she thought she recognized a flash of question on his face. He enjoyed her conversation?

"Esme, I'm sure, will be delighted to see you."

He looked away, and the wind threatened to steal her hat. "Esme and I shared few words even when we were children. It was with you I laughed."

She didn't know why, but his words stirred deep inside her.

"Esme has her charms."

"I think you and I both know the nature of my betrothal to Esme. I do not beguile myself to believe it is more than simply a mutually advantageous agreement." He slowed then and turned to skate backwards, now holding her hand. "It is left to me to find friendship elsewhere."

She stared at him, and had he not had her hand, she might have stopped skating. "I—I should go to the warming house. Amelia is waiting for me."

"Are you cold? My sleigh is waiting. I have a buffalo robe, and the weather is beautiful for a ride."

A ride.

With Foster Worth.

"I have not yet been presented into society. I need to return home, practice my quadrille. I cannot get the form of the hobbyhorse steps."

"I could help you. Perhaps you need a partner?"

He still had her hand and she stared at it now. "I—I don't know what to say."

"Say that my marriage to your sister won't extinguish the spark of friendship between us. Indeed, I can admit that I look forward to seeing your smile even more than Esme's, heaven help me. And I will ensure, dear sister-in-law, that you will have the most advantageous match in society that I can manage."

He had stopped and they stood in the center of the ice. Alistair swished past them, chasing Lizzie, who waved at her.

"I am cold."

"My sleigh awaits. I promise to deliver you home warm and safe. It is the least I can do after knocking you over."

"I think it was I who knocked you over, sir."

He again slipped her hand into the crook of his arm as he led her toward his sleigh. "Indeed."

* * * * *

Certainly she could learn to love Foster. Jinx obviously did. Esme watched her laugh at Foster's comments, hiding giggles behind her hand as he regaled the family—no, Jinx—with stories of catastrophes down at the shipyard. Esme picked at the boiled lamb's head her mother had decided to serve for dinner, trying to act informal. Never mind the shimmer of the crystal chandeliers above the table that cast a prism of light upon the gilded chairs, turning the spray of roses and orchids to gems. Hickory logs crackled in the hearth, as if the Price family took dinner every night in the dining room, a pastoral dinner.

Esme wished herself into the music salon, at her piano, or secreted away in her room watching spring bloom across Central Park, scribbling her thoughts—forbidden as they were—into the only journal her father hadn't confiscated from her room. He'd tossed her books, her magazines, her writings, one by one, into the fire, oblivious to her pleading.

She'd stopped begging after he'd thrown in her copies of her articles, folded and secured in a scrapbook. She'd watched wordlessly as the fire blackened the leather book, curled the pages, and soured the room with the acrid odor of incinerated leather.

Even her copy of the *Chronicle* disappeared from her morning tray. She'd discovered the announcement of her engagement through Jinx, who recited it word for word while Esme tried to close her ears.

While Jinx's world brightened with her oncoming debut, Esme's only seemed to darken. Never mind that she hadn't seen nor heard from Oliver. He once made a habit of stopping by the servants' quarter to inquire after his father, their butler, especially on Sundays. But although she'd asked, discreetly, about his attendance, no, Pierce Stewart hadn't seen his son in months.

An absence that should probably stop gnawing at her, especially with her fiancé seated at the dinner table.

"Have you heard anything of a grain shovelers' strike brewing in Buffalo, Mr. Price?"

Foster had initially given a feeble attempt to engage Esme in conversation, stopping by often for tea or to invite her for a stroll in the park. But it was Jinx's witty spirit that had filled the silence during the ride home from church he'd given them last Sunday.

Not that Esme minded.

Her father ate in silence.

Foster finished off his lamb's head. "We had men stop by the shipping yard talking about heading up to work as strikebreakers."

"Why would they strike?" her mother asked. "Aren't they well cared for?"

Foster wiped his mouth with his napkin, his gaze darting to her father, then back to her mother. "Depends on how you look at it. The brewery set up the workers' food and lodging at the local saloon, and the charges are taken out of their paychecks. But the workers claim the saloons are owned by the brewery bosses and they end up getting cheated."

Esme put down her fork. "What about their families?"

Foster looked at her, surprise in his expression. "Most of the men are single, just like the men we have working for us down at the docks. We provide their lodging, their food. I hope they don't get any ideas from the unions up north."

"But shouldn't they have a right to spend their paycheck where they choose?"

"Esme, don't be contrary. This is men's talk." Phoebe motioned for a server to take Esme's plate of uneaten food.

"But Mother, have you seen those saloons? The families live in tiny, unventilated rooms. Children die of dysentery and cholera. It's filthy, unchristian conditions and—"

"That's enough, Esme," Father snapped from the end of the table.

Foster stared at her, unblinking, as if he'd never heard her speak before.

"Mother, isn't it time for the May Day baskets to go to the Children's Home Society?" Jinx allowed her server to remove her plate. He replaced it with a custard.

"Indeed, Jinx. Perhaps you and your sister will join me this week for the presentation?"

Esme didn't know what took possession of her mouth, but, "Don't forget to invite Father's pressmen. You would hate to have the gift diminished by lack of fanfare."

"Esme!"

"I feel unwell, may I please be excused?"

"No," her father said. He turned to Foster. "I apologize for my daughter's tongue."

But Foster was watching Jinx as she ate her custard, a strange expression on his face. Amusement perhaps, or...

Was Foster in love with her sister?

Her stomach tightened as she looked from Jinx to Foster, at the way they stole glances.

Jinx. What had she done?

"Why don't you men retire to the drawing room for your port? We will join you presently." Phoebe signaled to the butler to follow the men to the drawing room and attend to their conversation.

Foster caught Esme's eyes, nothing of a smile in his expression as he pushed away from the table.

The maid closed the doors behind them and her mother waited one beat before, "Are you trying to cause him to retract his offer of marriage?"

"In my wildest dreams."

"Hush your tongue. Yes, you may be excused." Her mother threw her napkin to the table then rose and strode from the room.

Jinx finished off her custard. She licked her spoon, put it back in the dish. "I know I shouldn't finish my meal, not with my trousseau already ordered, but I just love our chef's custard—"

"What are you doing, Jinx?"

Jinx looked up at her. "Eating?"

"Don't be quaint. Foster looks at you like *you* are custard. You laugh at his jokes—"

"He's funny, Esme. You could get to know him more, you know. That's why he's here. You would like him. He's educated and well-mannered. And handsome."

"He's arrogant."

"He's a millionaire. He has a right. Besides, he's just like Father. I thought you adored Father."

Esme pushed her dish away. "He isn't Father." She didn't know what to think about her father. With her declaration at the newspaper, they'd lost all rapport. He seemed a stranger to her.

"You're going to be married to him. Have his children. Share his life... his home. His bed."

"Don't talk that way. It's bad enough that I barely know him. I refuse to think of spending my wedding night with a stranger."

"Then talk to him. He has beautiful eyes, and he's an amazing dancer—"

"Have you been dancing with him?" She hadn't expected those words to turn inside her like a knife, to have them cut, and bruise.

Jinx froze. "Just...a few times. For practice. I needed help with the steps of the quadrille, and the waltz."

She saw them then, Jinx in his arms, him smiling down at her, caught in the music.

The pose of a couple in love.

She stared at Jinx, the words boiling out of her. "Jinx, are you in love with my fiancé?"

Jinx recoiled. "No! Of course not. But I don't understand why you're not."

Esme drew in a long breath over the nettles in her chest. "I...will be. Someday." Please, please. But perhaps she'd had her chance for love, and walked away.

Do you love me? Because I think you do. She couldn't escape the haunting of Oliver's voice. He found her in her sleep, in the morning as she watched the newsies hawk their papers, in the familiar presence of her father's butler.

Did she love him? The question wrapped around her at night, noosed her breath from her chest. Indeed, she missed him so desperately, the answer seemed suffocating.

Jinx had risen from the table. "Give Foster a chance to win your heart. You may not find him as repulsive in reality as your despair has conjured."

She watched Jinx leave. Probably she'd never understand what it felt to have another determine her future. To be powerless. To feel as if she'd wasted her life before it had even begun.

To be a coward.

Lilacs and jasmine scented the April air as she walked out into the garden, the last tendrils of twilight etching the sky. Perhaps she should attempt to allow Foster to win her heart. Perhaps with time, she'd forget the echo of Oliver's voice.

After all, her parents wouldn't have sold her into marriage with a monster.

She sat on the bench under the cover of an empress tree, listening to the city just beyond the gates, the *clip-clop* of the horses' hooves, the chirrup of crickets rising from the park. A breeze raised the flesh on her bare arms, her mother requiring her green satin evening gown for tonight's dinner.

"You seem cold."

The voice startled her, especially when Foster stepped out into the garden. He wore a quilted Turkish smoking jacket—she recognized it as one of her father's.

She found a repentant voice. "I'm sorry for my behavior this evening. Perhaps I read too much of Jacob Riis's work."

"I read him also, and I'm not unaware of the plight of our working class. But it is not a sin to be wealthy, Esme. It is our businesses that give them employment."

He sat on the bench, next to her, the smell of her father's cigars rising from his skin not entirely unpleasant. "But when Alva Vanderbilt or Mrs. Astor throws a ball that could feed the city for a year—"

"They have that right; it is their millions. But forget not that to throw such a ball, they must employ hundreds. They are feeding the city."

Esme ran her hands up her arms, whisking away the cold. She nearly jumped when Foster traced his finger down the back of her neck. It was fleshly and bold, especially when he turned her to face him.

"I have always known you were outspoken and bold, Esme. I remember from those few times when we played lawn tennis. I won't ask you to temper your comments unless we are in public." He smiled at her, and she searched for warmth in his eyes.

"Th–thank you?"

"I think you'll find that I can be quite agreeable to a woman's whims." He touched her chin. "When she is agreeable to mine."

She stilled, and he held her chin as he moved toward her.

What—no, wait—she pressed her hand on his chest to stop him, but he brushed his lips against hers. She stiffened, "Fos—"

He curled his hand around her neck, held her in place as he moved his mouth against hers, forcing his kiss upon her.

She fought his grip, pressing both hands against his chest, but he held her tight, finishing his kiss before he released her.

She reeled back, staring at him, her lips bruised. "I—you—I didn't give you leave—"

"You will get used to my kisses." He ran his hand down her face. "Learn, even, to enjoy them."

She pressed her hand to her lips as he rose.

"Jinx has asked me to join her in the library. Apparently she has a poem she's penned for my amusement. Will you join us?" He held out his hand. She wanted to slap it. Instead, she shook her head.

"Very well. I'll call on you tomorrow. Perhaps we can take a carriage ride."

Watching him leave, she held her breath, her heart webbed in her chest.

She waited until she heard his footsteps vanish then fled to her room, locking the door behind her. She tore off her evening gown, unhooking her corset from the front, and slipped into her nightgown.

She scrubbed her face, pulled down her hair, brushed it through, tears shaking her. Why hadn't she run away with Oliver? She dropped the ivory-handled brush, put her face in her hands. Oh God, she'd lived such a fairy-tale. Thought she could somehow live in both worlds.

Now, she belonged in neither.

Father cheated on Mother. He had children—illegitimate children. And one of them lives right here, in this house.

Jinx's words gnawed at her. Maybe she hadn't lied. Maybe—maybe indeed, Esme wasn't the daughter of Father's wife, but the offspring of some illicit union, one she was destined to pay for. What if God, because of her father's sin, had turned His back on her?

Be the woman you were meant to be.

And who, exactly, might that be?

If you don't start behaving like a Price, you just might end up in one of those tenements, right beside your whore mother.

What if she didn't belong in this family? What if her mother had been a working-class maid, someone her father had betrayed, just as he'd betrayed her?

She watched the fire crackling, devouring the hickory Bette had laid in the hearth. *Please don't marry Foster Worth.*

Oliver again, and this time she let him linger in her mind, despite the barbaric pleasure of it. She saw him hiding behind the piano in the solarium, the winter sun in his ebony hair, stolen moments playing hide-and-seek.

"You found me, Esme! You always find me!" he'd said.

He smelled of the stables, where'd he'd no doubt assisted the footmen in caring for the horses, but he'd found her reading in the garden and the chase ensued.

"It's because I can smell you all the way across the house." Laughter always came so easily when she teased Oliver.

He came out, sat on the bench. "My hands are clean."

She took them, examined the scrapes, the reddened skin. Compared them with her own, creamy white.

"You have pretty hands," he said, and for a moment pressed his against hers. His wounds scraped, but she pressed back, folded her fingers between his.

They sat there, her legs swinging under the piano bench as the dust motes swam through the sunlight.

Footsteps in the hallway drove him away, back into the shadows, but his voice lingered.

"You found me, Esme! You always find me!"

She got up, went to her bureau. Inside was the picture Oliver had taken of her the night of Mrs. Astor's party. Regal in her white dress, she saw a woman undaunted by the scrutiny of the camera, a smile unfamiliar in recent days upon her lips.

I love you, Esme. I have for years.

What if he really did love her? What if he looked at her like—like Foster did Jinx? She pressed her fingertips against her lips, tender now after Foster's assault. Her first kiss. The gorge rose in her throat. Nothing like the moment when Oliver had searched her face, so much longing in his eyes.

She closed her eyes, remembered his breath, so close she could nearly taste his lips against hers. Why hadn't she let him kiss her?

Fear.

The truth shook her through to her bones. She wasn't so much different than Jinx, was she? She simply disguised it with a sort of righteous indignation.

She didn't want to be poor, live in the tenements, scraping out her life from day-to-day. But she didn't want to live trapped inside Foster's cruelty either.

Esme studied her picture again, then took it out and set it upon the bureau. Under it lay her Bible. She pulled it out and took both of them back to her divan before the hearth.

"Miss Price, is there anything you require of me this evening?" Bette stood in the doorway.

Esme sighed, ran her hand over the Bible.

"Ma'am, if you will permit me, I remember what Mr. Moody said that night."

Esme glanced at her. "Mr. Moody?"

"When he visited a year or so back? Your family attended the evangelical soiree. A fundraising event?"

Of course. Which meant Bette also attended. "What do you remember of the evening?" Esme remembered the man: portly, with a receding hairline and a dark beard. He spoke with a tone of command that made his words sink into her tissue, her bones.

Bette took a step into the room. "'God never made a promise that was too good to be true.'"

"And what did He promise you, Bette?"

"That night? 'Blessed are the poor in spirit: for theirs is the kingdom of heaven.'"

Of course Bette would be poor in spirit. What did she have but the clothes the Prices gave her, the room in the attic? How did she suppose to see the Kingdom of God?

But, just in case, "And have you seen it?"

"Every day, ma'am. Being poor in spirit means we need God more than we need ourselves. He also said, 'If we are full of pride and conceit and ambition and self-seeking and pleasure and the world, there is no room for the Spirit of God.' He said that many of us are praying to God to fill us when we are already filled with something else. Things, however, that leave us bereft."

Like, perhaps, her own ambition? Esme let her thumb shuffle through the Bible's pages.

Bette took another step toward her. "He also said that seeking to perpetuate one's name on earth is like writing in the sand by the seashore; to keep it, it must be written on eternal shores."

Bette picked up the poker, pushed the logs back into a pile.

Esme watched the embers glow red. "I remember, 'We can stand affliction better than we can prosperity, for in prosperity we forget God.'"

She glanced at Bette, looking for condemnation in her eyes. Strange, she'd always felt an affection for her maid, only a few years older than herself. She recognized nothing but a strange compassion in her expression as Bette said, "Yes, he said that too."

"Thank you Bette, that's enough for tonight."

"Very good, ma'am. Pleasant dreams."

Blessed are the poor in spirit: for theirs is the kingdom of heaven. Esme let Bette's words soak into her as she watched the fire burn. She hadn't needed God, not really. In fact, she'd spent most of her life thinking God needed her.

She opened the Bible, found the verse in Matthew 5, read it again, then the entire passage, ending with, "'Let your light so shine before men, that they may see your good works, and glorify your Father which is in heaven.'"

She pressed her hand into the filament pages, cold and smooth, letting the words churn inside. She remembered that night, remembered Moody's words stirring her to fresh awareness of heaven, of her own desire to do something more with her life.

In fact, her writing had started with the verse she'd scrawled on the program. She took it out, read it. "'Commit thy way unto the Lord; trust also in Him; and He shall bring it to pass.'"

Had she committed her way that night?

Ever?

She slipped over to the window, pressed her head against the cool pane. Outside, electric lights lit up the city, pushing back the darkness.

She wanted to push back darkness. But she couldn't, trapped in a marriage to Foster Worth, could she?

No. The word sank deep inside, reverberated. No.

Not when she loved Oliver.

In fact, just like he'd intimated, she'd loved him for years. The truth heated her through. Oh, why hadn't she seen it earlier?

Maybe she simply hadn't wanted to.

In the fireplace, the fire crackled, popped. She turned toward it, hearing again Oliver's childhood laughter. *You found me, Esme! You always find me!*

Yes, she did.

She got up, walked to the fire, and dropped the photograph of her debutante self into the flames.

Chapter 4

So this was how the other half lived. Esme clutched the paper on which Mr. Stewart had written Oliver's address and eased into the foyer of his building, located on the shore of the East River. In years past, this area of town housed George Washington and society's elite. Now, the steps of the stone dwelling crumbled beneath her shoes, the gated windows like eyes etched with age. She tucked her reticule closer to her, thankful she'd chosen her fading school cloak, something less than flamboyant. Imagine if she'd worn her fur....

The brine of beer and urine, the wail of a child in the dark recesses of the building curdled her courage. Oh, why hadn't she brought Bette?

Worse, she'd lied to Oliver's father—the first of her many sins tonight—when she'd said she only wanted to post Oliver correspondence.

If Mr. Stewart knew she intended to find his son, he would have never betrayed his employer. She had to hope her father would never discover his indiscretion.

Even if he did discover her absence.

Maybe she *should* have simply posted a letter. But then she couldn't see Oliver's face when she told him...what? That she loved him?

Perhaps she just wanted to confirm his words. *I love you, Esme. I have for years.*

She'd imagined a cheerier boardinghouse for him, something that didn't scurry with rats, one where the old tile floor from bygone days didn't echo her entrance, the ornate oak molding hanging with dirt and cobwebs. A gaslight flickered in a dim hallway that had once hosted a grand corridor, now partitioned off to create rooms. Somewhere in the catacombs of rooms the whine of a fiddle attempted cheer.

She lifted her skirt for the stairs, her gloved hand sliding on the decaying railing. A dog barked, possibly from the street. Shouting, in German, emerged from a door at the top of the stairs.

Why had Oliver given up a perfectly decent position in her father's home—he could have been a footman, or a valet—to live in squalor? She heard the scratching of insects and shivered.

She took the next flight, then another, and came to the attic. She could barely make out the numbers carved into the door. He'd ended up in attic's quarters anyway.

She knocked, heard low voices, and knocked again. "Oliver?"

The door jerked open and he stood there, outlined by a glow of lamplight. His hair had grown, his shoulders seemed even broader in his muslin shirt, rolled at the elbows, his pants held up by suspenders. He blinked at her. "Esme?"

She tried a smile, something quick that didn't betray her fear. But she felt eyes behind her, as if something vapid had followed her up the stairs, perhaps all the way from Fifth Avenue. She'd disembarked from the train at Penn Station, creeping along the sidewalks, past the dark alleys, the gated entrances to tenement buildings harboring street children with dark, lifeless eyes. She'd turned away from a policeman and nearly tripped over a rummy bedding down with a lamppost in front of a saloon.

But, she'd found him. Just like a journalist might do.

"What are you doing here?"

Not the words she expected, but she clutched her reticule to herself. "I—I had to see you."

He looked past her, as if expecting Bette. "You came by yourself? Here? Into Hell's Kitchen? Have you lost your mind?"

Her smile vanished.

He sighed then, and it was the way he glanced back, behind him, that shook her out of the kind of fantasy she'd entertained for nearly a week now. She'd imagined his delight, those beautiful brown eyes lighting up, him pulling her into his arms—yes, she imagined her hands on his shoulders, lifting her face for a kiss.

A kiss.

Sitting at his table, outlined in the light, sat a young lady, her long red hair down, her shirtwaist open at the neck, tucked into a simple skirt. She stared at Esme, bold. Unafraid.

She'd never had a scullery maid gaze at her so.

"Oh. I—I didn't realize you had a guest."

A guest? Esme's manners didn't allow her to suggest anything else. But suddenly, she felt sordid, as if perhaps she didn't know him at all.

"Come inside."

"No, I—"

"Come in, Esme. Now." He practically yanked her into his apartment, closed the door, and bolted it behind her.

Oh. She couldn't look at him and examined the room instead. It seemed cleaner than she expected, with a simple single bed along the wall made up with a blanket, stovepipe stove attached to the wall, a shaft of moonlight waxing the floor. But her gaze stopped on the woman at the table.

"I am sorry to interrupt—I should go." She turned, but Oliver gripped her arm, his voice cutting low.

"You shouldn't be here, but it's not what you think. I'm teaching Colleen to read."

"Read? But you can barely re—"

He gave her a hard look and she shut her mouth.

She just wanted to slink away. Why had she ever thought...

Yet, a book lay open on the table, the lamplight illuminating a notebook and pencil.

"We're finished for tonight."

Colleen rose and, regardless of what Oliver might want her to believe,

Esme had no problem reading the look on her face as she took in Esme's attire then turned to Oliver. "Aye. Tomorrow, we will finish our lesson." Then she leaned up and kissed him on the cheek.

He didn't look at Esme as he let Colleen out.

Oh, she was such a fool. She closed her eyes, hating how they burned, how her throat tightened. She would not cry. Would not—

"Sit down, Esme. Tell me why you're here."

"No. I'm going home."

She felt his hand take hers and opened her eyes to his pained expression. "Why did you hunt me down? I thought—well, you made your feelings for me clear at the paper."

"I didn't know my feelings, Oliver. You—you surprised me. I was confused."

"And now?"

She looked around the room, taking off her gloves. From an overhead window, moonlight puddled onto the floor. His camera lay in a bag on the chair. A pot of coffee sat on the stove. The room smelled faintly of Oliver, his scent, wild, safe, dangerous. "I don't know."

He nodded, his jaw suddenly tight. "This is how it is, Esme. Reality."

"Why do you live here?"

"It's across from the police station, if you didn't notice. They let me tag along on calls. I get the best, freshest photos in town."

"I saw men on the streets. Drunkards. And children."

"You'd see more than that if you lived here. Which you won't."

She took a breath. "I could."

He did her the courtesy of not laughing in her face. Instead, his mouth curved up in a wry smile. "For a day. Or two. Maybe even a week or a year. But eventually you would hate me for taking you away from your life on Fifth Avenue. We come from different worlds, Esme. I was fooling myself to think I could provide for you. I can barely provide for myself."

He looked away then, as if his words cost him.

"What if—what if we went west? To Oklahoma? Or Montana? Started over? We could run a newspaper—"

He rounded on her with more emotion than she'd ever seen of him. "Stop! Just stop, Esme."

She stiffened. He shook his head, his eyes slick. "Why are you such a dreamer? Don't you get it? We don't belong together."

"But, you're the only one who…" She put her hand to her mouth. Looked away as tears filmed her eyes. "Who knows me. Who—who still loves me."

Or, maybe he didn't. Not anymore.

But she heard a groan and looked back at him just in time to see him reach out for her. He cupped her face with his hand, ran his thumb down her cheek, his eyes tracing her face. His voice softened, and in it she found the man she'd feared she lost. "I do, Esme. I always have."

Then, he kissed her.

Although she'd hoped to find herself in his arms, however forbidden, she hadn't expected it to feel so right. As if she'd always belonged there. This was what a kiss should be—something urgent and kind, gentle yet confident. Something that told her that, indeed, he loved her, had hoped that she might find him.

She slipped into his embrace and wove her arms around his waist, ignoring propriety's heed, and surrendered to his kiss. He tasted of coffee and smelled of the city—oil and dust and his own hard-working scent, but it combined for something bold and wild. His arms had a perfect strength, capturing her, holding her safe, and she let the kiss awaken something inside her she'd never known.

Longing.

She longed to be with this man, to wake up every morning in his arms, to see his smile at the end of the day. She longed to forge out a life with him, something they could be proud of, something wrought from their own talents. Perhaps they'd have children, replicas of Oliver, with dark shanks of hair, bright eyes, smiles that spoke of mischief.

"Esme."

She didn't want it to end, didn't want him to pull away, so she held on, laying her head on his chest, listening to his heart thunder.

"Esme." His breath was close and eddied across her cheek. "I'm sorry. I shouldn't have taken advantage—"

No, no. "Please, Oliver. Don't say that." She looked up at him, at the stricken look on his face. "I've longed to kiss you since…well, longer than I probably realize." She ran her hand down his whiskered chin. "Don't push me away."

But he took her arms, pulled them away from him. Didn't meet her eyes. "This can't work, Esme."

She shook out of his grip. "Why not? Because I'm privileged?"

"And I used to be your houseboy, your footman! Yes! I can't bear to see you living like this."

"Shouldn't that be my choice?" But a strange heat webbed her chest.

"No. Because you truly don't understand."

She stepped away from him. "Enlighten me."

"Fine. Yesterday, the family downstairs lost their ten-year-old daughter. I knew something was wrong because I heard wailing. I went into their room and found her on the floor, delirious with fever, pale, and thrashing. I begged them to let me take her to the charity ward, but they had already been there. The ward sent the girl home to die. To die, Esme. The father is blind—hasn't worked for a year, and he and his wife both have lead poisoning. Their youngest son is a newsie, and the two dollars he might make every day is barely enough to feed them and keep their rent paid. I never, ever want to see your child die in your arms. So, yes, I am taking you home right now, and you must forget that you know me."

"I'm not going home!"

But he had shoved her reticule into her hands.

"No!"

"Esme."

She wrenched away from him, plopped down on his bed, her face fierce despite the flush of tears, the wobble of her voice. "I love you. I'm not leaving."

He just blinked at her. "You love me."

"Yes."

"You love me."

"Yes!"

He turned away, and then with a shout that scared her, he slammed his hand onto his table. She jumped.

Then he rounded on her. "You can't love me, okay? I was a fool when I saw you last. I should have never said what I said."

"Then you want me to marry Foster Worth. You're fine with me having his children."

He flinched. But, "Yes."

His word landed like a fist in her chest. *Yes.* "I hate you."

He nodded. "Good. Hold onto that thought."

"I shouldn't have come here."

"You're right about that." He grabbed her arm, pulled her to her feet. "I'll deliver you home, Miss Price, and then I never want to see you again."

His words cut her through.

"Don't bother seeing me home."

"Esme!"

She pushed past him, into the hallway, gathered up her skirt, and raced down the dark stairs.

"Esme!"

But he didn't follow her out the door, didn't follow her as she slowed her pace to a walk, clutching her bag to herself.

The street had turned dark, only the flicker of gaslights pushing back the night. She nearly tripped over a man lying on the sidewalk, then she crossed the street at the sight of a cluster of men around a barrel fire. A dog howled, the odor of gin oozed out of an alleyway. She ducked her head, hating her tears.

Fool.

I never want to see you again.

She brushed her hand across her face, realizing she'd left her gloves in his room.

The shadows loomed at her, hands that could yank her into a dank alleyway. The redolence of refuse and human waste seeped into her skin as she turned down a street, darker than the last. She'd ridden the elevated train for the first time ever, thinking herself clever. Now, the streets looked the same. Why hadn't she taken a carriage? Although that possibly might be more dangerous than walking.

"What do we have here?"

The voice slurred, drifted over her, dark and vile. A hand grabbed her arm, whirled her around. She screamed as she looked up into the face of a man not much older than Oliver with tangled, oily hair scrabbling out of an old, dented bowler. He reeked of unwashed flesh, his breath emitting something foul as he pushed her against a building.

Hands groped for her reticule. She let it go and he dropped it to the ground. He pressed his hand around her throat as he moved his body against her. She closed her eyes, turned her face away. "Please."

He had whiskers; they scrubbed her neck as he drew in a long breath against her skin.

She screamed.

And then, someone jerked the man off her, slammed a fist into his face, blood exploding from his nose.

"Oliver!"

The man crumpled onto the sidewalk as Oliver picked up her bag. Then he turned and scooped her up into his arms.

She locked her arms around his neck, buried her face in his chest, and let him ferry her from Hell's Kitchen.

Three blocks later, he finally slowed, his breath still coming hard.

"You can put me down."

"I don't think so."

She lifted her head to watch him, the tight cut of his jaw, the way his eyes flickered over her, shiny, dark.

"Put me down, Oliver."

He acquiesced then, righting her, not letting go of her arm. "Are you okay?"

She managed a nod. "I—I am a fool. My father said that someday I'd find myself in over my head. He was right."

Oliver pressed a hand on her cheek. Brushed away the wetness. "You scared me."

She leaned against his touch.

He sighed, blew out a breath. "Think this through for one second, Esme. Even if I do this right—even if I ask your father for your hand in marriage, he'll throw me out onto the street."

"He might not."

He gave her a look.

"I don't need my father's blessing."

"I think you do."

"I came after you, didn't I?"

He took her hand, ran his thumb over it. "And what was your plan? To find me, and then…"

She watched his strong hand cover hers. "I didn't have a plan. I just thought you'd be glad to see me. I guess that was foolish too."

He made a funny noise and she looked up to find his hand cupped over his eyes. He made another noise, something short, like a groan, and his shoulders shook.

"Oliver?"

He let go of her and held up his hands as if to stop her. "I'm trying very hard to be a gentleman here, Esme. I…" He looked up at her, his eyes reddened. "Yes, I want to take you home with me. I would marry you tonight. I would be that selfish, if I didn't fear the morning. If I didn't fear that someday you would die in my arms from some tenement disease, or—or actually come to despise me."

"Never. I would never despise you."

But his eyes didn't believe her. He took her hand, and she clung to his warmth. "I am taking you home, Esme. Right now."

"And then?"

"It would be best if you forgot about me."

She shook her head and her heart nearly burst when he offered her a slight smile of surrender.

"You are so stubborn."

She grinned then.

"I need time, Esme. Time to figure out what to do. How to marry you properly."

"Marry me?"

He glanced at her, his smile wider, and she met it. Nodded.

So, she rose on her tiptoes and kissed him. He caught her there, and let the kiss linger.

When she stepped away, he took her hand. "Shall we walk through the park?"

And as they walked into the greening commons, for the first time in her life, she knew what it was to be rich.

* * * * *

"Foster, look out! Don't hit anyone!" Jinx gripped the arms of the tufted leather seat, not sure if she should scream for fear—or joy. Through the tall pane of glass, and in the glow of the singular lamplight, a pedestrian leaped out of the path of the Dion Bouton as Foster steered the wheel protruding from the floor of his motorcar and swerved them out of the way.

"Sorry. I'll get the hang of it." He wore a black leather jacket, matching pants, and a pair of goggles. He'd also attired her in goggles, although she felt conspicuous as they motored up and down Fifth Avenue, coughing a black trail of smoke. She would have much preferred a walk through Central Park's winding trails.

Then again, could Lizzie or Del claim they'd ridden in an authentic motorcar, imported straight from France? Indeed, she could easily become accustomed to the gaping stares, the expressions of envy.

Too bad Esme had snuck away—and Jinx had a feeling where she'd gone, although she hadn't exactly minded when Foster extended the offer to her to accompany him on an after-dinner ride in Esme's place.

They splashed through a mud puddle, probably dirtying the beautiful yellow wheel spokes, the punched red tin on the front of the car. With its gold handles and polished mahogany, she couldn't wait to ride it down Oceanside Avenue in Newport this summer.

"You will bring it to Seacrest, won't you?"

"Of course. Esme and I will most likely be scouting for a summer cottage of our own. And I heard rumor of Alva Vanderbilt hosting a motorcross race on the grounds of Belcourt. I wouldn't miss it." Foster turned at the end of the park.

A motorcross race. How she longed to be the one wearing a chic Parisian dress, under an umbrella—although, what did one wear to a motorized event?—cheering on Foster as he bested a Vanderbilt in a race.

But, no. Esme would be among the ladies, cheering her husband. Jinx tried not to think about how he'd come to fetch her sister, to show her his newest acquisition. How, in fact, he would spend his evenings with Esme, hold her in his arms at night.

Jinx pressed a hand to her stomach, drew in a breath of springtime fragrance to scour away the burn.

She could probably console herself, however wickedly, that Foster had brightened when she covered for her sister and told him Esme wasn't emerging from her room.

Surely her sister would be more affectionate after she and Foster married.

They motored past the chateaus that sprawled over entire city blocks, past electric lamps glowing into the night. Foster's frame, close to her on the seat, warmed her, his leather outfit creaking as he steered.

"I saw her in France, and I couldn't wait until she arrived. Are you cold? I have a blanket in the compartment under the seat."

He glanced at her, the faintest hint of exhaust darkening his skin. He'd obviously decided to start the crank engine himself rather than ask a footman. But when he smiled, those white teeth, looking like an adventurer, pride in his eyes, she couldn't help smiling back.

No, she wasn't cold at all.

They pulled up to the house and he stepped down from the car. She braced her hands on his shoulders and he lifted her down, his hands on her waist.

He reached for her goggles. "Let me help you with these."

She closed her eyes, letting him remove them. When she opened them, he had removed his own and now stared at her, something tender in his eyes. "Thank you for going motoring with me. I really wanted to show..." His mouth tugged up. "Well, you, actually. Esme has no interest, I fear, in motorcars."

She wanted to say something—anything—in defense of her sister, but words abandoned her. Especially when Foster caressed her cheek with his gloved hand. "I am thankful we will be family." His voice softened, emotion in it.

Her throat tightened but she managed a nod.

Too soon, he stepped back. She wanted to lean into his touch, perhaps clasp it to herself, but what if others saw her movements?

What if they could read her heart?

"Give my regards to Esme. Perhaps I will stop back later tonight—your father has invited me for brandy."

"Thank you again," she said as he climbed back into his contraption.

The motorcar grumbled as it pulled away.

I am thankful we will be family.

She stood watching him go, the black exhaust making her step behind the columns that bordered their entrance.

And there, across the avenue, at the entrance of the park, just inside the rim of lamplight…no, it couldn't be.

Esme stood in the arms of a man. Kissing him. Sure, they were hidden by the body of an empress tree in bloom, if one peered straight out the window, but from Jinx's position…

Oliver.

She stilled, her grip tight on her reticule.

Of course. No wonder her sister didn't want to marry Foster Worth. She'd already given herself away—her heart at least, if not her body—to Oliver Stewart. The untidy footboy who had been chasing Esme and her money since the day his father, their butler, brought him into the house to live with them. Poor, motherless child, they allowed him too much freedom in the Price halls, and now the rogue had stolen Esme's honor.

Jinx couldn't watch.

She turned, shaking, and barely heard the footman's greeting as she entered the hallway. She unwrapped her coat, dropped it into the hands of the maid, and then stood in the marble hallway, listening to the ticking of the massive clock's echo against her heartbeat.

Someone had to do something.

Her movements felt natural, even heroic, as she knocked on her father's study.

The door creaked open, and Jinx stood there, letting the light from the hallway flow past her where her father sat at his desk. Her shadow cast a larger gloom upon the floor, and for a moment she shrank back from her betrayal.

But Esme didn't deserve her birthright, her millions.

Jinx did. Moreover, she would rescue them all.

And finally, her father would love her best.

August looked up from his desk. A soft glow of his lamp illuminated an edition of Pulitzer's *New York World*. "Jinx? I'm in the middle of something."

Jinx took a breath. This might even turn out for Esme's good. She'd be rescued from a penniless fate—shipped off to Europe, perhaps, but eventually married to someone who would allow her to spout her suffragette biases. Maybe even let her write those dime novels. Preferably from some chilly castle in northern Germany.

"Esme's betrayed us."

He stared at her. "What are you talking about?"

"She—she's run off with someone."

He stood up, came around the desk. "I don't understand. Esme's in her room. She wasn't feeling well."

"She snuck out."

He seemed nonplussed by this information. Oh, why did he love Esme so? Didn't he see that she couldn't carry on the Price legacy? "Where to?"

She took a deep breath as her father stared at her. "I think she went to see Oliver."

August frowned at her. "Oliver? Who is—"

"Father, you cannot be serious. Tall, dark hair, used to run through our home smelling of the stables?"

August shook his head.

"He's your butler's son."

"Yes, Ollie. Of course. I recommended him for a job with Bryant, the photographer. Why would Esme want to see Oliver?"

"Father, don't tell me you didn't know. Oliver has been in love with her for years. And I think—I think she's run away with him."

He stared at her so long it seemed that she might have to repeat herself. Then, "Stewart!" He looked at Jinx, and for the first time in her life, what looked like real fear entered his eyes. "Stewart!"

"Here, sir." The butler stepped into the open doorway.

"Do you have any knowledge about a friendship—perhaps a forbidden one—between your son Oliver and my Esme?"

Something flickered in Mr. Stewart's eyes. "Not directly, sir."

August's mouth closed into a tight line. "Do you know where your son Oliver lives?"

Mr. Stewart drew in a long breath. "Hell's Kitchen, sir. On the Cherry Hill side."

A trickle of ice went through Jinx. Certainly Esme hadn't ventured that far from their world. For what? Love? Had she listened to nothing Jinx had ever told her? Love couldn't pay for a home, servants. A life of value.

"Get my carriage. And all the footmen."

"Immediately, sir." The butler left them. August walked to his credenza. His hands shook as he poured whiskey into a glass. He took it and threw it back.

She wanted to tell him that Esme and Oliver were right across the street, in the park, but his tone had stripped her courage.

Esme deserved discovery, certainly.

She watched his reflection in the window as he closed his eyes, shook his head. "Why would she do this?"

Jinx almost let out a laugh but gulped it back. "You can't possibly think she really wants to marry Foster. She hates him. She has some idea that she will marry for love—"

"Love is a distraction."

She couldn't agree more. Clearly, she was her father's child.

Except, inside, her words pinched, just a little. Still, "I know. But she believes she loves Oliver."

"Love won't keep our family from ruin."

His words jolted her. He poured himself another glass, lifted it to the window, as if toasting his reflection. "Did you know that my first newspaper failed?"

She stilled, not sure if he wanted an answer.

"I invested my father's money in a paper in Buffalo. It failed and I was penniless. So I borrowed money to buy the *Chronicle*."

"But Grandfather is wealthy."

"Yes, he is, but he thought I should learn my lessons, grow up on my own. Well, I have, but the *Chronicle* has run into trouble."

"What about Mother's allowance?

"Deeded to me. And, all gone."

Jinx's hand tightened on the chair in front of her.

"The *Chronicle* has been losing money for years. We need advertisers and an injection of investments to keep it afloat until we happen upon something scandalous that will sell papers."

Something scandalous.

"Esme must marry Foster Worth, or our family, our fortune, will not survive."

Jinx drew in a soft breath. Now. She'd ask him now. "What if...I—"

"Sir, I believe Esme has returned." Mr. Stewart stood in the doorway, his face drawn. He looked at the floor as August brushed past him.

Jinx rushed after him, found Esme standing in the foyer. Two footmen held Oliver by the arms. He wore a wild, unruly look that made Jinx tarry behind the oak doors.

"Sir, I can explain."

August held up his hand. "Don't speak, or I'll have you arrested." He turned to Esme. "What were you thinking?"

For her part, Esme seemed...changed. Something radiated from her, a confidence, perhaps, that had died the night of her engagement to Foster. She lifted her chin. "I was thinking that I—I am not going to marry Foster. I want to marry Oliver."

Jinx's heartbeat thundered in the silence.

Then her father took a deep breath, and in a voice that seemed dangerously quiet, possibly emboldened by his second shot of whiskey, "Throw him out into the street."

"Father!"

He rounded on Oliver. "Don't ever come back here again. If I see you, if you try to contact Esme, I'll have you arrested. Or whatever it takes."

Oliver's eyes widened, then, "Esme, come with me. Right now."

She turned, but August grabbed her arm so hard she cried out. Esme clawed at his grip, and Jinx trembled as she watched her father shake her. "Stop these games, Esme! Don't you know you will be the wreck of us? You will marry Foster Worth. Tomorrow night or sooner, if I can manage it."

"No!"

He pushed her toward a pair of footmen. "Take her to her room," he thundered. "Post a man outside her door and don't let her out until the ceremony."

Then he turned his back to Esme. She tried to wrest free of the footmen's grasps, as others opened the door and threw Oliver onto the dark, muddy street.

"Esme! I'll be waiting right here for you. I'm not going anywhere. Esme!" They shut the doors, her name on his voice silenced. Then the footmen wrestled her around her waist, dragging her up to her room.

Jinx didn't move, horror stripping her of all thought. Esme would be made to marry Foster. Tomorrow night. Or sooner.

Her father stopped as he passed her, pressing a hand to Jinx's shoulder. "Thank you, Jinx. Well done."

Well done. She suddenly wanted to retch. Whirling around, she ran across the cold marble, up the stairs, and down the hall. She neared her sister's room, heard Esme slamming her hands against the door, screaming. The footmen couldn't hide their misery as they held the door shut.

Jinx closed her ears, running past them, casting open her doors. She shut them behind her and sank to the cold floor.

Tomorrow night or sooner.

Down the hall, Esme let out a wail.

Jinx felt it to her bones.

Then she pulled Esme's ring from her pocket, slipped it on her finger, curled into a ball, right there in front of the door, and wept.

Chapter 5

As if the heavens understood her misery, they opened and unloaded a torrent of tears upon New York. Jinx sat in her room in her bloomers, corset, and dressing gown, the rain pinging the windows, listening to the growl of thunder and wanting to flee.

How could she watch her sister marry the man she loved? And oh, how she loved Foster. She could close her eyes and lean her cheek into his touch, lose herself in his smile, his low tones, the smell of him as he held her as they waltzed.

Tonight and every day after, he'd hold Esme in his arms.

How would she ever learn to love another when she had given her heart to Foster?

Perhaps she understood Esme, after all.

Outside, lightning flashed against the gloomy pane. Thunder followed, far away over the river.

The servants readied the drawing room for the wedding—bowers of roses brought in to flank the marble fireplace, ivy and lilies hanging from the chandelier. Mother had sent out hurried invitations to a handful of close family friends, arranged a dinner for thirty to celebrate.

Unfortunately, Jinx couldn't possibly retire to her room, given the fact that she would be the next Price to marry. Her mother had already ordered her vellum calling cards, already begun the invitations for her debut ball.

Just this morning, her trousseau arrived from Paris. Ball dresses, dinner dresses, tea dresses.

Jinx couldn't look at it, knowing she'd be required to dance, flirt, and win the affections of a man who could never love her like Foster did.

Not that he'd professed it or—oh! She pressed her hands to her eyes.

"Ma'am, are you ready for your gown?" Amelia returned from the storage room, holding her new gown, the blue one with the rosettes along the neckline. She set the gown on the bed, began to open the muslin that protected it.

Amelia had already gathered Jinx's hair up on her head—nothing so adorned as when she would enter society, but it would be her first appearance with her hair up, ushering in her new identity as a "bud."

She stared at the mirror and wished she had half of Esme's beauty. Probably she wouldn't even make a match.

Maybe she should start looking at careers. Being a companion. Or a teacher.

"Jinx?" Her mother stood at the door, regal in a blue satin gown, her corset cinched tight, to accentuate her curves. On her head, she wore a tiara, diamonds at her ears, around her neck, a dog collar of diamonds. "Why aren't you ready? And it's freezing in here. Amelia, please light a fire."

She swept into the room, stood behind her daughter. Jinx stared at their reflections. Perhaps she did have her mother's features—at least the shape of her chin, the perfectly puckered lips. Someday she'd probably have her mother's tragic marriage too, if she didn't…if she…

"Mother, Esme should not marry Foster. She doesn't love him. And, if their marriage ends in divorce, it will be a scandal for us all."

"She won't divorce Foster."

"Are you so sure? She ran away to be with Oliver. Father had to post guards for the past two days to keep her secured in her room. What makes you believe she will keep her vows?"

She'd hit a mark. Her mother's mouth knotted, her eyes narrowing. She squeezed her gloves in her grip. "Perhaps you are right."

Jinx turned on the ottoman, keeping her voice schooled. "It's not a good match, Mother."

Her mother met her eyes then turned away to the window. "Then what will we do?"

Jinx took a quick breath, cast a look at Amelia, now striking a long match into her fireplace. She cut her voice low as she said, "I'll marry him."

Her mother rounded, stared at her. "But you haven't even yet been presented to society."

Jinx found her feet. "But you can admit it would be a perfect match. He and I share so many…interests. And you know I finished school with high praise from Mrs. Greenly. I can manage society and the balls, and the dinners—and you could teach me, Mother. I'm ready. I've been ready for two years."

"Indeed." Phoebe stepped up to her, lifted Jinx's chin to meet her eyes. "But are you ready for marriage? For—for the challenges, the…indecencies?"

Oh. Her mother raised an eyebrow.

She remembered Foster's hands on her waist when he'd helped her from the car, the thrill that went right through to her bones when he touched her face. "Yes."

Her mother considered her a moment longer. "Perhaps you are."

Jinx inhaled her Mother's words, let them sink through her, turn her body to light. *Perhaps you are.*

"But what if Foster doesn't agree?"

Jinx couldn't help herself. "I believe he'll agree, Mother."

Phoebe gave her a sharp look. Outside, lightning crackled against the pane. "Really. Well, what about Esme?"

A darkness fell through Jinx. She stepped away from her mother's grip, ran her hands up her bare, chilled arms. Thankfully, Amelia had lit the fire, but the immense room gathered the heat at the ceiling, warmed her toes last.

"She has Oliver." Not really—for what indeed would Esme do with her wayward heart? She couldn't marry the footman.

But her mother seemed to consider her words. Then she smiled. "Yes, she has Oliver. Get dressed." She turned to Amelia. "Fetch the white gown, the one we were to use for her debut ball."

The white gown, with the gold rosettes along the bodice, the lacy straps at her otherwise bare shoulders, a matching lace hem. In it, she felt fresh and bright and beautiful.

Amelia disappeared to the storage room.

Her mother took Jinx's hand, led her back to the ottoman. "Now you listen to me, Jinx. In order for this to work, you must keep your mouth closed. Say nothing to anyone, even your father. I will handle this."

Amelia returned with the gown, laid it on the bed, untying it. She pulled the gown out. The gold threads shimmered against the flames of the fire.

"Perfect," her mother said as Jinx stepped into it.

Jinx stared at herself in the mirror, the way the dress perfectly cascaded over her curves, accentuated by the corset. Just wait until Foster saw her.

Perfect, indeed.

She caught her mother's eye once, found her expression pinched.

It nearly strangled the euphoria bubbling up inside her.

Amelia finished arranging her dress then handed her a bouquet of lilies and roses.

"Remember, do not speak."

They passed Esme's room, her door still shut, the footmen staring blankly as they guarded her door.

Esme would be just fine. Perhaps Father would allow her a time of mourning, send her to Europe to paint, or write. Yes, she'd enjoy that. Perhaps she too might even find love.

They descended the stairs, the blooms from the florists scenting the foyer. It could be her debut night, her hands in her gloves hot, anticipation stirring in her stomach. If it were, she'd stand in the drawing room with her mother, greeting guests, then lead the first quadrille.

Yes, she'd gladly surrender her debutante season to marry Foster, to dance every night in his arms.

Her mother opened the drawing room doors, and by the fire stood her father, dressed in his tailcoat, an ascot at his neck. He held a brandy, swirling it, the amber liquid as if in flames.

"August, we have a situation," Phoebe said, gesturing to Jinx to close the doors.

Her father turned. He appeared aged, deep crevices etched into his brow.

"It seems that Esme may have compromised herself with Oliver."

Compromised herself—but no, Esme's wouldn't have...

Jinx glanced at her mother, who didn't spare her a look. She sat on the divan, folded her hands to keep them from shaking.

Her father flinched, his jaw tightening.

"August, you know she can't marry Foster, knowing she has...well, what are we to do?"

He shot back his drink. "Are you sure?"

"It may be worse than we suspect."

Jinx looked at the floor.

"What are you saying?"

"She may be with child."

Jinx closed her eyes, unable to believe her mother's tone, her words.

Her father's intake of breath made Jinx wish she could stop this. Except, well, what if it were true?

"I always feared something like this with Esme. She has a rather...untidy personality," her mother said. "We will have to arrange passage for her immediately for Europe, spend the season there while she...comes back to us."

Jinx didn't miss the narrowing of her father's eyes as she glanced at him.

"But, fortunately, Jinx is willing to"—she drew in a breath—"take her sister's place. She will marry Foster Worth, keep our family from ruin."

For the first time in her life that she could remember, Jinx saw her father look at her. Really look at her. As if she might be more than an annoyance, a mistake, a jinx.

"And would Foster agree to such an arrangement?"

"I believe he would be amicable, but of course, you'll need to ask him."

Her father's eyes hadn't left hers. She drew in a breath, held it.

And then, very softly, he gave her a tight-lipped smile. Nodded.

Heat washed through Jinx, her breath leaking out. And this time, when he patted her on the shoulder, she didn't want to weep.

In fact, she could probably soar.

* * * * *

She could live in poverty. Really.

For Oliver.

Esme stared at herself in the mirror, at her hair upswept into a concoction that made her appear as if she had wings, and hated the sliver of cowardice inside. She hated the memories that slid into her sleep last night, sour breath prickling her cheek, dirty hands groping her, the sound of her own breath, quick and sharp, waking her in a sweat.

She hated that, with relief, she'd awakened in her own wide, cotton bed, Bette knocking at her door with her breakfast tray. As Bette opened her door, Esme looked past her, just to confirm her footmen stood sentry.

Most of all she hated her father's voice in her head and how it could exonerate her, if she wanted. *If you try to contact Esme, I'll have you arrested. Or whatever it takes.*

Oh, why couldn't Oliver have been born to privilege? She cupped her face in her hands a long moment before she surveyed herself and the mess she'd made.

She looked like a princess in her wedding dress, the miles of tulle and satin puddling around her, the jewels sewn into the bodice capturing the twilight. Her hair coiffed, pearls at her ears, the dog collar laden with jewels around her neck. Bette had even affixed a tiara on her head.

Behind her, the fire flickered in the hearth, shimmered gold against the chandelier.

At least it had stopped raining, the rose gold of twilight sliding in across the parquet floor. She'd watched the wind lash Central Park, strip the trees bare, scatter the new buds upon the ground under the flashes of jagged light, turning over the touch of Oliver's hands in hers, his kiss, his eyes holding hers.

She could live in the tenements with Oliver, couldn't she? Share his tiny room with the moonlight scouring the floor, the scurry of rats behind the walls? She twisted her ring on her finger—apparently, she'd lost it, for it appeared on her tray this morning with breakfast. Diamond and platinum, it could buy food for the entire tenement house for a year.

"Esme."

A footman let her mother in, and Esme didn't look at her. She'd measured the distance to the ground last night, a desperate thought pressing her to the darkened window. *If you try to contact Esme, I'll have you arrested. Or whatever it takes.*

The thought burrowed inside her, turned her cold. If she married Foster, perhaps she could assist the families she saw in Oliver's building. Employ Oliver.

At least he'd be fed. Maybe he could move from that decrepit room.

Her throat tightened, her eyes stinging. "I'm almost ready, Mother."

Her mother walked up behind her. Esme turned and caught her strange expression. Almost a smile? "No need. You don't have to marry Foster." Her mother gestured to Bette. "You may remove her gown."

"What?"

Phoebe took the dog collar from Esme's neck and ran her hands through the pearls dripping from the ribbon. "I understand you better than you think, Esme. I know what it is to be in love, to be forced to marry another."

She sat on the divan before the fire, the dog collar still in her hand. "I loved a man who promised to marry me. But like your Oliver, he lacked social standing and money. He asked my father for my hand, but…" She shook her head. "I understand, Esme."

She stared at her mother, a slice of the night's chill rippling through her. "What are you saying?"

Bette had begun to unbutton her dress. Esme watched it fall from her shoulders. She caught it, held it to herself. "Wait."

Her mother looked at her.

Wait. Did she mean that? What if Foster courted her? They barely knew each other.

No. She pressed fingers to her lips, feeling Oliver's touch.

Phoebe rose, walked over to Esme's wardrobe, and pulled out a small valise, the one she'd used as a schoolgirl, visiting her friends on weekends.

"Pack her things—a skirt, some undergarments. We'll have the rest sent."

"Mother, what are you doing?" The words came out half panic, half disbelief.

She walked over to Esme, removed the tiara from her head. Then, carefully, she unpinned Esme's hair. It fell down, the hair rats dropping to the floor. Her mother reached down, removed the ring from her finger.

"I'm freeing you. But you must go before your father discovers your absence."

"Freeing me?" Her stomach swirled, her head lighter—probably from the lack of finery. "But Father said he would—that he would hurt Oliver."

"Shh. I'll handle your father. Bette, hurry, please."

Bette had already fetched a shirtwaist, a petticoat, bloomers. She layered these plus Esme's day skirt into the bag. Meanwhile, her mother unbuttoned the gown. Esme stepped out of it, gooseflesh rising.

"Her traveling costume, Bette. Now."

Bette found the brown skirt, the matching jacket, the shirtwaist, and helped Esme into it. "I don't understand—"

Phoebe took her face in her hands, icy against her flushed checks. She met Esme's eyes. "Be well, daughter." Then she kissed her on her forehead. "Use the servants' entrance as you leave. You may take a carriage, as long as you send it back."

Then, as she stared at Esme, a softness crossed her face, again that enigmatic smile. She opened Esme's hand, dropped the dog collar into it. Closed it. "For your dowry."

Then she shifted out of the room.

Bette bent to tie Esme's shoes. Esme sank down on the ottoman, staring at the dog collar. "I don't understand. Why would my mother send me away?"

Bette looked up at Esme. "Isn't this what you want?"

Esme flattened the collar out in her hand. "I...yes. But...what if it..." She leaned down, held Bette's hands. Not soft like her own, they had strength to them that Esme held onto. "I want to be happy. To do something powerful with my life. To...receive God's blessings. But I—I don't want to live in poverty."

Oh, she hated the truth, so bare and raw. She turned away from it, staring at her warm fire.

Bette cupped Esme's hands in hers. "What makes you think that poverty isn't God's blessing, also?"

"How could it be a blessing to watch your children die, living hand-to-mouth?" She slid her hands out of Bette's.

Bette folded her hands. "Ma'am. Is it possible that God is giving you exactly what you want? You just don't know how yet. Trust Him."

Trust Him.

Commit thy way unto the Lord; trust also in him; and he shall bring it to pass.

She got up and Bette retrieved her cloak then picked up her valise.

Esme watched her. "What will I do without you?"

Bette smiled. "You will learn to tie your own shoes." She met Esme's eyes, a smile on her lips.

"Indeed," Esme said and reached out for her valise.

She took the back stairway, as her mother instructed, and found a Victorian waiting for her at the servants' entrance. Giving Oliver's address to the footman, she climbed in, settled back in the shadows, her bag at her feet.

Bette stood at the window, her gaze on her as Esme pulled away.

A fresh breath upon the city caused her to draw her cloak around her. She clutched her reticule in both hands, the dog collar inside. The pearls and diamonds would be enough for her and Oliver to purchase an apartment, perhaps not on Fifth Avenue, but in Chelsea. They wouldn't have to live in the tenements.

Perhaps God had blessed her way already.

The smell of fire, probably from the coal furnaces and wood boxes in the slums beyond Fifth Avenue, scented the air. Storm water pooled in the streets, splashed up on the wheels. She could taste Oliver's smile as she let her circumstances flood through her.

Indeed, she would be happy. Blessed.

She drank in the sudden, wild sense of freedom as they cut past Penn Station. Maybe he'd find a job at a paper.

Maybe she'd even write too.

They traveled toward Hell's Kitchen and she watched the city darken. No more gaslights, no more trees laden with buds dripping onto the fresh grass. No more houses, their ornate windows peering onto the cobbled streets.

Alleyways like tunnels gaped at her, homeless men squatting under makeshift shelters made of crates, the sputter of fire flickering at the depths. The rain turned the streets to clay, scoured up a smell of waste.

She fisted the cloak tight. Perhaps she would ask her driver to wait while she found Oliver. And then—where would she spend the night? She hadn't thought far enough to consider her lodgings. Her mother didn't expect her to stay with Oliver, did she?

She glanced at the valise. What, indeed, did her mother believe about her?

Wait. What, in fact, did her mother intend to tell Father? She drew in a quick breath, leaned forward to tell the driver to turn around—she'd return home, get her father's blessing, or at least his forgiveness—

Light bathed the street before her. She heard shouting, screams, the breaking of glass.

A roar.

She leaned out the window as a stream of sparks swirled beside her carriage.

"What is it?"

"Fire, ma'am. One of the tenement buildings." Her driver stopped the carriage. "The street is filled with people. They seem to have abandoned the building."

As they neared, she got a view of firefighters in long coats pumping water out to hoses and spraying from horse-drawn steamers onto—

No. She reached for the door handle. Stumbled out onto the muddy street. Didn't even bother to hike up her skirt—just stumbled to the edge of the crowd, the heat burning her face as smoke poured out the windows at the top of Oliver's building. Flames licked like tongues around his dormer window, black smoke pouring from the ones below it. From the front door, a man, his face sooted, stumbled out, holding a little girl in his arms.

"Oliver!" She pressed forward, searching for him in the crowd, past firemen, women clutching their children, saggy-jawed men in suspenders and derbies reeking of alcohol, others in cotton shirts bearing the build of workingmen. A broad-chested man in a great coat and top hat, someone who could have been from her side of town except for his rickety-rack nose, stepped in front of her. "Whoa there, missy, you're going to get hurt."

She pushed against him, her eyes on the roil of flames as they burst out a lower-story window. "Oliver!"

"He's dead."

The voice, spoken loud enough to cut through the roar of the flames, the screams, stilled her. She whirled around.

The redhead—what was her name? Colleen. She held herself with her arms crossed, her hair long and tangled, her face puffy. "He was in his room when the lightning struck the house."

"How do you know?"

"I had just left him. He told me…" Colleen's face tightened, something frenetic in her eyes. Then her hand came out, up as if to slap Esme. Esme recoiled as Colleen made a fist, held it to her breast.

"You wouldn't have been happy," she said then pressed her lips together, her body shaking. "He wouldn't have been enough for you."

Esme stared at her, everything stilling, turning numb.

"But to me, he was the world." Colleen cupped her hands to her mouth, shook her head. "Go home, Miss Price. You don't belong here."

The words shook Esme through, winding down her body, seeping into her bones.

Dead.

She stared at the inferno. Glass exploded and the crowd gasped, screamed. She bore it without moving, even when the spray from the fire hose slicked her skin, turned her dress soggy. The mud seeped into her shoes as the night fell around her, shrouding her, only the glow of the fire upon her skin.

He couldn't be dead. She refused to believe it.

She wrapped her arms around herself. She'd stay until she knew. Until—

A great roar shook her as the house caved in, the skeletal frame charred, flames rising up to the blackened heavens.

He could be out taking crime photographs. Which meant he'd turn them in tomorrow…at the *Chronicle*.

You're an amazing writer, Esme. Prove to him that you can write—better than any man in his city department.

His voice found her behind the growl of the fire, his words calm and solid. She gritted her jaw, swallowing back her tears.

He won't care.

Make him care.

Her gaze landed on a group of three, a man holding a child, coughing, a woman stoically watching the destruction. Another man held his head, his eyes glassy. Firemen wet the houses nearby, the mist like the steam from the underworld as it floated into the night.

To me, he was the world.

This had been Oliver's world. The one he'd tried to capture, to not only survive in, but redeem.

"Ma'am, we should go." Her driver—she looked at him, saw that he couldn't be any older than Oliver, the hint of shadow on his skin, his eyes darting to the crowd around them.

She watched the fire begin to die, the embers like eyes, blinking through the night.

"Take me to my father's paper. Take me to the *Chronicle.*"

* * * * *

"You never told me you had a yacht."

Jinx held onto Foster's shoulders as he lifted her out of his landau and onto the pier.

"It's a recent acquisition. For our wedding trip to Europe."

Their wedding trip. She glanced at him, trying to read his face. He seemed unfazed by the substitution of a different bride, almost as if her father had suggested she might be a racehorse, one that could accomplish the derby as well as the first. Foster had entered the drawing room after meeting with her father in his study and taken her hand. Then he bent before her and slipped the ring he'd presented to Esme onto her finger. She'd watched him for any hint of a twinkle in his eyes, but when he looked at her, she saw nothing. No charm, no smile, not even triumph.

Perhaps he, like she, didn't want to betray an untoward jubilation.

He did, however, squeeze her hand, just enough to calm the battle inside.

Surely he loved her. After all, he stood before the judge and committed himself to be true to her, to care for her, in sickness and health, for richer or poorer.

Hopefully for richer. "Europe?"

"You said Esme wasn't going to visit Paris, so I thought…" He lifted a shoulder as he held out his hand to help her up the gangplank.

She rather wished he'd sweep her into his arms, carry her across the proverbial threshold. But perhaps he wanted to wait until they had privacy.

He did help her manage her way over the deck, sweeping up the train to her wedding dress—or rather, her debutante costume. But it felt like a wedding dress, the way the guests had admired her attire. She'd eaten nearly nothing at the dinner, and now, at midnight, hunger clawed at her insides.

But she had nothing of food on her mind.

"It's a beautiful ship." Three-masted, with a steamer pipe in the center, she gauged it nearly two hundred feet long. An observation lounge spanned the center of the deck. She peeked inside, noticed padded chairs, long windows that overlooked the ocean.

The yacht listed gently, a delicate memory of today's storm, and overhead, diamonds of light sparkled in the scrubbed sky. The slightest tinge of smoke seasoned the air, caught in the breezes of New York harbor.

"Our salon is downstairs." He cupped her elbow and escorted her down the mahogany stairs. Rooms off the main gangway opened to porthole windows, most with a fireplace and maple wainscoting, overstuffed gold and green chairs.

He led her to the end of the boat, to the room at the bow. Porthole windows like eyes peered over the ocean. He turned on the tiffany chandelier, the gold thread in the seafoam-green damask wallpaper sparkling like an undersea chamber. And at the far end of the room, sat a carved walnut canopied bed, its linens fresh and tufted.

On top lay a box, wrapped in bright paper.

"You got me a wedding gift?"

She glanced up at him and he nodded, his smile tight.

"I'll change, but…" She turned. "You'll have to unbutton my dress."

She had hoped for something gentler as he worked her buttons free. She held the dress to herself then scooped up the box, glancing over her shoulder as she headed to the dressing room. "I'll be right back."

But he had moved to the fireplace, as if to start a fire. Well, it did seem chilly, and…

She shut the door to the dressing room, leaned against it, and tried to swallow the webbing in her chest, the dark thread that wound through her.

She'd rescued them all, hadn't she? Her father walked her down the stairs, into the drawing room, gave her hand in marriage to Foster, and for a moment, her hand on his arm, she'd felt safe. Protected. Wanted.

Blessed.

She stepped out of the dress and, not knowing what to do, laid it out on the carpeted floor. Then, she unhooked her corset, letting her body breathe.

Finally, she opened the box.

Inside, wrapped in brown paper, she discovered a two-piece lingerie suit. White cotton, with lace across the bottom of the drawers, and pink ribbon sewn into the edge of the corset bodice, which hooked in the front. Eyelet lace trimmed the neck and sleeves. She pulled it out, ran her fingers across the fabric.

Tears filmed her eyes. What a kind gesture from her husband. She reached up to take down her hair, missing Amelia's ministrations. She should have insisted her maid travel with her. Perhaps she could request her in the morning, before they left port. Her hair fell, and she finger-combed it out, gathering up the rats, setting them with the tiara her mother had presented to her next to her dress.

She stepped into the drawers, tied them at the waist. They seemed longer than normal, bagging nearly to her ankles. Then she pulled on the bodice, hooking it in front. It pulled against her chest, bagged at her waist. Still, she felt oddly pretty, despite the shiver that ran up her bare feet.

Good thing Foster had built a fire.

She smoothed the fabric over her stomach then looked at herself in the mirror. She seemed older, just in the few hours since she'd become a married woman. Her eyes wiser, her body more womanly.

She fashioned a smile, her lips puckered, then opened the door.

Foster stood with his back to her, one hand braced over the mantel, a poker in hand, staring at the flames.

"It's beautiful, Foster," she said softly.

He turned.

His eyes contained no warmth of the man she'd thought she knew, as if he'd been far away and yanked back too soon. He let his gaze scour over her. "Indeed. It was made for Esme."

Esme. Of course it was. Jinx pressed her hands to her arms, rubbing away the gooseflesh. She looked down, wishing suddenly she could change back into her debutante dress, wishing that the flimsy fabric didn't make her feel naked.

She turned toward the dressing room, not sure—

Foster caught her, wrapping his hands around the tops of her arms. His hands were warm, almost sweaty. He leaned down, and as she drew in a breath, staring at her reflection in the mirror, he brushed her hair aside and pressed a kiss at the base of her neck.

Then met her eyes in the mirror.

There was the smile, the one she'd fallen for. Something full of mischief, of charm. She caught his hands on her arms, wove her fingers into his grip. "We'll have the perfect life, won't we, Foster?"

He gave a low chuckle and turned her to face him. He cupped his hand beneath her chin and raised her face to meet his.

As he moved in to take her lips, he stopped a moment to meet her eyes, his so gray, like the smoldering sky right before dawn. "Yes, Jinx. Absolutely perfect. I promise."

* * * * *

Her father had a magnificent view of New York from his office, the way the sun gilded the cobblestones, the statue on the roof tolling the early morning hour. Here, seated in his leather chair, hands on the armrests, Esme could see why people feared him.

Not her. Not anymore.

She watched the pigeons alight on his statue, others pick at crumbs at his feet. Across the street, newsies scuffled their way to the alleyway to pick up their papers, a man wheeled an apple cart into the square. Inside the corridors of the office, the city desk began to stir with voices, stringers stopping in to sell their stories, the night photos of local crime.

No Oliver.

The truth began to settle in her bones, a pervasive chill that tasted of grief.

She closed her eyes, itchy and cracked, and leaned her head against the chair. No second thoughts.

Ma'am. Is it possible that God is giving you exactly what you want? You just don't know how yet. Trust Him.

No, she was through trusting God. So far, with every step of faith, she'd found grief instead.

From now on, she'd trust no one but herself.

Footsteps through the reception room stilled her and she drew herself up, not turning to greet him, staring a moment longer at the view.

"Who's here?"

The voice shook her, the violence in it, as if he'd arrived to the *Chronicle* already churning the stress of the day.

You're an amazing writer, Esme. Prove to him that you can write—better than any man in his city department.

She didn't have to prove anything to anyone but herself.

She turned his chair around. "Hello, Father."

He looked as if he hadn't slept either, his eyes reddened, cracked, his face lined. She hadn't before noticed the stoop in his shoulders, the way his hands shook when he took his watch from his coat pocket, checked the time.

"How did you get in here?"

"The night editor let me in. He remembered me." She folded her hands on his blotter. He just stared at her.

"When did you get here?"

"After midnight, after watching Oliver burn to death."

She clipped out her words without emotion, pushing the ball of flame deep inside her chest. Later.

Her father stared at her. "Has something happened to Oliver?"

She caught her voice before it escaped her. "His tenement caught fire last night. He was trapped in his attic apartment."

"I'm very sorry, Esme, but I still don't understand. What were you doing there? I thought…your mother told me you were unwell. Of course, that's to be expected I suppose. And now…I suppose we will have to provide for you in your situation."

She frowned at him. "Unwell? Why would I be unwell? What situation?"

He stared at her a moment longer, his eyes finally narrowing. "Aren't you expecting…a child?"

His voice shuddered at the end and she saw what his words cost him. As if, with that question, everything flushed to the surface. Suddenly, she saw it all in his eyes. Hurt. Worry. Grief.

The truth settled on her. Of course.

"I don't know what you have been told, but no. I have not been with a man. Including Oliver."

He pressed his hand to his heart. Closed his eyes. Reached out to palm his credenza. "Oh no."

It was the way he sagged, how he turned to her, horror in his expression, that made her breath hiccup, made her want to rise, to rush to him.

Instead she watched him make his way to a chair, sag into it.

"Father, you've been lied to. But never mind. Oliver is gone, and I will do my duty for the family, on one condition."

He had his face pocketed in his hands as if overwhelmed, despairing. She couldn't agree more. But now wasn't the time to grieve. "If you require me to marry Foster, then I want to write for you. Be a journalist for the city. I know I can do it, and you do too."

He still hadn't looked up at her.

"I saw those people at the fire last night, and they need a voice. Families without homes, living in squalor. Children dying of cholera. And high society sits by and lets it happen. We should be ashamed of ourselves, having dinners for our dogs and horses and going to Hell's Kitchen on guided tours. Makes me ill." She stood, picked up the notepaper she had put on his desk, and handed it to him.

He looked up at her.

"What is that?" His voice seemed to emerge from far away.

"My first article." Somehow she held it without her hand shaking.

He reached out and took it.

And, as she lowered herself back into his chair, he read it. The clock ticked behind him. So, this was how it felt to have an editor read your material. She tried to study his face.

It shook her when he cupped his hand across his forehead, hiding his eyes.

"Father?"

He said nothing, finally sighing. "It's very good. A few sentences I might change. Overdramatic."

"Thank you. I will return home and dispatch my apologies to Foster immediately—"

"He's already married."

The words clipped her, fast and hard.

"What?"

"He married last night."

She leaned back in his chair. "I don't—I don't understand. Who did he marry?" But even as the question left her, she knew the answer. Heard the name in her head before he said it.

"Jinx."

Of course, Jinx. Finally ascending to her birthright.

She spread her hand on his desk. Felt the smooth wood, with the other hand, the worn creases of his chair. Someday, she would sit here. Rightfully.

For Oliver.

Her father set the article on the desk. "I can't publish this, Esme. You're a talented writer, but it is not your place in society to write articles for my paper, like some stringer. We will need to find you another suitor—"

"No." She got up and picked up her reticule, the one holding the dog collar. It would buy passage somewhere, even to a new life. Oklahoma, or even Montana. She didn't belong in New York. Not without Oliver.

She would go somewhere that allowed her to be the woman he believed in.

Her father looked up at her, eyes reddened. "I love you, you know."

"I'm sure you did. Take care, Father."

He caught her arm as she passed by. She glanced at his hand, the strength of it, on her arm. "Love has many faces."

"I know, Father. The one I knew was Oliver's."

She reached the door before he turned. "Esme?"

She pulled out her gloves, fought the tremor in her hands as she worked them on.

"I don't know what to do."

She turned and traveled back to Delmonico's, to her father's voice in her ears. *I expect great things from my Esme.* She found a smile.

"Keep an eye out for my byline."

JINX

NEWPORT, RHODE ISLAND
1900

Chapter 6

News traveled too fast, even in the seaside town of Newport. Jinx should have had the right to tell Foster the news, should have been entitled to see his face.

Trace it for a hint of remorse.

"How long will you wait for him to come in from the harbor?"

"I don't know, Mother."

Jinx sat in the dining room, the bronze and crystal Doré-style chandelier dripping light like tears upon the table. Landscape panels depicting a dark and fertile French countryside suggested a more baroque existence than her own. A clock—a wedding gift from the Astors—chipped away the late hour. She should have ordered a fire in the marble-carved fireplace, for the early July breeze had a bite that had collected in the corners of the room before they'd closed it for dinner.

"You'll just let him sit out there, scandalizing you with his boatloads of trollops, chorus girls, and cabaret singers." Her mother put down her fork, letting it rattle on the Dresden china, a purchase from Jinx's last trip abroad.

Upon her own plate, Jinx's broiled quail had turned chewy. She had no appetite anyway and lifted her hand for the footman to carry it back to the kitchen.

"I won't be needing dessert," she said. Indeed, with Foster's arrival in port three days prior, she'd sworn off all sweets, aware that since the miscarriage, she hadn't yet fit back into her standard corset. In fact, she should probably reorder her winter season wardrobe, since she wouldn't need the adjustments the maternal condition would have demanded.

Her throat burned and she drew in a breath, wishing for the tang of the salty air, to lose herself in the sultry night. She would have taken dinner on the terrace, but her mother regarded that sort of al fresco dining barbarian.

"He went to Paris to pick up his brother. I am sure they are simply friends of Bennett's. You know his reputation."

"Perhaps his reputation has infected his brother."

"Mother—"

"I saw his sins with my own eyes as I rode with Mamie today down Ocean Avenue. A sloop setting out for the *Jinx* with a couple of strumpets on board."

"Mother, please!"

"He's as much of a scoundrel as your father."

Jinx stared at her mother. One had to consider her closely, past the powder, the diamonds and pearls at her neck, the flourish of her dark, padded hair, to see the marks of despair, the finite lines troweled into her face over the past four years. But no one could miss the flashing dark eyes, the contempt barely veiled when she spoke of August.

Indeed, Phoebe had all but moved into Rosehaven the moment Jinx finally announced her renovations completed. Never mind that her father resided in New York—even during the height of the social season of Newport. Phoebe apparently couldn't bear the notion of his belongings leering at her.

Jinx gladly gave her mother rooms at Rosehaven. She had no one else to fill them. And, her mother made for an adept party planner. She had stood beside her in the gilded ballroom for the past two seasons to host Jinx's annual motor chase cotillion.

"Foster is most likely conducting business and is too busy to come ashore." She refused to believe that he might be simply punishing her for the loss of their child. He couldn't be that cruel, could he? "I no longer wish to discuss this." She stood, smoothing her shirtwaist into her skirt, then rose and walked out toward the ballroom.

Without guests, the chandelier unlit, the massive room gathered the shadows, the windows dark, the electric lamplights outside illuminating the fountain. The place mocked her.

Four years without an heir. No wonder Foster had fallen out of amour with her.

Her shoes resounded across the parquet floor, and for a moment, she saw herself in Foster's arms, the few times in the past two years when, for society's sake, he belonged to her.

She opened the doors and stood on the veranda. The sky was dark with mystery, the nuance of the sea beckoning.

Her mother's steps tapped across the floor, so she stepped out onto the terrace, past the potted ferns and ivy twining across the Corinthian balustrades that bordered the terrace. In two month's time, she'd have the footmen erect columns, entwine them with silk and electric lights, perhaps sprays of hydrangeas from the gardens. Then, three hundred of her closest friends would dine alongside her and Foster, she in a new Worth gown, bedazzled with some diamond choker Foster had gifted her. He always found a way to soothe her wounds, and this night, these past two months of reading his name in the tattler's pages of the *Newport News* would be abolished.

"You need to give him an heir."

Her mother's voice, kept low, cut through the swath of her assurances, and Jinx drew her arms around her waist.

She drew in a breath. "You know I've tried."

Phoebe stood beside her, staring out at the fountain where two swans swam, their wings clipped. "You must keep trying. Your standing is insecure unless you produce an heir."

Jinx closed her eyes, fighting the ache that swelled inside her, the one that could curl her into a ball in the wee hours of the night. Or cause her to walk out onto the grass, barefoot in her nightclothes, when she knew the house slept.

She didn't bother beseeching God. After all, she had stolen her sister's husband. Maybe she deserved the loss of three babies from her womb.

"I can't make him come home. Can't force him into my bed." Couldn't make him love her. "He might not even know that I lost this child yet. He might not want to risk the child's survival." She had no illusions that he really loved her, but he did want a son, and so far he hadn't neglected his marital duty. Like he might be conducting a business transaction, an invitation appeared on her plate on the designated morning before their assigned meeting, an appointment designed to produce someone to carry on the Worth name.

"Then go to him. Certainly you are not ignorant to a man's weaknesses."

Jinx glanced at her mother. Phoebe didn't look at her.

"Mother, I...no. Foster is not very..." Gentle. He'd never been overly amorous with her, not even on their wedding night. She'd almost suspected anger, although she couldn't admit that. Brutal would be too harsh, but sometimes she slipped away from him feeling hollowed out, as if he'd stolen yet more of herself from her. "Affectionate."

"A woman does what she must. It is part of the marriage contract."

She had kept her part of the contract. Usually, however, she crept off before the dawn, unable to see his face when he awoke and found her sleeping beside him. She would never forget the morning after the wedding for as long as she lived, the smile upon his lips as he'd awakened, only to vanish as he'd looked at her in the light of day.

She blamed herself for their conjugal estrangement. She wasn't, after all, beautiful like Esme.

The image of her sister bubbled up, stole her breath.

"What is it?"

Jinx longed to remove her shoes, run her toes through the blades of sweet, thick thatch. Wind stripped her hair from its bounds, tangling it around her face. Beyond, in the darkness, waves pummeled the shore.

"I smell a storm coming."

"Indeed. You should hurry if you intend to board the yacht tonight."

Jinx glanced at her. "I will not. I hate the yacht. It makes me sick."

"I thought you loved the sea. You spend more time in Newport than any other society woman. I feared you would be attacked by ruffians, coming down here without a full complement of house staff before the season opened last week."

"I hoped the sea air would help me...would help the..." Baby. But she couldn't say it. She had to stop thinking of the pregnancy as a child or she might simply fold into herself, let despair take her like the currents below the cliffs.

Phoebe drew in a long breath. "I had three miscarriages before I had you, Jinx. You are not without hope. You simply must take to bed the moment you know you are pregnant. It was the only way I had you. Complete bed rest."

"And Esme? How did you fare with her?"

Phoebe pressed her lips together.

Oh yes, the forbidden topic. "Mother, you can't simply erase her from your life. She's your daughter also...isn't she?" She took a breath, searching her mother's face. She refused to interpret her stoic expression. Her voice softened. "Don't you wonder how she is? Where she is?"

"I know where she is, Jinx."

Jinx studied her, the way her mother opened her mouth, drew in a long breath. Blinked.

"Where?"

"She doesn't have your life, I promise you that." She turned away. "I will retire to my room while you fetch your wayward husband."

Jinx stiffened as her mother pressed a hand to her arm. "Bear him a child, and then, even if he divorces you, you can demand he provide for the child. You will still have the means to care for yourself."

And your family. Her mother didn't say it, but Jinx caught the undertone. Her allowance would be enough to keep her mother in style as well. Of course, childbearing had been reduced to security.

Have a child. Then she could close herself away from Foster forever.

Away from love, forever.

Oh, why had she stolen her sister's life, thinking it should belong to her? Perhaps if she'd waited, she would have found love, someone who wanted her. Not Esme.

Not beautiful, brilliant, courageous Esme, who had run away with the boy she loved to live happily ever after.

Jinx toed off her shoes, leaving the slippers in a pile on the terrace steps. Then she stepped out on the cool stones, past the swans, their heads tucked under their wings, and into the curtain of darkness.

Away from the house, with the windows like eyes peering out over the lawn, she could tear out her hair, let the husky lick of the sea coat her skin, draw her into the secrecy of the sea. Sometimes, when bathing at Bailey's Beach, she longed to tear off her black stockings, feel the sand between her toes. To dive headfirst into the waves like the men.

The purpose of visiting Bailey's is not to froth around in the waves, but to be seen. Her mother's voice cut into her ears, reminded her of decorum. Indeed. Society would cut her so quickly, she might as well move to Philadelphia, or even Baltimore. If she had the excuse of a child, she might withdraw from the lawn parties, the dinners, the coach races, and the afternoon carriage rides along Bellevue Avenue, at least until her shame at Foster's behavior pulsed less fresh.

Perhaps, if he had a child, he might not look upon her with such disgust.

She walked out to the edge of the lawn, where their property tumbled into the sea blow. A walkway along the cliffs gave voyeurs view of their estate, but no one hazarded the sand-cast rocks this hour of the night. Jinx sat on the ground, the cool of it seeping into her skirt. She leaned back on her hands, staring at the dark sky, searching for stars, wishing to unravel her mother's words. *She doesn't have your life, I promise you that.*

Lightning bugs pulsed around her, the cicadas sawing against the thrash of waves. She smelled a storm in the scurry of air lifting her hair from her neck.

Esme, where are you?

She longed for some relief to whisk through her, but she only tasted dread welling in her mouth. *Please let Esme be happily married to Oliver, have a child, or perhaps two.* Certainly her mother had bequeathed her enough means for her and Oliver to start a life. Perhaps nothing of stature, but enough for their own estate, a meager staff. Oliver surely could find a way to support them, perhaps as a photographer.

Esme wouldn't be destitute, right?

Jinx longed to close her eyes, to lift a petition toward heaven, but she had annulled that right years ago.

Instead, her gaze fell upon the ships anchored off shore. She didn't recognize the *Jinx*—the fact Foster named the ship after her only skewered her through with his mocking—but it drew forth the familiar longing. She didn't want to simply bear Foster a child. She wanted to earn his love, figure out how to win back his smile, his laughter.

The soft words of affection that had cajoled her to hand over her heart.

She wanted to feel his arms around her, just once, in love instead of duty, and to live happily ever after.

The sky lit up, a splinter against the pane of night, and behind it, a growl. She should leave, perhaps, but didn't, even at another shock of lightning.

I can't make him come home. Can't force him into my bed.

Her own pitiful tones rushed at her and she closed her eyes.

Then go to him…

The sky broke open and began to weep upon her. She sat in the cloak of darkness until it saturated her through, down her bones, turning her numb.

Go to him. Yes.

* * * * *

The storm drove Foster home.

Jinx lay in her bed, the canopy casting shadow upon shadow as the rain lashed the window, and heard his steps in the hallway. The door to the adjoining room opened, closed.

She held her breath, her heartbeat filling her ears. She didn't hear his valet, so perhaps he'd come ashore alone. Occasionally, after a night of too much bourbon, Foster simply commandeered a waiting landau and instructed the driver to repair him back to Rosehaven.

At least he knew where he belonged. At least he didn't take rooms at the Newport Casino.

She listened to him tharrumph about his room, then silence as he must have climbed into his bed.

What had Doctor Thornton told her after her second miscarriage? Something about being more apt to conceive within the three-month window afterwards? She had, of course. And lost that one also.

But, that had been only a month ago. Perhaps…

Outside, the rain drenched the lawn, pulsing over the cliffs in great waves of fury. Lightning flickered against the pane. She wouldn't need a candle, or an electric light, however foreign the path between their rooms. She rarely used their adjoining door—only once that she could remember, even after four years of marriage.

She half expected it to be locked. When she turned the handle, eased the door open, she could barely see into the room. His velvet drapes shuttered the paladin windows, blotting out even the barest of light.

Maybe it would be best not to see the cruelty in his eyes.

Her throat parched, her breathing webbed in her chest.

Drawing in a breath, she reached out into the darkness, her hand bumping a long bureau. She tracked her fingers across it, stepping gingerly across the floor, and they brushed his array of bottles. Her fingers trickled up the slim neck of a whiskey—perhaps it might be brandy—bottle. She stopped, drew it to herself. A tremor went through her.

Last time they'd been alone, he'd called her a name, ordered her from his embrace. Humiliated her.

She uncapped the bottle, brought it to her lips. Made a face at the pungent odor then tipped up the bottle.

The liquid hit her throat like fire, tearing through her, burning her belly. She slapped a hand over her mouth to stave off a gag, her eyes watering. But she steeled herself and took another draught.

This time, it burned less, although her stomach roiled. She closed her eyes, let it settle. Yes, her heartbeat seemed less thunderous in her ears. She didn't bother capping the bottle, just set it on the bureau.

Her skin prickled, the cool air finding the gaps in her silk corset, the bloomers she'd ordered from a boutique in Paris. She didn't need Esme's castaways. Foster was her husband.

She shuffled across the floor, her toes finding the carpet edge then smoothing across it until she found the bed frame.

The hint of a snore at the apex of his breathing told her that he'd already dropped into a sound sleep.

Perhaps that would be best. Awaken him with soft kisses, allow him to believe this moment a dream, something lovely and rare.

She tasted the brandy she'd drunk—probably brandy, from the sweet, albeit fiery, tang in her mouth—and let it embolden her as she lifted the bedclothes and climbed in.

He had his back to her, his skin radiating heat even before she touched him. She ran her fingertips over his smooth back, the wide shoulders she had loved, his muscular arms, strong from lawn tennis and golf. She pressed a kiss to his spine, felt him rouse.

"Shh, Foster. It's me. Welcome home. I've missed you."

He stilled, and for a long moment she thought he might spurn her, say something cruel.

In the bottom of her stomach, she expected it.

She didn't expect him to roll over. To reach for her. Didn't expect his kisses to be so sweet, so languid and kind. Didn't expect him to hold her, or to make her feel beloved in his gentleness.

He smelled of the sea, salty and fresh, and kissed her like he'd missed her, as if they hadn't spoken cross words before his journey to Europe to retrieve Bennett. He said nothing, not even her name, and she tasted the whiskey on his breath. She decided he must believe himself back on the boat. Or dreaming.

She certainly was.

He seemed thinner, but perhaps he'd lost weight at sea, and his hair, longer, shifted through her fingers. He needed a shave, but she had expected that, although not the missing mustache. She imagined what he might look like without it—the way he'd appeared when they'd first met—and relished it.

He wrapped her in his arms, covered her with his warmth, and for the first time ever, she didn't fear him.

Never had she felt so perfectly whole.

Nor so utterly bereft.

So, this was how it was supposed to be between them. So this was how it felt to be loved, even briefly.

Don't wake up, Foster.

He shuddered in her arms, as if sighing, then his breathing became thicker as he settled back into slumber.

She longed to stay, but something—perhaps the errant slip of fear—shivered through her, whisking with it her relief, compelling her to flee. She slipped out of bed, pressing a final kiss to his whiskered cheek. Tomorrow, perhaps he'd remember.

She would never forget.

She closed his door behind her and found her bed cold. Shivering under the sheets, she watched the storm flash and bellow outside her window. Then she cupped her hands over her womb and prayed for a miracle.

* * * * *

Morning slid into her room like a waltz, bold and triumphant, the storm having scrubbed the sky to a classical blue. Jinx awoke early, wrapped herself in her peignoir, and stood at her window, watching the sun on the sea, the waves now calm as they rode to shore, breaking on the unseen cliffs below. She heard nothing of movement next door but couldn't erase the images she conjured—the ones unseen except in her imagination, thanks to the blanket of darkness.

She couldn't wait to see him today, his gray eyes, hued with what she hoped might be the affection of their courting days.

Except, they'd never really had a courtship, had they?

She'd pressed the bell for her lady's maid what seemed ages ago, and finally Amelia knocked then opened the door, her face freshly scrubbed, her dark hair pinned up. She wore her morning attire—white dress, a princess apron with the bib, apron, and shoulder straps made as one and edged in lace, a matching lace cap pinned to hair. She tipped her head to her mistress and added a shallow curtsey. Jinx had read of that behavior in the *English Ladies Manor Handbook* and instituted it for her household. She'd also upgraded the uniforms of her staff to more formal attire in the afternoon, with black dresses, embroidered cuffs and stiff collars, and lacy aprons and caps. One had to set high standards to establish a reputation of culture.

Amelia carried a tray furnished with tea and toast, a copy of the *Newport Daily News* folded on the tray. She set it on the breakfast table then left to draw Jinx's bath.

"I'll be eating breakfast in the dining room this morning with Mr. Worth, Amelia. Please inform the cook."

Amelia emerged from the adjoining bathing room. "Yes ma'am." She slipped out.

Jinx poured herself a cup of tea, added two cubes of sugar, and sank into a divan. She'd have to replace Amelia soon—the girl was going on twenty-seven, nearly too old for a lady's maid. But she'd been with the family since she was twelve, starting as a scullery maid. Perhaps Amelia could fill the position of a second housekeeper.

It took so long to train a competent lady's maid. What a shame that Jinx couldn't keep her attendant like Foster kept his valet. Lewis had been with Foster before Jinx had met him, although with his dark eyes, his ugly, broken nose that made him appear like some back alley ruffian, she could admit that she feared him. He watched her like she might be something scurrying across the floor.

Jinx finished her tea before Amelia returned. Amelia helped her bathe then slip into a corset—not too tight, just in case she might already be with child—and a bell skirt and white blouse with the new pagoda sleeves, flouncy and tied at the wrist. She wasn't sure she liked the way they sometimes caught in her soup, but today she must be most delicately attired.

Hopefully, beautiful.

She exited her room, light sweeping from the two-story ballroom down the dark, paneled hallway, and followed it down the stairs. The dual staircase, split in the middle then rejoined at the bottom, carved out a heart shape when viewed from the bottom. She'd worked with architect Stanford White, competing with Alva's beautiful Marble House for the largest ballroom in Newport. She'd laid marble floors, erected Corinthian columns, and found the perfect chandeliers to cast kaleidoscope colors captured by the sea. She'd designed Foster's billiard room with bleached English oak and a chimney piece carved with the visages of Irish Kings. Decorated with a nautical theme, including an oil of his beloved *Jinx,* she'd thought, foolishly, that the room might call him home.

But maybe those days of merely hoping were over. Maybe, after last night...

The smells of breakfast—bacon and eggs, the oil on the griddle—seeped up from the basement, filling the hallway. She would have to instruct the housekeeper to open the windows, let in the salty air.

She didn't expect her heart to hiccup in her chest when she saw him, and for a moment, she stood entranced in the doorway, tracing the cut of his wide shoulders, the curl of his dark—except, it seemed lighter, almost sun-bleached—hair.

Too many days at sea. Or, some fancy Paris salon.

Most likely, his brother had thumbed him into it.

Along the length of the table, her mother sat attired in a stiff, high-collared, blue day dress. She sipped watery oatmeal and read a morning issue of the *Newport Daily News*.

Jinx scraped up her voice. "Hello, darling."

He turned, and her world halted, her breath caught in her lungs, her eyes widening.

"Hello, darling, to you."

She didn't recognize this man. He had the features of Foster, the high cheekbones, the regal nose. But his smile—almost playful, and the tease in his blue eyes, suggested a man unencumbered by marriage, by responsibility.

Bennett. It had to be, and she voiced her suspicion. "Bennett?"

"At your service. And you must be the mistress of the house, my brother's wife. Charmed to finally meet you." He'd risen to his feet, and now, as she stood, rooted at the door, he came over and took her hand.

Indeed, he looked a younger version of Foster, his crisp white shirt outrageously rolled up to the elbow, although he'd buttoned his gray waistcoat, his pinstriped pants neatly pressed.

He bent and kissed her hand.

What? She felt his lips, sweet, gentle on her hand, and the touch shivered through her.

Oh…no…he hadn't…

"Where's Foster?"

Taking a closer look at him, she saw that he wore no moustache.

"He stayed in town to attend to some last-minute duties." Funny how his voice fell when he said it, and she could recognize the texture of a lie.

But that meant…

"When did you get here?"

"I arrived late. Foster's valet brought me home, repaired me to one of your guest rooms. I apologize for the suddenness of my arrival." He walked her to the table, held up a dismissive hand when the footman stepped forward to escort her into her chair. He pulled it out instead and helped her sit.

She nearly toppled into it, her knees suddenly liquid.

Oh no.

"Jinx, are you well?" Her mother looked up from her paper, frowning.

She pressed her hands to her stomach, now roiling. Swallowed and tasted bile. "No, I don't think so. I think I need a walk outside. Some fresh air."

"I'll attend you," Bennett said. Nothing of the inebriation of last night reflected in his clear blue eyes, especially when he offered his arm.

She stared at it, at the kind hand, and a flash of memory went through her, something so rich that, for a second, she felt his hands on her, warm and kind.

She might be ill. "No...I'm fine. I'm sorry." She stood and pushed past him, nearly running down the corridor, through the massive, shadowed ballroom and out onto the terrace.

She gulped in the salty air. The heat of the sun, piercing in the unveiled sky, bore upon her, pressed through the cotton of her shirt, into her skin, her pores, her bones, as she sank down onto a chair and pressed a shaky hand to her lips.

Along the edge of the terrace the gardener tended the roses, cutting them back, petals falling like droplets of blood onto the grass.

Oh, please. Please. She hadn't really—couldn't have—spent the most important part of the night with her husband's brother.

Chapter 7

"Jinx? Are you okay?"

Of course he hadn't obeyed her. Of course Bennett Worth had followed her out to the terrace, probably to drive deeper her shame, the betrayals of the night. How had he ended up in Foster's bed?

"Don't come out here. Don't talk to me." She gripped the arms of the chair, steeling herself at his voice. She couldn't look at him.

"Your mother is worried about you—"

"How could you?" Oh, she hadn't meant for the words to lurch out of her like that, but oh... "You lecher!"

She turned and caught his expression at the tail end of her words, the way he recoiled, as if they slapped him.

"What did you call me?"

Bile filled her throat. "You deserve it, and more. I'm not some chorus girl easily wooed into your chambers. I—I am not that girl."

"Of course you're not." His tone mocked her, as if he might actually be confused.

"You make me sick. All the way through to my bones. I can't believe... oh, what will Foster say?"

Dawning slipped over him slowly, she read it in his face. The frown, the flicker of memory in his eyes, the intake of breath, again a frown. "Wait a second. Last night. That was you?"

She shut her mouth, her jaw tight. "Don't tell me you didn't know."

"Stop. I need to think." He held out his hand to her, or rather to

123

steady himself on a nearby chair. "I—no, this isn't right. Listen, Jinx. I…" He seemed to have a difficult time breathing, because he pressed his hand to his chest. He shook his head. "When I awoke this morning, I wasn't exactly sure what happened."

"You weren't sure that…" She pressed her voice low, her breath knotted in her chest. "That you'd had a visitor in the night?" Her tone scared even her.

"I was…not exactly sober. And very tired. So yes, when I woke this morning, I had a fuzzy memory, something that lingered as a pleasant experience—"

"A *pleasant* experience?" She needed to keep her voice down lest her mother or any of the babble-mouthed servants hear her, but… "A pleasant experience?"

He stared at her, as if he might be choosing his words carefully. "Yes. Very…pleasant. Well, wasn't it pleasant?"

She closed her eyes, wishing herself anywhere else. "Just who did you think I was? Some servant girl, compliments of the house?" She stared at him, trying to skewer him, make him bleed. "Just what kind of household do you think we run here?"

He lowered himself into the chair next to her. Stared down at his polished shoes.

No, no, no. Fury—or perhaps shame—turned her voice to a fine, sharpened point. "I have to admit, Bennett, the stories I heard of you turned my ears red, but to meet you and your womanizing ways face-to-face? You come sneaking into my home—"

"Just one second here, Mrs. Worth, but just who did the sneaking around here?"

"Keep your voice down!"

Out of the corner of her eye, she noticed his jaw tighten, his face hardening, a look she recognized from the Worth legacy. Here it would come—some sort of remark meant to cut her to the quick, something brutal and eviscerating. *You trollop.* She heard the slur in her own head in the voice of her mother.

But his voice emerged soft, almost hurt. "I don't know what you've heard about me, Jinx, but I think perhaps my brother has been feeding you inaccuracies. I was overseas managing our father's business. I had one or two girlfriends, French women, yes, but I...I'm not the kind of man who finds himself in the late-night company of women. Not usually."

Did he think her an idiot? "Not usually? Then what about the parade of women to the yacht the past four days?"

His mouth tightened. He looked away.

Oh, she hated Foster then. The disgust burned inside her. He'd never find her knocking on his door late at night again.

Ever.

Last night had been a cruel, horrific mistake, the kind she'd have to bury inside her so deep Foster could never see it in her eyes. She'd have to tear from her mind the memory of the way she'd felt, as least for a slice of time, like she belonged in his arms.

As if he wanted her.

It was all a lie.

Her eyes burned as she watched another gardener gather hydrangeas. "If the cabaret girls weren't for you, then why? Why did you..." She couldn't even say it. *Pretend you were my husband.*

"I swear, Jinx." His voice softened, and he looked at his hands. "I didn't know it was you."

Another memory raked up, so that she had to measure her breath lest a gasp leak out. How could she have mistaken him for Foster? He'd been nothing like Foster. He'd been tender, and sweet. No moustache, and now that she thought of it, he'd smelled different, his body thinner, his hands woven into hers.

What if she'd known? Deep inside her heart—what if she'd known and surrendered anyway?

Sweat trickled down her back, dribbled under her corset.

"You were just there." His voice lowered, the tone soft and gentle. "And you smelled like roses, and you were soft and…" He actually lifted his hand as if to touch her hair. She jerked away.

He tightened his hand to a fist. "I'm not a lecher, but I don't know what I was thinking." He buried his hand back into his lap. "I haven't been with a woman for a while, and maybe I just lost myself. I know it was wrong. But you acted like you wanted to be there, if I recall."

"Of course I did. I thought you were my husband."

"Yes, of course. You're right. I—I don't know what to say."

She glanced up at him then, at the texture of his blue eyes. He did look sorry, the way he looked at the sea, back to her, the bob of his Adam's apple in his throat.

"Foster can never know. Ever. It's erased. It never happened."

"We'll never speak of it again." He blew out a breath, rubbing his hands now on his legs. "But, really, you couldn't tell the difference between Foster… and me?"

She tightened her lips into a knot. Glanced at him. Tried to find words that wouldn't scour up her shame. Finally, "Foster and I don't often… have marital relations." She turned away as her face heated.

"But you've been married for four years."

"Yes. He travels a lot. And I summer in Newport." She looked away, just barely stopping herself from fleeing the terrace, running across the lawn, perhaps throwing herself from the cliffs. "And I've been pregnant three times. There was a waiting period after the miscarriages."

"Naturally." He was silent then. Drew in a long breath. "I wish I could convey how truly repentant I am for what I did, Jinx. My inebriation was no excuse. I forgot where I was, and in the moment, simply gave in to my loneliness. I should have been honorable."

He met her eyes then, the blue in them so piercing she couldn't breathe. "I also apologize for my brother's neglect of his wife that would drive her to find solace with him in the middle of a stormy night. He should have been home three days ago, should have invited you to his chambers, or asked admittance to yours. He should not neglect you."

The words burrowed in like a blade and turned her voice crisp. "I'm not a pet that he should attend to me. I'm his wife. I run his household. Keep his name in the social register. He doesn't neglect me. He's simply busy."

"He's simply a buffoon."

"You can leave anytime."

She glanced at him and tried to add daggers to her eyes.

He met her gaze, held it, anger in it. "You're a beautiful woman, Jinx, and I'm sorry it was me in Foster's bed last night. I'm sorry it wasn't your husband. And I'm sorry I took advantage. And, this is probably despicable, but I've gotten to know my brother over the past few weeks, so I'm hoping that it *was* a pleasant experience. It was for me."

"Get out of my house."

"I'll have Lewis collect my things." He rose and she bit her lip to keep it from trembling. "It was nice to meet you, Jinx."

She turned her face away from him, listening to his steps echo across the parquet floor of the ballroom.

Even his footsteps sounded lighter. She again pressed her hand to her mouth, to stave off the scream building inside. What if she had known? She searched her memory for a moment when she might have suspected he might not be Foster.

No. Never. But what if she had? Would she have pushed herself out of Bennett's arms? After the relief of him not turning his back on her, after the tenderness of his attention awoke something dead inside her, would she have had the courage to turn away?

You're a beautiful woman, Jinx.

She feared the answer of her thirsty heart.

The gardener, bearing a bouquet of peonies, approached the terrace and replaced the sagging stalks in the vase on the table. She inhaled the fragrance. Foster could never know. If he did, he'd divorce her.

And without an heir, she'd be left penniless.

An heir. She closed her eyes, pinching away the prayers from the night before. No, no, no, she could not have conceived last night.

"Ma'am? Mr. Worth has asked for your presence in the salon." Her butler, Neville, stood in the terrace doorway.

She turned away. "I don't care what Mr. Worth has requested. You can gather his things and tell him to get—"

"Jinx?"

She jerked, the voice raking through her. There was a time when she longed for the deep tenor of his greeting, the way her name rolled off his tongue. Now, it just made her stiffen, made her fight for a smile.

Foster.

Perhaps if Bennett had said her name in the swaddle of darkness, she would have known, because there was no mistaking the difference in the delivery of her name.

She drew in a breath. Dredged up a smile, although she didn't expect one in return, and rose from her chair. "Foster, darling. Finally. I'm glad you made it home."

He looked older. More tidy. A pinstriped bow tie at his neck, he wore a dark frock over a black waistcoat, his boots sandy from the harbor, his dark hair oiled back on his head. His cool gray eyes held hers, an arrogant smile at his lips as he bent over and pecked her cheek. "I sent my brother on ahead last night. I take it you've met?"

He stepped aside, and Bennett looked past her as he nodded. She, however, kept her smile in place. "Of course. We had breakfast. Got acquainted. I'm just sorry we didn't meet sooner." The words tumbled out like grease, thick in her throat.

"Perfect, because he'll be summering with us here at Rosehaven. I've asked Neville to prepare his rooms. I told Lewis to repair him to my chambers last night, given the late hour. I hope he didn't disturb you."

"Of course not." Her glance went to Bennett, who made a significant attempt to stare through her to the ocean. "But are you sure he would like to stay here and not in town?"

Please, Bennett?

He seemed to rise to her inner pleas. "Yes, brother, I'm just as happy taking rooms in town. I hate to disturb you and your wife. I know you must have missed her. And she, you."

Jinx cut a look at Bennett, and the way he stared at her—finally looking at her—her throat tightened. He didn't take his eyes away from her, holding her gaze as Foster laughed, something harsh and bright. "Oh, we'll be fine, Bennett. As you see, her mother has taken a suite as well. I hardly think Jinx has been lonely."

He clapped his brother on the shoulder. "Your trunks are being unloaded as we speak. My house is yours. Besides, in a few days, I must continue on to New York. I have shipments to greet and accounts to settle."

"But you've only just returned."

Had she said it? She'd thought it, yes, but the protest issued from Bennett.

"Business calls. Someone needs to keep my wife in gowns and jewelry, right Jinx?"

"But—but I have to talk to you. It's about…" She glanced at Bennett, who was now inspecting the gardeners' work, a real horticulturist.

Foster glanced at him, back to her.

Fine. She cut her voice to low. "I am no longer with child, Foster."

He made no response, just breathed in the news. Bennett closed his eyes, something like a wince on his face.

Finally, Foster nodded. "I expected it, frankly, Jinx. It seems you can give me nothing of worth."

She flinched.

"But fear not, I heard the news in port a few days ago. I trust you're feeling better?" His gaze ran over her, and she knew he had to be comparing her.

"Somewhat."

"Splendid. I'll return in time for the motor coach cotillion," he said. "As long as work doesn't tarry me." He winked at Bennett.

She watched Bennett's mouth tighten, just a bit, on the edges.

"In the meantime, Bennett can fill in as your escort to your summer soiree and fripperies. Introduce him around. I've already paid his fee for the Casino—he loves a good game of lawn tennis, don't you, Bennett?"

"I don't need a nanny."

"Jinx plays a passable game of lawn tennis. And she's brutal in croquet, aren't you, peach?"

Bennett looked at her again, compassion in his eyes.

Clearly, he'd heard her confession. She wanted to dissolve into the terrace.

However, a lady didn't air her pain before guests. "Do you know how to drive a car, Bennett?"

"I haven't yet had the pleasure."

"Great idea, Jinx. Take him motoring. And to all the lawn parties and to Bailey's Beach." He boxed his brother on the shoulder. "Maybe you'll get lucky and find yourself a wife."

Bennett glanced at him, but Foster hadn't finished. In fact he rounded on Jinx, something dark and sharp in his eyes. "If anyone can marry you off, it's Jinx."

* * * * *

She could lose herself under the glitter of the Newport night sky. Jinx sat on a chair, her gaze more on the way the moon flowed like syrup across the ocean than Puck's soliloquy in the final scene of Shakespeare's *A Midsummer Night's Dream*. The back lawn of Beechwood Estates, the milky white mansion of Caroline Astor, spilled out to the sea, the moon turning the grass to silver. On the terrace, a stage and light showcased a private group of players shipped in for the Astors' amusement.

"'If we shadows have offended, Think but this, and all is mended...'"

"Penny for your thoughts?" Bennett leaned close, his voice low, sending a tremor through her. She glared at him and he sat upright as, on stage, the player Puck finished then bowed to the applause of his audience. It seemed Caroline Astor had invited the entirety of Newport to her gathering under the clear August skies for the Shakespearean festival.

At least Foster had finally left for New York City. He had managed to turn a few days into two interminable weeks that stretched out into painful silences and a fog of cigarette smoke drifting from his billiards room. He and Bennett jaunted off to the port every day, lost in some business transactions. They left her to plan the motor chase cotillion, make her daily coaching tour along Bellevue, attend one of Mamie Fish's lawn parties, and take in her daily dip at Bailey's Beach.

Fully clothed and under the canopy of the bathing cart, of course.

She'd also managed to spread the word that Foster's younger brother had returned to the States in need of a wife.

An influx of calling cards appeared at her door that very afternoon.

Jinx applauded with the crowd then allowed Bennett to help her to her feet. She slid her hand through his cocked arm, necessary to keep up appearances.

"You were daydreaming at the end, Mrs. Worth," he said, nodding to Alice Vanderbilt. Jinx had spent the past three days introducing him to as many of society's notables as she could, making a list of the eligible ladies still unspoken for, responding to calling cards. If Foster wanted his brother married off, yes, she could manage that. Anything to get Bennett out of the house and out of her thoughts.

Especially her thoughts. It didn't help that the sultry night captured the fragrance of the salty sea, the aroma of the freshly manicured grass, stirring romance. Not to mention that Bennett wore a Parisian male fragrance that she found particularly distracting. Annoying, even.

"I'm thinking that I find this particular Shakespearean production frivolous. Imagine having a potion that makes a man fall in love with you.

It's ridiculous. Poor Helena. No wonder she felt as if the men were mocking her when they professed their love. It was just a game."

"At least she and Hermia married the men they loved."

"But did the men truly love them back?" Jinx said, not looking at him.

"It was supposed to be a dream."

"A dream it was, because the girl who regards love as a serious matter is a girl who has never been in love." She tried to keep the hurt out of her voice.

He slid his hand over hers. "People do stupid things under the light of the moon."

"Come, I'll introduce you to Her Grace the Duchess of Marlboro, Consuelo Vanderbilt. Her mother locked her in her room for two weeks until she agreed to marry the Duke. I wonder what she might think of this play."

She angled toward the dark-haired only daughter of Alva Vanderbilt, her body swollen with child, and cut her voice to a stage whisper. "The woman gave birth to the heir to the Spencer-Churchill legacy only a year ago. She refers to this child as 'the spare.' Her duke she left conveniently at Blenheim Palace in England."

"You women have a delicious view of marriage."

"And you men seem to think it a game."

Beside her, Bennett smiled at a number of young women, clearly the gaggle having spent most of the evening circling the eligible bachelor, hoping for an introduction, as evidenced by the way they used their fans to hide their smiles.

Jinx had never played at the game of debutante flirting.

Consuelo was occupied by a group of aunts, so Jinx allowed Bennett to guide her across the lawn, toward the edge, where the dark waves splattered upon the rocks below.

Jinx suppressed a yawn, then couldn't help it and covered her mouth.

"I should get you home."

"Not until you tell me whom you would like to call on. I can make the arrangements."

"You don't have to find me a match, Jinx."

"I think Foster would like to see you married. I know your parents would. They are getting older—"

"My father's mind slipped away years ago. And mother is more interested in the bottom of her whiskey bottle than my advantageous marriage."

"Bennett!"

"I'm sorry, but they decided long ago that the only Worth they trusted was Foster. I failed out of West Point, and they sent me away to Paris to forget my name."

"But you made a name for yourself. Foster said you tripled the company's worth in the past two years."

He glanced down at her, surprise in his eyes. "Foster told you that?"

"I listen to his conversations sometimes. He speaks highly of you to his friends."

"Too bad my father didn't have the mind to recognize it."

"I learned long ago not to hope in the approval of a father." The words sounded harsh, even bitter in her ears.

He said nothing, the chamber music of Mrs. Astor's orchestra lilting across the grass.

"Why do they call you Jinx?"

She removed her hand from the crook of his arm. Her body felt sticky with the heat, despite the breeze off the ocean. "My father called me Jinx. At first, I loved the name, thought it was a term of endearment. Only later did I realize he meant I had brought him bad luck."

"Jinx…" Bennett turned to her, the texture of kindness in his eyes.

"Please, don't. I have long come to believe we make our own luck, design our own fate. No one will look after us but ourselves."

"That's not true, Jinx."

"Really? My father is a cheater and a cruel man, and he married me off to one of the same. My mother and I have had to fight for every piece of this life I've attained, and Foster hasn't a clue about what I do to keep him in good society. Shall we walk?" She turned, and he drew in a long breath before he held out his elbow.

"Foster doesn't mean to be cruel."

"Of course not. He just despises me because he believes I conspired to make him marry the wrong sister."

"The wrong sister? I don't understand."

"He was engaged to my sister, Esme. But she eloped with our butler's son and—"

"You married him in her place. I always wondered if I read the paper incorrectly."

"We were friends, and I misread his affections."

"I'm sure he was agreeable, or he would have never said yes. I know Foster. He's a stubborn man, set in his ways."

"He wanted Esme, and settled for me to get his hands into my father's newspaper and influence. I used to think he wanted to run for a public office, and having the newspaper would only advance his cause. It's made it worse that I haven't been able to offer him a child. I fear he's tiring of trying. And of me."

"Jinx."

Her name, again, on his voice, in that tone, could unravel her. She looked away from him. "I shouldn't have told you all that."

"Yes, you should have. Foster is stupid not to see what he has."

She hated how he could find the kindest things to say at the most raw of moments. She drew in a breath. "Tell me which of these women here you want to meet?"

"I've already—"

She nearly tripped, and dug her grip into his arm.

"Are you okay? Did you turn your ankle?" He led her to a folding chair, settled her upon it, kneeling before her.

She slapped his hands away then cut her voice low at his startled expression. "That's the last thing I need—for Mrs. Astor to see my brother-in-law lifting my skirt."

"I'm hardly lifting your skirt. You twisted your ankle."

"I'm fine." She leaned back, stifled another yawn. "Just exhausted."

He took the chair next to her. "You haven't been sleeping?"

"Too hot outside." She fanned herself for practicality only. "Sometimes, I stand at the window and stare at the fountain, wishing I could be like the swans and splash through the cool water." She fought a smile. "I have this wild dream of showing up at Bailey's Beach in my bare feet and wading into the water."

Oh. Whoops. She hadn't quite meant to share that. Heat flushed her face, and she glanced at Bennett, hoping he hadn't really heard.

Unfortunately, he was regarding her, those blue eyes on her, as if trying to unravel her words. The wind tousled his dark blond hair, ruffled his tie. Then, "Come with me."

"What?"

"Please, Jinx." Her heart tripped, thumped in her chest, an unfamiliar tingle in her veins.

She couldn't rightly make a scene, could she? Especially with him standing over her, extending his hand. She took it and he helped her up then led her through the house, signaling their footman at the door for their landau. He shooed the man away and helped her with his own hand into the carriage.

"We didn't say good-bye to Mrs. Astor." She felt oddly mischievous, even naughty.

"I promise you, no one noticed." He leaned back against the seat, staring at the stars.

She did the same. Let her heart trip then settle into a regular, albeit quicker beat.

"Can you trace the Big Dipper?"

"No."

He pointed it out, then the Little Dipper. "And those three bright stars are Orion's Belt."

"Where?"

He moved over beside her, pointed to the sky. She nodded but didn't see, his nearness suddenly befuddling her senses. He smelled dangerously sweet.

She finally sat up and saw that instead of turning left, to Rosehaven, they'd continued down Bellevue Avenue, past the Breakers and the Chateau-Sur Mer, past Alva's Marble House, and toward the center of town. "Where are we going?"

"Just a little place I know about. I promise, no one will know."

No one will know. Well, they had already kept one secret.

Instead of turning toward the wharf, they went east along Memorial Drive, into the middle-class section of town, the older, smaller, sea-beaten homes, then onto the peninsula connecting Newport to Aquidneck Island.

Bennett leaned up as they came to a rutted two-wheeled path. Beyond the scrub of the wispy beach grasses and tangle of wild roses, the ocean glistened under the moonlight.

"Stay here," he instructed the footman, and helped Jinx off the landau, holding her around the waist, his hands firm on her as she sank into the pearly sand.

"Where are we?"

"Foster and I used to come here when we were younger, when my parents took rooms in town. It was the only place we could swim without our knickerbockers."

"Bennett!"

"Shh. I promise to keep my knickers on." He glanced at her, grinned.

Sometimes, like now, she could easily grasp that he was only a year older than she.

He helped her to the beach and to a pale, skinned piece of driftwood. "Sit, please." He held her hands as she sank down onto it.

Then he knelt into the sand and reached for her hem.

"Bennett."

"Trust me. I won't look." He raised her hem enough to slide her slippers from her feet, roll her stockings off.

"Put your feet in the sand."

She lowered them to the earth, expecting something harsh and cold. Yes, the cold nipped at her feet, but as she burrowed her toes into the milky sand, she began to giggle. "It's...creamy. No, it's like sugar. Wet sugar."

Beside her, he untied his own shoes, set them aside, dug his feet in. She stared at the creamy white flesh of his feet, the strength in his ankles, his legs.

He held out his hand. "Hold up your skirt." Then he hoisted her up, and before she could protest, dragged her to the surf.

"Bennett, wait—"

But he didn't. Just pulled her right in up to her ankles, where her feet sank into the sand and the waves frothed their cold batter around her ankles.

The sea.

Another wave spilled over her then tunneled out the sand beneath her feet. She laughed, nearly fell, and Bennett caught her.

"I love it." She glanced up at him, saw herself reflected in his eyes. Saw her smile, her laughter. "I love it."

"Me too," he said, grinning, holding her hands as another wave poured in. "I could get lost in the sea."

They stood in the surf as the ocean tugged at them, cajoling them into its mystery, the moon the only witness to the truth as it settled into Jinx's heart.

This man was the Worth son she wished she'd married.

Chapter 8

"That was absolutely not out."

Jinx approached the net, pointing where Bennett's serve had landed in the opposite court. The morning sun shown down upon the clipped, pressed grass of the court, ringed inside the horseshoe courtyard of the Newport Casino. The dewy smell of earth and fresh-cut grass had long surrendered to the rigors of their early morning match.

Elise Donahue met her on the other side. "It was on the line. And on the line means out."

Jinx glanced from her to Grayson, Elise's brother, laughing as he backed up to the service line. "Jinx, you don't have to argue every call."

Maybe not, but she had to do something to salvage their match. Jinx felt as if she might be combusting from the inside out, beads of unsightly perspiration glistening on her skin and rolling down her corset, dampening the stiff white collar of her cotton shirtwaist and her flannel tennis skirt, while Elise appeared unblemished by the August morning sun, her white tennis shirt and skirt stiff with starch, her veiled sailor's cap neatly pinned.

Bennett had been watching the unmarried debutante all morning.

At any moment, Jinx's own hat might fly like a clay pigeon off her head. She wanted to claw the veil, tied neatly at the back brim, from around her face and allow herself a good look at the game.

Maybe then she wouldn't miss so many shots.

Maybe then Bennett's gaze might find itself back on her.

"It's okay, Jinx. Their serve. It's still forty-love." Bennett moved into position, readying himself for Grayson's serve. But he glanced at her and winked.

Something dangerous took flight inside her.

He appeared every inch the gentleman sportsman this morning in his cream linen tennis suit with the blue stripes, the white tie and a dark blue derby, a pair of suede court shoes. She'd given him Foster's racquet—a nearly unused Slazengor Demon. "I had the catgut restrung by my footman when he worked on my racquet," she said when she handed it to him.

"You mean to win," Bennett said, offering his arm. Her hand fit so neatly, so easily into it after two weeks of jaunting around Newport, making introductions at luncheons, competing with him during coaching contests, pairing with him in croquet at lawn parties, and besting other doubles at tennis.

Never, however, had he shown any interest in anyone's company besides her own. Perhaps she had become spoiled with his attention.

His gentlemanly attention. Aside from their risqué wade into the sea, he'd done nothing to stir up memories of their clandestine night together. Nothing to make her feel sordid.

Nothing to indicate, in fact, that he even remembered holding her in his arms. Kissing her.

But he'd made her that promise, hadn't he?

"The Donahues hold last year's doubles title. Wouldn't it be lovely to dethrone them?" Jinx said, lining up at half-court. It helped that her father owned the Newport Casino—her presence at the tennis club seemed expected. Even with Bennett.

Grayson's serve landed in the service square and Bennett lobbed it back easily. Elise returned and Jinx stepped back, nearly into Bennett, to return the shot to Grayson. He scooped it up and sent it high over the net, the perfect setup for Jinx to smash it back to him.

Grayson let it go with a shake of his head. "You going to let Bennett play, or should we let him retire to the bar?"

Jinx glanced back at Bennett. He shrugged.

"Sorry."

"You can't help it. But I'm here, just in case you want a partner."

He finished off the game with two neat aces.

Elise met her at the net. "You play beautifully, Jinx. I daresay you've been practicing. Will you attend the Open next week?"

"Of course—my best to you and Grayson."

"I think you and Bennett should enter." Grayson shook Bennett's hand. From Irish influence, he had kind eyes and an estate of millions. Recently widowed after his young wife passed in childbirth, Grayson had been eligible during the season she would have debuted.

Jinx might have been his wife.

Elise slipped her gloved hand into Bennett's, smiled up at him. "Newport is lucky to have such an accomplished sportsman among us."

Jinx didn't miss her smile, the way she held Bennett's eyes. Something twisted inside Jinx when Bennett smiled back. "I believe the same could be said about you, Miss Donahue."

Her smile affixed, Jinx shook Grayson's hand. "I think we'll simply watch you two win, won't we, Bennett?" She let go of Grayson, slipped her hand under Bennett's arm, despite the fact he still seemed transfixed with Elise's smile.

Her golden hair.

Her willowy body.

Of course she bewitched him. "Bennett, we have luncheon plans." She gave his arm a tug.

"Indeed." He seemed to come back to himself then, traded his racquet into the other hand, crooked his arm. "Perhaps I could call on you later, Elise?" He looked at Jinx, as if for permission.

The unexpected urge to wail filled Jinx's chest, but she nodded. He'd need a society escort, and since she was his married sister-in-law, she could easily fill that role. "Perhaps this afternoon?"

"Lovely. I'll be at home today," Elise said. She looked at Bennett, such glorious hope in her eyes. "Thank you for besting us."

Jinx barely stopped herself from rolling her eyes.

A court attendant gathered their racquets, secured them in the satchels, then followed them out as Bennett walked her back to the Casino meeting rooms in silence. His smile had vanished. "Would you like some lemonade?"

"No. I need to return home and repair my toilette if we are going out calling today."

He said nothing as they exited the building to their landau. He let her grip slide from his arm and allowed the footman to help her into the carriage, climbing up across from her.

He glanced at her, his voice tight. "Did you know Elise was a debutante when you arranged this match?"

"Yes."

He nodded, his lips knotted, suppressing all other comments.

He didn't look at her as they drove home.

And why not? He knew a beautiful woman when he saw one.

Jinx tried to drink in the sight of the harbor, so many yachts glinting in the sun, dappled upon the water. The smell of fresh fish, wet nets, gas, and oil obliterated the sweetness of the sea, and shoppers, their baskets full of fruits and breads, made her stomach roar. She'd been famished after tennis, but now—

She pressed a hand to her mouth.

"Are you okay?"

His tone nearly made her want to cry. What was her problem that she flitted from one extreme emotion to the next? One second she wanted to fight Grayson for points, the next, pummel Elise and Bennett for their smiles, and now she just wanted to cry.

And, she felt ill. She reached up, untied her veil, and lifted off her hat as Bennett watched, wide eyed. "What are you doing?"

"Fanning myself. I think I need to eat lunch. Too much exercise."

"What did you have to eat this morning?"

"I wasn't hungry. Toast and tea."

Bennett turned around in his seat. "Driver, please stop."

The carriage pulled up to the side of the road. "Stay here," Bennett said, and hopped down. She put her head back on the seat. Maybe she should instruct the driver to put up the top lest the *Newport Daily News* see her collapsed in her landau. But the sun seeped into her skin, kissing it, and the sounds of the village lulled her and—

"Jinx?"

The voice roused her and she opened her eyes. Where—

Bennett had his arms around her as she leaned into his chest on the seat of the landau. They'd returned home, the Rosehaven gardens perfuming the air, the movement of a fan—her hat—a light breeze before her face. As she pushed herself up, he scooped her up in his arms.

"Bennett."

"Shh. You're tired. Too much activity this morning, I fear. And it's so hot out. I left to purchase you an orange and returned to find you snoozing on the carriage seat. I just hope the sun didn't burn you." He glanced at the driver as he said it, but Jinx was too busy tucking her head against his shoulder, her arm looping up around his neck. He again smelled of that Parisian fragrance—woody, yet with a hint of citrus and the efforts on the court this morning. She had the terrible urge to press her lips against the well of his neck, to taste his skin, the sense of it stirring—

Oh.

Oh!

She leaned back, looked at him, and knew she wore her embarrassment on her face when he frowned at her as he carried her into the foyer. "What is it?"

"Nothing. I'm okay. You can put me down."

"No." He shrugged past the butler and her lady's maid and carried her up the stairs to her room.

He didn't need to ask where it was, naturally, and he pushed open the door with his foot.

"I'm really okay, Bennett. I was just fatigued after our match."

He set her down on the bed as Amelia rushed in after them. He turned to her. "She is hot and hungry. Draw her a bath and tell the cook to send some nourishment up immediately. She'll be retiring to her room this afternoon."

"But we have to call on Elise."

He rounded on her, something dark and unsettled in his eyes. "Please stop trying so hard to find me a match. I promise, I can manage just fine on my own."

He turned to go and the abruptness of his words, his departure, pushed tears into her eyes. She closed them, turned away.

She felt his hand on hers, then, closing. She opened her eyes and found his blue eyes on her, a kindness in them that she could never seem to slack her thirst for.

"I will see you tonight, at dinner, after which I promise to best you in a game of cribbage." Then he winked and strode from the room.

* * * * *

"I fear you have created trouble for us, Jinx."

Phoebe leaned up from the dining table where the butler had laid out the bookplates, which listed the descriptions and quantities of the china, silver, crystal, and gold services.

"What do you mean?" Jinx had already approved the menu for the motoring cotillion from the chef—terrapin, creamed oysters, lobster salad, salmon mousse, salad, bouillon, ice creams, cake, coffee, tea, and plenty of champagne. She intended to empty out Foster's supply.

She'd already met with the housekeeper, determining the rooms to be used as well as the floral arrangements—they'd feature the roses from their own gardens and ship in arrangements from Fleishmann and New York City. They'd secured Paul Whiteman and his orchestra for the evening.

Engraved, vellum invitations had already been sent, hand-scripted by Maris de Baril. "We only have the seating chart and the decisions about the footmen's livery to make. With nearly a month to spare. I believe this might be my best-planned motor coaching weekend ever."

Phoebe, still dressed in her shirtwaist and skirt, her dark hair coiled tight at the nape of her neck, shook her head. "That's not what I'm talking about. Surely this cotillion will be the finest of the season." She turned to the butler. "Please leave."

Neville bowed and left the room, closing the doors behind him.

"Mother?"

"You're in love with him."

Jinx let a beat pass, swallowed, and affected innocence. "Yes. He's my husband."

Her mother let out a sound that might have been a laugh had it not sounded so harsh. "You cannot play games with me, Jinx. Bennett. You're in love with Bennett."

Bennett. Yes. His winks, his laughter, his blue eyes in hers had been scrubbing at her mind all day since she awoke from her nap. Was he calling on Elise, right now? Taking tea with her? Walking with her through the gardens of her home? Perhaps he'd taken her for a carriage ride.

Jinx stared down at the bookplates, turning pages. "I think the Dresden might be too formal."

"Don't tell me you are unaware of your own feelings."

"He is my husband's brother. I am supposed to find him a wife. Of course that necessitates getting to know his personality, finding a suitable match. And escorting him to make introductions. It's all proper, Mother."

"I see how you look at him. How you smile when he enters the room. How you laugh together. You did this with Foster, when you first met."

"It's my nature to be kind to my houseguests."

Phoebe closed her eyes, took a breath. If Jinx didn't know her better, she might believe her to be praying. She slid into a chair opposite her daughter and took her hand, meeting her eyes. "I understand happiness in marriage has eluded you, Jinx. I understand disappointment and the need for affection. But this affair will destroy you and everything you have attained."

Jinx pulled her hand away. "I am not having an affair, Mother." She managed to press out those words without a hiccup, despite the tightening of her throat. "We are simply relatives."

"Jinx. Do not assume that I do not understand the situation."

It was the texture of her tone, so soft, so foreign, that whisked tears into Jinx's eyes. She tightened her jaw, drew in a shaky breath. Couldn't look at her mother. "He's just—he's just kind, Mother. And attentive. And he listens to me. And he makes me feel…" She closed her eyes, held in her word. Beautiful.

She brushed the wetness from her cheek. Found the appropriate word. "Happy. He makes me happy."

"Then he must leave."

Jinx looked up at her mother. No. No! "That is not necessary."

"Yes, Jinx. The longer he is in this house, the more the risk that he might recognize your affection. And that you might do something regrettable."

Regrettable.

Jinx looked away, turned another page in the book, despite the blur of the handwriting.

"Jinx. You haven't done anything Foster might not approve of, have you?"

"Of course not." But the words came out high, uneven. She tried again. "No." Although, Foster might have even disapproved of her wantonness that night, even if it had been him asleep in his chamber.

The lie lay in her chest, burning.

Oh, she'd done so much to betray him—and not just that night, but every day when she raced downstairs to breakfast with Bennett, or met him on the terrace for tea. Every night when she tried to burnish from her mind the memories of his touch, his smell, the sweetness of his embrace that forbidden night. She hated how often she stared at the adjoining door, wishing he might be on the other side. The fear that scuttled through her at the very allowance of that thought shook her to her core.

Regrettable? She didn't know how to articulate the word that embodied that night.

Many words, perhaps, but not regrettable.

Bennett, and his friendship, had awakened something dead inside. Made her feel alive.

"Good," her mother said, taking a breath, as if to rise. "That's very good. Then it's not too late. I'll arrange for Bennett to take rooms at the Casino. You can tell him tonight."

"No!" She held up her hands, hating the way the word lurched from her, but… "No, Mother. Foster wants him to stay here."

Her mother gaped at her. "Foster doesn't want to lose his wife to his brother!"

"Foster doesn't care about me. About what I want."

"Of course not. You're his wife, not his mistress."

Jinx recoiled. Stared at her mother, whose face had tightened, her own eyes reddened.

"Haven't you figured out yet the role of a wife? It is to manage her husband's life, to give him a legacy. He finds his happiness elsewhere."

"And me? Where do I find happiness?"

Phoebe's hand went to her neck, the pearls there. She rose stiffly, wandered to the window overlooking the front gardens. Finally, "You don't."

Jinx stared at her, an outline of darkness against the light of the window. "Mother, I know about Father's indiscretions. I know how he hurt you."

Phoebe drew in a breath but didn't turn.

Jinx softened her voice. "Did you never once have a friend who made you feel as if your words, your thoughts, your laughter, mattered?"

"Women in our position don't have the luxury of true friends. Male or female."

No. "That's not good enough for me. Bennett makes me…happy. Since he's arrived I've realized I want more, Mother. I want to know companionship, maybe even real love. I want a marriage like Esme and Oliver."

"Don't talk to me about Esme and Oliver!" Her mother rounded on her. "Oliver is dead, and Esme is lost. Living hand-to-mouth out in some feral land."

The words shucked Jinx's breath from her, and again she felt ill, her head light. "Dead. Oliver is dead?"

"He died in a fire in his tenement building. The night Esme left us." Her mother's jaw twitched. She turned back to the window. "Esme was stupid and headstrong and she destroyed her life."

"We destroyed her life, Mother. We lied. We sent her away."

"So you could marry Foster! So you could live this life. Rosehaven. Your chateau in New York. You are among society's elite; everyone wants to attend your cotillions, your dinner parties, your soirees."

"And everyone is laughing behind my back as I sit here, childless, while my husband cavorts his way around the globe with his yacht full of trollops. We conspired every bit of this life, Mother. We stole from Foster the bride he wanted. I probably deserve Foster's cruelty."

Her mother's shoulders rose and fell. Nothing of protest issued from her.

Jinx allowed the silence to linger, soothe their words. Finally she rose and joined her mother at the window. She wove her hand into hers, not acknowledging the wetness on her mother's lined cheeks.

"Fear not, Mother. I don't love Bennett. I am simply very fond of my brother-in-law. I find him to be everything Foster could be, if I could win his heart again. In Bennett, I see the man I thought I married." Her voice fell, almost to nothing. "Please don't deny me the pleasure of Bennett's company, for as fleeting a time as this. Please don't send him away. I promise not to disgrace Foster, to sully our reputations."

Outside, the sky had begun to purple with the twilight; long shadows from the oaks lay across the lawn.

"Your reputation is not what scares me most, Jinx." Her mother squeezed her hand. "Please don't lose your heart to Bennett Worth, for I fear you will never get it back."

Chapter 9

She wasn't in love with Bennett. Jinx watched him as he surveyed Foster's fleet of motor carriages, running his gloved hand over the olive-green fenders of Foster's newest acquisition, a Benz Comfort, fresh from Germany. Bennett wore the same grand expression of his brother so many years ago, when Foster had pulled up in front of their mansion to ask her to go motoring.

No, he'd wanted Esme to accompany him. Jinx had been his second choice. She sometimes forgot that.

No, she wouldn't love him. But sometimes, Bennett simply made her remember what it felt like to be noticed. Especially when he looked at her, a smile in his blue eyes. "It's beautiful. Are you sure Foster won't mind us driving it?"

"Not at all." She pulled her goggles over her eyes, adjusting them under her motoring hat, then allowed Amelia to tie the gauze veil under her chin. She already wore a fawn-colored alpaca duster, purchased especially for the sport of motoring, and now held up her arms for Amelia to fasten the cuffs tight around her wrists. "In fact, the Comfort belongs to me. It was a birthday gift."

She motioned her driver and his footmen to push the car from its stable in the garage house and onto the curved drive. She stood away as they started it up, cranking it to full power. It belched out black smoke, settled to a loud rumble.

Beside her, Bennett also affixed his goggles. "Do you like your new coat?" She'd ordered an alpaca motoring coat for him, in gray, weeks ago, when Foster first suggested she might teach him to drive.

"It's splendid. And a perfect fit."

She'd taken Foster's measurements and subtracted two inches from the waist.

Overhead, the sky suggested an intemperate day, patches of crisp blue being blotted out with bulbous clouds, the kind bearing trouble. In the distance, over the sea, a swath of dark suggested rain. But, for the moment, she'd grasp the cool August day with Bennett.

He'd been spending too much time with Elise.

In fact, their names appeared together twice last week—once at an afternoon tea thrown by Mamie Fish, another at a coaching tournament.

Society would have them married off in a week's time if he didn't school his attention to her. How could he possibly know if they were a suitable match after such a short courtship?

She shooed the footmen away, allowing Bennett's hand in assistance as she gathered her skirt and climbed aboard, settling behind the wheel.

Bennett stared at her, frowning. "Are you driving?"

"Of course. Did you not hear me offer to teach you when you first arrived?"

He stepped up on the running board. "I thought you were playing with me. You drive?"

"I am a better motorman than Foster." She patted the seat next to him. "You have nothing to worry about, Bennett."

He raised an eyebrow but sat next to her. She noticed his gloved hand curl around the edge of the seat and suppressed a smile.

Indeed, she had been the first of society's ladies to dispense of her footman and partake in the sport of motoring. Something about the power of directing her own course down the road, under the canopy of elms and oaks as they rumbled down Bellevue, set her free. In a motorcar, she could determine her own speed, her own course, decide her own destination.

The feeling had surprised her and wooed her quickly into the sport.

She removed the arm brake and stepped on the accelerator. The motor carriage eased forward and she bit back another smile as Bennett collected a quick breath.

"Certainly you have ridden in a horseless in Paris," she said.

"I preferred my own two feet in Paris."

They turned down the long drive and finally out onto Bellevue. She drove slowly enough to keep the nails and debris in the street from littering their clothing. Still, they passed a landau, the top up, and a Shay on their way to Bailey's Beach.

No Bailey's for her today. In fact, she'd lost her appetite for bathing at Bailey's. If she couldn't sink her naked toes into the wet sand, she preferred to not let it frustrate her. Let Duchess Consuelo bask in society's attention in her bathing hut.

Jinx would choose driving along the beach with Bennett over society's praise any day.

"You are a professional, Jinx. I am impressed." Bennett loosed his hold on his seat rail. "But I'm not surprised. You do everything well."

She kept her hands on the wheel, but her face heated.

"I mean it, Jinx. Elise holds you in high regard. In three short years you have managed to become a powerful lady in Newport, and your motor coaching cotillion is one of the most sought-after invitations of the season. You manage your household with efficiency, your staff is well-trained and attentive, and you have even acquainted me with a host of eligible debs. I am in your debt."

She hazarded a quick glance at him, shaken by his words, his smile.

"And you drive a horseless carriage."

They passed a landau carrying a company of bathers, clad in their dark dresses and hats.

"How are things going with Elise?"

"She is pleasant enough. Where are we going?"

"You'll see." She grinned at him. Pleasant enough. That didn't sound smitten, did it?

He folded one leg over the other, sat back in his seat as she turned at Webster then motored down to Spring Street, the mercantile district. "We'll cut over to

Thames and observe the ships in the wharf." Hopefully, Foster's yacht wouldn't be moored in harbor. She didn't even want to know if he'd returned. Please not. Please, never.

"Tell me about the motor coaching cotillion. I've been to several coaching weekends, but never a motorized event."

"It's a way for Foster to display his collection of vehicles, really. Everyone is required to bring their newest acquisition. We display them in the front courtyard, and then, a few select drivers agree to run an obstacle course down Bellevue Avenue. It's a grand event."

"Do you drive?"

She turned onto Thames, braking for a milk cart stopped in the road. The odors of the wharf, with the redolence of fish and oil and the brine of the sea, saturated the air. From here, she made out the shiny masts of the yachts moored in the harbor, bright spires against the darkening horizon. Overhead the sky seemed undaunted by the danger at sea.

She didn't spot the *Jinx*.

"No, I don't drive in the cotillion. Too much to oversee."

"Society not ready yet for a woman driver?"

"Perhaps."

He reached over and honked the horn affixed to the lamps in the front. Two schoolboys in knickerbockers looked up and waved. "I think you should drive this year."

She laughed and turned on Farewell Street, toward Memorial Park. So far to the north of Newport, no one would ever see her teaching Bennett how to drive. "And what would Foster say?"

"Perhaps Foster hasn't the right to say anything."

She drew in a long breath. "He has every right."

Bennett said nothing, letting the sound of the motor fill the air. Finally, "Of course he does."

They passed the cemetery, a thousand headstones at awkward angles cascading over the hillside. Then, finally, they came upon Memorial Park. Beech trees swayed in the wind, scattering their leaves over the rolling hillside. She turned off the dirt road onto a two-lane carriage path.

"What are you doing?"

"I'm going to teach you to drive. Hang on." She slowed the motorcar as it rumbled over the pathway, careful to keep it in the dirt rows. Once, when driving, she'd veered off the pathway and the uneven ground caused her to lose control. The car plummeted into a depression and stranded her for an hour until the Ernest Wilsons happened by in a carriage and rescued her.

It made the *Newport Daily News*.

Today, she'd stay on the path and find a secluded place to show him the steering mechanism, the brake lever, and how to work the gas pedal.

They topped a hill and she coasted down to the bottom, to a long stretch of scenic pathway that disappeared into the woods.

She braked and slid over on the seat. "Your turn. This is the brake lever, and you steer it here." She demonstrated the turning of the wheel.

Bennett just looked at her. "Jinx, I don't think this is a good idea. I don't want to destroy your birthday present."

Around them, the trees seemed to shiver in the approaching storm. Perhaps coming out this morning hadn't been the most judicious of ideas, but Bennett seemed to be away from the house so often, she didn't know how much time remained.

"It's grand fun, Bennett, I promise. And, when you get proficient, you can take Elise out in one of Foster's—"

"Please stop talking about Elise." His tone stilled her. "I don't want to talk about Elise when I'm with you." He drew in a long breath. "I'm sorry." A pained expression crossed his face.

She felt it all the way to her bones, a quickening, a scurry of forbidden hope that stirred up the taste of fear inside.

Somehow, she found the appropriate tone. "I don't understand. Isn't everything going well with Elise? You said she was pleasant." Amazing how her own voice could manage such a façade when inside her heart thundered.

"She is. And I—I suppose she is a good match for me." He turned to her, his eyes searching hers. "But Jinx, even when I'm with Elise, I think about you. I think about your laughter, the way you always try to best me in cribbage, how you have an answer for every social topic I raise, how you know exactly what to say to anyone, and how, when you look at me, I am completely undone. And, heaven help me, I think about that night. I remember everything now, and I can't dislodge it from my mind. You're in my head, Jinx, and I fear in my soul too."

Jinx couldn't move, couldn't breathe. She closed her mouth, swallowed, fear trickling through her at the forbidden desire now wildfire inside.

No, oh no—

He touched her hand then picked it up, held it. She didn't pull away—just stared at her hand in his.

Indeed, that night came back to her too. Oh.

"I'm in love with you, Jinx. Probably since that first night, although that's not why. You are so beautiful, and it's not just your eyes, or your hair—I can still feel it in between my fingers. You have no idea how I long to unpin it, let it fall around your shoulders, to see it in the light instead of my imagination."

"Bennett…" Please, stop.

"I hate my brother. I hate how he treats you, and I hate that you are entangled in this marriage that will only bring you suffering. But most of all, I hate that he found you first. That I never had a chance to win your heart. That I will never again know that night we shared."

Oh, Bennett. She pressed her free hand to her lips, her eyes burning. "I…" She closed her mouth before the words could betray her.

No, she'd lived a terrible lie. She wasn't just fond of him. She loved him. Of course she loved him.

Oh no. She closed her eyes, shaking. "Bennett, please stop talking."

"Shh. I know this is wrong. I feel nearly ill at my jealousy for my brother. For my sins against you, Jinx, that night, and every day when I wish you were my wife." He drew a breath. "God must think me a terrible man."

"And me, a wretched woman." She wasn't sure how the truth emerged, but it lay there, shaken out of her. She couldn't stop herself from the rest, her tone low as the confession sneaked free. "If I had known it was you that night..." She met his eyes, poured her heart into her gaze. "I would not have left."

His intake of breath told her just how she ached to give him her heart.

He took her hand then. Closed his eyes and didn't speak as he ran his thumb over her glove. She longed to take it off, to feel his touch.

"Maybe," he said softly, "maybe we could leave. Move to Paris."

The images rose inside her with such force she cried out. "Oh...no..."

"Or Berlin. Or London. I'll go anywhere, do anything to be with you, Jinx." He stared at her, the earnestness in his gaze scaring her a little.

No, not a little. His gaze scared her right to her bones. She couldn't leave Foster—and move to Paris! What about her life, her homes, society? "Please, Bennett, don't say such things to me."

"I know you're afraid of Foster, but I'd protect you."

"How? He has unlimited resources. He would ruin you. And he'd never forgive me. Please, stop talking."

"Jinx, I love you, and I would never hurt you. I swear, I would be true to you every day of my life."

"No—Bennett! No." She pushed against him, gave up, and pressed her hands to her mouth. The word shuddered out of her, down to a whisper. "No."

He stiffened then, something cold, heartbreaking in the expression in his eyes, the tight form of his lips. "I see."

No, he didn't. She heard the voice screaming inside her. *Yes, Bennett! I love you. I will come with you.* But truly, he didn't understand. "My sister ran away with the man she loved," she said softly, "and he died."

He gave her a terrible look then, something of horror. "You're afraid I'll die?"

"I'm afraid of Foster." She whispered the words, let them fall between them. "He's capable of many despicable things. He would hurt you."

"He already has, by taking you as his bride."

She drew in a long breath, wanting to curl onto the seat, to put her hands over her head, her ears. To weep. "Why do you say this to me? You sneak into my house, into my husband's bed, you love me in the middle of the night, you make me..." Fall in love with you. No—she'd already gone too far. "Care for you. Of course I care for you. But I can't love you. I can't run away with you!"

He recoiled as if she had pummeled him.

Her voice dropped, turned cold, for her sake as well as his. "This is the life I have, the life I created. It's the one I must hold onto."

He shook his head. "No, Jinx. You can start over. You can have the life you were meant to live. With me."

Inside her rose the inexplicable, crazy urge to hurt him, to throw herself at him and rail upon his chest, or leap off the motorcar and run, anywhere, screaming.

Instead her voice tightened, sharp and crisp. "You are even crueler than your brother."

He flinched. "Jinx—"

"Get out. Stay away from me. Please, just stay away."

She willed herself not to cry. Not yet. Her throat burned, her breaths came fast.

Mercifully, he got out of the car.

"I will send a driver to fetch you," she said and released the brake. Then, before she couldn't see anymore, she lurched the car forward down the path.

She didn't look back as she left him in the grass. Didn't care that he'd looked bereft.

Overhead the sky shuddered, a roll of thunder beyond the trees. Water spit upon her as she guided the car between the ruts, crying full out now, hearing only his words in her ear. *Jinx, I love you.*

She'd gotten herself into this mess. She had to live with it.

But oh, it just wasn't fair.

It wasn't fair.

She jerked the veil from under her chin, threw it off, and wiped her eyes.

Oh, God was mocking her and her glorious hopes. She'd tried to be the heroine, to save her family, to grab the blessings of her station.

And now God mocked her.

Before her, the world wept, the shower turning the path slick and muddy. She wiped her hand across her face as she crested a hill, reaching for the brake as the carriage careened down the other side. It slid and lurched off the path, onto the grass.

Maybe God mocked them all—their grand lives, their glittering stations. The blessed were destined to live lives of clandestine misery.

She fought the tiny wheel, but the motorcar jerked in the wilds, the brakes nothing as the motorcar slid down the hill toward a thicket of gnarled beech trees.

The car jerked, bumped her off the seat.

Throwing her hands over her head, she screamed as the motorcar crashed into the forest, upended, and threw her into the sky.

* * * * *

"Come back to us, Jinx."

Her mother's voice, the authority in it, drew Jinx from the folds of darkness, from the cocoon of safety where she could find herself inside Bennett's embrace with impunity.

She opened her eyes and the throbbing in her head made her want to sink back into the folds of unconsciousness. Her mother sat on a chair beside the bed, her hands clasped on her lap. At the foot of the bed, Doctor Hanson dictated his findings to a nurse.

"What happened?" Jinx's hand went to her head and she found a bandage.

"That infernal horseless carriage you love so much—you ran it into a tree," her mother said. "Bennett found you and flagged down a carriage to rescue you. You're so fortunate you didn't break a bone—"

"Or lose the baby."

The doctor looked up from his dictation.

Met Jinx's eyes.

"The...what?" No. Oh no. Her hand went to her belly.

Doctor Hanson glanced at her mother, back to Jinx. "You're with child, again, Jinx. Didn't you know this?"

"Of course she did. She is just shaken," her mother said, her hand cradling her arm. She met Jinx's eyes, a hardness in them that sent a chill through Jinx.

"Do you know when you might have conceived your child?"

Heat burned her cheeks. Yes. She swallowed, her voice faint. "Foster was here in July, about six weeks ago." The lie seemed to burn coming out, her throat thickened.

"You'll have to start bed rest immediately," he said.

Bed rest? "But I have the motor coaching cotillion."

"Perhaps society will have to forego the cotillion this year." Hanson closed his satchel, turned to Amelia. "Immediate bed rest, and please continue to monitor her alertness." Then he placed his hand on her shoulder, the warmth touching her bones that were so brittle with his news. "You're a lucky woman, Jinx."

She nodded and Amelia followed him out.

Her mother closed the door. Turned. Folded her hands across her chest. Smiled. "I admit, I lost faith in you when Bennett showed up. Something about your demeanor with him, the way you two seemed to share a camaraderie, threatened my confidence that you would approach Foster. I should have trusted you, Jinx. I raised a lady like myself—you know what you must do in order to survive."

Jinx stared at her, praying her expression didn't betray her. Praying that the wailing inside her head wouldn't escape.

Pregnant? How could she not have noticed? She did the math, realized that she hadn't even considered how much time had passed. But the clues, oh, she saw them now. The fatigue. Her upset stomach. Her moods.

The sudden urge to weep. In fact, even as she affixed a smile on her mother, her eyes brimmed. She pressed a hand to her cheek to catch the tear.

"I know you're afraid, darling." Her mother perched on the side of her bed. "But you will stay right here, and this time you will have this child." She pressed her hand to Jinx's cheek. "You'll see, everything will work out."

Jinx nodded, trying to keep the horror from her eyes. Pregnant.

With Bennett's child.

Her breaths fell over each other.

"Are you all right? Shall I call back the doctor?"

She shook her head. Don't panic. She could figure this out, fix this. *Jinx, I love you, and I would never hurt you.*

Bennett's voice rose, the texture of it wheedling inside. *I swear, I would be true to you every day of my life.*

"Jinx, what is it?"

She found her voice, hating how it shook. "Is Bennett here?"

Her mother drew in a long breath. "I suspect he is waiting to see if you are okay. Your accident deeply upset him. Certainly seeing you in such a condition unraveled him—he wouldn't let anyone else touch you as he carried you to your room. You know how I feel about you driving. It's simply not a sport for women."

"Mother—"

"He prowled the hallway for a while, and I heard him ask the butler to gather his things so he could take rooms at the Casino."

"What? Why—no. He can't leave." She pressed her hand over her mouth, cut her gaze away from her mother, toward the window. They hadn't drawn the drapes, and the sun simmered above the horizon, bleeding over the ocean. "Please ask him to stay."

Her mother considered her. "No."

"Mother, this is my home, and he is my guest."

"And you're my daughter. I will not see you destroyed by falling in love with another man."

Jinx flinched and her mother's eyes widened.

"I knew it. You do love him."

Jinx tried not to move her hand over her womb, to the child inside. Bennett's child. A child conceived, if not in love, at least not in fear.

But Foster would know the child wasn't his. She hadn't exactly greeted him as a wife should. She drew in her breath, probably too sharply.

"What is wrong, Jinx? Are you having pain?"

Yes. "No."

But her mother gave her a long, hard look, finally drawing herself up. She rose and walked to the window, her back to Jinx. "It's his child, isn't it?"

Jinx wound her hands into her bedclothes.

"Jinx?"

"I don't know what you're talking—"

"I am not stupid, Jinx. I know what infidelity, what betrayal looks like. I see the frame of guilt in your eyes. And the naive hope that Bennett will burst through those doors and declare his love—"

"He does love me! He told me in the park. He wants to marry me."

"You are already married. To his brother." Phoebe rounded on her. "Do you know what Foster would do to him—and to you—if he knew?" She drew a long breath, her voice emerging low. "How could you?"

"I didn't mean to." Jinx pressed her fingers to her eyes. "I made a fool of myself, going to his room that first night, when he came home. Only it wasn't Foster. Bennett slept in his bed and took me into his arms."

Her mother stilled. Then, in a voice Jinx recognized, something cool and sharp, a tone her mother reserved for her father, "He is a scoundrel of the worst kind. He is leaving, immediately."

Jinx had no words as she stared at her hands, at the ring Foster had put on her finger, the one that belonged to Esme.

She'd never been his bride, not really, and suddenly, with everything inside her, she wanted to leap from the bed, to throw herself into Bennett's arms. *Yes, yes, I will leave with you!*

Her mother sat on the bed, took her hands. "We can fix this, Jinx."

Maybe he was outside the door right now. She could call his name—he'd rush in.

"There is an easy answer." Her mother cupped her hand on her face.

What would he say when she told him about his child? She could see his smile, feel his arms around her, the taste of him on her lips.

"You need to invite your husband back, make sure you have marital relations."

The words stopped the tumble of what-ifs and Jinx stared at her mother, horror in her expression for sure. "No. Never." Not after being with Bennett. Not after knowing… "I hate him."

"You love him. Or you pledged to. He's your husband, and you owe him honor. At the very least, you must make him believe this is his child."

"No, Mother. I can't." She wanted to fold into herself at the thought.

"You must. For your good." Her mother pressed her hand to Jinx's belly. "For your child. Imagine what life this unwanted child would have. Foster would hate your child, divorce you. Ruin our family. I have no doubt he would cut Bennett off, destroy him as well. You would have nothing, nowhere to live, no one to turn to." Her mother left the rest unsaid, gathered in her eyes.

Jinx moved her mother's hand away. "I see." For a moment, she saw her mother standing in the study, telling her father of Esme's disgrace. Heard the tone. Tasted her father's disappointment, his anger. *Oliver is dead, and Esme is lost. Living hand-to-mouth out in some feral land.*

"And, you have no guarantees that Bennett would even marry you. Consider his reputation."

"It's a lie, Mother. He isn't the playboy Foster has made him out to be."

"So he says. Considering your situation, I might argue otherwise." Her mother moved over to her desk, opened the drawer. "You will invite Foster home." She pulled out stationery, a quill pen, and ink. "You will throw yourself into his arms and beg for his love."

Jinx burned inside at her words, tasting the shame.

"You will make sure that when he leaves again, he believes this child is his."

This child would never, ever be his.

Jinx found her voice, somewhere under her disgust. "He won't come home to see me. He must have a reason to return to Rosehaven."

"You have one. The motor carriage cotillion. He won't refuse your reminder to be the charming host of Newport's most coveted ball."

"What about the bed rest?" The other solution lay in the unspoken. Getting up and going about her daily activities, even strenuous ones, might guarantee that Foster never discovered her indiscretions.

Which indeed might be God's will.

"If I go to bed, word will leak out. Foster will discover the truth. Perhaps—perhaps I should let God determine my fate." But even as she said it, she wanted to weep.

Oh, indeed, she was a wretched woman. She couldn't lose this child.

Her mother drew in a long breath. "Very well. We will leave it to fate. She piled the stationery on a bed desk, moved it over to Jinx. "No more driving."

No more driving, indeed.

"I should tell Bennett."

Her mother stared at her as if she'd announced she might bathe naked at Bailey's Beach. "Have you lost your mind? Bennett must never, ever know." She took Jinx's hand. "If he finds out, he will want to woo you, to make it right between you. I promise you this, Jinx, no good can ever come from following your heart. You must be clever, my daughter, and don't let fate betray you, or your sins will follow you forever. This is the only way out. Your future is in your own hands."

Chapter 10

Never had Newport seen such a party. And never had God provided a more beautiful night for a woman to betray her heart.

After all, what choice did she have? She hadn't miscarried, which seemed a divine joke, of sorts. The stars glittered overhead, scorning Jinx as she watched her guests dance in her glorious ballroom to the orchestra from New York City, the waltzes and polkas of Debussy and Chopin swirling through the marble hall and spilling out on the open doors of the terrace.

Parked in the front circle, around the fountain, motorcars of all styles decorated her yard—De Dion Bouton's model L's from Germany, and Peugeots from France. Even a Ford quadricycle. Foster had his stable of motorcars polished and bedecked with wreaths of flowers, vines and ivy twined into the spokes of the wheels. Among the wreaths, glow lights sparkled, capturing the greens and reds and gold edging of the vehicles, accentuating their magnificence.

For the cotillion, Jinx had salvaged a gold-edged dress from her pregnancy trousseau, with an accompanying picture hat, swaths of red and gold ribbon at the brim to match Foster's driving clothes.

He appeared the master of his kingdom in a black satin jacket, black leather pants, and a plaid derby he wore during the parade. He'd swept in two days before the ball as if he hadn't spent the past month away, and spoken as few words as possible, it seemed, to accomplish his orders. Now he stood on the terrace, engaged in conversation with men from the Newport Reading Room. She recognized William Vanderbilt and John Jacob Astor, who had driven their newest acquisitions, their wives beside them on the leather seats.

Jinx rode with Foster, despite her mother's silent objections. But really, she had no choice if she hoped to stay in Foster's favor.

If she hoped to woo him into her charade.

She'd survived the past two weeks without Bennett's dangerous companionship, her secret growing inside her, waiting every day for the cramping, the grief.

She hadn't miscarried. Which meant that God indeed intended her sins to be displayed, to follow her all her days.

She knew she should be afraid. Instead, she wanted to weep with gratitude.

Meanwhile, Bennett and Elise's social appearances in the *Newport Daily News* dug a furrow through her.

What would Bennett do if he knew? She longed to tell him, to see his expression. Would he feel the same sweet agony that swept her to tears in the thin hours of the night? How could such a terrible sin reap such joy?

She already loved the child inside her. And if she had to behave like a wanton chorus girl to seduce her husband, to conceal her secret, she would find the strength.

"You look most lovely tonight, Jinx." Grayson Donahue edged up to her, his flute of champagne glittering against the electric lights on the terrace. He appeared regal and very eligible in a gold-threaded black waistcoat, top hat, and a pair of pinstriped breeches.

"Thank you, Grayson. I noticed your new De-Dion Bouton outside. It's beautiful. I love the gold-fringed cover. Very practical."

"I heard about your accident in the park. I'm so sorry about your carriage, but I'm thankful you are unhurt."

"I suppose you read about it in the *News*?"

"Actually, Bennett related the story to me not long ago during a tennis match. He is an adept singles player."

Just the mention of Bennett's name could send a thrill through her. She drew in a steadying breath. "Indeed."

"Perhaps we could challenge you and him to another match," Grayson said. He had kind eyes. "Or better yet, we'll best Elise and Bennett."

Elise and Bennett. After a month of seeing their names appear together, certainly she would have grown accustomed to the cadence of it, but traitorous tears burned her eyes and she had to force a smile, turn into the night. "Unfortunately, I will be closing Rosehaven early this year. Mr. Worth has obligations in New York City."

"But certainly you'll stay for the wedding, won't you?"

She tried to bite back her gasp, the way the words she should have expected dug into her even before she asked, "Whose wedding?"

"I shouldn't say anything—their engagement isn't yet announced." Grayson winked at her. "But I think we both saw it coming, didn't we? Bennett is a splendid match for Elise. I am happy for them both." He lifted his glass, as if to toast them, and she nodded in agreement.

The night dipped around her, her stomach light. Perhaps she should sit down. She opened her fan. "When is the wedding?"

"They wanted to accomplish it before the end of the season, but since the marriage agreement was only made two days ago, I suspect they will have difficulty securing the arrangements." He took a sip from his champagne flute. "Then again, you managed to prepare a wedding in two days' time, didn't you?"

She glanced at him, searching his expression for malice. Nothing but innocence, even admiration, in his eyes, and she supposed he didn't know that, in fact, her arrangements took less than an hour's time.

Sometimes she went back to that moment and wanted to rewrite it. To stop at the edge of her father's study, as Foster met her eyes, his solemn countenance hinting at her ruined future, and run.

Why hadn't she waited for her own match, someone to win her heart? Or perhaps she'd been so set at designing her own future, she couldn't take her chances at a happy fate.

"Jinx, are you okay? You seem flushed."

"I'm simply fatigued. I believe I will check with my butler on the evening's final event."

"There is more?"

"Of course." She flashed him a smile.

The dancers were engaged in a German, social coordinator Harry Lehr calling the moves as Jinx moved through the ballroom, toward the dining room. She found Neville there.

Yes, the fireworks display would be lit precisely at midnight, below the cliffs. She wandered out to the front driveway, running her gloved hand over the chrome fender of a beautiful Benz.

"Hello, Jinx."

The voice trickled through her, set something deep inside on fire. She drew in a breath to extinguish it and turned. "Bennett."

She'd greeted him, of course, when he entered, breathtaking in the motoring suit she'd ordered for him, adding his own blue pinstriped shirt, a gold threaded ascot, and a matching derby. His blond hair curled out the back and his blue eyes pressed into hers, barely a smile on his lips before he'd taken Foster's hand in greeting. The two men shared a warm moment and Jinx had to turn away with shame.

Bennett stepped up to her, his gloved hand rising as if to touch her then falling back. "I had hoped to talk to you tonight."

"It's a lovely evening, isn't it?" She turned before he could see the wreckage his movement wrought on her resolve and wandered past a Peugeot. The moonlight cascaded over the shiny, gilded lanterns, the leather seat. She plucked the petal of a white rose woven into the wreath.

Bennett stepped up behind her. "How are you?"

Wounded. Breaking. Wishing I'd had the courage to say yes to you that day in Memorial Park. "I'm well." She fabricated a smile. "I hear congratulations are due?" She couldn't look at him, not fully, but managed a glance.

He didn't smile, didn't even acknowledge her question. "I was so worried about you. But your mother said you didn't want to see me. That you preferred me to leave. I know I should have come to see you, regardless."

"No, she was right." She wanted to weep. Her mother, not his own hurt pride, had sent him away. Had her mother's lies about Esme taught her nothing? "I was fine. Thank you for finding me, for rescuing me."

He looked at his shoes, properly shined. "I will always rescue you, Jinx, if you allow me."

Oh, his words had lethal precision. She moved away from the Peugeot, walked out to the fountain, watching the spray weep into the night, dapple the surface of the platinum pond.

"I don't need rescuing. Besides, I believe Elise would have something to say about that."

"I don't love Elise."

She turned then. "You don't love your fiancée?"

"It's just a match."

Before she could stop herself, her hand lifted to slap him. He recoiled and she jerked back. "Don't you say that to me!"

"I'm fond of her, of course, but she is not you."

She gritted her teeth, closed her hand into a fist. "Then don't marry her. Don't do to her what Foster did to me. He hates me."

"I will honor Elise. I am not Foster. But I am not married, yet. And… my brother is a fool."

She wanted to tell him, then, wanted to spill out the truth, to cling to him, just for a moment.

I'll never betray you, Jinx.

"Perhaps I was the fool," she said. "But what's done is done."

Bennett said nothing, examining her face before she finally turned away. "You're right. What's done is done. We'll announce our engagement this week. I wanted to prepare you."

"I hope you both live happily ever after." She moved away from him.

He caught her arm. "Jinx, don't do this. You spurned me."

Her jaw tightened, and she yanked herself away, out of his grip. "Don't touch me. Ever." But her voice betrayed her and she pressed her hand to her mouth.

"Jinx—"

She turned and strode out into the darkness, away from the luminous eyes of Rosehaven.

"Jinx!"

Footsteps in the soft grass behind her made her speed up, made her nearly trip. Bennett caught her, swept his arm around her waist. "Please, don't run from me." He turned her to face him.

She couldn't look at him. "I have to, Bennett. Don't you see? I have to. You're going to marry another, and I…I'm going to have a baby."

The words tumbled out and lay there, brutal. He let her go as if she might be on fire, so fast that she nearly fell. But she should have expected the pain on his face. The look of betrayal.

And right then, she knew. He believed that she belonged to him. Believed her to be his.

And, oh, she wanted to be.

But she needed his hurt to churn up her courage, to push him out of her life before she did something truly foolish. She added a fine edge to her tone. "Yes, Bennett. I'm going to have a child. Foster's child. So you see, you need to stay away from me. Marry Elise. Make her your wife and please, learn to love her."

He stepped away from her, whitened, shaking his head. "You can't be pregnant. Foster hasn't even been here…."

His mouth opened. Closed. And he gave her an awful, soul-searing look, one that shook her clear through. "It's mine. The baby you're carrying is my child."

She didn't expect his softly spoken words to make her want to weep, to throw herself at him, let him hold her. *Bennett must never, ever know. If he finds out he will want to woo you, to make it right between you. You must be clever, Jinx, and don't let fate betray you, or your sins will follow you forever.*

Yes, Bennett. "No. It's Foster's. Of course it's Foster's."

He held her gaze until she nearly surrendered, until the truth pulsed at her lips. But she was a woman of society, of power.

She knew how to tell a lie.

Or, not.

His voice shook. "I don't believe you." He reached for her hand, but she jerked it away. Still, his voice had the power to hold her captive. "Come to me, Jinx. I will wait for you. I won't go anywhere until you are with me."

"Then you will wait in vain."

A crackle, then a bang sounded in the sky behind her. She jerked as a spray of red fire exploded over the back of the house.

It was reflected in Bennett's eyes. Then his voice cooled, crisp and quick. "Congratulations, Jinx. I wish you the best."

He turned and left her there, in the cool, damp grass, as the fireworks destroyed the midnight sky.

* * * * *

Foster was in a good mood. Jinx stood at the edge of the terrace, bidding farewell to the last of her guests, the Wilsons, and heard his laughter twining out of the billiards room, through the ballroom, and out into the night.

It sounded so young, so unencumbered, it roused a long dormant memory. Ice skating on the pond in Central Park, his hand around her waist, laughing as he caught her in his arms, saving her from crashing onto the ice.

She watched the Wilsons take their leave, then the movement of the servants as they collected the debris of the party from the lawn. They wound up the damask table linens, extinguished the electric lights on the back lawn, and left only the stars for luminance.

Jinx drew in a breath, smelled the earthy bouquet of cigar smoke and some exotic fragrance, and turned to see Foster strolling up behind her. He had loosened his bow tie, unbuttoned his waistcoat, lost his derby. In this light, he appeared younger, the man who had driven her up and down Fifth Avenue in his sparkling new motor carriage or held her in his arms in the ballroom.

"I never danced with you this evening," he said, his gray eyes on her. His soft tones rattled her composure.

Perhaps the party had broken him free of his contempt. She had managed the cotillion of the season.

"I apologize. I gave the first dance to your brother, as a welcoming gift, and allowed him to choose his partner. He and Elise make a lovely pair." There, she managed the words without malice, without betraying the burn scraping her throat.

"I agree." Foster came up to stand beside her, a softness in his eyes. She smelled brandy on his breath as he leaned down, brushed his lips against her cheek. "Thank you."

She glanced up at him.

"For finding my brother a match. I am most pleased with Elise. She is the daughter of a banker, and her connections will benefit our family well." He cupped his hand on Jinx's cheek. "Sometimes your ascension to the pinnacle of society has been less than endearing to me, I admit. I had thought you might be less capable, might need me more. But in this endeavor, I find your accomplishments most...fetching."

He leaned down again and pressed a kiss, albeit it a touch sloppy, to her neck. He wrapped his hand around her neck, angled her face up to his.

She swallowed, met his kiss.

He tasted of cigar smoke, of the bittersweet tang of brandy, and as he deepened his kiss, her chest tightened. He was never a gentleman when he drank too much. He drew back, his voice slurred. "I've missed you, Jinx."

Oh, even his words could bruise. She'd stopped hoping for such affection. Now, it brushed over the wounded places of her heart like silt. "Really?"

"Mmm-hmm."

She hated the tears that burned her eyes as he kissed her again. Not exactly gentle, but not as much anger inside of it. Even, perhaps, a hint of longing, that earnestness inherent in every groom desirous of his bride.

What if it could have been like this from the beginning? Perhaps she'd tried too hard to earn his esteem. Perhaps if she'd been less capable, he might have seen her as he had before—a young girl, dazzled by his elegance, his power.

She could do this. "I've missed you too, Foster." She dug deep, tried to find something of truth. "I'm so lonely without you. And afraid."

He leaned back, his lips twisting into a smile. "What are you afraid of, peach?"

She drew in a breath, stirring up her courage. What if—what if she told him the truth? Let him see her heart? "I'm afraid you'll never love me, Foster. Never forgive me for not being Esme. Never look at me the way you did when we first met, when you held me in your arms at the ice rink, or when you taught me to dance. That you'd never see me as..." She drew in a shaky breath, slipped her hands up to his chest. "Beautiful."

Time seemed to stop, her heart laboring in her ears, her face hot in the darkness. *Please.*

Please tell me you are glad you married me, that of all the women at the ball tonight, you would have chosen me.

He laughed. She couldn't detect the texture of it—malice, or adoration, but he shook his head as if in disbelief and bent down to kiss her again.

She let his touch, his ardor, soothe the hollowness inside. She surrendered herself, almost fled into the belief that he saw her again as naive and delectable. Most of all, she let his husky invitation to join him in his chamber be the affirmation she needed.

However, as he closed the door behind her, as he brought her into his embrace, as he reminded her to whom she belonged, never once did he affirm, *Yes, Jinx, you are beautiful.*

Tears ran into her ears as she yielded to him, but he never asked why. Never even stopped to inquire about her comfort.

Never spoke words of tenderness.

Her hope died in the silent business of the union. She cursed herself for wanting more.

Most of all, as she endured him, she realized that, indeed, she'd known. That night, in Bennett's arms, she had to have known.

I love you, Jinx. I always will.

Bennett's voice haunted her, as she suspected it would, and she lay in the darkness, finally alone, Foster's breathing heavy beside her. She curled herself into a ball, debating an escape back to her chamber, and pressed her face into the pillow. Why hadn't she left with Bennett? Run away?

Esme had chosen wisely, even if it had been fatally. Although Oliver had died, certainly Esme had a few moments, days, years of joy.

Too well, Jinx understood the passion that had driven Esme to despair. Too easily did Bennett's touch sweep into her thoughts.

Foster would never be Bennett. Foster would never love her, never see her as Bennett did. Never hold her as Bennett had.

Never make her feel beautiful.

Her mother's words resounded through her, echoing, driving her to press her face into her pillow, muffle her sobs.

Please don't lose your heart to Bennett Worth, for I fear you will never get it back.

She waited until she'd stopped her hiccups, until Foster began to snore, before she finally escaped to her own bedroom.

Then she stared at his closed door, her knees to her chest. At least now she was free. Foster would claim the child as his own. She'd arranged her own fate, and, once again, made her own luck.

Because that's what Jinx did best.

She finally lay down, cupped her hands over her stomach, and waited until the sun slid across the parquet floor of her room, until she heard him rise, and leave.

She felt brittle, as if she might shatter. She rose and stepped onto the cool floor. She dressed herself in a loose tea gown, left off her stockings, and descended from her room before Amelia could bring her tray.

"Ma'am, I didn't know you had risen." Neville stood at the bottom of the stairs, panic in his expression. "I will summon your lady's maid."

Jinx raised her hand. "No need, Neville. I will take my tray on the terrace, however."

No trace of last night's cotillion remained—she'd trained her staff well. The planters flanking the broad steps overflowed with ivy and geraniums, the pond glittered with goldfish, the back lawn glistened with the dew, groomed and free of litter. She stepped off the terrace and ran her toes into the thick, silky sea grass. It tickled the soft flesh on her feet. She lifted her skirt and waded out into the thick of it, lifting her face to the sun, letting the heat wash into her.

Anything to not feel so empty, so hollow.

Anything to erase the feel of the sea on her feet.

She didn't even realize she was crying until she heard the voice behind her. "Jinx? Are you all right?"

She turned. Whisked her hands across her cheek. "Father. I didn't know you were in town."

He had aged since Esme's departure, his dark hair streaked with gray, his eyes tired. He rarely left the newspaper, and when he did, he stayed most often at his private rooms at the Casino. Today, he wore his typical black suit, waistcoat, and jacket, a bowtie at his neck, a pocket watch strung across his belly into his side pocket, fully attired, even in the early morning hours. "I need to discuss something with you. However, you seem upset?"

The unfamiliar tone had the power to unhinge her. She shook her head. "I'm fine. To what do I owe this call?"

Her father walked out beside her. Faced the ocean. "Your husband came to me this morning." He waited, and she watched a pelican search the currents for breakfast. "He wants an annulment."

She stilled, unsure what words to form. But just last night…

"He says, since you have been unable to give him a child, he needs to find someone who can provide him with an heir."

She burned with the swell of shame inside her. She stared up at her father and must have worn something wretched in her expression, for his face softened, his voice kind.

She nearly didn't recognize it.

"I know of your situation, Jinx."

That rooted her still. "What situation?"

He drew in a breath then lowered his voice. "I know you are in a family way. And your mother suspects that it is not Foster's."

Jinx looked away but her father caught her arm. "Jinx."

She rounded on him, yanked her arm from his grip. "Don't you dare stand here and judge me. Don't you dare."

Instead of the rise of fury she expected, however, he met her eyes. "I fear my sins have become yours."

Something snapped inside her. "My sins are nothing—nothing like yours."

He continued to hold her gaze. "Yes, in fact, they are. But perhaps you don't have to live my fate."

She narrowed her eyes at him. "I don't understand."

He tore his gaze from hers then, to the ground, and walked ahead of her. She didn't move. Didn't breathe.

Finally, "I betrayed your mother."

The edges of her mouth hardened, her teeth clenched.

"I should have never done it, but, like you, she couldn't bear a child. And the pain of that bled into our marriage. Kept us apart. I—I found solace in the arms of another woman."

She knew this but said nothing. Let him confess, tell her what he'd done. Tell her which of his daughters was illegitimate.

She steeled herself for the truth.

"She bore me a daughter. And I brought her into my barren, dead marriage and asked my wife to raise her as her own."

Please, don't let it be—

"Esme was the light of my life, Jinx. I couldn't hide it, I know, and for that I apologize." He glanced at her, and the pain in his eyes made her want to forgive him.

She'd let out her breath too.

He continued walking, and she followed. "I should have divorced your mother, perhaps. Taken Esme and raised her with the woman I loved. But I feared being cut off from my family, from our means. And I feared your mother's father. He would have ruined me."

Yes, Grandfather, what little Jinx remembered of him, would have brought her father to his knees. At the very least run him out of town, socially, if not economically.

"I was a coward. And then—then you were born." He stopped at the edge of the yard, where the grass tumbled into the sea. Below, the waves splattered against the rocks, receded, threw themselves again.

"You were the only good thing to come out of our loveless marriage, Jinx."

She looked up at him, caught his gaze on her.

"You were the other light of my life, Jinx. But your mother wouldn't let me near you. Said I didn't deserve you—which, of course, I didn't. But I did love you, Jinx. I still love you. I'm sorry I never told you that."

She looked away, afraid of the emotions on his face. Of the way her breath caught, her throat tight, burning.

He stood, watching the waves climb the shore and then fall in a mass of frothy defeat.

"I knew from the beginning that you and Foster wouldn't be a good match."

"You knew?" Her voice emerged as a fractured whisper.

"I didn't want either of my daughters to marry Foster. I knew of his philandering. But my desire to protect Esme from scandal pushed me into arranging the marriage. I thought Foster's pedigree would protect her. But he has instead ruined you also."

His voice betrayed him. "I am sick of my own machinations. Sick of trying to arrange and deceive and pretend." He drew in a breath and looked at her in a way she didn't recognize. "I lost Esme. And I fear losing you too, Jinx.

"Jinx, if you want to have a life with Bennett, I will protect you. I will have your marriage annulled and provide Bennett with a job. You will not go hungry. Yes, you may lose your position in society, but you will not have to look over your shoulder with regret. Marry Bennett with my blessing."

With his blessing.

She couldn't breathe. And then, yes, she could. Could breathe full and thick and glorious, and for a long moment she thought she might take the drafts with the pelicans.

But, "Bennett is engaged to Elise Donahue."

Oddly, his face curled into a smile. "Can it be that I know more of society gossip than Jinx Worth?"

Her pulse had the power to deafen her. "Stop toying with me, Father. What do you know?"

He checked his watch. "Bennett and Elise had a terrible row last night in the yard of Rosehaven. Something ugly and having to do with him being in love with another woman."

Jinx closed her eyes.

"She didn't mention you—I'm not sure she even knows. But she did tell him that she would not abide a marriage of convenience."

"Then she does not know society."

"Indeed. I fear her brother's marriage spoiled her. Put ideas into her head."

"Is it so terrible to love and to want to be loved? To share something…"

She bit back her words, pushing away the images, the senses that rushed at her.

"Perhaps not. Perhaps...not." He tucked his watch back into his pocket. "As I rose this morning, I saw the Casino porters loading Bennett's trunks onto a carriage. He has hired a yacht to ferry him back to Paris."

The words dismantled her. She pressed her hand to her lips, hating the cry that nearly issued.

This was for the best. Surely, for the best. But she pressed her hands against her stomach, at the lurching there, the way she wanted to crumble.

Her father caught her arm again. This time, she allowed his support.

"I know you care for him. And with Foster set against you... Go to Bennett. Have his child. Live happily with the man you love." His eyes glistened, and she knew he longed to say those words to Esme. "I will support you as I can. You may not have the power you now possess, but perhaps that won't matter." She stared up at him as he cupped her cheek then leaned over and kissed her forehead. "You have my blessing, my daughter."

* * * * *

"What are you doing, Mrs. Worth?"

Amelia stood at the door of Jinx's room, holding her morning tray. She entered the room, set it down on the bureau. "Are you and Mr. Foster leaving?"

A bag lay on her bed—she'd found it in a storeroom down the hall, where they kept her summer ball gowns, stuffed onto dress forms. Now, a few of her things—a corset, a pair of bloomers, her jewelry cases—lay upon her bed.

She had no idea how to pack for her escape from this life. Maybe she should take nothing.

Maybe she should leave it all behind, just like Esme.

She turned to Amelia, not sure what to say. "I...I'm leaving Foster."

Amelia gave her the expression she expected, wide eyes, the intake of breath. Indeed, she might have reacted the same to those words, laying out so naked, if they hadn't already been burning through her head for the past thirty minutes.

She was leaving Foster. She let the words slide through her again, unlock something deep inside.

"I'm going with Bennett to Paris." At least, she hoped so. She turned to stare at her scattered items. "I don't have much time before Mr. Foster returns." Maybe she didn't need them. None of them, none of this life.

She heard Amelia close the door. "He has already arrived." Her voice shook. "Mr. Foster has such a temper. How will you leave?"

She looked at Amelia and must have worn a desperate look, because her lady's maid drew herself up, nodded. "I'll get your bathing costume."

"But I'm not going to the beach." Except, Foster didn't know that, did he?

"You're brilliant, Amelia," she said as the maid returned, holding her bathing attire: the black-sleeved tunic, tied at the neck, her corset, full-length cotton drawers, and the shorter skirt.

Amelia loaded the clothes into the valise. Closed it. Paused. Then, "I will be happy to accompany you," she said. She met Jinx's eyes, something rare, bold. "I cannot stay here with Mr. Worth and his—his valet. There is an evil there that disturbs me. His valet watches you, miss, and sometimes follows you when you go out, even when Mr. Worth is at home."

Jinx had always harbored a fear of Lewis O'Farrell, with his cauliflower ears, a nose that jagged down his face. She had noticed his black eyes that followed her with a sort of undisguised contempt.

She wanted to forbid him from the house when Foster wasn't at home. But, he was still a servant. "He is a vile man, I admit, Amelia, but—"

"Please, ma'am. I will be happy to serve you, even in Paris. I have no one here."

For the first time, Jinx considered her, the young girl who had turned into a woman while serving Jinx. She'd cared for Jinx after her miscarriages, fitted her into her finery, made herself invisible in their home, always alert for her mistress's needs.

"Yes. Of course." Jinx had the sudden, mad urge to touch Amelia's hand, to squeeze it. But they weren't exactly sisters.

"Help me dress then fetch your things. I will wait by my carriage for five minutes."

Amelia cinched Jinx inside a day dress then left with the valise.

Jinx pressed her hand to her chest. Took a breath. She ran her hand over her body, where Bennett's child grew. Closed her eyes and heard her own voice. *Is it so terrible to love and want to be loved?*

Perhaps not.

She didn't look for Foster as she left, although she was glad he wasn't in the dining room, nor the front salon. Perhaps he'd gone out.

With his valet.

She waited inside her covered landau, the glass windows and convertible top up, curtains pulled just enough so she could shrink back should Foster see her.

The door opened and Amelia climbed inside. She held Jinx's valise, now bulging, to her chest. "I haven't much," she said, and opened the valise.

Inside, a small bag, tied at the top, was tucked inside.

Jinx drew in a breath. She hadn't realized she'd given Amelia such a small life.

She signaled to the driver, holding her breath, but he pulled them out of the driveway, toward Belleview Avenue, without fanfare.

Without the faltering of her heart.

She clasped her hands on her lap, mostly to keep them from shaking. She couldn't look at Amelia.

"To the harbor," she said to her driver once they'd reached Belleview.

You have my blessing, my daughter.

She tried not to let those words taste bittersweet in her mouth.

But perhaps her father had found his own healing in surrendering those words.

They finally turned onto Thames, and she drew back the curtain to locate Bennett. In the harbor, shiny yachts caught the sun and she spied the *Jinx* listing at anchor out in the marina.

Farther on, in the shipping port, fishermen would be hauling in their morning catch, ships waiting to be loaded.

Here, however, porters loaded trunks into a yacht moored along the long pier. She read the name—the *Shamrock*, a beautiful three-masted yacht bound for Paris. She spotted Bennett on the dock, the wind in his hair, wearing a white linen suit, his hands in his pockets as he talked with the captain, and her heart gave a rebellious, joyous lurch.

He hadn't left without her, just as he promised.

She tried not to listen to the voice pulsing inside, the one that told her that Foster would find them, hurt them.

No. He wanted to annul their marriage. Those words, from her father, had woken her, finally, to the truth. Whatever marriage they had was a disgrace to their vows, however selfish they'd been. Foster hated her. In fact, she had no doubt he'd be relieved if—

They pulled up across the street to the wharf, and as she watched, her breath caught.

Amelia leaned up, stared out the window. "It's Lewis."

Foster's valet stalked down the pier toward Bennett.

Bennett looked up, his expression not welcoming. Lewis handed him something, Bennett took it, shook his head.

He turned away and flung whatever he held in his hand into the sea.

Lewis turned and walked away. Positioned himself at the end of the dock.

"Foster knows," Jinx said quietly. He had to know. He didn't want her for himself, but he didn't want his brother to have her either.

"Mrs. Worth—"

"If I go out there, Lewis will see me." She looked at Amelia then back to the valet. He hadn't moved, and she thanked the shades she'd drawn, hiding her.

"We must go, now, Mrs. Worth."

Yes. What did it matter that Foster knew? She'd be with Bennett, in Paris. She reached for the handle, opened the door.

On the dock, Bennett was boarding the yacht.

No. She glanced at Amelia, shook her head. "No!"

Workmen on the dock turned to stare at her, gulls cried overhead, the sea lapped against the pilings. Motorcars braked, a horse reared, snorting as its driver yanked back the reins.

Lewis turned her direction; she could see him searching.

"Mrs. Worth!" Her driver disembarked, pulled her back toward the curb. "Be careful."

Bennett hadn't heard the commotion, hadn't turned, hadn't run after her.

And, as she looked around her, she couldn't move. Her own actions made her tremble. What was she thinking?

"Let's go, now, ma'am!" Amelia had pushed out of the landau behind her, holding her valise. "Run!"

Eyes still watched her. The sailors were casting off the ropes.

No. A lady didn't run. She didn't make a scene. She didn't... She couldn't run out on the dock like a wanton woman after her seafaring man.

She drew in a shaking breath. She couldn't live as a tarnished, shamed woman. She'd worked too hard to create this life. Her life. She could live with her husband ignoring her, without his love, with his indiscretions— what Fifth Avenue woman didn't? But she couldn't live with the stamp of adultery, of betrayal upon her. She couldn't be the fodder for Page Six.

And if she ran out on this dock, in the middle of a blue-skied Newport day, in full view of every tongue-wagger...

Jinx pressed her hand over her mouth as the yacht drifted from the pier, the motor stirring the waters to carry it into the marina then out to sea.

"Where are we going, ma'am?" Her driver jolted her from the view of Bennett's yacht disappearing toward the ocean. Dressed in last night's livery of a black leather waistcoat, a topcoat of suede, a top hat, only the best attire for her footman. A trickle of disgusting sweat dripped down his cheek.

She ignored the distress on Amelia's face and found her voice. "Bailey's Beach, please."

He nodded then helped her back into the landau.

The landau jerked, and she caught herself on the handle inside the door. They pulled along the marina, and Lewis turned.

His dark gaze fell upon the carriage. Jinx drew back, shaking.

It didn't matter what Foster suspected. She had a child now—his child, for all he knew. A child she would love and who would grow up to be strong and healthy. A son of Worth.

The sun's full attention bathed Bailey's Beach as her coachman helped her down at the entrance into the hands of the Bailey's porter, a footman in gold livery. He knew her by sight, of course, and let her enter the grounds.

If she wanted to dispel any rumors kindled from Bennett and Elise's debacle last night, she needed to make an appropriate appearance at Bailey's Beach.

It would be her last before she took to bed rest.

Amelia had said nothing and now acted as if they had intended, all along, to bathe. She set to work securing the bathing machine, and Jinx waited in the shade until the four-wheeled, donkey-drawn carriage was erected. When she entered, she found a pitcher of orange juice and a basket of fruit waiting.

Amelia would serve as her dipper, and she helped her change into her bathing costume. Jinx even donned the required rubber-soled bathing boots, lacing them up the leg.

"Ready, ma'am?" Amelia asked, her voice strangely cool.

Jinx nodded and they sat as their attendant drew the carriage toward the sea. She heard the waves scraping the shore and looked out the front as the donkey waded into the waves until the water reached the level of the wheels. Then the attendant unyoked him and drew the animal around to the front.

The attendant drew down the awning in front to afford her privacy, then Amelia helped her into the water.

Jinx stepped down, dipping one covered foot, then the other, into the surf. The water swelled around her, lifting her skirt, but even as she waded deeper, the wool kept the freshness of it from her skin.

The cover of the bathing machine obscured the view of the ocean, but Jinx imagined it, stretching out beyond her enclave, an immense blue, waves free to roam from shore to shore. And somewhere in that expanse, Bennett had sailed away from her.

She wet her hands, drew the water to her face. Oh, to dive in. She longed for the chilly lick upon her legs, the mortar of sand between her toes, the salt in her mouth.

To let the sea baptize her.

Instead, her costume weighed upon her, tossed her off balance in the rile of the waves. She lurched forward and Amelia caught her.

"Careful, Mrs. Worth, you don't want to fall."

Jinx let Amelia steady her, dug her rubber-booted feet into the sand, then took a long breath, staring down at the darkness swilling around her knees, at the dark, tented puddle of sea that belonged to her. "I won't fall." No, not ever again.

ESME

SILVER CITY, MONTANA

1903

Chapter 11

The *Butte Press* had scooped her again.

Esme sat at the long, polished oak bar of the former Trammers Saloon-turned-headquarters for the *Copper Valley Times*, her hands still black with ink from her single-plate printing press, and read the Butte sixteen-page weekly cover to cover.

The Butte paper had covered the recent vigilante hanging of two highway robbers on the road between Virginia City and Butte, the mining accidents from the Copper Valley mine just outside Silver City, an unsolved murder of a gambler found in the alley behind the Nickel, and the recent looting of Annie Doyle's homestead. All articles found in her own eight-page *Copper Valley Times*.

But the Butte paper also had headlines from Washington, New York, and San Francisco. She hadn't known about President Theodore Roosevelt's upcoming visit. No, that she found on page 1, above the fold, and read it three times, hating Ellis Carter for every ounce of backdoor, underhanded shenanigans that allowed the Copper King/newspaper baron/senator to trickle down information to his staff at the *Butte Press*.

She needed an insider in the halls of Washington, or even the state seat in Helena, if she wanted to compete with the *Press*'s circulation.

And, with their advertising power.

She propped her chin on her hand and flipped through the paper again, counting the ads, the space. Paid-for space comprised half the paper. No wonder Carter could afford the mansion on Fifth Avenue in New York when he wasn't in Washington, or paying off senators in Helena.

And, as if to grind salt into her wounds, there, on the back page, a quarter-page ad from Adelaide's Mercantile, just three doors down from Esme's office, advertising a shipment of Heinz 57. As if any of the immigrant workers down at the Silverthread mine could relate to an advertisement of a showy high-society woman and her daughter admiring their housekeeper's recent purchase.

The advertisement just reeked of Carter's grimy fingers creeping toward her little town, greenbacks in one hand, a copper collar in the other.

"Miss Essie, I thought you went home." Hudson came from the back room—which used to hold the kegs of beer, the bottles of whiskey back when Silver City boomed, years before copper was discovered in the defunct silver mines. Then, miners and gamblers, and even highway robbers-bellied up to the long bar, staring at their grizzled mugs and bloodshot eyes in the mirror, hoping for substance before heading back out into the lawless and unorganized territory of southern Montana.

Esme had rolled into town ten years too late for the silver boom, but in time to acquire the saloon for the price of one of her pearl earrings. She'd purchased the linotype machine, the printing press, and the opportunity to prove her father wrong with the other.

Hudson came with the place. Once a miner, he bore the years of frustration in his baggy eyes, the bow of his back, and knobby worn hands. He had long ago lost his dwindling silver claim to a pair of jumpers who paid off the sheriff's vigilante crew of bone-breakers for protection. Esme had peeled him off her front steps, where, like a dog, he'd returned as if lost.

She'd finally offered him a job—in return for sobriety. He kept his promise on Sundays through Thursdays.

But the man could fix anything, especially a broken vise or elevator bar, and defended her as if she might be his own daughter.

"I can't help it, Hud. I have to read the *Press*."

"Put it down. You know it ain't nothing but gossip."

"Only page four is gossip. The rest is the same news we print. Except this." She turned the paper to the front page, flipped it onto the counter. Pointed to the article. "President Roosevelt is coming to town."

Hudson, wearing a pair of overalls that betrayed the night's scurry to put their five-hundred-circulation paper to bed, leaned over and read the article. "I voted for the reverend." He pushed the paper back to her. "Don't get upset now, Miss Essie. Folks around here don't care about no president coming to visit."

"Of course they do, Hud. It's the closest thing we have to royalty. Back in New York, there'd be balls and dinners and parades—"

"There ain't none of that here."

Indeed. The last party she'd attended had been a social at the Copper Valley mining camp. If one didn't count, of course, the many wakes she'd attended, mostly out of courtesy, as a member of the press. Eulogies never seemed as lively as when told by a man with a glass of whiskey in his grip.

It seemed, however, everyone loved a good obit, and she hated the fact that a mine catastrophe meant a run into the black for her paper.

She wanted the hard news. Something that caused a rush on the paper. Something that put her in the big leagues.

Something her father might somehow see, read first sentence to last. Let himself realize that he'd been wrong.

Maybe even ask her to return.

She got up, wiping her grimy hands on her wool pants, hazarding a glance in the tarnished mirror. She'd streaked ink along her jaw.

Hud seemed to be reading her mind because from behind her, he handed over a handkerchief. It seemed clean and she did her best to wipe off the residue of her profession. "If I could just get an interview with the president, imagine how many copies we could sell. We could print double runs, maybe get ourselves some scratch money to pay for a folding machine."

Not to mention newsprint and ink. And someday she should tally up how much she owed Ruby for her photographs. And bookkeeping. And compositing.

She handed back the handkerchief, ready to crawl under the counter and sleep for a week.

No wonder her father obsessed about Pulitzer's *World*. No wonder he'd been so desperate to sell Esme off for a final grasp at their fortune.

She might have sold herself if she knew just how much a newspaper could consume a man—or woman's—soul. Her paper had become her child.

Her husband.

Her family.

The *Copper Valley Times* just might be her very heartbeat.

"Arty and his brother are out back, ready to start filling in the newsstands," Hud said.

"Perfect. Will you run a bundle out to the camp?"

He pocketed his handkerchief. "If you promise to get some shut-eye. And don't bother tellin' me that you aren't exhausted—you look like you spent a week huddled up with a bottle of whiskey."

"I don't drink, Hud, you know that. But thanks for the honesty."

Hud winked at her, tease in his expression, and headed into the pressroom. Or file library. Or loading dock. Sometimes, when scrutinizing her two-room operation, and laying it beside her father's glorious Chronicle Building with the angelic clock...well, she'd left divine providence long behind in New York when she traveled out West, in search of some elusive independence that had nearly starved her that first year.

She'd survived, however. Barely, but with enough to keep herself and Hud fed. Enough to hire Ruby. And someday she'd file for a homestead claim, build a house, and move out of the room upstairs, next to Ruby's.

The bell above the door jangled and like clockwork, Agnes O'Shaunessy billowed in, her red hair braided under a wide-brimmed hat, ostrich feathers tufted at the crown. She had tucked herself into a Sears & Roebuck day dress as if she fancied herself a lady, despite the mud-caked cowboy boots. Now she slapped a list down on the bar. "I got a fresh crop of catalog women needing husbands."

Esme reached under the bar, pulled out a manila envelope, pressed a copy of her folded *Times* into it. "Agnes, we've been through this. The *Copper Valley Times* is not a social page. I am not going to advertise your mail-order brides like they were parasols, or Heinz 57 ketchup."

"Parasols?"

"I'm not selling your women for you."

Agnes's mouth dropped. "I'll have you know I screen every single one of these men who come calling. And I hardly make any profit off my troubles. But the fact is, these women have come out West to secure themselves a happily ever after, and there are plenty of lonely men here needing a good wife."

Esme sealed the envelope. "They need someone to get the soot and grime off their pants is what they need. And tell them to shave. And maybe even get a haircut. They can get that from Cats Alley. Thank you, but I'm not in the business of selling women to the highest bidder in search of a wife. They'll only shackle her to a life of poverty, fear, and an early death."

"They need someone to come home to after a day twelve hundred feet under the earth, smelling the stench of hell and facing the grim reaper with only a hardhat, a lamp, and a hammer is what."

Esme looked up at the tremor in Agnes's voice, drew in a long breath. Agnes looked away fast, pressed manicured nails under her eyes.

"I'm sorry, Agnes. That came out wrong." Two years after Agnes's husband's accident, and the wounds on her expression seemed as fresh as when Esme watched the company men lower her Clancy into the earth. Lines of grief whittled into Agnes's face made her seem decades instead of only two years older than Esme.

Only, perhaps that's exactly how Esme had appeared when she'd arrived in Silver City. Lined. Desperate, and more than a little ready to take on the world and make sure she never got hurt again.

"I just don't abide arranged marriages, is all," Esme finally said, trying for an explanation.

Agnes drew a long breath. "I think you don't abide love. Look at you, a single girl, out here for the past five years—"

"Seven, Agnes. I've been here seven years."

"Long enough to find yourself a husband, maybe have a few children."

Esme came around the counter, wishing away, for a moment, her finishing school lessons. She wanted to snap back at Agnes—*Maybe I don't get a second chance at love. Maybe I had my opportunity and lost it.*

But none of those words emerged. Instead, she smiled. Esme tried to soften her voice, add compassion to it. "I know you believe you are helping these girls, and perhaps I have judged you too quickly. But as long as I'm the owner and the editor of the *Copper Valley Times,* I cannot print your advertisement."

Agnes grabbed up the list. "Fine. You may write fancy articles, Miss Essie Stewart, but you haven't a clue how to run a business. See you at the church social on Sunday."

She turned and marched out, rattling the pane of glass behind her, the gold COPPER VALLEY TIMES etching on the door obscuring her exit.

"You know, Agnes has a good heart. She's matched half the men in town—or at least, the good ones." Ruby came down the stairs. Dressed in a split skirt and shirtwaist and with her hair in two long braids, she looked as fresh and bright as the day she marched into Esme's office and begged for work.

She needed a job before she got married off to a man twice her age. Or worse. But what choices did an orphan girl have out here in the unforgiving West? Until that moment, when Esme had seen her quick, wounded smile, Ruby considered her only commodities her long chestnut hair, golden brown eyes, and the fact she knew every miner that worked the Silverthread Mine. Which meant she also knew how to sniff out a story.

Esme had dropped a camera in her hand and put her to work.

"Agnes O'Shaunessy is running nothing more than a glorified brothel. Or a mercantile where the women are merchandise."

"Agnes is a good God-fearing woman who specializes in matters of the heart. Nothing but conversation and parlor games are permitted. Believe me, before Agnes took it over, the O'Donnells had a very different purpose for the place. You should give her credit for cleaning up the town."

"Right alongside Sheriff Toole."

Ruby picked up the envelope, studied the address on the front. Shook her head. "Take it from me, the 3-7-77 vigilante squad put the fear into the highway robbers. Whether the sheriff's at the heart of the vigilantes or not, they've made the ride from Butte to Silver City survivable." She held up the envelope. "When are you going to stop sending these?"

Esme took it from her hand. "Go find me a big story for next week's paper. I need something that will sell ads."

"The Copper Camp is having their annual miners' dance in a few weeks. I'm sure I could come up with a list of women needing dates. Or perhaps a recipe or two."

"Ruby, please—I need news. I'm not running a gossip magazine here. If I hope to compete with the *Butte Press,* I need to scoop them with something hard-hitting."

"We're not the *New York Chronicle,*" Ruby said softly.

Esme drew in a breath. Caught a glimpse of herself in the tarnished mirror, recognizing the blue eyes, the wisps of blond hair pulled back with a lanyard. The rest of her—from the men's pants to the boots—seemed like something she'd only read about in one of her dime novels.

She picked up the envelope, grabbed her hat, something bequeathed to her from under the dusty bar, and headed for the post office. "No, we're not the *Chronicle.*" She stopped at the door, her hand on the brass handle, staring at her inverted freshly painted lettering. "But with the right story, we could be."

* * * * *

Sometimes, like now, Esme could hardly believe she lived on the edge of the frontier, in a country where she hid a pearl-handle revolver in her desk, where she rode a horse—not sidesaddle—and where she'd become a woman she'd dreamed up in the back of her Fifth Avenue mind.

But Silver City was most definitely not Fifth Avenue. Corralled in a thumbprint alpine valley, edged on all sides by a rough-hewn scattering of foothills, pinched and drawn forth around the edges like one of Cook's Christmas pies, and liberally dolloped with sage, mountain grasses, and groves of pine, Silver City served up all manner of Wild West legend.

From gunslingers to forty-niners to catalog girls to card-sharking black legs to Bible-thumping converters, they all found their way to Butte—and when the big city wrung them out, they crawled twenty-six miles west, over the ridge to Silver City.

Esme had taken one look at Butte, with its arsenic- and sulfur-poisoned skies blackened by the two dozen smelter stacks burning ore—courtesy of the Anaconda and Amalgamated mine companies—the sea of wooden shanty towns from Dublin Gulch to Chinatown, the row of brothels on Venus Alley, and enough saloons and breweries to slake the thirst of all New York, and decided to stay aboard the Northern Pacific Railroad.

Besides, she'd already circled Silver City on her railroad map, charmed by the way the words slid off her tongue. Silver City.

Then, she watched the plains of South Dakota turn from golden expanse of undulating ocean to ragged black hills to rolling prairies gullied out with furrows and rivulets of land and grassy buttes hacked off as if a giant shovel descended from the heavens, to finally the glorious rumble of white-painted mountains to the south and west. Halfway through Montana seemed exactly the right measurement to disembark and begin her Calamity Jane life.

Indeed, the sky overhead stretched so far she thought she might see all the way to the edge of America; and under it, a man—or woman—could rename themselves and start over.

For seven years, she barely looked backwards, barely narrowed her eyes to make out faces in the shadows, the ones that knew her real name, not the one she'd adopted for cover as well as honor. Esme Stewart.

Yet, after seven years, she could still find herself in Oliver's arms that stolen evening as he walked her home. And, in soft dawn, with the meadowlark calling outside her window, he came to her with the taste of his kiss upon her lips.

You're an amazing writer, Esme. I believe in you.

What would he think now, to see her in a pair of pants, mucking through the muddy streets of a mining town, the sole proprietor of the only newspaper in a town of six thousand, chronicling the lives, the deaths, the villains, and the heroes of the West?

Oliver, you might have been proud.

The six blocks of Main Street, Silver City, threaded through the center of town, dividing the homesteaders where their parcels dumped into Silver Creek from the townsfolk whose tiny soot-covered, wood-framed shanties resembled in miniature the boroughs of New York City. Irish, Welsh, Italian, and Serbians all found themselves in the Copper Valley, most of them wrung out of the mines in Butte, holding onto the rumor of something better twenty-six miles away to the southwest.

They found it, for the most part, in the Silverthread Mine. Owned by a former miner, Archie Hoyt. Esme knew him as solid, fair, and dependable. And, in failing health.

The last thing this town needed was for Archie to die and for the mine to be swallowed up into the maw of the Anaconda Mining Company, or even the Amalgamated.

With their dubious working conditions and history of tragedy, the Copper Kings would only tarnish Silver City.

"*Dobray ootra*, Miss Stewart." Russian Oogie Popovich, bald-headed and the size of a buffalo, emerged from his barbershop. He had a nose broadened with too many fists, wide hands that betrayed the life of a mucker. A blast in the Neversweat Mine in Butte had taken his foot, sent him in search of a more gentle occupation.

"Morning, Oogie."

"I hear there was a ruckus down at the rec center last night." He stood, his apron tarnished with hair and old shave cream. "Sheriff's got a couple BMUs down at the calaboose, cooling off."

"What else is new?" Esme said as she passed by. The miners seemed to be always itching for a fight, and the agitators from the Butte Miners Union knew how to stir them. So far, they hadn't accomplished their goal of banding together the Silverthread miners, but they never appeared to fatigue in their efforts.

This morning, the sun slid over the rim of foothills to the east, turning the ice-skimmed puddles to onyx. A western wind cleared the sooty skies over Butte, their smelters delivering sulfur and arsenic gasses into the blue-skied day, but over the mountains and away from Silver City.

It was a pretty town. She'd arrived just as the Silverthread Copper mine began to flourish, and chronicled the town's growth from a mercantile, a saloon, and a very small Presbyterian church to a metropolis with three general stores, two saloons, a blacksmith, numerous grocers for every nationality, a butcher, a livery stable, a brewery, a cafeteria, two hotels, a trading company, a smattering of boardinghouses, the Cat's Alley, a miners' recreation hall, a courthouse, and a school, not to mention a boomtown of churches pledging to save them all from the dark habits cultivated by miners trapped too long under the crust of earth.

They even had a library, an opera house, and…a weekly newspaper.

From far off, she heard the piercing whine of the shift bell, and she could almost see the men ascending from the maw of the earth, black-faced, whitened eyes, smelling of sweat and grime, gulping in the sunshine as they trudged home, sandwich tins in their gnarled grips.

Another whistle signaled that this shift emerged without injury. No fires, no cave-ins, no faulty detonations, no falls.

Esme stood in the street and drank in the sound.

It died on the wind, stinging and brutal, as it delivered particles of the earth against her face. She pulled her hat down and trudged toward the post office.

The bell dinged over the door.

Neely Button stood at the counter, his hair gray and long, and grinned up at her. "Is that the latest issue of the *Times*?"

She handed him the package and dug out the appropriate coinage. "What's the news?"

Neely took the package, stamped it, moved it to the outgoing mail. She watched it just a second longer. Never an acknowledging note from her father, not once, in seven years.

"Sheriff has a slew of rabble-rousers in the pokey. Picked them up from the recreation hall last night."

"Oogie told me. BMUs again."

"They're agitatin' for a strike."

"The Silverthread's never going to strike. Hoyt's a decent man. The Silverthread miners don't need a union—they know if they strike, it'll shut down the mine, put Hoyt out of business, and then they'll have to work for the Anaconda." Esme walked over to the wanted posters, scanned the faces. She knew most of the homesteaders in this area, but one never knew when she'd meet someone on the road. Besides, in her line of work, it behooved her to know the faces and names of the wanted.

"They might strike now that Hoyt's passing on the mine to his son. Daughtry Hoyt might not be as agreeable as his old man."

She froze, glanced over at Neely. "Archie Hoyt is passing the reins of the Silverthread?" She hadn't seen Archie since the Christmas service, but the long Montana winter had driven nearly everyone inside to barred doors and boarded windows.

Neely shrugged. "Daughtry got off the afternoon train a couple days ago."

"He's back?"

"You know him?"

"Just the legend, but yes." So, maybe someone could return home again. Put things right.

"The scuttlebutt is that he's here to sell off the mine."

Esme froze. "He wouldn't."

"Why not? He's been living back East for the last ten years. Running Hoyt's stocks in New York after his Harvard education. Got a real way about him—come in to town yesterday wearing a top hat, tails, a real gent, like them you read about in the papers, you know?"

She did, and the image conjured memories she'd banished long ago.

Daughtry Hoyt couldn't sell the mine.

But if he were planning on it, then that was news she aimed to find out first.

Esme pushed outside, bracing herself against the crisp spring breeze. Already, men fresh off their shift lined up at the recreation center, probably looking for hot coffee and eggs from the cafeteria. The saloons wouldn't open until noon.

A man had set up a soapbox, climbed on top of it, and a crowd jockeyed close as his oration rose over them.

"If we are to be a force against the Capitalists, we must join together. There can be no peace between the working class and the employing class so long as they have all the benefits of life. We must organize and wage war, take ownership of production, eliminate the system of wages, and live as one class."

Union agitators. But, a newspaper woman could recognize a notable moment. She estimated the crowd, pushed forward to the front as the man, a rakish charm about him with his dark hair that fell over his blue eyes— she guessed him to be Cornish, maybe, and the English twist of the vowels confirmed it—raised his earnest tenor vibrato in song.

"When the union's inspiration through the workers' blood shall run,
There can be no power greater anywhere beneath the sun."

With the passion of his voice, he reminded her, crazily, of Oliver.

"Yet what force on earth is weaker than the feeble strength of one,
But the union makes us strong."

Around her, men—some she recognized from a few of the wakes, Irish and Cornish, and one Italian—began to hum to the contagious melody of the "Battle Hymn of the Republic." Her stomach knotted as they joined in the chorus. She'd heard rumor of this song belonging to the International Workers of the World, a much larger movement than the BMUs.

"Solidarity forever,
Solidarity forever,
Solidarity forever,
For the union makes us strong."

"Stop!" The voice cracked the air as the leader began the second verse. He searched for the dissident as he sang.

"Is there aught we hold in common with the greedy parasite,
Who would lash us into serfdom and would crush us with his might?"

"Don't listen to him!"
A murmur of discontent started, like a locomotive. The voices in the crowd lost steam even as the union man bellowed out his response.

"Is there anything left to us but to organize and fight?
For the union makes us strong."

"The union will only destroy you!"

The owner of the voice pushed through the crowd, tall, with an aristocratic look in his high cheekbones, his dark eyes, and an expression that could part crowds. He turned, a derby clutched in his hand, a shadow of dark whiskers layered upon his dimpled chin. Esme placed him about her age, and something about him—his diction, perhaps, or even his calm, commanded attention.

It niggled something inside her.

"We don't need a union," he said. "They're out to destroy the Silverthread! They don't care what it costs. They don't care about your children or your homes or your jobs! They'll starve you all when they force you to strike, and it'll be your bodies rotting from the pit heads!"

He'd ignited a dangerous murmur, and yet she heard others, the whisper of stories about the strikebreakers fighting the Pinkertons, and labor leaders found murdered.

"What about the six men who died two weeks ago when their cage crashed?" the union man shouted, his eyes sparking. "Who paid for their funerals? Who will feed their families?"

"The Silverthread looks after its own."

More murmering began, someplace low and behind her, and she heard the name in the well of her mind even before it emerged on the tongue of the union man. "Daughtry Hoyt. Come back to finish the job?"

His tone, perhaps, stunned the crowd to silence. Or maybe the way the two men stared at each other.

Daughtry Hoyt, blue blood from the East. Indeed—she should have recognized his confidence, the kind wrought from a vast supply of resources, unaffected by life's lower-class tragedies.

As if in confirmation, he stared, unruffled at the union man, his voice steady. "No, Abel. I've come back to fix—"

It seemed she alone heard him because even as he said it, the crowd erupted into a surge of fury.

Men pushed and kicked, fists finding flesh, shouts and cries. Esme had seen plenty of fights—mostly the flavor of inebriated men spilling out of the Nickel. But this felt different—as if the union man's song had plucked a string already too taut.

Someone knocked her to her knees and she scrambled back to her feet, ran toward the direction of her office.

She caught a fist in her back and cried out, pushed against another man, then ducked when he turned on her, his fist swishing past her cheek.

"Miss Stewart!"

She heard the voice but couldn't find it in the mass of bodies, the sense of panic that roused inside her, turning her body to liquid.

Blood splattered on her jacket, across her face.

She wiped her hands down her face, stared at them. Stumbled and fell into another man.

He whirled, grabbed her up by the collar of her jacket.

She screamed, covered her face, and braced herself for the blow.

Chapter 12

"Do you think it's broken? It looks broken." Ruby peered over Doc Samson's shoulder at Esme's swollen ankle as if she'd like to push the frontiersman-turned-physician aside and doctor the swelling herself.

Esme gripped the stool and gulped back a cry, seizing her breath between her teeth as the doctor examined her foot, moved it ever so slightly in a circle. "Can you walk on it?"

"Absolutely. Just give me back my boot. Sorry to have bothered you—"

"She can't walk on it, and ten minutes before you got here, she was in tears, so don'ya listen to her, Doc."

The doctor glanced at the man standing behind Esme, his arms folded. "I suppose we should all thank Abel here for picking her up out of the mud."

"I can take care of myself." Esme shot a glare at Hud. He leaned against the bar, arms folded, not in the least intimidated. In fact, he even rolled his eyes.

Well, she could take care of herself, thank you very much. Except, she had to admit to a moment of relief that when the blow came, it didn't hurt as much as she feared, more glancing as it spun her around. She'd slipped in the mud then crawled until she saw daylight, dragging behind her an ankle the size of a grapefruit.

She didn't have so much pride, however, that she couldn't take the hand offered to her at the edge of the angry mass.

A hand that belonged to the rabble-rouser himself.

"Does this hurt?" The doctor pressed his thumb against the bones in her ankle. Pain shot up her leg, nearly to her eyeballs.

"Nope." Her gaze ran to the union man, now straddling an office chair backwards, scrutinizing Esme's expression. He wore the makings of a smirk on his unshaven face, his brown eyes alight with humor.

"Okay, maybe a little. But I'll be fine."

Doc Samson stood up, grabbed his hat. "I don't think it's broken." He glanced at Ruby, who looked dubious. "But you'd better stay off it a couple days."

"Hardly. I'm heading out to the Hoyt ranch to talk to Archie, find out what he thinks about all this rabble-rousing."

She glanced at the union man, who pursed his lips. Well, she had a bruise on her cheek, thanks to his agitating.

"The story will keep for a few days," Hud said to her, then turned to the doctor. "We'll make sure she behaves."

Doc Samson let out a laugh. "I don't expect that much, but I'll come by in a couple days to check on you. Try to stay out of the miners' street brawls, will you, Miss Stewart?"

She waved him away and reached for the snow-filled cloth the doctor had used to take down the swelling. Ruby dropped to her knees to help her. For a second, a memory skidded through her mind—her lady's maid, Bette, fixing her hair, helping her into her dress, tying her slippers. She brushed Ruby's hands away. "I can do this. Thanks, Ruby."

Ruby stood, rounded on the man in the chair. "And I want to know, Abel White, just what you were doing leading that union meeting? Have you taken leave of your senses?"

Abel seemed well acquainted with Ruby's demeanor. He grinned up at her. "Don't go getting your knickers in a knot. I was just drumming up support for the Butte Miners Union. We're going to need one with Daughtry back in town."

His voice slid into a dark tone at the name of the owner's son.

Ruby shook her head, grabbed up her hat. "Ten years seems too long to hold a grudge."

"Too long to forget my brother?"

Ruby shook her head. "No one is forgetting anyone. Including your brother." She glanced at Esme. "You want me to go see who else got hurt?"

"Yes. Please go talk to the sheriff while I interview the troublemaker here."

A ghost of that smirk returned, one that Esme might have found fetching if not for his cryptic, acerbic words ringing in her mind. Forget his brother?

Hud must have sensed a confrontation, because he walked over to the stove, added another log, and stirred the coals to life. "If you need me, you know where to find me."

Normally, on a Friday morning after the paper was out on the streets, he'd be tapping a keg at the Nickel. But today, with her reminding him of her mortality, she knew he'd be sitting in the back room, with his ear pressed to the door, listening for trouble.

Just as she thought, he headed to the back room.

"Is he your father or something?" Abel said, watching him go.

"An uncle of sorts." She hopped over to a chair, held up her hand when Abel stood to help her. "He came with the place." She lifted her leg onto another chair and managed not to let the pain show on her face.

Maybe. Abel gave a small shake of his head. "I know you like to act like you're a man, Miss Stewart, but you might consider letting someone help you."

"Act like a man? What are you talking about? You don't even know me."

He gave another cryptic smirk and moved over to the fire, held out his work-worn hands. Strong hands, as far as she could remember from his brief help as he ferried her over to the *Times* office. He'd smelled clean too, like he'd bathed after his last shift, although the redolence of the earth, of hard work, and smoke embedded his clothes—his shirt, the woolen pants. "You don't remember me, then?"

She stared at his back, his words stilling her. "Have we met?"

"At my cousin Alton Wallace's funeral. You interviewed me and a bunch of the boys for his obituary. I even bought myself a paper, just to read it."

"I hope I did him justice." But oh, she couldn't remember. Was he the boy who'd been trapped in a cave-in?

"He left behind a wife and two daughters."

Oh yes, a fall—part of the wall had caved in on him. She remembered the daughters, little dark-haired beauties who hid behind their black-attired mother. "Gretchen and Leah?"

"You did him just fine."

"How's his family?"

"She married again, a widower who had a son. Her new husband's a trammer—works on the second shift." He turned. "But I remember how you tromped down to the graveside and stood in the snow as we lowered him back to his mother's bosom. Then you came over to the Nickel." His eyes fixed on her, unmoving. "You listened to us wind tales of Wally, raising the rye with us."

"Actually, I toasted, but I don't drink."

"I thought so, because you were the only one standing after five hours."

"Hud made sure you all got home."

"I thought he looked familiar."

He gave her a smile, something fragile in it, and drew in a breath. He reminded her of Oliver, the way he looked at her, such earnestness in his eyes. "I bet you look real pretty in a dress."

She stilled.

"Sorry, I've just been thinking that ever since that day. That you'd look pretty in a dress."

She didn't know why, but she felt the compliment, husky and unrefined as it was, all the way to her toes. Yes, long ago she had looked pretty—very pretty—in a dress. But she'd left those days behind, and a woman on her own didn't survive the West with a trunk full of dresses, in need of assistance from a maid and a footman.

He held her eyes a long moment then smiled as if he'd accomplished a sort of victory, and wandered over to a stack of papers. "So you're going to write about today's shenanigans?"

"Seems newsworthy. Especially with the fact that Daughtry Hoyt is back in town. You want to tell me what happened between you two?"

"What makes you think anything—"

"Please. I'm a reporter, and I know what I've heard—that his father sent him away after he caused an accident at the mine. But I don't deal in rumors. I want the truth. And I saw the way you were looking at him as you sang. What do you know, Abel? Now, you have a choice—I can ask Ruby, or you can tell me in your own words."

He closed the paper. Turned and braced himself against the bar. Considered her. Finally, "Daughtry Hoyt murdered my brother."

She studied him for guile, but he met her gaze with his own, dark and solid.

"How?"

A shadow crossed his eyes, a ghost from the past, perhaps. She'd seen it before, in Hud's eyes before he told her a story, as he considered which half of the truth to tell her. For a moment, she thought Abel would turn away, even toss out a full-out lie—she'd confirm it later with Ruby anyway. But she held his gaze and hoped for honesty.

He swallowed. "You've lived here long enough to have heard of the Silverthread mine explosion, right?"

"Killed thirty-eight miners. It happened about three years before I got here. You're telling me he was involved in the accident?"

"I was fourteen. And just starting work. They put me on my brother's shift so he could help me. We were trammers, along with Daughtry."

"Daughtry worked in the mine?"

"His old man started out as a miner—thought it might do his son good to get his fingers dirty. He'd only been around for a few weeks. He was working with Orrin and me, transporting a couple boxes of powder. Daughtry and Orrin took a break, and Daughtry was smoking a cigarette when the shift boss came up. He didn't want to get caught, so he flicked his cigarette away. It must have landed in the powder box in the car, and smoldered there.

"Later, Daughtry and I left to go change his carbide because the idiot didn't check his supply before he went down, and it went out. While we were gone, the box exploded. The blast caved in the drift, trapping Orrin and the rest of our crew. We dug for hours, but by the time we got to them, they had all died."

She had never been inside a mine—the thought of working so far under the crust of earth could turn her cold—but she saw everything: the dank walls glistening with tears of water, the suffocating heat, the tremor of the earth as it convulsed.

Abel clawing away the rock, desperate to free his brother.

"I'm so sorry."

Abel leaned up from the bar, walked over to the stove, warming his hands there. "I'll never forgive him. Daughtry killed those miners. It wasn't long after that when his father sent him away. I can't believe he had the courage to return."

I've come back to fix— Daughtry's voice slunk back to her, the tremor in it. "What if he's come back to make things right?"

Abel glanced at her then, nothing of mercy in his expression. "Can he bring me back my brother? Or Ruby's father? Or the sons and brothers and husbands who left families behind?"

Ruby's father had been among the thirty-eight dead?

"How old was your brother?"

"Sixteen, same as Daughtry."

"I'm so sorry, Abel."

He grabbed the chair, again straddled it. "I'm sorry you got hurt in our assembly today."

"You mean brawl?"

"Don't you see, that's what we have to do to get them to take us seriously? The muckety-mucks that control the Silverthread need to understand that we're not going to let them cut our wages or work us to our deaths. But we gotta organize, be one unit, if we hope to shut them down."

She stared at him, those wide hands he used to gesture with, his earnest eyes. "But if you shut them down, you won't have a job."

He considered her a long moment. "You clearly don't understand the purpose of a strike. But I sure would like to see you in a dress." He gave her a smile, something that might be devastating to any other woman. Indeed, he had a mischief in his eyes that made her smile as he lowered his voice, turned it sweet. "Would you come to the miners' dance with me?"

A date? Oh… "Abel, I—"

"I promise to be on my best behavior, really. No fighting." He held up his hands in surrender.

She smiled, shook her head. "I don't have a dress, Abel."

But what if Abel and his fellow miners were planning a strike? She could find out about it before the *Butte Press* got the story.

Scoop them.

"But I think Ruby might have a dress I can borrow."

A smile slid up his face. "That'll work."

"But only if I get to come to one of your union meetings."

His smile fell. "I don't think so. They get kind of rough, and—"

"I'm not afraid of getting hurt."

His eyes narrowed. "Keep your notebook at home?"

"No. But I do promise to be fair."

He got up. "Fair. That depends on your perspective. But, Miss Stewart, I do want to see you in a dress at that dance, so it's a deal."

* * * * *

Archie Hoyt had chosen the best piece of real estate for his home when he'd built the three-story house with the white-painted siding, the front porch, the gable roof with the peek-a-boo window. It overlooked Willow Creek, and beyond that, the lacy edge of white-capped mountains. A working ranch. Esme didn't spot the vast herds of angus ranging over the land—

she guessed they might still be in winter pastures. Hoyt did have one of the prettiest red barns she'd ever seen, situated away from the house and back-dropped by the crisp blue Montana sky. She reined in her mare, Dixie, and drew in the smells of spring, the mountain grass stirred by the wind, the hint of cattle embedded in the land, the sting of the air on her ears.

Soon, the meadowlark would call, tumbleweeds be chased by the wind. She felt that sometimes, chased by the wind. Or perhaps she was chasing it. But Daughtry's words, and Abel's tale, had driven her out to the Hoyt home-stead, despite the doctor's warning, in search of answers. Or, at least, a story.

She had seen Archie Hoyt, owner of the Silverthread Mines—with its three shafts, the Pipe, the new Neck, and the now closed Horn—at city council meetings and courthouse hearings. She had even interviewed him here at his home after he'd shown up at the opening of the new mineshaft a year ago. He'd seemed tired, then. Thin, with a narrow face, a shock of whitened hair, and a beard that obscured most of his sallow face, he bore a scooped-out appearance. His second wife had died only a year prior, in childbirth, along with their child. To her knowledge, Daughtry, the son of his first wife, Jane Morninglory, was his only descendant.

The only one to whom he might will the Silverthread Mining operation.

She hauled in a couple of swift breaths before she eased off Dixie, the old mare so patient with her it seemed she understood Esme's wounded ankle. Pausing to absorb the pain, she took a breath and hobbled up the front steps then pressed the bell.

She heard the sound of it deep inside the house, then footsteps, and the door opened to a housekeeper, a woman who might have scared her years ago with her dark eyes, her black hair in a long braid. But the dime novels did no justice to the character of the Indians she had met in the flesh. "Good afternoon, Dawn. Is Mr. Hoyt in?"

"He's napping, but I'll tell him you stopped by." Back in New York, Esme might have left a calling card. Dawn started to close the door.

"Is Daughtry here?"

"Charlie's down at the barn."

Charlie?

She took her time going down the stairs and onto the path, aware of the pockets of snow that still blackened the ground. She eased open the barn door, the musty redolence of hay escaping. Inside, shadows darkened the massive room. She saw no one. "Hello?" She stepped inside, her boot, so tight she had barely managed it on, now scraping on the dirt floor. "Daughtry Hoyt?"

Back in New York, her father kept a stable of horses, a shiny row of thoroughbreds in their spic-and-span stalls, waiting to be hitched to a landau or brougham, ready to ferry her and her sister through the park, or to church.

Only a few horses remained in this stable—a mare nursing a foal, a working horse flicking its giant tail against the stall, an appaloosa chewing hay. At the end, a farrier sat, mucking out mud from the hooves of a beautiful black Arabian.

"Do you know where I could find Daughtry Hoyt?"

He looked up. Even in the shadows, she recognized that same lean, aristocratic face, the ebony hair, the keen expression of confident interest. "No Daughtry here," he said. "But my name's Charlie." He let down the horse's hoof and grabbed a towel, wiping his hands. "And you're the lady in the middle of a nasty fight this morning. Esme Stewart, is it? Newspaperwoman?"

The afternoon sun shafted through the high windows and he stepped into a blade of light. Oh, he was dangerously handsome. He had dark eyes, a smile that curved up to a perfect divot in his cheek, and sculpted shoulders that suggested he knew how to sail, or row. Tall and trim, yes, she could see him in a waistcoat, tails, a gray ascot, white gloves, and a top hat, and he wouldn't look for a moment out of place.

She stepped away from his outstretched hand, also seeing, for a moment, Foster.

"I'm sorry. Of course, I should wash up." He withdrew his hand. "I suppose you came out to interview the prodigal son of Archie Hoyt?" He said it with a wry smile, something of pain in his voice.

"People want to know why you came back."

He shut the stall then turned and started out of the barn.

"You said something at the assembly. Something about wanting to fix—"

"I was wrong." He rounded on her, his eyes dark. "Some things can't be fixed. And maybe prodigals can never go home."

She stood frozen, his words digging through her unprotected places, finding soft soil.

He left her there and strode out ahead of her, across the shadowed terrain of the barn. She sprinted to catch up with him—

Her foot caught in a divot of ground and crumpled beneath her. "Oh!" She put out her hands but landed hard, pain spiking up her leg. She drew in breath between her teeth, pulled her leg to herself, rocking.

Daughtry crouched before her. "What happened?"

"Someone hit me in the fight today and I turned my ankle. I think I just injured it further."

His face contorted in a sympathy show of pain. "May I carry you to the house?"

The courtesy of his request—the fact that he hadn't simply swooped her up—resonated inside her. She found herself nodding.

He swept her up without a pause, as if she might fit perfectly into his embrace. Nudging open the door, he brought her out of the barn into the brisk sunlight. She groaned at the mud caking her arms, her legs.

"I'll have Dawn draw you a bath, find you a change of clothes. Although, you might find my attire a bit…enveloping."

"I can ride back to town—"

"Of course you can. But should you?" He smiled down at her, his elegant brow raised.

Opening the door, he stood in the hallway. She had loved this home the first time she saw it—the grand two-story entryway, with the polished oak floors, the scrolled and curved dark alder banister leading to the second floor. He carried her past the oval grand room with the green marble fireplace and up the stairs to the second story. Dawn appeared from the upper level, moving aside as he reached the landing.

"Would you please get Miss Stewart some ice? She's been injured."

He turned down the hall and nudged open a door. Inside the expansive room, a grand brass featherbed, a rolltop desk, and a deep mahogany two-door wardrobe conjured up memories. Everything, from the red damask coverlet on the bed to the green velvet drapes, all swept her back to Fifth Avenue. It smelled too of dried rose petals, as if they might be lifted from the tiny rosebud wallpaper.

"This was my mother's favorite room," Daughtry said.

"It's beautiful."

He walked toward the bed.

"No, I'm filthy. And that's French damask!"

He stared at her a second, curiosity flashing across his face, then set her down on the hard-backed desk chair. "Hold onto something, this might hurt," he said as he knelt before her.

Taking a hold of her boot, he looked up at her. "And, for the record, I'm sorry."

He took the boot off as gently as he could. Even so, she had to bite back a cry, her body trembling by the time he got it off. "You may have broken it."

She wiped her cheeks, staring at the swollen mass. Whatever she'd done before, the fall in the barn made it worse. "Doc Sampson already said it was sprained."

"A bad sprain. But Dawn will know what to do." He stepped back as the woman came in with ice in a basin of cold water. She lowered Esme's foot into it and Esme sucked back her breath.

"I don't think you're going anywhere for at least a couple of days, Miss Stewart," Dawn said.

"Call me Esme." She looked at Daughtry and closed her eyes as the ice worked its way into her bones.

Dawn picked up her other, booted, foot. "Leave us, Charlie. I'll call you when she's ready for guests."

Indeed, Esme had been transported back to a life of ease, right here in the wild hills of Montana.

Dawn drew her a bath, filled it with rose petals, and helped her clean up. Then she let her choose between a pair of Daughtry's wool pants or a crimson brocade dress with creamy lace sleeves and a collared bodice, a gown Esme might have worn to a Vanderbilt dinner party.

Something inside her made her choose the dress.

She sat on the settee as Dawn did her hair—nothing fancy, like Bette would have done, but swept up with a pair of pearl combs. "Mr. Hoyt gave these to his second wife. I know he will enjoy having someone wear them again."

Esme stared at her bare décolletage and imagined the pearl and diamond dog collar around her neck, the one tucked away in the safe at the *Times.* Someday, she might wear it again. When the prodigal felt ready to return.

"You're beautiful, Miss Stewart," Dawn said.

A knock came at the door. Dawn opened it, and Daughtry stood in the hallway, wearing a western brocade vest, a pair of pressed black woolen pants, a gold ascot at his neck. "I heard we had a guest for dinner," he said, and something about his smile sent heat through her.

"Dawn suggested I stay."

"I agree with Dawn." He drew in a breath, a smile pushing at his mouth. "You look breathtaking."

She ran her hands down the dress and allowed the compliment to sink through her, warm her in a way she hadn't felt in years.

"My father said he'd join us at dinner." He stepped inside the room. "May I?"

She frowned and he held out his arms. Oh. She nodded.

He smelled spicy—bathed, yes, but with a hint of the woodland and alpine breeze, and she realized he was wearing an imported scent. He carried her with ease to the parlor and settled her on a crushed velvet divan. A fire coaxed warmth into the room, and over the mantel hung an oil of a woman, Indian descent in her features.

"My mother. She was a half-breed, from the Crow tribe. My father married her when he was just a teenager, when he came out to pan for gold down in Virginia City. She died when I was twelve."

"I'm sorry. Was this her dress?"

"Yes. My father had it made for her in Paris. Now that he had money, he wanted to turn her into one of those fancy New York Knickerbockers."

Esme thought she recognized the handiwork of a Paris house.

He stood at the window, staring at the sun setting over the far white ridge. "We visited New York two years before she died. We took the train and I remember wondering how so many people could live in such a tiny place. The streets were muddy, the skies dark. But she loved the shops and the hotels. We took rides through Central Park and she bought so many dresses I thought we'd need another train car to haul them home. She simply ignored the expressions of those who questioned her presence, who made assumptions as to why she assumed the right of my father's arm."

His voice turned dark and he stopped, swallowed.

"One night, though, we took a carriage to the Metropolitan Opera. My father allowed me to join them, and we waited in our hotel lobby until my mother appeared. In just that dress." He looked over at her, but he had only his mother in his eyes. "She was radiant. That night, she wasn't the Crow wife of a miner from Montana. We were society. Footmen helped us into our rented landau. We took an opera box. And, we dined later at Delmonico's."

"It sounds glorious." She remembered nights like that. Glorious might be the word she would have used back then if she weren't intent on escaping matrimony.

His smile fell and he returned to her. "It certainly wasn't Montana."

"Is that why you moved there?"

He glanced at her, turned his back. "My father sent me away."

Her gaze returned to the woman over the mantel. "She sounds like a lovely woman."

"She was. She loved my father—would have done anything for him. I think that's why she put up with all the scorn in New York City. All our money couldn't buy her respectability."

"New York can be a fickle city, caught up in appearances rather than substance."

Her words turned him, and again he frowned at her. "What do you know of New York?"

Oh. She stared at her hands, debated her response. "I read the *Chronicle* sometimes. The society page." It wasn't a lie, exactly. But the truth swelled before her—what if he found out she descended from the Price family? The miners, Silver City considered her one of their own. But if anyone— especially Abel—found out she came from money, from power, from the elite set, he might not let her attend the union meeting.

She might lose her scoop.

Which meant she couldn't tell anyone—not even Daughtry.

"You read the society page?" He gave her a wry smile. "I very much doubt that. What would you care of the society page, the frivolous party life of the rich and foolish?"

His words stung her, despite their accuracy, despite the fact that she herself had thought them, once.

"They're not all rich and foolish—"

"Let's see, shall we? I'll be right back."

He disappeared across the hallway and she stared at the sunset, the way the reds and oranges bled out over the vast horizon.

He returned, holding a copy of her father's *New York Chronicle*. She folded her hands in her lap and refrained from leaping to grab it.

"Here's a gem," he said. "'Mrs. Astor Hosts Glittering Ball to Ring in the New Year. All the fashionable of New York attended last night's annual ball at Mrs. Astor's residence at 842 Fifth Avenue. Everything was done to the most perfect taste. Large vases of American Beauty roses adorned the vestibule and the entrance hall and decorated the handsome ballroom, the grandest of all New York.'"

Esme tried not to the let the image fill her mind, but once there, the grandeur of Mrs. Astor's ballroom revived her memory. The gilded walls, the lilt of the orchestra, the gold-embroidered ball gowns.

"'It was nearly midnight when the guests arrived, following the opera *The Magic Flute* at the Metropolitan Opera. Mrs. Astor did not attend the event. After greeting her guests in the Louis Sieze drawing room, Mrs. Astor enjoyed Landers Orchestra playing from the ballroom. Supper was called at 1 a.m. The menu was as follows: Filet de Boeuf aux Champignons farcies, Pommes Surprise, Terrapin...'"

She could see the dinner before her, the small tables with cover for six or eight, the white-gloved attendants, the smells of sumptuous, rich meats and gravies. "That's enough."

"There's more. Don't forget the guest list. 'After supper, the cotillion was danced. It was led by Mr. Foster Worth, dancing with Mrs. Orme Wilson. And Henry Lehr, dancing with Mrs. Cornelius Vanderbilt. Mrs. Astor's gown was a trailed robe of dark velvet, trimmed in pointelle lace, garnished with her array of diamonds, tiara, stomacher, and necklace. Mrs. Foster Worth, with child, wore a white gauze robe embroidered with silver. Her ornaments were diamonds and rubies.' And..." He put down the paper, waggled his eyes at her, and for the first time, she looked at him and saw the tease in his face. "'Mrs. Rosamond Street wore a white mousseline gown over silk, trimmed with lace.'" He glanced at her again. "Simply riveting news. What is mousseline, anyway?"

"It's a sauce, I believe. Or a fabric of fine film."

Oops. He stared at her, one eyebrow high. "Interesting."

"Can I see the paper, please?"

He handed it over and her eyes tracked to Jinx's name. With child. A few years ago, she'd read an announcement of the birth of a son, Jonathon. This must be her second child then. She ran her finger down the guest list. "I see here the name Daughtry C. Hoyt." She gave him a look. "Rich and foolish?"

"It's the most fashionable party of the season," he said, winking. "I do it for my mother, I think. They didn't want an Indian among their elite sect. So, I join them with my secret."

Indeed, if Mrs. Astor knew his genealogy, she might have his name blackened from the lists. "That you secured an invitation at all is something. I hear her parties are quite elite."

"I'm friends with a number of politicians. And my friend Grayson Donahue asked me to escort his sister, Elise."

"So, you didn't suffer too poorly." She closed the paper. "If you have a life in New York, then why did you return to Silver City?"

He sat down opposite her. "I'm not a fool. I saw you fall—tried to get to you, in fact, but I lost you in the crowd. Thankfully, I spotted Abel helping you to the newspaper." He looked at his hands, now cleaned from the work in the barn. "I have no doubt he also filled you in on the past. And the accident."

A good newspaperwomen would ignore the pain in his gesture, despite his kindness to her, and would go for the jugular. But she tempered her words. "He blames you."

"I blame me. And every week I search for reports of accidents from the Anaconda and Amalgamated mines, not to mention the Silverthread, as reported in the *Copper Valley Times*." He didn't wink and she believed him. "And every single time I read about one, I feel responsible. Which is why I returned. I am hoping to convince my father to sell Silverthread."

"You're going to sell Silverthread?"

"I want to get out of the mining business. Erase the past."

"But what about all those miners who need jobs?"

He got up, walked to the window. "They won't be the responsibility of the Hoyt family."

"But the Amalgamated is twice as dangerous. Butte is a town of sin—and it's the main industry in Silver City…you can't take their livelihood away from the miners."

He rounded on her. "Why? You heard Abel. *He* wants to take the livelihood from the Silverthread. We're already overextended, and a strike could put us in debt, cause us to lose everything anyway. And then Anaconda could buy us for the smell of the Montana air."

"I thought the Silverthread was flush?"

"My father only makes it seem that way with his benevolent gifts to the widows, the Christmas endowments to the miners' children, the scholarships. But every bit of it comes from his investments. Silverthread hasn't been profitable in three years. It might help if my father didn't pay the Silverthread miners twenty-five cents more per day for their base pay than the Copper Kings of Butte, or if we produced more than one-tenth what the Amalgamated and Anaconda mines produce. Or, if we had a smelter of our own instead of shipping the ore out to Anaconda. But see, I could take the sale and invest it in the stock market. I've spent the last year keeping our stocks alive and preparing for our bankruptcy. I could move my father out to New York City and invest in celluloid film. Did you know they showed the first motion picture in New York, just before I left?"

She stared at him, seeing Abel and Ruby, Agnes without their homes. "What are you talking about? Celluloid film? What about the livelihood of your miners?"

"I can't have thirty-eight miners' deaths on my conscience anymore."

She studied his face, the lines etched around his eyes. Yes, she knew what it felt like to live with regret. "If there were another way to save the mine, would you do it?"

"Mr. Hoyt, dinner is served." A butler Esme hadn't seen earlier appeared at the door, white gloves and all.

But Daughtry just stood there, considering her words. Finally, "I don't know if I believe in second chances. Do you?"

Chapter 13

"Are you buried in Page Six?"

Esme looked up to Daughtry's question. Back to the *Chronicle,* which she'd commandeered after dinner and stolen to the parlor for a thorough read-through. "Actually, no. I wanted to read the news."

He came in, bent down, and stoked the fire. Funny, in that moment, he reminded her of her father, an old memory scurrying up of him finding her tucked into a book in his den. "I'm afraid it is old news. At least three months."

"Old news from New York is recent news for Montana." The lamplight flooded over the page onto her dress, glinting against the golden threads. She should take it off, escape this fantasy before it took root.

"Are you warm enough?" He sat down on the settee opposite her.

"Yes." In fact, getting much warmer, with him sitting across from her, his dark eyes considering her.

"May I see your ankle? I promise not to look at anything else."

There went a blush. But she raised her hem enough for him to find her ankle. He took it into his wide hands, ran his thumbs lightly over the swelling. "It's still quite injured. I fear you should stay here until it is recuperated."

"Stay? Here? But what about—"

"Dawn is here, of course. And Francine—our cook. You won't be abandoned to two crabby bachelors."

"Your father is hardly crabby."

He smiled at that. "He found you quite fetching. I am sorry he couldn't eat with us."

"How is he feeling?"

"Much better once we settled him back in his bed. He becomes overzealous, believes he can do more than he should, with his heart condition. But he wanted to meet the beauty in the house."

Oh. She closed the paper, smoothed it on her lap. "I fear our meeting taxed him too greatly."

Daughtry's smile vanished. "He won't be with us long. I wish I'd known sooner how serious his condition had become, but he only released Dawn to write to me a month ago. Perhaps he didn't want me to relive the nightmares."

Nightmares. She presumed from the accident.

He got up, moved her ankle to the settee. "You should keep it elevated."

"Are you a doctor?"

"I grew up with a mother who knew everything. When she passed, it took us years to figure out how to live on our own. I should never have left. I could see immediately that I should have returned much sooner. And not just for the mine, but for him. He missed me desperately. And I, him."

"You two sound close."

"As close as two grieving men can be, I suppose. I believe it was a relief for him when I moved away, however."

The journalist inside her wanted to prod.

The former deb knew to offer a conciliatory silence.

"When I received Dawn's letter, I feared I wouldn't return before his passing. I couldn't bear not to say good-bye, to have him go without hearing his final words to me."

His quiet words, the urgency in them, pulsed inside her. She knew exactly his sentiments. Please, her father couldn't pass away until she had the strength to return. Until she could personally bring her *Copper Valley Times* to the *Chronicle*'s door.

"Esme?" Oh. She'd been caught in time, seeing her father again—broken and distraught—as she walked out of the Chronicle Building. "I'm sorry. I was thinking about—"

"People you left behind?"

She drew herself up. "What do you mean by that?"

He sat on the divan, lifted a shoulder. "I remember hearing about your arrival in town. My father said you simply appeared one day, like a fresh wind. Bought the building and the paper with a couple of drop pearl earrings."

He raised an eyebrow at that.

"They were a gift."

"I didn't assume otherwise."

Oh, she had sounded too defensive. "I just needed a place to start over. To do things my way."

"And you certainly have."

It was her turn to raise an eyebrow.

He held up a hand of surrender. "No offense intended. The *Copper Valley Times* is a solid newspaper. I have it sent to me every week."

He did?

"I'm just saying that there is more to you than meets the eye, Esme, and if you would permit me, I'd like to find out what it might be."

She didn't let his words show on her face and instead found her society smile. But what if he did find out who she was? It might change the way the miners saw her, they might stop letting her into their lives, might see her as—how did Abel put it in his song—a greedy parasite?

No.

Still, the way Daughtry put it, softly, nudged under her skin. What might it be like to become Esme Price, debutante, courted again?

She closed the paper, rose to her foot, balancing herself on the arm of the divan. "I really shouldn't stay."

He stared at her. "Why not? Would it be so terrible to ask for help? To have someone take care of you?"

"I am perfectly capable of—"

"I know—taking care of yourself."

He stood up and wrapped his hand around her waist.

"The sunrise is beautiful from the breakfast verandah."

* * * * *

It frightened Esme how quickly she could become accustomed to luxury. Two days of pampering by Dawn as her ankle healed had revived all the memories of having Bette greet her with her morning tea and toast on a tray. Of being tucked into bed at night with a crackling fire in the hearth. Of proper dinners with white-gloved waiters to clear her plate. Of listening to music in the parlor after dinner.

She might be able to stay forever in the copper tub, steam rising from the surface like a Montana lake in the middle of winter.

Fine, she would admit it—she missed her Fifth Avenue life. Missed the sound of horses' hooves upon the street, the golden lamplight spilling out into the night, the smell of Cook's rich French concoctions rising from the basement. Missed her glorious clothes, the diamond tiara, the pearl chokers, the bowers of roses.

Her mother.

Her father.

Jinx. Especially Jinx. She'd poured over the entirety of Page Six of the *Chronicle* for any other mention of Foster and Jinx and finally resigned herself to her imagination. Jinx would have blossomed into a regal beauty on Foster's arm, the mother of his child, and by now they would have built their own house, hosted their own parties. Jinx had inherited the world meant for Esme.

But Esme had inherited the rest. The pewter-blue sky flowing over foothills and beyond the frosted mountains to the north. The frothy rivers, the pale pink bitterroot flower peeking from the earth, the tang of the pine in the air. She sat now astride her mare, following Daughtry across his land. He'd given her one of his boots to wear and one of his mother's split riding skirts. If the set in New York knew she rode a horse like a man...

She'd inherited freedom perhaps also.

"Are you cold?" Daughtry looked over at her. "We could stop, if you'd like."

"It's the end of April, and I'm dressed for a trip to Butte and back at the height of January. I'll be fine." He'd had Dawn dig out a worn buffalo jacket for the ride out to a remote section of their land. But his protectiveness didn't seem condescending—rather, he seemed thoughtful. She didn't expect a gentleman out on the frontier.

She urged her mare up behind his horse—he rode the glorious Arabian he'd shipped back to Montana. "Where are we going?"

"I want to show you something." He glanced back, gave her a wink. "Something you don't see in Silver City." He paused. "Or New York."

She met his gaze. He'd winked. He hadn't asked—or suggested—anything about her interest in the social set of Mr. Astor's 400 since that first night, confining their conversation over the past two days to Silver City, the newspaper, his father's health, and the war of the Copper Kings for control of the mines in the region.

Perhaps he simply meant the wink as a friendly gesture.

She said nothing as they topped the ridge. He reached out, reined in her mount. "Shh."

Below them, thirty or so giant shaggy-shouldered boulders lounged on the greening pasture, corralled on three sides by canyon walls. A soapy river blocked escape to the south. The animals, impressive even at this distance, wore horns and heavy beards, their massive bodies twice the size of her mare. "Are those buffalo?"

She glanced at Daughtry, the way he rode easily in his stirrups, gloved hands leaning on his saddle horn, his reins loose but firm in his grip. He looked like a Charlie—she remembered his comment in the barn, the name Dawn called him by. He too wore a buffalo jacket, dark, with a fur collar turned up against the wind, a buckskin cowboy hat, his hair curling from the back, and leather breeches with fringes that made him appear a working cowboy instead of a silver-spoon heir.

"My mother started the herd with just three we rescued. The Crow depended on the buffalo for their livelihood, and when they were hunted to near extinction, my mother hoped to help restore them to plenty. Her dream was to see them roaming the ranch like they did when she was a child. My father told her it was impossible—they were just too few, but she refused to believe it. She knew in her heart they could be rebuilt. She would ride down here, especially after calving, and shoot the cougars that hunted them. In the winter, she dragged hay out here with the ranch hands, cut holes in the river ice. She believed she could grow them into a powerful herd. They're magnificent, aren't they?"

"Yes, they are. I've read about them—I even heard that President Roosevelt is starting a national herd. But you're right, Silver City has very few buffalo, unless you include the fellas at the Nickel after their shift."

He laughed at that. "The men do have a way of winding down that might be less than tame."

"I've awakened to men sleeping on the boardwalk all the way to the *Times* office, even in February."

She watched the herd, singling out a calf as it moved away from its mother. "I'd love to write an article about the herd."

He drew in a breath. "I don't think so. If things get difficult down at the mine, the union boys just might decide on payback. Buffalo fetch a hefty price and still make good eating." He turned his horse around. "Let's go."

His shift in demeanor rattled her more than she would have liked. Probably just because he'd been such a kind host. "I'm sorry, Daughtry. Of course I'll keep your secret." She caught up to him.

He rode in silence, as if contemplating her words. "And I'll keep yours."

She stared at him, her breath tight. "I—I don't understand."

"Where are you from, really, Esme?" The question in his voice, as if he didn't already know, untied the knot in her chest.

For a moment, she longed to tell him. Longed to give him the truth, to ease back into the skin of Esme Price, the heiress. Or, former heiress. But then what? Would he stop seeing her as the frontier newspaperwoman? Would he start seeing her as a wealthy woman who could save the Silverthread from bankruptcy?

She couldn't tell him and not lose this curl of delight that kept building in her chest. She wasn't sure why, but she suddenly longed for him to enjoy the company of Esme Stewart, without the expectations and limitations of the Price name.

"You guessed right—I grew up out East. Close enough to New York to enjoy the society page. But I came west to leave that all behind, to start a new life."

She ended there, let the wind emphasize her silence.

After awhile, she had to fill it. "Why does Dawn call you Charlie?"

He guided them down a ravine then took her reins in hand as they crossed a creek. "My mother called me Charlie, after an older brother she lost to Custer. I like it—it makes me remember who I am."

"Who are you, Mr. Daughtry-Charlie Hoyt? Montana cowboy, or New York gent?"

He let her mare go, urged their mounts up an incline. "I'm both. And, neither."

"What do you mean?"

"I'm not a society man, although I know how to behave. I simply don't care about society's nod. It's a curse, I think, to trap yourself into living by the whims and opinions of others."

Oh, she couldn't agree more.

"But I'm not the half-breed whelp who got pummeled at school by the miners' boys, either."

"The miners' kids hurt you?"

"My father thought it would be to my benefit to attend school with the kids from Silver City. It's how I met Abel—his brother and I were friends. Orrin took up for me before I learned how to fend for myself."

"I'm sorry for his death; it sounds like he meant a lot to you."

"Listening to him call out my name as we tore into the rock separating us nearly undid me. My father sent me to Harvard just so he wouldn't have to hear the nightmares as they woke me in the middle of the night. But they followed me and eventually drove me to recklessness. I started fighting on campus, boxing and then brawling. I got kicked out of school my second year."

Abel had left out that part of the story. Or maybe no one knew it.

"After that, I sort of drifted until a friend took me under his wing—he'd attended Harvard also, and his family ran a shipping company. He introduced me to Wall Street and taught me how to buy and sell stocks. Soon I was managing the stocks for the Silverthread and watching them explode. We even managed to ride out the crash of the past three years."

"So, you're a speculator."

"Perhaps. Or maybe I'm simply an optimist." He caught her reins again, stopping them. He had strong arms, and sitting on his horse beside her, he seemed every bit a hero she might find in one of her hidden Old West dime novels. "And, I do believe in second chances."

She stared at him, trying to place his words.

"The other night, before dinner. You asked me if there were another way to save the Silverthread, would I take it? I think the answer is yes. I do believe we can start over, if we want." He seemed to hold something more in his gaze. "Because, even if I do sell, I'll never truly leave the mistakes of my past behind."

"You don't believe in forgiveness?"

"Absolutely. I've made my peace with God. But like my scars"—he lifted his chin and pointed to a pucker of flesh along his jaw—"the effect of those mistakes won't leave me. Still, I'm not the person I was back then. I'm not desperate for approval, wanting to make my own mark, wanting to atone for my crimes. I know who I am, know who I'm supposed to be now. And that man is ready to cut ties with the past."

His words burrowed inside her, a coal against her bones. "Nobody can really break free from their past."

He glanced at her. "Yes, they can. They can start over, become the people they were intended to be."

"It seems to me that you are two different people. In New York, you're Daughtry. Here, you're Charlie. You can't be both at the same time."

"I disagree. It's not about my name, Esme. It's about my character. And about the fact that no matter where I go, what name I put on, I'm the same man. Redeemed."

She'd never heard a man talk this way before. Well, once, but he was an evangelist.

He smiled. "I'm simply a man rescued from the wrath of God for a divine purpose. I'm no longer that poor, desperate sap needing to prove something. I know who I am, who I belong to. I know my future. That's the blessing of belonging to God. Security."

She stared at him. "You sound like D. L. Moody."

"You heard D. L. Moody?"

"As a child. He came to our town." Oh, keep it up and she'd give it all away.

"I read his sermons sometimes. 'If we are full of pride and conceit and ambition and self-seeking and pleasure and the world, there is no room for the Spirit of God. It's better to be poor in spirit than be rich in self.'"

She stared at him, seeing Bette, hearing her own voice in prayer. *Commit thy way unto the Lord; trust also in Him; and He shall bring it to pass.*

There was a time when she'd trusted God with her future, her hopes. Her heart. He had hardly been trustworthy, had He? She'd lost Oliver. And God didn't stop her from running to the far West, hiding in some muddy mining town, trying to eke out a living. She'd run too far—all the way across the country—for God's blessings to find her.

She shivered.

"You're cold. We need to get back. All this riding isn't good for your ankle."

She didn't protest; his words, however, heated her through. *I know who I am, know who I'm supposed to be.*

After seven years, she longed to know too. Perhaps it was time to stop hiding. To return, like Daughtry had, to repair her mistakes.

To reclaim the blessing—the birthright—she left behind.

She imagined walking into her father's *Chronicle* office, his back to her as she entered. Would he turn and smile? Open his arms to her?

From her mother she expected no rejoicing, but perhaps Jinx would kill the fatted calf. They'd been sisters, hadn't they?

"You're very quiet."

"I'm thinking about your buffalo. Nearly extinct. But they're such resilient creatures."

"The hunters simply ran them over a cliff. They had nowhere else to turn and fell to their deaths. If only they'd stopped running—I imagine more might have survived. They're buffalo, after all."

The house came into view, lovely and white against the red barn. They rode into the barn, and he dismounted then moved over to help her.

She looked down at him, those dark eyes that suddenly seemed to possess the ability to look clear through her and make her catch her breath.

"I can help myself."

"I know you can," he said, his hand on Dixie's shoulder. "But if you would permit me, I'd like to assist you."

Oh, she shouldn't say yes. She'd spent seven years shrugging off help.

She put her hand on his shoulder, allowed him to catch her as she dismounted, to steady her as she put weight on her ankle. He had strong hands, and his smell—fresh air, leather, the scent of a man—lifted off him.

Perhaps being needy wasn't such a terrible condition after all. Still, "I need to go back to town, Daughtry."

He nodded. "Of course you do."

A small piece inside her wished he hadn't assented quite so easily.

An hour later, she stood on the porch before the gleaming gentleman's brougham, with its shiny black exterior, glass windows, the berry-red wheels. "I can't ride back into town in this. Every miner from the Silverthread will see me and—"

"And?" Daughtry came around the back of the carriage where he'd just tied Dixie for their trip into town. "They'll know you were with me?"

She clipped off her words. But, yes. However, she couldn't exactly mention the miners' union meeting, could she? What if Daughtry thought she was conspiring against him, searching him for information? She made a face, not sure what to say.

"I understand," he said softly.

She hated herself then, just a little, but she couldn't align herself with him and keep her footing with Abel.

From behind her, two of his laborers emerged with a trunk, setting it on the back of the carriage. They secured it into place.

"What is that?"

"Your things," Daughtry said, a funny frown on his face.

"I have no things," she said. "I came here with nothing."

"Yes, but my father insists that you take the dresses you wore. They're beautiful on you, they fit you well, and we have no need for them."

But, "What of your future wife? Wouldn't she appreciate them?"

The moment the words left her mouth, she wanted to gulp them back for the look he gave her. "I hope so," he said, drawing in a breath.

Oh. She pressed a hand to her face, suddenly feeling like a deb who'd been asked to dance. Oh.

Daughtry too seemed suddenly shaken by his own words. He cleared his throat. Looked at the ground, back to Esme. "You intrigue me, Esme. I've very much enjoyed your presence here. It's like the house was alive again. Your laughter at dinner and your keen conversation. I've never met a woman who was at once so feminine and yet so capable. I..." He blew out a breath. "I don't suppose you would agree to allow me to call on you."

She had drifted back to New York, half expected her mother to be standing in the shadows, watching. If she were a debutante, she would see a game behind his request—something that measured her family's finances, their legacy in this request. But with Daughtry, she sensed nothing of guile. Indeed, she had met a gentleman.

One who just might cause her to lose everything she'd worked for. He didn't want to live here. He wanted to sell the mine and return to New York.

Despite her longings, she couldn't go back to that world. Not yet. "I—I don't think that is a good idea."

He winced, and the expression tore through her. For a brilliant second, she wanted to take back her words, to tell him that yes, she wanted to know him better, to see if she could belong in this world, again. To even slide into his arms, to press her lips against his.

To be held by this gallant, handsome man.

But that wasn't the woman she'd become.

"Thank you for doctoring my ankle."

Daughtry stepped back, trying to hide his wounds. "You're welcome."

"And I can't take the dresses, I'm so sorry."

Another wound.

"If you insist. But I will leave them trunked for you in case you change your mind."

No. She was done with that world.

At least until she figured out how to go home.

He untied Dixie, and she allowed him to help her into the saddle. "Thank you for the interview."

"Was that what this was?" He patted Dixie's shoulder, not meeting her eyes.

She turned Dixie and didn't look back.

* * * * *

Maybe she could go home, back to New York City. Esme sat at her desk in the chilly office of the *Times*, looking over the articles Ruby, as well as the few other stringers she regularly used, had submitted over the few days she'd been holed up at Daughtry's.

What if she let him into her life, to court her?

She could too easily fall in love with Daughtry—the way he cared for her, let her into his dreams. She'd so easily slipped back into the world she left behind, she wondered just how much she'd really despised it. More than that, he wasn't a man thirsty for wealth, for a name, for power.

He wasn't Foster Worth.

But she couldn't return to New York as Esme Hoyt. No, she wanted to march into the *Chronicle* offices under her own byline, holding an article that even her father would run, front page, above the fold.

Like an interview with President Roosevelt. The idea had taken root, settled deep as she rode back to town. Sure, she might be able to scoop the *Butte Press* on a possible strike, but an interview with Roosevelt would not only scoop the *Press* but would be picked up and reprinted across America.

Even in her father's *Chronicle*.

"Where have you been?" Ruby banged into her office, wearing a split skirt, a tan shirtwaist, a long duster. Her black hair she'd tied back, low at her neck. "I was about to ride out to the Hoyts' place to look for you. You had Hud nearly out of his mind."

"Sorry. I turned my ankle again when I visited Daughtry. I wasn't fit to ride back until today."

"Um-hmm." Ruby raised an eyebrow. "Did you get your interview?"

"Did you know him when he attended the Silver City School?"

Ruby made a face. "Some of the boys weren't real nice to him. Orrin took up for him."

"He said that. Orrin's death really took him apart."

Ruby considered her a long moment. "You fancy him."

Esme looked up at her. Ruby smiled. "Don't even try and lie. You're a terrible liar."

Actually...

Ruby shook her head. "He lives in a different world than we do, Esme. He has servants and a fancy life in New York City. He's going to sell the mine to Anaconda and leave as soon as he can."

"Where did you hear that?"

"Abel. He was talking to Dustin this weekend, said that if he does, then we would join the Butte Miners Union."

"We?"

Ruby smiled. "Dustin and I are getting married."

"Oh Ruby, that's wonderful." Esme moved to get up, tested her ankle, then leaned forward to hug Ruby. "When will you do it?"

"In two weeks. After the miners' dance." Ruby returned her hug. "I want you to be next."

"What?" Esme leaned away from her.

"Abel. I think he likes you. He was looking for you this weekend. He couldn't stop talking about you."

Abel. He had a passion about him, coupled with enough confident tease to make him dangerous to her heart. Most of all, he reminded her, right down to his easy smile, of Oliver. Except, look where that ended. She shook her head. "Abel is handsome, but—"

"Good men are hard to find in this town, Esme. Isn't it about time for you to fall in love, to be happy?"

Happy. She was happy, wasn't she?

No, most of the time she was just scared. Scared that she'd walked away from any chance of happiness. Scared that no matter how she tried, God simply couldn't bless her. Scared that, truly, she was on her own.

Esme looked at her choice of articles—a robbery at Adeline's, Aggie's list of eligible women, a notice about the upcoming miners' dance, Ruby's article about the union brawl, the mine report and her so-called interview with Daughtry—

A shrill cry pierced the air.

Ruby jumped, turned pale even as Esme recognized it as originating from the mine.

Trouble.

The whine of the whistle rattled the flimsy windowpanes in the front of the saloon.

Ruby whirled around, ran for the door, Esme behind her.

They stood in the street watching the plume of dust rise from the Pipe mine, choke the air, and darken the town of Silver City.

Chapter 14

"These accidents are going to keep happening unless we unite and strike!"

Abel stood at the front of the assembly of miners, many of them still black-faced and wrung out from a week of digging through the dust and rubble for the survivors.

A cage had broken free as it transported a shift of miners to the surface. They'd fallen a half-mile.

Sixteen men dead. Esme had interviewed the living, wrapped her arms around the grieving, written countless articles about the loss, and stood at the gravesides as, one by one, young men returned to the earth.

She'd seen Daughtry that first day, just hours after she'd left him at the ranch, his jacket off, his shirtsleeves rolled up, dirty and sweaty as he worked alongside the miners for rescue. He'd even attended the funerals— standing away from the graveside grief, but close enough to offer the Silver-thread's condolences and hand over an envelope of sustenance on behalf of the mine. Usually, Archie sent one of his representatives—she had no doubt Daughtry's past accounted for his presence at the gravesites.

That, and he might have been trying to avert the very event happening in the Miners' Recreation Hall. The room stank of earth and sweat and not a little whiskey, and for the first time, Esme questioned the wisdom of her attending the meeting.

"Don't you see, if we don't band together and strike, we will die for the same pittance our brothers did? The Silverthread owes us, owes our families. The Hoyts sit in their mansion, eating off golden plates, while we go to bed with dirt in our mouths."

Abel made a passionate leader, with his brown eyes on fire, his shirt-sleeves rolled up, jacket off, suspenders securing his workpants. He gestured with his hands, probably working up a sweat as he prowled the front of the room, stirring up their anger.

"What about our families?" someone yelled from the audience. "If we strike, how will we buy food? They'll shut down the mine store."

"That's why we plan ahead. We store up for trouble. We don't play their games. The Silverthread can't stay idle forever—"

Another man: "The Anaconda brought in strikebreakers—Pinkerton men. I don't want to hang!"

Near the back, Ruby stood slightly behind Dustin. He'd barely made it out, having ascended with the first half of the crew.

"This is our fifth accident in as many weeks. Ground falls, misfires, explosives accidents with the caps and fuses, a ladder fall, and just a few days before the cage fall, an unbalanced load of timber crushed two of our guys. No one wants to say it, but this mine is jinxed. It's time for the Silverthread to close, to make repairs, to pay us a decent wage for our work. All we want is a fair shake."

These miners made twenty-five cents a day more than the miners at the Anaconda. But was there ever a decent wage worthy of the miners' lives? She wrote down Abel's words, not sure Daughtry might ever find a way to appease them. He couldn't guarantee their safety, their lives. And no amount of money could buy peace of mind.

"We've gone six years without a major accident, suddenly we're having one a shift. A miner never knows if this shift might be his last, if he might end up toes up."

Ruby wound her fingers around Dustin's hand.

"Strike!" The word punched through the crowd and started the murmur. Another cry for strike. Esme eyed the door.

From the front, a man standing next to Abel stepped up onto a chair, held up his hands. He seemed familiar, but she couldn't place him. "Strike, and let the brothers at the Butte Miners Union join you."

Yes, she knew him now. Brawny, dark hair, a reddened nose from years of drink. He had been one of the first to throw a punch at the street brawl.

So, he must be a member of the Butte Miners Union. "We'll help you fill the lines, defend you from Hoyts' Pinkertons."

Esme tried to imagine Daughtry employing Pinkertons. No, he'd let the mine go to Anaconda, despite his losses. And then, who knows what condition the mine would fall into? "What if you owned the mine?"

Oh, why had she said that? The words just erupted out of her, and every head turned. But it seemed they wanted the answer to be easy and— "What would you do to make the mine safe, to make it more profitable?"

"It's already profitable!" a voice said just as she found Abel's gaze upon her. She couldn't read the look he gave her.

"Yes," Abel said above the crowd. "They're making money off our broken backs. They just want to work us until they crush us."

He didn't raise his voice, but it had the effect of a blade, slicing through the crowd, through her. More murmurs, more anger.

The Butte man began a chant for strike.

She had enough for her article, and Ruby would fill in the rest, from Dustin.

Outside, Esme gulped in the fresh night air, the smell of the explosion having finally dissipated over the hills. No machinery grinding in the distance, no smells of fire burning. Stars spilled overhead like tears, the steel headframes over the mine entrances in the distance like silver skeletons.

She pulled her coat around her, headed toward the *Times* office. Maybe Daughtry should sell—walk away from the deaths, the anger. But she feared that in the hands of the Anaconda—

"Esme?"

The voice, now quiet, even filled with hurt, stopped her. She turned, and in the cool starlight stood Abel, his jacket off, his eyes on her, breathing hard as if trying to catch her. He had such an earnestness on his face, something moved inside her. Had he been trying to impress her?

"I thought perhaps the meeting part had ended, the rabble-rousing beginning. I'm just starting to walk right."

He cupped a hand behind his neck, glanced at the recreation center. "They're just angry. And hurting. And…scared."

He let his emotions show then in his eyes, and she drew in a breath. Scared. He, too, was scared.

In a second, however, he'd flushed it away. He stepped closer, caught her arm. "Can I walk you home?"

The gallantry in his request touched her. "Yes."

He held out his arm and she slipped hers through it, not unaware of the strength there. After all, he did shovel ore for a living.

"Do you really think Daughtry wants to crush you?"

Abel took a moment in answering. "The Hoyts live out there in their castle—"

"It's just a farmhouse, Abel. Yes, they have a couple of servants, but they're two bachelors living alone. They need help and hands to run the place."

"Daughtry lives a glittering life in New York City off our hard work. He doesn't care who he kills to make his millions."

She considered her words a moment before she allowed them. "Is this about Orrin? About how much you hate Daughtry?"

He stiffened under her hand. "I know you went out there. Spent time with him." He turned to her, stopped them. "Don't you see that he's just using you to get to me? He saw me helping you away from the brawl that day and ever since, he's been after you. To take you away."

Take her away? "But Abel, I barely know you. And I went out there to interview him."

"I'll bet he told you how we bullied him in school."

She stilled.

"What he didn't mention is how he bullied us too. He rode to town in his shiny red-wheeled carriage, in his New York clothes, and talked about how someday he'd own us all."

"He's not that boy anymore—"

"And now he wants you too. Well, he can't have you."

She should have seen it in his eyes, heard it in his tone, but he cupped his hand behind her neck and kissed her. Hard, and passionate, and with a hunger that she understood.

And, for a moment, she let him. Because she longed to be wanted, to be lost again in Oliver's arms, to know love.

But this wasn't love, and it took her only a moment to come to herself, to put her hand on his chest, to push. "No, Abel, please."

Abel leaned away, breathing hard. Her heart lodged in her throat, her heartbeat evaluating his expression.

"Sorry. I thought..." He shook his head. "I'm sorry, Esme."

She stepped away from him, fighting the rush of her pulse in her ears. Anger spiked her words. "Stop trying to make your grief into a sporting event. You're more interested in winning against Daughtry—"

"And robber barons like him—"

"Than feeding your miners. Than making sure they're safe."

Abel froze. "That's not true."

"Then you tell me—isn't it odd that the Silverthread has gone six years without an accident, and suddenly there are five in the past five weeks? Could it be that someone wants to do the mine harm?"

Her words seemed to sink inside him. "Who would do that?"

"I don't know. Someone who wants to force you to strike?"

His mouth tightened just a little around the edges. "Anaconda?"

He whispered it, but she felt the implications rustle through her like the fragments of winter still remaining on the breeze. "If the miners went on strike, you just might force the Silverthread into bankruptcy. And then they'd be forced to sell to Anaconda."

"But I heard that Hoyt wants to sell the mine anyway. Maybe he's doing this."

Her heartbeat had settled into a hard, solid thump now, and standing in the darkness, heat stirred inside her. "I can promise you that Daughtry Hoyt would not be behind any mine sabotage."

Abel considered her.

"Before you strike, prove that it's not sabotage. Please. You don't want to work for a company that's been killing you."

That made him draw in his breath. "I'll find out the truth. Because I do care more about the safety of my fellow trammers than Daughtry Hoyt and his crimes."

"He's sorry, you know. That's why he left—because of his guilt."

Abel shook his head. "We're all sorry. But it doesn't change anything."

"You don't believe in second chances?"

"Sure I do. Just not for everyone."

She shoved her hands into her pockets, walked away from him.

"Do I still get to see you in a dress?"

She glanced back at him. "Abel White. You don't ask for much, do you?"

He grinned at her, his hands in his pockets, rocking back on his heels.

* * * * *

President Roosevelt had turned down her interview request. Esme stared at the telegram.

> *Pres. Roosevelt unable to accept interview request. Thank you for your inquiry.*
> *Office of the President.*

Clearly Esme Stewart hadn't ascended the journalistic hills she'd hoped. Probably she shouldn't have signed the request as from the humble editor of a small town weekly in Nowhere, Montana.

She should have used her name, Esme Price, daughter of August Price, owner of the *New York Chronicle*.

She crumpled the telegram, dropped it into the waste bin under her desk. The next issue would go to bed tomorrow night, and she still had about thirty thousand characters of type to press into the linotype machine, not to mention layout of the slugs onto the plates that would go to press. She sat at the hulking machine, the keyboard just above her lap, her apron dark with powdered graphite, the text clipped to a board above the keys.

Ruby and Hud sat at turtles—metal stone tables—laying out the slugs from the galley mat onto the form, called the chase, on their way to the lead mold.

"I'm out of line rules," Esme said.

Hud handed her a tray of long lead slugs that separated the galley type in the final printed page.

She picked one out, ran the makeup rule over it to clean out any traces of extra lead before placing it in the chase.

"Your article on the miners' strike is nearly half this paper," Hud said.

She measured out the picas for the next line with her line gauge, reached for the next slug, and measured it out. Then she grabbed the slug cutters.

"It's because it's big news. You were there—the BMU leader nearly had them ready to pick up signs, not to mention the hubbub Abel caused."

"This issue is going to sell out. We might want to print extras." Next to Ruby, Hud filled up any spaces in the galley with spacers called reglets, then added the wooden blocks where the photographs would appear. He also added the set galleys of advertisements onto the bottom of the pages, the gaps left by Ruby to the appropriate size.

"Don't forget to give me a proof," Esme said as she collected the next mat filled with loseo linotype and delivered it to Ruby, along with the article.

Hud ran ink over the type with a brayer then pressed a blank sheet of paper over it, hammering on it with the planer so every nuance of ink might sink in to create a proof. He tightened the "quoins" or rods that held the chase tight. How many times had she gone to press with misplaced words or even sentences out of order? She hadn't dared send those back to New York.

Esme always caught her breath, just a moment, when Hud lifted the chase from the turtle to the press. If he hadn't tightened the quoins or added enough filler slugs, the entire page would fall from the chase. Thankfully, in his magic, Hud had only "pied" the type a few times. But they'd had to reset the entire page and put their production schedule back an entire day.

"Someday, we'll be able to afford a rotary press," she said as he loaded the chase into the press. The rollers would ink the paper, and then, the paper, manually fed, would move under the stationary bar as Hud cranked it. Sometimes she manned the pages.

So far, they'd managed a print run of nearly two thousand every week of their eight-page, four-plate paper.

He handed her a copy of the printed front and back page.

MINERS TALK STRIKE AT RECREATION HALL. She scanned through the article. She'd left out her conversation—and speculation—on the road with Abel. Mostly, because it screamed conjecture, but…what if they were correct? What if someone was sabotaging the mine?

The thought had her asking questions to her ceiling long into the night.

"So this is where the news happens."

The voice startled her, and even Hud looked up from where he worked on another galley.

Daughtry had donned his cowboy aura today. A charcoal-gray hat, a pair of trousers, a dark cotton shirt, a leather jacket. He seemed worlds away from his mention on the *Chronicle*'s infamous Page Six but perfectly right for Montana. He looked down at her with those dark eyes. "So, no strike?"

She handed the page back to Hud. "Not for now, no."

Daughtry tipped his hat to Ruby. She gave him a smile, only a hint of warmth in it. Perhaps all the union talk had spoken to her heart.

"Can I speak with you privately?"

She glanced at Ruby, at Hud. They effectively pretended that Daughtry had vanished.

"I have to put this paper to bed. It comes out tomorrow."

"It'll just take a moment." He lowered his voice. "Please?"

Oh, his voice could tunnel right under her skin, through her brain, take possession of her common sense. "I'll be right back."

She stood up, led him out of the press area into her cluttered office, the former kitchen. Glancing outside, she noticed his shiny brougham wasn't parked out front. Perhaps he had decided to live undercover as well.

"You look nice today," he started.

"I'm covered in graphite, I'm tired, and I look like a man. What can I do for you?"

He drew in a breath, and she immediately hated her abruptness. It was just he'd also been the reason for her fatigue, the fact that he'd done exactly as she'd asked and stayed away from her. Didn't call on her.

Made her feel as if she wasn't worth fighting for.

She closed her eyes, ran her fingers over them. "I'm sorry, Daughtry."

"It's okay. I know I'm not the most liked man in town right now. And, you'll never look like a man, Esme."

The texture of his voice made her open her eyes. He was smiling. "Who put that in your head?"

"I don't know. Man's job. Man's world. I'm a man."

He reached out, pushed her hair back behind her ear where she'd tried to contain it into a braid at her back. "You'll never, ever be a man."

Oh, he possessed powers to undo her. She looked up at him, those dark eyes, and for a moment wished it had been him that had kissed her under the stars. Then, she might not have pushed herself away, might have lost herself in his embrace.

But—and the thought needled her—what if Abel had Daughtry's refinement, his resources? Would she prefer Abel, with his passionate eyes, his vibrancy?

She stepped backed from Daughtry before she did something to give herself away, picked up a towel, and wiped her hands. She probably had graphite under her eyes.

"How would you like to go to dinner with the president of the United States?"

She stilled, searched his eyes for tease. Had he been reading her mind, her mail? "What?"

"I just got an invitation for dinner at Ellis Carter's mansion. For next week. Would you like to attend with me?"

See the president? Oh—maybe then he'd agree to an interview. Except—and she'd considered this when she'd sent the interview request—what if he recognized her? Maybe didn't remember her name but recalled her father? What would Daughtry say?

Or Abel?

Certainly there'd be no more invitations to the miners' meetings.

"Why...me?"

"Because I have the feeling you know how to use the proper fork." He raised an eyebrow and she felt all her lies rise to the surface. "And, because I miss you. I saw you every day last week at the mine, and longed to talk to you. But I knew that if I did, you'd become a pariah too. And that's not helpful for the newspaper woman in town, is it?"

Oh, why did he have to be so—so...thoughtful? "No, I guess not."

"But I can't help myself—I would like to go to dinner with the most beautiful woman in Montana." He took her hand. "Will you accompany me, Esme? Please?"

The most beautiful woman in Montana. On any other man's lips, it might have sounded ridiculous, but it seemed almost regal from Daughtry.

"I—"

"And in case you're suggesting you have nothing to wear..." He winked. "I have that covered."

She couldn't help but stare at her current attire. For a moment, the image swept through her—her hair up, a dress that fit her every curve, long gloves, a glittering choker at her neck. And Daughtry, in a waistcoat and tails, waiting by his shiny brougham to take her to dinner, his gloved hand out, a smile playing on his lips.

Good men are hard to find in this town, Esme. Isn't it about time for you to fall in love, to be happy?

It was the quickening of her heart to that image that made her shake her head. "I'm sorry, Daughtry. I can't."

She had to turn away from his disappointment.

"I don't understand."

"It's simple. We live in two different worlds, and soon enough you're heading back to New York City, and I'm staying here, with the miners of the Silverthread."

"With Abel."

The sudden hardness of his voice rocked her. She looked up at him. "What are you talking about?"

"I know he kissed you after the union meeting the other night."

"What, are you spying on me?"

He flinched at that. "No. I was working late. The Silverthread offices overlook the recreation center."

Yes, they did.

"I didn't know he was courting you."

"He wants to, but—"

"He kissed you without your permission?"

"No, but—"

"Then you wanted him to kiss you."

"No! He just did it."

"Then he did steal a kiss!"

"Yes, but that's not the point—"

"I'm going to kill him."

"He kissed me because of you!"

Daughtry stared at her. "Because of me."

She shook her head. "I refuse to get between you two, be used as some sort of taunt for the other."

"I never saw you as a way to hurt Abel. That's absurd!" Daughtry looked genuinely hurt, and she nearly reached up, pressed her hand to his face to soothe the wound from it.

"Abel is still so angry with you, he actually accused you of sabotaging the mine. Orrin's death is still horribly fresh."

His voice dropped. "What do you know about someone sabotaging the mine?"

"Nothing, but it seems strange that the mine has gone for years without a serious accident. Then, suddenly, they start occurring, right about the time your father falls ill and you return to sell."

"Did you tell this to Abel?"

"I did. He promised to look into it."

Something like panic, or even horror, crossed Daughtry's face.

"What is it?"

He shook his head. "I feel sick. I actually thought Abel was behind all this."

"Behind what?"

"Take off your apron and come with me."

"Where are we going?" She untied the apron around her waist, set it over the chair, propelled by the earnestness in his voice.

"You may want to stop the presses for this."

* * * * *

"We're going down…into the mine?"

Esme stood in the lamp room, a one-story corrugated metal office filled with all manner of mining equipment—boots, drill shields, shovels, gloves. With this entrance to the mine shut down, the room empty of miner's voices, the shadows of the twilight sawed eerie lines across the floor, as if daring her to cross into man's territory.

"I want to show you something." Daughtry turned and handed her a soft cap outfitted with a hook for the carbide headlamp about the size of her hand.

"How far down are we going?"

"All the way to the bottom, three thousand feet."

Oh. Oh. She pressed her hand to her chest and for the first time, Daughtry paused. "I assumed you wanted to go in there. But we don't have to."

"Will it prove the mine is being sabotaged?"

"Maybe not. Maybe it's my imagination."

"Let's go."

He steered her out into the graveyard of a workplace, toward the opening of the mine.

"Is this the Horn?"

"Yes. We officially closed it years ago, but it could still produce ore."

The portal, with its timber header over the opening, appeared a guillotine over her as she passed into the blackness, the wood timbers like ribs as she entered the throat of the mine. The headlamps striped the dark tunnel of rock, the horizontal boards with earthen hubris pushing through the slats.

A large plate metal box hung directly ahead, the door open. Another opening next to it gaped, a gate cordoning off the darkness. A young man waited, standing next to the hoist lever, dressed in a pair of cotton pants, a grimy shirt.

"Ready, sir?"

Daughtry nodded. "Thanks, Crandall. We won't be down long."

He stepped up to the box, extended his hand to her.

She hesitated a moment before she stepped onto the floor, bracing her hand on the wall.

"The lift cage is safe. I've been using it."

It didn't feel safe to suspend yourself in a tiny box over a shoot of darkness that fell a half-mile. Her expression must have broadcast her thoughts.

"This carries twenty-four men. Sometimes more. And, on occasion, a cart of ore. I promise it can hold us." Daughtry closed the metal doorway. Only a tiny window revealed the dim light from the mouth of the mine. "Ready?"

"No. But go ahead."

"Next stop, a half-mile down." He gestured to Crandall.

She pressed herself to the back and closed her eyes.

The cage dropped, and her stomach with it, and she wondered for a moment if it had been cut loose from its moorings. Oh, please don't let them free fall into the gullet of the earth. The cables whined, the box clanking against the wooden guides of the shaft. Her courage abandoned her, and had Daughtry not reached out to take her hand, she might have dropped to a ball right there on the grimy floor.

It seemed to take half her lifetime, although perhaps only two minutes passed as they descended. The temperature fell at first, the breath of the cave cool on her skin. Then, as they descended deeper into the tomb, it heated, the humidity beading upon the back of her neck.

"I expected it to be colder," she said, hating how the darkness ate her voice.

"Wall temperatures down here are about one hundred thirty degrees. The ventilation cools the air down to about ninety-five, but the one hundred percent humidity makes the air thick. A man's smell can curdle your stomach by the end of a shift." He squeezed her hand. "Sorry. I should have mentioned you'd need a bath after this."

"Why do you come down here?"

He looked at her, frowned. "I own it. I need to know the mine well enough to make sure the inspectors are giving the miners a fair shake for their ore contracts. And, I like the geology of the earth, seeing God's handiwork from the inside out. Most of all, I'm fascinated by the engineering of the miners. Sure, the Silverthread company drills the shafts and provides the equipment, but the miners design the inside of the mine, creating the drifts, or the tunnels that connect the stopes."

"Stopes?"

"The chambers where the mine is ored. We do contract mining here— the workmen are assigned to a stope, and the miners of each stope are in charge of taking the ore out. They're paid a base wage plus an incentive, calculated by the tonnage of their ore. So, the harder workers might get more tonnage, more money. Sometimes, however, they take shortcuts on reinforcing their stope."

"Every miner has their own stope? Is there enough to go around?"

"Not everyone that works here is a miner. Some are timberers—they work to reinforce the drifts and stopes. Trammers help haul the ore out in cars, and mawers, or shovelers, and drillers and blasters—they all work with the miner and get a portion of his haul. The drift miners—those that create the tunnels—are paid by the foot, as are the raise miners—those men who make tunnels vertically between levels and into stopes."

"How big are the stopes?"

"They start out small, but they get bigger as the ore is mined out of them. They can grow to be as large as sixty to eighty feet high, about two hundred feet across. The men finish clearing a stope, then dynamite out another section above it, then mine out the ore that is loosened. The problem is, the highest grade ore comes from the weakest rock, so the best stopes are the most dangerous."

"You're not afraid?"

"Not if the mine has been properly timbered."

The cage slowed then stopped with a hard jerk, bouncing and shuddering as all three thousand feet of cable stretched.

"Are we here?"

He let go of her hand and opened the cage door, then the gate at the shaft station.

Sweaty heat rushed into the cage as her eyes adjusted to the small timber-girded room. Electric light from the fixtures in the walls cast a shadowy glaze.

She stepped off the lift into the domed room. From the chamber ran a series of tunnels, their mouths black with secrets, dangers. Moisture glistened off them like tears. On the floor of each tunnel, steel rails aligned in the center of the shafts, where the mining cars ran. Despite the pervasive heat that slithered into her pores, she shivered.

"I'm going to light your lamp," Daughtry said, and turned to her, unclipping the little bronze pot and lamp from her hat.

"It won't light my head on fire, will it?"

He laughed. "No." He unscrewed the bottom portion of the pot. "I'm putting a piece of calcium carbide into the bottom chamber. Then I'll pour water in the top. The chemical reaction between the water and the carbide forms calcium hydroxide and creates a flammable gas called acetylene. The gas then flows out through a small hole in the burner tip at the center of the lamp reflector."

"Which you light?"

"Yes. Then the constant drip of water into the carbide keeps your lamp lit." He put the carbide—pale little pebbles—into the bottom of the chamber then screwed it back to the top. Then he opened a tiny portal in the top chamber and poured water from his canteen into it.

"Without catching my hair on fire."

"You know it's considered bad luck to bring a woman into a mine." He looked at her with a grin. "I promise, your hair won't catch fire."

He took a match, stuck it against the rock floor, and held the blaze to the lamp. It caught, and he adjusted the flame with a lever on the top of the canister. The flame shot out, flared, the light so bright it appeared almost blue. She squinted against it as he continued to adjust it down to a bold glow.

He fitted the cap back onto her head. Smiled down at her, lifting her chin. "Not as dirty as a miner, and definitely more beautiful."

Suddenly, the ground below, the very walls began to quiver. She nearly leaped into Daughtry's arms as a piece of the ceiling shook off, crashed onto the rock floor. Dust boiled up around her feet and she covered her mouth, her eyes smarting. Her headlamp barely cut through the debris now filling the chamber as thick as fog. Her nose burned with the smell of smoke.

Daughtry had his arm around her, moving her away from the edge of the cave. "Best not to be standing under a Creeping Pete."

She glanced up and spotted an overhang carved out by the explosion.

"What happened?"

"Blasting in one of the tunnels. You never know how it's going to affect the entire Silverthread mine. The drifts are all connected down here. They blast at the end of the shift. By morning, the air will clear."

"I didn't think the mine was open."

"This shaft isn't, but we haven't closed down the entire mine. The shaft I brought you down was the old Horn. The blasting is from our new shaft, the Neck. All the shafts are owned by the Silverthread Mining Company."

He slid his hand down to hers again. She clung to it, coughed, but it didn't clear her throat. She pressed her hand to her mouth.

"I won't let you go, I promise. Come with me, we have a bit of a hike."

He led them down one of the dark portals into the catacombs under the earth, their boots scuffing, kicking out stones. Every few feet, the mine had been braced by great twelve-by-twelve timbers. In between, smaller slats kept the walls from trickling in.

"This drift needed more cribbing than others."

"Cribbing?"

He pointed to the ceiling, then to the sideboards.

Now and again, she stumbled, her boot catching on larger rubble. The pitch blackness, even with her headlamp, seeped into her skin, the musty, dirty heat of the cave embedded her pores. Sweat ran in rivulets down her spine. Daughtry's hand turned moist in hers, sealing their grip.

The tunnel seemed about eight feet wide, the same distance tall. Sometimes other tunnels jagged off it; rough-hewn ladders, crudely lashed together, would lift now and again off the floor, and when she looked up, they vanished into darkness.

"Those are rises between levels. We can take a ladder all the way to the top of the mine if we have to."

"They don't look very safe."

He said nothing as they walked along. She took it as an assent. She'd never felt so soggy, so rank. Her lamplight didn't seem to possess the strength to push back the edges of the tunnel and the farther she went, the more the darkness pulled her in, closed around her.

Her eyes teared, probably from the smoke, but she refused to whimper.

A person could wander these tunnels forever, perish in the darkness when his carbide ran out.

She cupped her other hand over Daughtry's, her fear nearly audible by the time Daughtry finally led her into another domed area, the Pipe's shaft station. Timbers again lined the wall, shoring back the smaller rocks. The electric lights shone, her eyes blinking in the shadowy brightness as she came out of the pitch darkness.

"This is it. The lowest level of the Pipe shaft, where the accident happened."

She didn't release his hand as she surveyed the site of the accident. Five feet away, the debris from the destroyed cage lay crumpled, as if someone had taken a hand and pressed down, the metal plates contorted and in pieces on the dirty, greasy floor, the steel hoist rope in a tangle nearby.

"This is where they died?"

"No, they died seventy feet below, at the very bottom of the shaft. We rigged up a jib and dragged the cage up to investigate."

He took her over to the carcass of the lift. She noticed the gnarled metal where the steel cable had sheared off from the top of the lift. Claws on the sides of the cage appeared as mangled hands, ripped and torn.

"What are those?"

"Those are the dogs. It's a braking mechanism. If the hoist rope breaks, it'll stop a fall. But look at this." A spike protruded from the hinge point on one of the dogs. "It looks like this one was tampered with. And there's more."

He pointed to where the hoist cable's frayed edges had loosed, broken from the line. "Right here, see this? The cable's been cut."

She tried to angle her headlamp down, to see where he might be looking. Indeed, the metal seemed to have been shorn, or sawed into a crisp line over halfway through.

"After hauling men up and down so many times, it would have broken free."

"Dropped them to their deaths." She said it on a ghost of a voice. "Sabotage. Someone could have done this in the middle of the night, after the last shift of the day. These men were murdered."

"Indeed. But by whom?"

"That's a very good question, Hoyt."

The voice seemed to echo through the chamber, slide over her skin. She turned to the glaring lamplight of a miner.

"Abel," Daughtry said, without warmth. "What are you doing here?"

"You brought a woman into this mine?" Abel advanced on him, his eyes glittering. "You know that's bad luck."

"Esme needs to see this, and so do you." Daughtry showed Abel the hoist cable then the dogs. Esme watched as Abel's expression turned to fury.

"I was just down at the site of the last ladder fall," he said, his voice lethal. "Or rather, the scene of the murder."

"What?"

"The ladder between level 2900 and 3000 was all but cut through. It didn't break, it was cut. We thought it was rotten until I took a good look. Two men fell eighty feet."

She held his gaze, saw the grief in it. "Abel."

He marched up to Daughtry, put his finger to his chest. For his part, Daughtry didn't move. "You swear to me the Silverthread had nothing to do with this."

Daughtry's voice came out low, even. "I swear."

I swear. His words sank into her as they trekked through the drifts back to the Horn shaft. Abel walked behind them, his breathing hard, as if trying to sort through what truths he could believe.

She wanted to weep with relief when they came out to the shaft room, saw the cage waiting for them. But as they walked toward it, suddenly it jerked, the gears at the crust of the earth grinding.

"Hey!" Daughtry said, "Stop!"

And then, even as Esme leaped for it—to do what? Grab a hold of the bottom and ride it to the top?—the cage lifted and disappeared into the shaft.

"Can you make it come back?" She didn't even bother to disguise her panic.

Daughtry ran to a box mounted at the side of the shaft. A rope hung down, and he pulled on it. A bell rang. Next to the box, a chart listed the bell signals. "It should ring on the surface, to Crandall in the hoist house. It's the bell signal, and every level of the mine has its own signal." He gave it eight rapid shots. "That's our emergency signal."

Esme stood there, tasting her heartbeat. Looking at Abel, back to Daughtry.

The men stared at the empty shaft.

Daughtry rang the bell again. And then, a third time.

They stood, headlamps flickering, waiting for rescue.

"Where's Crandall? Where's the cage"

"I don't know, Esme. Shh." Daughtry glanced at Abel, who shook his head.

"We've been abandoned," Esme said, her pulse so thick in her head she thought she might collapse. She looked up the shaft again, felt the cool lick of fresh air snaking down from the surface.

"Who would do that?"

"The same person who would kill our miners," Abel said. He looked at Daughtry. "Now what?"

She felt her knees start to wobble. Was that another blast? She put her hands against the wall. And then, as she watched, Daughtry's carbide lamp flickered out. His face darkened in the shadows. She stifled a hiccup of fear, her breath leaking out in a whimper.

"Esme. It's okay. We'll get you out of here."

"How?" Oh, she didn't mean to sound so delicate, so needy, and her voice echoed off the walls, probably down every chamber. "What if my carbide runs out? We'll die down here."

Daughtry reached out and she didn't care that Abel watched as she clung to him. "Shh."

"We're trapped!"

"We're not trapped. All the shafts are connected by drifts. Abel, can you get us to the new Neck shaft?"

Esme stared at the dark maws. "Go through those tunnels again? What if my light goes off?"

"It's either that or we can climb up three thousand feet of ladder," Daughtry said. "And Abel has a light." He took her hand. "Abel, you're the boss. Save us."

Something flashed across Abel's face, a flicker of surprise, perhaps. "Follow me."

He took them down yet another tunnel, this one rougher, filled with boulders and the broken timbers of the ore car rails, earth dribbling through the cribs, some of the bracing timbers broken. She wiped her hand down her cheek, hating her tears.

Abel led them through passages as wide as a street, others that might turn a man sideways. Other passages led off the first, but Abel led the way without pausing.

"How do you know where you're going?" she finally asked, because speaking seemed better than listening to their breathing or their feet scrubbing on dirt.

"I grew up down here. I know every nook and cranny of this mine," Abel said.

Her light flickered out then, and it took every ounce of strength for her not to cry aloud.

They finally emerged into another open chamber.

The gate over the entry to the shaft was closed.

Abel walked over to the bell box, pulled on it, a series of short then long signals. The sound was returned. From the top, she heard the clanking of the lift cage.

"Welcome to the Neck," Abel said, a smile edging up his grimy face.

Daughtry extended a hand. "You saved us, Abel. Thank you."

Abel stared at the offering a long time, and just when Esme thought he might turn away, he took it.

She nearly leaped into the cage when it settled on the ground. Daughtry followed, then Abel closed the gate, then the door behind them, then reached through the window and pulled the bell signal.

The cage started slowly, bouncing as they rose.

As the darkness settled around her, she found herself in the pocket of Daughtry's chest, her ear pressed to his jacket. His heartbeat seemed even more thunderous than hers.

"Were you afraid?"

He looked down at her, his eyes white against his now dirty skin. "Terrified."

She laughed, more of an avalanche of emotion than humor. "I never want to do that again."

His face sobered. "And yet these miners do it every day."

She looked over at Abel. He was considering her, his eyes white in the darkness, his expression grim.

"We have to find out who's sabotaging the mine and stop them."

The cage slowed as it reached the top, finally lurching to a stop. Abel opened the doorway, then the cage.

Even from behind Daughtry, Esme heard the rabble, felt the tension as they piled out. A hoist man met them, his gaze going from Abel, then to Daughtry.

"What's the matter?" Daughtry said. Behind him, she heard shouting, saw what seemed like a mob outside the entrance.

"Crandall Norman's dead—and we caught the murderer. It's the man from Butte Mining. They're gonna lynch him."

Daughtry glanced at the mob then at Abel. They shared a moment, something they'd lost, perhaps, years ago, and had only found again under the crannies of the earth.

Daughtry turned to her. "Please. Go home. I promise to tell you everything that happens." He looked at her with those dark eyes, the ones that had told her to trust him, the ones that believed in her.

Esme nodded.

* * * * *

Esme waited, stopped the presses, pacing in her office. The moon had already risen, the light pale upon the floor.

"What if he doesn't come? Why didn't you stay? You know it would have been a front-page story." Ruby sat on the edge of her desk, having spent the last hour typing Esme's article into the linotype machine and reformatting the entire front page.

Hudson waited to run it through the press.

They'd left room for the update from Daughtry. So, the paper would go out late. She'd finally scoop Ellis Carter.

But more, she wanted to know who'd been sabotaging the mine. Who had killed Crandall, and so many other men.

"He asked me to go home," Esme said, not sure why she'd obeyed him. But something on Daughtry's face had convinced her that he would tell her the truth.

He just didn't want her to watch it.

For the first time in a long while, years maybe, she wanted to trust a man, to let him protect her.

Ruby was staring at her. "You have feelings for Daughtry Hoyt."

Esme had bathed, scrubbed the mine's breath from her skin, but she couldn't dislodge the way Daughtry had made her feel. The firm grip of his hand over hers, sweetness in his gaze when he'd called her beautiful under the glow of a carbide lamp.

I would like to go to dinner with the most beautiful woman in Montana.
She should have said yes.

Clearly, it showed in her expression. "I…maybe I do." The confession of it uncoiled something inside her. A grief, or maybe a fear.

She could fall in love again. Be happy.

But Ruby didn't smile. "Are you sure, Esme? He's not one of us. He's a rich man's son."

Esme shook her head. "But he is us, Ruby. You should have seen him down there. He asked Abel for help, even though I think he might have known his way back. And he understands the miners, the mine. And you should have seen his face when he found out that Crandall had been murdered."

Ruby folded her arms across her chest. "I just hope he doesn't break your heart."

A step sounded outside on the boardwalk, and Esme met him at the door, her hand on the latch when he entered.

Daughtry appeared wrung out, burdened, as he walked into the room.

She let her emotions lead and wrapped her arms around him, not caring about the sweat embedded in his shirt, the greasy dirt on his face, his hands. He curled his arms around her and, for a second, leaned down and seemed to draw in the smell of her.

"They didn't lynch him," he said. "But they wanted to." He put her away from him, met her eyes. "He was the agitator from the union meeting the other night. Apparently, he's been on-site for the past five weeks."

"He's our saboteur."

"Yes. He shot Crandall at the Horn. But Crandall managed to sound the distress whistle before he died. He identified his killer to the miners just coming off shift from the Neck shaft. They caught up with the man, and we got a confession. The Butte Miners Union has been committing the sabotage. But he said they were paid to do it…by Ellis Carter."

"But why?"

"So I'd be forced to sell to Anaconda. And the Silverthread miners would have to join the union. It means more dues, more power for Butte."

"They killed people so they'd have striking power?" Ruby's voice had a dangerous, lethal tone.

"I knew Ellis was behind this," Daughtry said. He sat down, ran his filthy hands through his hair. "But we only have the word of the BMU. We can't prove it."

"We have to expose Ellis Carter and his crimes," Esme said quietly.

"How?" Daughtry said, his eyes tired. She'd never seen him so shaken, so defeated. "He is above the law. He'll deny it and just send more saboteurs, and it won't matter if we catch them. He owns the Butte sheriff. He even bought his own senate seat."

"He doesn't own President Roosevelt." Esme crouched before him, reached up, and wiped dirt from his chin. "Clean up, Daughtry, because you're taking me to dinner."

Chapter 15

"Welcome to the 'Richest Hill on Earth.'" Esme stood back to allow the porter to open the door to her suite.

"This hotel is so grand," Ruby said, her eyes wide. "I always knew Daughtry was wealthy, I just never knew how much."

Esme hadn't the heart to tell her that this room could fit twice into her room back in New York. But then again, she could fit her current bedroom three times into this top-floor suite of the McDermott Hotel in Butte.

Esme entered the room behind Ruby. "Yes, grand, if you concentrate on the red brocade wallpaper, the velvet drapes, the sitting room, the white marble hearth." Indeed, she had been transported yet again back to her youth, with the golden chandelier dripping with the hues of twilight, the smell of roses on the round table by the window. "But don't look out the window."

Even from here she saw the steel headframes rising behind the hotel, the dark smoke of the smelters hovering like a hand over the city, turning it dusky. The city smelled of rotten eggs, and even breathing the air seemed poisonous.

Behind her, yet another porter ferried in her trunks with tonight's accoutrements. The first contained one of the grand dresses Daughtry had bequeathed her. The other held her undergarments, her clothes for tomorrow's ride home, and her dog collar she'd taken from the safe at the *Times*. She'd kept a weather eye on it as they'd traveled from Silver City to Butte, not sure why she'd brought it.

Certainly she wouldn't need it tonight. But some errant urge inside her compelled her to bring it, to fit herself back into the mold, if not the name, of Esme Price.

"I don't care. It's glorious." Ruby flung open the double doors to the bedroom, tossed herself onto the large, silk-covered bed with fluted pillars rising to the frescoed ceiling. "I could live here."

Esme caught her smile. "Then I guess I won't have to worry about you getting into trouble tonight while I'm at dinner."

"I'll be waiting with anxious breath for you to tell me everything the president says." Ruby came over to the trunk, opened it, and gasped. "This dress is breathtaking." Over a flowing, royal-blue satin skirt lay an embroidered crepe overskirt, all of which tucked into a white gauzy top, low cut and gathered at the apex of the waist with a blue floret.

Esme watched Ruby draw it out slowly, stuffed as it was for travel. Dawn knew how to pack a dress, and this one had survived the twenty-six-mile journey without damage. Ruby caught it up and carried it to the wardrobe, hanging it inside. It would have looked more spectacular on a dress form, but still it caught the light, the silver and gold threads shimmering.

"I've never seen such a beautiful dress. Or slippers!" Ruby had returned to the trunk to pull out the crinoline then opened the other trunk to discover the white satin high-heeled shoes. She set them beside the trunk and dug back in. "And what's this—a corset?"

She turned to Esme, mischief in her eyes. "Don't tell me that Daughtry gave you this too."

"No, thank you very much. That's mine."

Ruby got up, set it on the bed. "It's so fancy, so much lace."

"It's imported. From France."

Ruby stared at her. "How did you get an imported lace corset? Did you work for one of those high society women?"

Esme walked to the trunk, withdrew the case with the pearl dog collar. Perhaps tonight wasn't the best night to wear it after all. Too many questions. Too many memories. "Something like that."

She tucked the dog collar in the drawer beside the bed. "Ruby, do you know how to do hair?"

"I can braid, but—"

"No matter. I'll teach you how."

Two hours later, she'd bathed, instructed Ruby on an elemental hairstyle that swept her hair up from her neck, with a long braid that wound into the back. Dressing seemed more complicated than she'd remembered, from the bloomers and the crinoline, to the chemise and corset—how she'd forgotten her posture over the past seven years!—and finally the magnificent dress.

The dress hugged her body, flowing over it like it had been made for her.

"You're breathtaking," Ruby said, and Esme felt it as she considered herself in the mirror. And not only the dress—something had changed inside her since the last time she wore a dinner costume. No longer the woman who cowered inside her attire, she saw herself, suddenly, as an accomplished woman.

She belonged in this dress. And, perhaps, also in pants and an apron behind the linotype machine.

A knock at the door echoed through the suite.

"It's Daughtry."

"I need my gloves. And my jewelry."

Ruby stared at her. "You have jewelry?"

"Please tell Daughtry to wait in the parlor. I'll be out presently."

Ruby shut the doors behind her and Esme retrieved her gloves. Then she pulled out the jewelry box with the dog collar. For a moment, she wished she still had the pearl earrings to match, but then she wouldn't have this life. Her birthright had purchased her future.

Standing before the doors, she took a breath. *Commit thy way unto the Lord; trust also in Him; and He shall bring it to pass.*

Once upon a time, she'd given God her future, her hope.

Perhaps, tonight, He'd bring it to pass.

She opened the doors and mouthed the word "prism."

Daughtry turned, and for a moment the world stopped on his smile. His eyes shone. "You are more beautiful than anything I've ever seen."

Oh. He stood and extended his hand. She allowed him hers.

"You managed to get the dirt off," she said. Indeed, if she'd been a debutante, she would have hoped that he'd scrawled his name on every line of her dance card. In his gray and blue silk waistcoat, his cutaway jacket, the dark pants, and a bowtie, he appeared fresh from the Metropolitan Opera.

She handed him the jewelry box. "Would you carry this for me?"

He searched her eyes then nodded, putting it into his inner jacket pocket without looking at it. She began to work on her gloves, but they tangled in her hand.

"Allow me," he said, and took them from her, holding them open. She worked her hand in and drew the glove up above her elbow. Then the other. She took his arm.

Outside, the lights glittered beneath the cloud of smelter smoke. His shiny brougham waited at the entrance, and a footman helped them into the carriage. He climbed in beside her.

It seemed incongruent for them to be ferried in their finest attire through a city populated with saloons and brothels, with women displayed in large windows and raucous music drifting into the streets.

"I despise Butte," Daughtry said and handed her a handkerchief for her to press to her mouth.

Carter's mansion sat on a hill overlooking the city, a red-bricked, gabled house that could equal anything on Fifth Avenue. Still, it seemed too elegant, too gentry sitting above the tiny wooden houses of the working class boroughs of Butte.

They pulled up to the gabled entrance, the house lit up, light spilling into the darkness. Through the window, she spied men already seated at a long table, the blinds open to the street. Strange. Mrs. Astor always obscured the public from a view of the wealthy.

A footman met them, although Daughtry helped her down.

She took a breath.

"You look nervous."

She glanced at him.

"I hear there will be everyone from senators to miners here tonight. But you will be the belle of the ball."

She had heard that Carter's young wife of twenty-three years—to his sixty-two—might be in attendance tonight. At twenty-seven, Esme felt ancient.

Daughtry knocked at the door.

The butler, of course, answered, and Daughtry presented his name.

The butler asked them to wait and closed the door.

She shivered in a breeze from the mountains. "I should have brought a wrap."

"You can wear my jacket on the way home."

The door opened.

The butler stared at them, and for a moment, Esme returned to the moment when her father, so many years ago, had discovered her with Oliver. She'd opened the door, and Oliver's father, the butler, stood there on the stoop, behind him Father's footmen, bearing his orders, his anger. She stiffened on Daughtry's arm.

Then, "I'm sorry, sir, but you are not on the guest list."

Daughtry just stared at him, nonplussed. "But I am. I received an invitation."

"Apparently, your father received an invitation. You, however, did not."

Daughtry stiffened and Esme felt a muscle pull in his arm. "But I am attending in his stead," he said very softly.

"I'm sorry, sir. Mr. Carter has ordered you sent away." He closed the door.

Esme heard Daughtry's breath, tremulous, and in her heart, heard his words about his mother, in Esme's New York. *All our money couldn't buy her respectability.*

But Daughtry was, in her estimation, the *only* respectable Copper King.

"I'm sorry, Esme. Perhaps we can find a nice dinner someplace." He made to move away. She held his arm.

"No."

He looked at her.

"We're getting into this dinner party. We are talking to the president. We are holding Ellis Carter accountable for his crimes."

She turned her back to him. "There's a necklace in your pocket. I wasn't sure I wanted to wear it until now."

She heard him reach into his pocket and pull out the jewelry case. A pause. He cleared his throat. And then, "Oh my."

She lifted her chin as he secured the collar around her neck, the cold jewels prickling her skin. Then she turned back to him.

His face was solemn. "What are you doing?"

"Knock again, please."

"I don't understand."

She looked up at him and suddenly wanted to cry. "Would you still care for me, still want to court me, if I were rich?"

He stared at her, even more flummoxed, if that were possible. "But— aren't you poor? Because, last time I looked, you lived above your newspaper. You seem poor."

"I have a newspaper."

"That you sleep at. You don't even have a proper house."

"I'm not poor." She drew in a swift breath just as the door opened. The butler stood like a gunslinger, backlit by the entry hall lights. "Please tell President Roosevelt that Esme Price, daughter of *New York Chronicle* publisher August Price, would like to present herself for dinner at his table."

She managed not to touch the jewels at her neck but noticed that the butler's gaze ran to them a moment before he nodded. "Please, come in," he said. "It's cold out."

She couldn't look at Daughtry as they waited in the hall, but he leaned in to her ear anyway.

"I honestly thought you were just a very avid scholar of Page Six."

She smiled as the butler returned to escort them for dinner.

* * * * *

She didn't expect the dinner company around Ellis Carter's massive table. Mayor Mullins, of course, and she recognized the owner of the Amalgamated Copper Company seated at the far end, along with the president's aides. But seated at the table along with the dignitaries was a cross-section of every face in Butte. A negro man, a Chinese man, an Englishman who reminded her very much of Abel, a red-haired Irishman, a Greek, and an Italian. And finally a man who bore the fair coloring of a Swede.

They all stood and introduced themselves. She could nearly swim in the whiskey on their breaths.

From everything she'd heard about Ellis Carter, she doubted he would impress her. She sat opposite the senator—he ogled her décolletage, or perhaps her jewelry—and thought she just might lose her appetite if she had to watch him shovel quail soup into his bearded maw.

She hadn't come for the dinner anyway.

She'd come, perhaps, for the look in every man's eye when President Roosevelt greeted her with warmth, like she might be his long-lost daughter. He hadn't changed severely in seven years—still robust, still the handlebar moustache, the way he peered through a person, disarming her even as he offered her a seat. "What is August's daughter doing out here in the middle of mining country?"

"I moved out here seven years ago to start a paper. In fact, I cabled you to ask for an interview but was told you were too busy."

He glanced at an aide. "I wasn't informed of any interview request."

"I used a different name. My…Montana name. Esme Stewart."

He raised an eyebrow, and in that moment, her courage scattered.

She couldn't look at Daughtry. What if she made a fool of both of them with her request? What, was she running to the president like he might be her father, about to solve her problems?

Around the table, the miners presented gifts to the president. She clasped her hands in her lap and tried not to touch her necklace, tried not to run from the room.

When the negro miner presented his gift, Roosevelt held it up, a pair of sliver scales. "This comes in the shape I appreciate—scales of justice held even. I served with many colored soldiers in Cuba, and they all honored themselves." He turned to him then. "It's my duty to help you get a square deal."

She glanced at Daughtry, saw a sort of hope light his face.

The waiters finally served the first course, and she turned her skills to the art of small talk.

She hadn't been a debutante for nothing, it seemed.

She made Roosevelt laugh, his aides grin, and Daughtry shake his head with her story of riding a horse astride for the first time. They turned solemn at the story of the time during Christmas when four children showed up at the *Times*' doorstep, hungry after their father had died of consumption. She had them nodding in agreement over the cleanup of the Butte highway by Montana vigilantes, and Roosevelt's eyes widened at her account of seeing a buffalo for the first time.

"Daughtry has about forty head," she said. She glanced at him and found his eyes on her, the sort of smile on his face that might make a woman blush. For all his desire to see Roosevelt, Daughtry seemed more intent on her every word.

The president turned to Daughtry. "I'm sorry to hear about your father. Send him my regards. Your family runs the Silverthread Mine Company, is that correct?"

"Yes sir. But we may be shutting down."

Esme drew in a breath. "In fact, that's why we wanted to talk with you tonight." She wouldn't look at Carter, the way his dark eyes speared her. "We believe that one of the men at this table, one of the Copper Kings, is sabotaging our mine."

Silence drilled into the room. Roosevelt sat back in his chair. "That's a serious accusation."

"Men are dying. We're extremely serious. But we believe the local law might be…compromised. We need your help to keep our miners safe."

Roosevelt considered her, and she held his gaze. And it occurred to her then that she hadn't been born a Price, hadn't spent the last seven years scraping out a life in Montana, to scurry under the table. She drew in a breath.

Finally, he nodded. "I'll have my men look into it." He looked up at the men around the table, let his words sink in.

She somehow managed not to throw her arms around the president of the United States. She glanced at Daughtry. He wore pride in his eyes.

"About that interview, Miss Price," the president said. "Join me after dinner. I believe I may have some thoughts for you."

* * * * *

"I think I'm in love with you."

Daughtry spoke the words softly, earnestly, into her ear as he draped his coat over her shoulders, drew her to himself. "You were magnificent, Esme Price." He kissed her hair. "But I still can't believe you didn't tell me your real name."

She leaned away from him, settled herself into the seat of the brougham. Overhead, the sky had cleared, the stars spilling out like diamonds. "I couldn't. I didn't want my name—or my family's money—to taint how you saw me."

"I couldn't care less about your money, Esme. I care about you— the way you laugh, the way you make me feel like I belong in your world. "

She slid a hand to his cheek. "I think you're the only one who could." And somehow, the words felt exactly right. Only a man who straddled both worlds would understand hers.

His smile dimmed, his gaze growing serious. He took her hand from his cheek, wound his fingers between hers. "I meant it. I love you, Esme Stewart."

Suddenly, her name hovered between them. "Esme Price. Stewart belonged to a man I once loved. But he died before he could really live. He had passion, and loved me, and I was more thirsty for what he could give me than for him, perhaps. But I couldn't find what I needed with him."

"And what is it that you need, Esme?"

"I—I don't know." She looked away, but he brought her face back to him.

"I do. You need to know you're loved."

And then he kissed her. Nothing like Oliver, or even Abel, Daughtry took his time, his lips on hers so soft it might be a whisper. Then, as she moved toward him, as his touch awakened something locked inside her, he deepened his kiss, moving his hand behind her neck, exploring her mouth. He tasted sweet, of the chocolate dessert and the after-dinner cognac, and smelled husky and dark, the cowboy hidden under that refined waistcoat. She let her arms move around his waist, let herself hold him.

Let herself be held.

Daughtry. His name seemed so right, so rich in her mind. Daughtry Hoyt.

"Marry me." His voice was in her ear, soft, urgent. "Marry me, Esme. Marry me tonight. Right now."

She leaned back, the words rushing through her.

He caught her face in his gloved hand. "I know we haven't known each other very long, but I can't stop thinking about you. You are in my head, in my heart, and in my hopes for the future. And, yes, you were amazing tonight, but I fell in love with you when I saw you in dirty britches lying in a puddle on my barn floor. You're strong and trustworthy and brave and I don't care what your name is as long as you're my wife."

She hooked her hands on his arms, stared up into his face, those eyes that could see right through her. "You forgive me for my secrets?"

"I told you I knew you had them. Why would I be angry?" He tipped his forehead to hers. "Marry me, Esme. I'm not afraid of your secrets."

Oh, she longed to say yes. Maybe it was time for her to fall in love. Except... "I can't move back to New York, Daughtry. Not yet. I'm not ready."

He searched her face. "Then we'll stay. I'll figure out a way to keep the mine open, make repairs so that it's safe."

He would stay, for her? "How much in debt are you?"

"We can cash in our investments. Maybe fifty thousand?"

She reached up and unlatched the dog collar. Pressed it into his hands. "Will this cover it?"

He stared at her, back to the jewels. "I can't take this."

"If I'm going to be your wife, then what is mine is yours. We're in this together. Take it. I don't need it anymore."

"Are you sure?"

"I'm sure, Daughtry. I know who I am."

Still, he asked twice more as they drove through the city, as they tracked down a judge.

Asked her one final time before he agreed to be her husband.

They made it back to the hotel before dawn flushed into the sky, and she left a note for Ruby under the door, from Mrs. Daughtry Hoyt.

* * * * *

"Are you nervous?" Daughtry sat on the bench beside Esme in their train compartment, looking out the window as the train cut through the greening hills and gullies of Montana. Behind them, the Rocky Mountains rose crisp and white, parting the sky. "You are so quiet today."

"I just don't want it to end." She slid her gloved hand onto his on her shoulder, squeezing. It seemed right to have procured a new toilette—two split skirts, a blouse. She couldn't continue to wear Daughtry's mother's clothing, but she hadn't felt like slipping back into her britches either.

"What do you fear will end?"

"This happiness." She turned, pressed his face between her hands, finding his eyes, seeing herself in them. She liked what she saw—a woman unafraid to be in two worlds, a woman at peace. "I think God has finally forgiven me. Finally decided to bless me."

He drew in a long breath, frowning. "Esme, God has always blessed you."

She shook her head. "No. I disappointed Him. He gave me so much, and when I rejected my family, my duty, He took Oliver from me. But now He's given me you." She leaned up to kiss him, but he drew away.

He took her hands in his. "Oliver's death was not about God not blessing you. He wasn't punishing you because of something you did. Oliver simply died. And I'm sorry. But it has nothing to do with God's love for you."

She pulled away from him. "No. No. God knew I'd turned away from my birthright, the life I was supposed to live. I had no choice but to run, to strike out on my own. Depend on myself."

"You've never been on your own, Esme. That's a lie that the devil wants you to believe. Don't you know that nothing you do can ever separate you from the love of God?"

She watched as they rolled toward Silver City, the outlying homesteads, the bitterroot flowers peeking their pink and white buds through the silvery grasses. "I grew up very wealthy. I could buy anything I needed, we lived with a host of servants. I thought we were blessed. But I never felt blessed. And, I was ashamed of that. How could I have so much and be so miserable? I thought maybe I should try to be poor—D. L. Moody says that it is better to live in suffering than prosperity, because you find God in suffering. But where is God's blessing when you make a living tunneling under the earth, making just enough to feed your family? Is that God's love? What does it mean to be blessed by God?"

He turned her, drew her to himself. "Esme, being blessed by God isn't being wealthy, or healthy. Nor is being poor a lack of His blessing. The Bible says the Almighty makes the rain fall on the just and the unjust. Being blessed is about being safe in His hand. It's about belonging to Him, and knowing you are secure in His care." He put her away from himself. "'O taste and see that the Lord is good: blessed is the man that trusteth in Him.' God's love, His blessing, isn't about getting things, it's about knowing that even in our suffering, He is holding us secure and can make good things come out of it."

"Like losing Oliver, but marrying you."

He cupped her face in his hand, a smile that told her he approved. "God has never abandoned you, my beautiful Esme. He has gone with you, cared for you, and protected you. And you will find everything you need, and more, as you trust in Him and His love for you."

He kissed her then, and she believed him.

As they pulled near the station, he gathered their bags. "Do you want to keep this paper?" He held out a copy of the *San Francisco Examiner,* with the front-page interview with President Roosevelt. "I like the byline."

She took it, ran her finger under the name. "Is it okay that I wrote it under Esme Price? I—I could start writing under Esme Hoyt."

He tipped up her chin. "You write every article under your name, Esme. You earned it."

She considered the paper then folded it and left it on the seat.

They stopped and he took her hand as they exited. But even as they stepped into the sunshine, even as the pigeons scattered before them on the platform, she heard the siren.

"The mine," she said. "There's been an accident."

Beside her, Daughtry's face tightened. "Come." He said nothing, his eyes on the headframes on the hill beside the mine as he helped her into the brougham. He didn't wait for their trunks, just headed toward the Silverthread.

Esme spotted Ruby in the crowd pressing against the fencing. Mine officials stood at the gate, the doors closed, yelling at the women, the other miners. Ruby stood with her hands pressed to her mouth.

"Stay here," Daughtry said. She gave him a look, and he reached up his hand to help her from the carriage.

They pushed their way through the crowd, to the gate. The guard there, a man whose fear rattled through Esme, let them through. Ruby pushed in behind her.

"What's going on?"

Ruby shook her head. "There was a cave-in. Dustin—he's down there. With six others."

Daughtry turned to her. "Was it sabotage?"

"No—they've had extra security on the mine since the federal investigators were here. This one is deep inside the mine—they blasted and a tunnel caved in. It's just an accident."

Esme read the flash of pain in Daughtry's eyes. He shucked off his coat, handed it to Esme. "I'll be right back." He stalked over to the office and emerged five minutes later holding a carbide light, wearing a pair of dirty overalls, Abel behind him.

Abel appeared as if he'd spent the last week underground, his reddish hair matted with dirt, his skin blackened. He carried a pickaxe.

When he saw her, she recognized a ghost of a smile, something sad. "I always knew you'd look pretty in a dress."

She tried to find a smile for him.

He glanced at Daughtry, now talking with the shift boss. "We're taking another crew down. But you might want to talk your man into staying behind. The drift they're trapped in is unstable, and it might cave in."

Even as Abel said it, Daughtry glanced at her. His eyes told her the truth. He wasn't sending Abel someplace he wouldn't go himself.

"Take care of him, Abel," she said softly.

Abel's mouth tightened into a solemn line. He looked at Ruby. "I'll find Dustin, I promise."

Ruby wrapped her arms around herself and nodded.

Esme did the same when Daughtry returned to her, his hat lopsided on his head. She wanted to wind herself tight, to hold in the words. *Don't go.* But she'd married a man who knew where he belonged. Who knew what he had to do. He cupped her chin. "I love you, Mrs. Hoyt."

She nodded, her eyes wet. "Come back to me, Daughtry. I'm not going anywhere. I'll be waiting right here until you return."

Then he disappeared into the dark cradle of the earth, carrying her heart with him.

HEIRESS

NEW YORK CITY

1917

Chapter 16

For a man who wanted to kill their son, Foster Worth managed a serene expression as he recited the Nicene creed.

"We believe in one God, the Father, the Almighty, maker of heaven and earth, of all that is, seen and unseen."

Jinx stood beside him, focusing her gaze on the light streaming through the glorious stained-glass windows arching over the chancery behind the altar of Grace Episcopal Church. Such a glorious Resurrection Day, the violets and lilies in bloom outside, the smell of spring in the air despite the early April nip of the wind.

Foster stood attired in his best—a gray waistcoat, charcoal gabardine suit, a bowtie at his neck, looking regal and righteous, as if he hadn't a sin in the world to chase him, to linger in his soul.

If anything, he lied better than she.

Behind their third-row, left-side pew—which he'd purchased early in their marriage—two hundred voices recited with them. "We believe in one Lord, Jesus Christ, the only Son of God, eternally begotten of the Father, God from God, Light from Light, true God from true God, begotten, not made, of one Being with the Father. Through Him all things were made. For us and for our salvation He came down from heaven...."

Next to her, Rosie refused to look at her mother—apparently punishing Jinx for not allowing her to escape to Eleanor Fish's house after the service. Perhaps she should have relented—Easter dinner would certainly be nothing short of suffocation for all of them.

If Foster even decided to join them.

"For our sake He was crucified under Pontius Pilate; He suffered death and was buried. On the third day He rose again in accordance with the Scriptures; He ascended into heaven and is seated at the right hand of the Father."

She glanced at her son Jack—Jonathon—and tried not to let the conversation she'd overheard before services curdle the moment of worship.

The one involving Jack's future appointment to West Point.

She curled her gloved hands over the dark wooden pew before her. "He will come again in glory to judge the living and the dead, and His kingdom will have no end. We believe in the Holy Spirit, the Lord, the giver of life, who proceeds from the Father and the Son."

Foster surely did it on purpose—routed her efforts to urge Jack into Harvard. She'd already arranged to buy out his enlistment. Sometimes she had to wonder if Foster knew the truth, if he deliberately intended on making her suffer.

On sending her only son to war.

Everything had changed the day she'd announced her pregnancy to Foster. She'd hoped for something amicable, even warm. Hoped for a truce.

Instead, Foster had gradually turned brutal. Mostly behind closed doors, and she was thankful he'd never turned his fists on their children—neither Jack nor the daughter he'd given her one drunken night in anger.

Beside her, Jack's voice raised, clear and solemn. "With the Father and the Son He is worshipped and glorified. He has spoken through the prophets. We believe in one holy Catholic and apostolic Church. We acknowledge one baptism for the forgiveness of sins."

The words on Jinx's own tongue tasted like ash. She had to be sorry to ask for forgiveness, didn't she? But she hadn't had one moment of regret since Jack's birth, despite Foster's hatred. Even now, looking at Jack's beautiful, strong face as he recited his salvation could root her to the spot with gratitude. She'd never known how to really love until she held Jack in her arms, until she pressed her lips to his damp, chapped cheek. Until she held him to her breast.

Jack had saved her.

And Foster meant to send him to war.

"We look for the resurrection of the dead, and the life of the world to come. Amen."

She sat in the pew and folded her hands on her lap, listening as the priest led them in prayer for the church, the world, the sick. She managed to concentrate with a list of things she thanked God for—Jack, and Rosie too. And her mother. She lifted a prayer for Esme, somewhere, when the priest began his petitions for the dead. She wasn't dead, but sometimes it seemed that way. Oh, to return to that day when Jinx had longed to take her place. Perhaps Foster would have loved Esme. She, certainly, would have never betrayed him.

But given the choice between betraying her soul and having Jack...

"And we pray for all those lost on the battlefields of France and Germany, of Belgium in this great, horrific war. Bring them into Thy peace."

What was peace, anyway? Did she have to die to get it? Because it seemed that her life had disintegrated into one endless cycle of betrayal, revenge, and fear.

She confessed her sins alongside Foster and her children, and her mind wandered to the upcoming sermon, then the psalm for the day as they received absolution.

"The eyes of the Lord are on the righteous and His ears are attentive to their cry; the face of the Lord is against those who do evil, to cut off the memory of them from the earth."

The words had burned into her brain, now caused her breath to washboard in her chest.

She couldn't count on God to help her keep her son out of war; she'd have to manage it herself.

The priest ended the prayer and raised his hands. "The peace of the Lord be always with you."

"And also with you," she responded then turned to offer peace to her fellow congregants—the Fishes behind them, the Astors across the aisle. Foster, she noticed, lifted a hand to the mayor.

"Are you sure I can't go to Ellie's house after services?" Rosie leaned over, her voice not as quiet as Jinx would have preferred. What was it about her daughter that managed to rankle her nerves? She simply refused to take no for an answer, pushed ahead with her own desires, despite the wounds to others.

"We are having lunch at Delmonico's. After that, perhaps," Jinx said as the congregation sat for the blessing of the Eucharist. She hesitated just for a moment, just in case—

"He's not here, Jinx," Foster growled, and reached for her hand to tug her down.

She turned, slipped her hand free. "I have no idea who you are referring to."

A muscle pulled in her jaw as the presider told the story of Jesus and how communion came to pass, and she swallowed hard against the burn in her throat. She didn't expect him to be here, not really. Bennett seemed to manage to avoid her every time he'd come from London in the last seventeen years—so few times she could probably count them on one hand. She ached to see him—had hoped to that first time, when Rosie turned two and she'd reentered the social scene. She'd heard that he had taken rooms at the Waldorf. She searched for him from her box at the Met, and on the dance floor at Alva Belmont's New Year's ball, and even at Elise Donahue's wedding. Perhaps, however, he didn't have the courage to attend after breaking their betrothal so many years prior and leaving poor Elise nearly an old maid.

But Bennett neatly managed to avoid her. She only knew of his arrival in New York from a tiny sighting at Delmonico's with Foster, listed on Page Six.

Foster, of course, said nothing. In fact, since his brother escaped Newport that summer, Bennett hadn't invited Foster back to their home once.

Foster knew. He had to know. Lewis's sudden appearance at the dock always itched at her, as if Foster might have sent him to threaten Bennett. And, it didn't help that Jack had Bennett's smile, his infectious charm, a way of listening as if he genuinely cared. Bennett had given all his best traits to his son, Jack.

The priest blessed the sacraments then they recited the Lord's Prayer. She watched as Jack reached out, took Rosie's hand, played with her thumb. Rosie stifled a giggle.

If Foster sent him away, to West Point, to become a soldier, she would tell him the truth. Jack wasn't his.

Jack had never, ever, been his. He'd never had Foster's cruelty, never his slithery charm, and never, either, his interest in business. Jack would rather spend his afternoon reading or driving or sometimes playing cricket or ice hockey with his St. Paul boarding school chums than join the military.

They rose and filed forward for the host and wine. Jinx took the host on her tongue, swallowed it, and then let the wine burn her throat.

The priest finally dismissed them to their lives of Christian service.

Foster left her in the pew and headed for the vestibule as Jinx again greeted the Fishes, the Wilsons, the Astors.

"Yes, you may go to Ellie's after lunch," she said to Rosie as she hooked her arm through Jack's. Rosie grinned, too much triumph in it, but Jinx didn't have the energy to fight her.

Jack tucked his hand onto hers as they eased down the aisle. He looked like a soldier already, with his broad shoulders, his dark blond hair, those blue eyes. He already had the attention of every young lady in Manhattan. Too bad the practice of social debuts had died with the war—he might have found himself the center of society's attention.

Jinx hadn't a prayer of pushing Rosie into a finishing school, however. Rosie had a mind of her own and it didn't involve learning French or how to dance a cotillion. Jinx couldn't even imagine forcing her into a corset.

Foster waited by his gleaming white Rolls Royce, with the red wheels and plush leather seats, something he purchased off the ballroom floor of the Astor's Hotel in January. He refused to allow a driver to do anything but polish it.

"Hurry up," Foster said as Jack opened the door for Rosie and Jinx. They climbed in the back. "I'll drop you at Delmonico's. I have business."

On Easter Sunday afternoon? Oh, yes, probably at the Knickerbocker Theater, the Winter Gardens, or perhaps even at the Casino, where his latest floozy awaited backstage.

"Of course you do," she said, considering her options. If she showed up at Delmonico's unescorted, it just might make the top news on the social pages.

But if she didn't, and Bennett also happened to dine at Delmonico's...

No. She had spent the last seventeen years pushing him from her mind. Or, trying to.

"Just take us home. Genevieve will manage to scrape together something for us."

They ate in the immense dining room, just the three of them, a simple lunch of eggs Benedict. Then Jack ferried Rosie to the Fishes' and left to play cricket with his pals.

Jinx spent the day in her room, reading the *Ladies' Home Journal*. It came to her as no surprise to hear Foster's steps on the marble floor long after the sun dropped into the Hudson.

It had taken her seven hours, anyway, to churn up her courage.

Jinx wrapped her dressing gown around her, padding down the stairs into the dark foyer. Foster stood in his office, a fire crackling in the hearth, holding a highball of bourbon. So much of their house reminded her of the one she'd grown up in—the smoking room opposite the stairs and the dining room, the ballroom in the center of the house with an overlooking balcony, the servants' quarters in the basement. She'd remodeled twice, planted a garden in the back, turned the stables into a motorcar garage. She'd then turned her attention to the suffrage movement, and along with Alva, Frances Perkins, and Anne Morgan, joined the Mink Brigade and picketed with the working class women of the Triangle Shirtwaist Factory.

Foster had stopped talking to her shortly afterward.

A year later, she'd walked in the funeral march of some of those same factory women.

She'd arrived home from the funeral march to find Foster waiting for her, surly on too much bourbon. It was the first time he used his fists on her.

She'd taken Rosie with her when the suffragettes marched on Washington two years ago.

Foster had moved into rooms at the Astor Hotel.

She'd hoped he'd stay there, but for some reason he'd moved back home six agonizing months ago.

Jinx held onto the mahogany doorframe, muscling up her courage. The entire room oozed power, designed after John D. Rockefeller's Moorish smoking room, from the black marble hearth, the rich red and gold leather wall panels, the black velvet slipper chairs, the exotic gold candelabra. She hated the room, the smells of Foster's cigarettes that oozed from it, and most of the time kept the doors open to the garden.

Somehow, she dredged up her voice. It sounded oddly unfamiliar. "I don't want him going to West Point."

Foster stood with his wide back to her, staring at the fire. "I don't care what *you* want. He's too much of a mama's boy."

"He'll go to war, Foster. Do you want him to be listed among the dead, to be praying for his eternal soul? He's already been accepted to Harvard. Why can't he—"

Foster rounded on her. "Because no son of mine is going to be a coward."

His words rattled her, and the retort nearly breeched her lips before she swallowed it back. "Jack is no coward. But he wants to be a lawyer."

"I don't care what he wants. He's my son—or at least you claim he is! And until you tell me the truth, he'll do what I say!" Foster threw his drink into the fire, the glass crashing against the hearth, the fire flaring. "West Point will make him into a man."

She ignored his accusation. "Will it turn him into the kind of man you are? Who hits his wife? Betrays her with other women?"

She should have expected it, but Jinx jumped as Foster rounded on her, his eyes glassy. She backed away, but he reached out and buried his hands into the flesh on her arms, pulled her close. His breath slid over her, filled with heat. His words slurred out, a growl. "You've wrecked him with your doting."

She pushed against him. "Let me go, Foster."

"Why? You're my wife, aren't you?"

Her eyes burned. Oh, she wished not. She stiffened, looked away.

He held her for a long moment, his fingers boring into her flesh. Finally, he flung her away. "Not much of one," he said, and returned to his sideboard, picking up a fresh glass.

His hand shook as he poured himself a drink. Then he sat down at his desk, opening a drawer.

He pulled out a cherry box, set it on his desk. "I bought these years ago. Perhaps we should finally find a way to end our differences." He opened the box, turned it.

Nestled inside crushed cherry red velvet lay two dueling pistols.

"You're drunk. And crazy. Stay away from me." She rubbed her arms, backing from the room.

She whirled around and nearly ran into Amelia, still attired in her housekeeper's uniform. "I heard a crash," she said softly.

"It's nothing, Amelia. Thank you." She'd become an excellent housekeeper after Jinx had to replace her for a younger lady's maid. And, for Amelia's part, she never spoke of that day in Newport when Jinx had nearly freed them both.

"Mama?" Rosie stood in the foyer, her coat in her arms. "Are you well?"

Oh, she had a beautiful daughter. At first, she'd seen so much of Foster in the girl, her tight brown curls, those cool gray eyes. But she'd blossomed into a beauty—not at all like Jinx, but not Foster either, with her heart-shaped face, her slender form.

In fact, Rosie reminded her of Esme.

Jinx held out her hand, caught Rosie's. "Go to bed."

Rosie handed off her coat to Neville, who had appeared as if from the walls. Jinx turned and saw Lewis in the shadows, his eyes on her raising gooseflesh on her skin.

Her legs shook as she climbed the stairs, her stomach in knots. She managed to hold in her breath until she reached her room.

She'd created a palace in here, with her bed the throne, the gilded walls, the purple velvet tapestries, white marble fireplace, chaise lounge, and French Renaissance writing desk.

She should have created a fortress.

Jinx lifted her sleeves, examined the marks of Foster's grip impressed into her arms. Good thing Jack hadn't yet returned. Once, Jack had seen her bruises and his teenage anger had scared her.

Downstairs, she heard yelling—probably Foster in one of his drunken monologues. Another smash, the sound needling through her. He'd go through an entire service at this rate.

Sitting at her dressing table, she wrapped her arms around her waist, stared at herself in her mirror.

No wonder Foster chased other women. Crow lines framed her eyes, tiny wrinkles around her lips. She had lost weight, her face sallow, but on her the loss only turned her severe. To her own eyes, she appeared wrung out, defeated.

At least Foster hadn't hit her. She ran her hand down her face, as if the last bruise still remained, but it had vanished long ago.

She closed her eyes, remembering his rage, how she'd tried to run from him.

How Lewis had stood in the corner and watched, a gleam in his eye. How Amelia cleaned up the crystal Foster had flung across the ballroom.

How Daphne prepared an ice pack to reduce the swelling and delivered her regrets to the final dinner party of the season.

Maybe, in fact, the bruises remained.

Jinx put her forehead on the dressing table and let a sob trickle out. No one would hear her anyway. Still, she cupped her hands over her mouth, pressed hard.

Her own weeping had the power to frighten her.

The knock came quietly, and she thought it might be the knocking of her own heart. But it came again, louder.

Jack couldn't see her like this, eyes swollen, nose red. She got up, pressed a cloth to her face. "Just a moment." Wrapping her robe around herself, she cinched it tight, got up.

Took a breath.

She wouldn't allow him to go to West Point. To war.

Not with young men returning in pine boxes. She would lose too much of herself if Jack went to war.

And the rest if he never returned.

She opened the door. "Jack, I know what your father—"

Not Jack, but the man who stood there took away her breath, just as handsome as Jack, just older, with his own fine lines of pain around his eyes. Tousled blond hair, blue eyes that could stop her heart, and an expression on his face that told her he hadn't forgotten her either.

Bennett.

* * * * *

Lilly Hoyt had too much of her father in her spirit. Esme stood at the window, dressed in her Easter attire—a simple shirtwaist with mutton-chop sleeves and a linen skirt under a long buttoned jacket—and watched her thirteen-year-old daughter ride into the yard on her father's Arabian. She wore a pair of britches, her braids flying in the wind, armed with a .22, and not in the least ready for morning services.

How her daughter could have inherited so much courage and downright stubbornness from a father she'd never even met baffled Esme. Drove her, in fact, to want to pack up their things and march her to Misses Graham's Seminary for Young Ladies in New York City where, at least, she'd learn some manners.

She met Lilly at the door. "So much for a morning bath. Your dress is laid out, and I don't even want to know why you were up at the crack of dawn armed with your father's shotgun."

Lilly had inherited all of Daughtry's dark looks too, with her sable brown hair, her dark exotic eyes. In fact, the only thing she seemed to have of Esme's was her sass.

"Abel spotted wolves in the south pasture. I didn't want them spooking the buffalo. There are three new calves." Lilly hung her hat on the peg near the door. Esme picked it up and handed it to Dawn, who also took Lilly's buffalo jacket, which was oversized and mannish on her. Dawn glanced at Lilly's boots and shook her head.

Esme grimaced. "Could you at least use the side entrance when you're covered in mud?"

Lilly gave her a look, stormed back outside to remove her boots. She left them on the porch and walked in, barefoot. She gave Dawn a narrowed-eyed look and headed up the stairs.

"She needs a firmer hand," Dawn said.

Esme had long ago realized that if she hoped to parent her fatherless daughter, she'd need more hands on deck. Dawn had become a grand-mother of sorts, making Esme ache for her mother's advice.

How Phoebe had raised her with such refined manners eluded Esme.

"She needs a father," Esme said. "And the buffalo herd makes her feel close to him. Especially since President Roosevelt declared it a national herd. She considers them her personal responsibility."

"She acts like a boy, and she's getting to the age where people are going to notice."

Esme drew in a breath. Yes, at Lilly's age, Esme had already begun attending finishing school, spending hours practicing her dances, learning German and French. She couldn't imagine Lilly attempting a waltz, let alone walking across the room balancing a book atop her head. "Could you ask Abel to unhitch the horse from the brougham? We'll have to take the runabout to town in order to make it to service on time."

Outside, the Easter morning sun ate away the last of the frost, climbing over the recently repainted red barn, tempering the lick of the spring breeze, still so rife with the winter chill. The bitterroot had yet to peek through the matted grasses, but this time of year stirred the memory of Daughtry like a fragrant wind. She saw him riding through the fields, tall and cowboy in the saddle. Saw him in his cutaway jacket, a gold ascot at his neck as he offered her his arm. Heard his whispers in her ear, his laughter nourishing her bones.

In the springtime, she felt winter melt away, saw herself stronger, surviving another season of loneliness. She spun her wedding ring around on her finger with her thumb.

"Fine. I'm ready. You know I hate wearing a dress, right?"

She turned to the lovely image of her daughter in her Easter attire— a white dress with a belted navy overcoat, her hair hanging long and wavy, freshly freed from her braids. And, she'd washed her face, leaving only a springtime freshness upon her skin. She looked like a girl who lived outdoors, more comfortable with the hands of the ranch—Abel and Hank, Thomas and Dustin, all former miners who had moved out to the ranch after the accident.

She didn't know what she would have done without Abel. After he'd healed from burns, learned to walk again without a foot—he'd become more than a ranch hand, a brother, really. For a while, she wondered if she loved him, but after knowing what real love felt like, she couldn't give Abel her heart.

And, as if he knew, he never asked.

"You manage to remind me every single Sunday," Esme said to Lilly and picked up her hat.

Outside, the wind lifted the collar of her jacket, cinched at the waist. Abel waited by the runabout, holding the door open for the both of them. She never noticed his scars anymore—there was no need to keep them covered with gloves.

She heard the singing even before they entered Trinity Methodist, the robust sounds of miners and their families, most of them German, some Cornish, blended as she arrived. Down the street, St. Patrick's Catholic Church tolled its bells. Archie had attended Redeemer Lutheran, so she'd accompanied him the two times he managed to attend—once for Daughtry's funeral. The second, just weeks later, for his own. But always she'd returned to Trinity. She needed the comfort of Ruby and Dustin, even of Agnes O'Shaunessy, who reminded her that God could reap blessing from darkness.

Thirteen years later, seeing her daughter settle into the pew beside her, Esme believed it. Lilly picked up the hymnal, paged to the number on the board in the front of the church, and lifted her voice as if she might be angelic.

Ruby glanced down the aisle at Esme, who rolled her eyes. Ruby shook her head, patting her oldest on his head. Beside her, Dustin held the baby over his shoulder as he sang.

"Low in the grave He lay, Jesus my Savior, waiting the coming day, Jesus my Lord!"

Esme couldn't help but think, every time they sang this song, of that day too soon after her honeymoon, waiting until darkness filled every cranny of the hillside, scattered only by the electric lights on the Neck's entrance, her breath crammed into her chest.

"Up from the grave He arose…"

She'd never forget how, suddenly, the earth trembled beneath her, a shudder almost, as if in witness to her worst fears. How Ruby took her hand as they fell to their knees. How a plume of black smoke spat from the gaping mouth of the mine.

"…with a mighty triumph o'er His foes."

As soon as the ash cleared, they sent down a second crew, worked through the night. By dawn, the first lift of survivors appeared.

"He arose a victor from the dark domain…"

Dustin, his arm broken, and Abel, his hands seared by the smoke, his legs mangled.

"…and He lives forever, with His saints to reign."

Daughtry, however, had never fully emerged, his body so broken they only recovered a portion. He'd been deep in the mine, drilling holes in the debris, hoping to loosen it to retrieve the men caught behind. Abel suggested, long after, that perhaps he'd been priming a stick of powder with a cap when it exploded.

However, the explosion had loosened the cave-in and freed the trapped miners.

"He arose! He arose! Hallelujah! Christ arose!"

She closed her eyes, imagined him beside her. He might be proud of what she'd done with the mine. She'd sold off half his shares to the miners, giving them a stake in their earnings. No worries with unions—they held their own futures in their hands, learned what it meant to manage a mine as it grew to feed a town that doubled in size.

The *Copper Valley Times* expanded to a daily. Then took over the press in three other small towns.

She might even consider herself a newspaper baroness if she let herself measure her profits. She slipped her arm through her daughter's.

"Vainly they watch His bed, Jesus my Savior, vainly they seal the dead, Jesus my Lord!"

Yes, Lilly could have benefited from a father, someone to dote on her, buy her dresses, treat her like a lady.

Esme glanced at her daughter then to her daughter's feet. From beneath the white skirt peeked her dirty boots from the porch.

She'd turned into a truly wild thing under Abel's encouragement. Lilly knew how to rope and ride and shoot and herd and…

Esme had raised a boy.

Her daughter had no idea how to behave in cultured society. Didn't know the legacy of her name.

Lilly had become her father's child. Perhaps it was time she became her mother's daughter. Oh, how Esme longed to have Daughtry's wisdom, his character. His ability to live in two worlds.

How she longed to truly believe his words, the ones she so long ago pocketed inside, "O taste and see that the Lord is good: blessed is the man that trusteth in Him."

"Up from the grave He arose; with a mighty triumph o'er His foes!"

She did trust in God. Had seen His goodness to her over the past thirteen years.

Had Lilly to prove that He could make blessing out of suffering, at least out here in the West.

"He arose a victor from the dark domain, and He lives forever, with His saints to reign."

Esme slipped her arm around Lilly. Imagined her father's face if she returned to New York. She'd like to show her daughter Central Park, take her to dinner at Delmonico's, perhaps to the opera. Dress her in pearls.

"He arose! He arose! Hallelujah! Christ arose!"

Perhaps it was time to go home.

* * * * *

"Bennett. What are you doing here?" After seventeen years, and spending too much time imagining this moment, Jinx had hoped for better, more emotionally accurate words to issue from her mouth. And possibly more ceremony than to grab Bennett by the arm and yank him inside her chamber.

Surely she'd lost her mind. And Bennett stared at her as if she had too, when she shut her door behind him. She didn't turn then, simply ran her hand over the door, her heart so far in her throat, she had no words.

Bennett Worth.

She turned and just drew him, head to toe, into her mind, afraid he might vanish. He wore a white shirtwaist and a black cutaway and tie, as if he'd been out for dinner. Time had only broadened his shoulders, darkened his bronze hair, made him more devastatingly handsome. Her memories hadn't done him justice.

"Are you okay?" Bennett spoke just above a whisper, as if wrenching the words from deep inside some sequestered place.

She stared up at him, trying to scrape up an answer, willing herself not to weep at the sight of him.

"You look like you've been crying."

She pressed a hand to her cheek, found it hot, wet. "I—I had a fight with Foster."

He drew in a breath. Nodded. "He's downstairs, drunk and angry."

"Was that you fighting with him?"

"Unfortunately, yes. I was—I was worried for you. I know how he gets when he's angry and drunk."

He smelled the same—that exotic, spicy scent that she'd never forgotten. Sometimes, if she picked up a whiff of it in Harrods or Macy's, she would stop, find herself again in his arms. Lose herself for a moment in the if-onlys.

"What are you doing here?" This time her voice held disbelief, short and shaky with emotion.

Bennett looked away from her, as if her question wounded him. "He asked me to stop by, when I saw him today."

"Where did you see him?"

He drew in a breath. "At the Knickerbockers." He cleared his throat. "But he asked me to stop by days ago too, when I returned to America. I should have come sooner." The reason for his absence rose in his eyes. His mouth tightened, his voice softening. "Are you all right?"

Oh, she'd missed him, and it all rose up inside her. But the past was lost. "I'm fine—"

But he reached out, touched her arm, and she cried out.

He yanked his hand back. Stared at her. She caught his gaze and couldn't bear it.

"I knew it—he's hurt you."

She started to shake her head but he took her hand and, before she could protest, drew her sleeve up all the way to the now purpling bruise on her arm. He stared at it, a terrible expression on his face. Cursed. "I'm going to kill him."

"He's my husband—"

"It doesn't mean he can hurt you." His words were clipped, but she felt the fury in them.

"He's spent his life hurting me," she said before she could stop herself. The look he gave her made her eyes fill, made her turn away.

"I should have never left. I should have *made* you come with me. Why did you turn me down, Jinx?"

"I wanted to come with you, more than you know." She closed her eyes. "I was afraid."

"Afraid of what?"

Losing her place in society. Losing her world. But she'd lost it the day he'd left.

"I missed you," she said softly.

He drew in a breath, as if reeling in her words. She wanted to look at him, but she feared the power of his gaze. The terrible longing that must be in hers. "But you still can't come with me, can you?"

She listened to him breathe, in and out, so much between them she didn't know how to breach it. Just stood there, her back to him, until she heard him move. She whirled around just as he reached and the door, and lunged for him. But he moved out of her reach, opened the door.

Then he turned, his eyes hard. "I would have given you a different life. A happier life."

His words hollowed her out as he shut the door behind him.

It took a moment, but the words hiccupped out of her. "No. Bennett, don't go…"

She didn't care what society thought, what Foster might do. She flung open the door, but Bennett had already vanished. She gathered up her gown, fled from the room, down the hall, bathed only by the moonlight.

She had nearly reached the stairs when she heard the shot. It popped, resounded through the house, shaking her to her bones. She stopped, caught her breath. Then— "Bennett!" She raced down the stairs, the light from Foster's office still spilling through the open doorway. "Bennett!" She heard footsteps down the hall but didn't look, fear making her lunge into the room.

But it wasn't Bennett who lay face down in front of the hearth, his blood oozing onto the Turkish carpet from the wound in his skull. Behind him lay a dueling pistol. Beside the fireplace, the garden door lay ajar.

"Foster!" She ran to him, rolled him over. His eyes already glassy, he stared at her unseeing, his mouth open. Blood puddled the floor, her robe. She pulled back her hands, stared at them, dripping. "Oh—oh…"

Behind her, she heard a scream. She turned. Amelia stood in the doorway.

A scuffling noise sounded in the garden. A shadow appeared, someone—

"Jinx!" The voice turned her again and Bennett stood in the foyer of the house, his coat on, his hat in hand. "Jinx, what happened?"

Words stuttered out of her, but she couldn't make them clear.

Bennett's mouth opened as he entered the room, horror on his face. "Jinx, what have you done?"

Chapter 17

Come home.

The words on the telegram pulsed inside her as Esme stepped onto the platform at Grand Central Terminal, caught at once by the pace of the city. Women pushed baby carriages, men carried cases, and soldiers in uniform, too many with the lines of war etched into their faces, bustled through the marble expanse. At the far end, the brass clock showed the early hour.

She couldn't wait to surprise her father.

"This station is enormous," Lilly said beside her. Esme had managed to coax her daughter into a dress, her long dark braids hanging down under a straw hat. "And it smells funny."

"That's the smell of the city. Of people. Of life." Esme took her daughter's hand, despite Lilly's efforts to dodge her, and pulled her through the terminal. The porters would ferry their trunks to her parents' home.

They emerged onto Park Avenue and a porter called them a taxi. A yellow Model A pulled up and Esme climbed with Lilly into the back. "The Chronicle Building, please." She'd debated since Chicago where to head first, and the words simply emerged. The *Chronicle*, to her father's office.

The driver turned down Forty-second Street and Esme settled back in the seat, pressed her hand on her stomach. She'd purchased a new suit in Chicago, a V-necked blouse, a skirt, a low-belted jacket. She'd long ago shortened her skirts to compensate for the mud in Silver City; now it seemed she fit right in to fashion.

"You used to live here?" Lilly pressed herself against the window as they turned left on Broadway. They passed trolley cars pulled by horses, walking alongside streetcars and open-cab Dodge and Buick tourers and four-door roadsters, shiny Rolls Royce runabouts, and delivery cars painted in fresh blue and red. Theaters—the Casino, the Winter Gardens, and the Knickerbocker—loomed above her, their bright lights chronicling the shows—*Oh! Boy,* and *King Lear,* the Ziegfeld Follies at the New Amsterdam Theater. As they passed The Metropolitan Opera House, rich memories washed over her—Wagner's *Huldigungsmarsch,* and Liszt's *Polonaise,* standing in the cold, the January wind finding her skin despite her mink coat as they waited for their carriage, her hand tucked into her father's arm.

"Yes, I used to live here," Esme said quietly.

She drew her breath in as the Chronicle Building came into view. It hadn't changed in nearly twenty years. Minerva and the bell ringers still graced the apex of the building. The arched doorways beckoned welcome. The pigeons took roost on the lamppost out front where the newsies once lounged.

The driver pulled over across the street and helped them out.

"Do you wish that I wait?" he asked in an accent she placed as Irish. Across the street, the elevated train rumbled by.

Lilly had a tight grip on her hand.

"No, thank you," Esme said, paying him. She stopped for a moment and simply smelled the city, the smoke and oil from the train, the trolleys, the animal scents still cluttering the street, the odor of gasoline, the smell of chestnuts roasting, the hubbub of pedestrians passing by.

"Extra, extra, read all about it! Local heiress accused of murder!"

Esme caught the ring of a local newsie, his voice rising from his perch on the corner. She glanced at him, tempted, for a moment, to press a dime into his hand, to buy herself a crisp paper, to smell the newsprint.

Read the headline.

But her father beckoned.

She waited then scooted Lilly across the street, between trolley cars.

Esme stopped for a moment under the statue of her father.

"Is that my grandfather?" Lilly asked.

"Yes," Esme said, and turned to see if he might be looking down on her from his round window. The window remained dark.

As they entered, her gaze went to the cloakroom, where Oliver had hidden her from her father, where he'd declared his love for her.

Unexpected tears pricked her eyes. So long ago, but the grief came at her, fresh, blunt. She drew in a quick breath.

"It smells like the *Times*," Lilly said, standing in the middle of the circular room.

"It's the newsprint," Esme said, finding herself again. "The pressroom is right through those doors." She pointed to her left.

She wasn't a desperate young woman any longer, afraid of her father's wrath. She had a business, a fortune of her own.

She'd been married, lost a husband, had a daughter.

She was long over Oliver and the effect of his memory running rampant through her heart.

"Let's go meet your grandfather," Esme said and led Lilly up the stairs to the *Chronicle* offices.

Although the *Copper Valley Times* had expanded into the mercantile next door, and although Esme had acquired three more linotype machines and a rotary press, the breadth of the *New York Chronicle*'s city department, the row of editorial offices on both sides of the building, the massive library, could cause her baroness heart to leap. The *Chronicle* had such power, such influence.

She could admit that she still someday hoped to helm it.

She entered the reception area, half expecting someone she might know. A broad woman in a suit sat at the desk, her dark hair piled behind her head. She looked up, offering a smile that didn't quite meet her gray eyes. "Can I help you?"

"I'm here to see the publisher," Esme said, tucking her arm around Lilly.

"He's not in yet."

Esme glanced at the clock. Nearly 9 a.m. "That's not like him."

"No," she said. "He had a family emergency of some sort. You may wait, if you'd like." She gestured to a bench along the wall.

Esme glanced at the closed door. "I'd rather wait in his office and surprise him."

The woman gave her a look. "I don't think that would be appropriate."

Esme smiled. "No, you don't understand. I'm his daughter. And this is his granddaughter, Lilly."

The woman's smile fell, her eyes narrowing. "I'm not sure what kind of trick you're playing, but he doesn't have a daughter. Or a wife, for that matter. Perhaps you should leave."

Esme's heartbeat quickened at her words, a hiccup of her breath. "Perhaps we're not talking about the same person. I'm looking for August Price. I'm his daughter, Esme."

The woman wore the pallor of a Montana winter. She swallowed, and it was the way her hands shook before she clasped them in her lap that unnerved Esme the most. She managed another smile, this one kinder than the last. "I'm sorry, Miss Price, but your father hasn't been the publisher here for two years. He's…"

Esme pressed her hand to her stomach.

"He's resting comfortably at home, waiting for his time."

The clocked chipped away at her heartbeat as she tried to find a response, anything but to stand there numbly, staring at the poor woman. Finally, Lilly took her hand. "Mama?"

Esme glanced at Lilly, saw her standing there, stricken.

At home. "He's not dead, then?" It sounded stupid to say, but the words issued from her before she could pull them back, the desperation in her tone making even the secretary wince.

"A stroke, ma'am. He has some facilities, but only on a good day."

A stroke. How could they not have told her, not have sent a telegram? Heat started in her stomach, spread out through her body, took over her muscles.

"Come, Lilly," she said, turning. Then, "I'd like a copy of today's paper, please."

The secretary handed it over and Esme folded it, tucking it under her arm.

They entered the street, the heat now turning to waves in her brain. She squeezed Lilly's hand and hailed a cab, not caring about decorum. She'd lived too long in the West to care that people might think she'd turned bohemian. Wild.

In fact, a part of her had.

She climbed into the cab. "Six forty-five Fifth Avenue, please."

Lilly tucked in beside her, very quiet.

Esme held the paper on her lap. "They couldn't send me a telegram?" She shook her head, stared out the window. The city seemed dirty, still emerging from winter, black snow lining the gutters. "I suppose this is what I get, what I should have expected. But if they weren't going to cable me when Father had his stroke, then why now?"

Come home. Only two words, and she'd just assumed they were from her father. The sender was, simply, *The New York Chronicle.*

Someone else from the *Chronicle* had sent it to her.

She'd stopped sending the *Times* thirteen years ago. How had anyone known where to find her?

They passed a brand-new hotel on the corner of Central Park, pigeons waddling around the fountain in search of sustenance. Lilly's gaze glued on the magnificent row of residences of high society's "400." She wondered if Mrs. Astor still had her New Year's ball.

Probably Jinx and Foster lived somewhere on this side of town.

Esme opened the paper. Stared at the headline, read it again.

"What is it?" Lilly leaned back, tried to read over her shoulder.

Esme could barely mouth the words. No, it couldn't be— "Your aunt Jinx is in jail for murder."

* * * * *

The last week had turned into such a snarl of events, Jinx could barely sort it all out. She'd been standing above Foster's body, his blood seeping into her dressing gown, her skin. Bennett had arrived—no, he came before, to her room. Then he'd left her, and—yes, he was wearing his coat, carrying his gloves, clearly leaving. And Amelia had appeared, then, behind her, Neville, and Lewis. Someone had screamed, and it seemed Bennett had pulled her away from the body, held her, although even when she recounted it to her counsel, Jinx couldn't be sure.

Yes, yes, she had been in her room. Yes, she'd seen the dueling pistols.

Yes, she'd wanted him dead. That confession came out in a rush, harsh and angry after the police had the impudence to drag her from her home—they'd barely allowed her to dress—to the Tombs, where they interrogated her.

Yes, she wanted him dead, but she didn't kill him. No, she didn't have a reason to kill him. Yes, sometimes he used his fists on her, but he had that right, didn't he?

Yes, she knew how to fire a gun—had done it for entertainment at a number of Newport picnics. Foster had even sent her to a private tutor.

And yes, okay, yes, she had wanted him dead! Yes, she'd fought with him just that evening over their son, over the war, over her fear that he would die in battle. Of course she loved her country, but she loved her son more—that wasn't so hard to understand, right?

She'd gone to her room after the fight. What brought her downstairs? Noises. Yes, noises. And…

No, of course she didn't plan it. No, she didn't wait until his back was turned, take the dueling pistol, point it toward his head, pull the trigger.

Who else could have killed him?

She needed a drink, licked her lips instead, not sure where to start. She thought they'd offered her a drink then, but she couldn't be sure.

Yes, of course she was alone, who else would she have been with? She remembered that statement, remembered the silence that echoed through the interrogation room, the way she folded her hands on the chipped wood table, praying her heart wouldn't betray her.

No one could find out that Bennett had come to her. Not without asking why. Not without discovering the truth.

Of course, she'd read about the Tombs, the Manhattan House of Detention, heard about the bridge of sighs that convicts would traverse on their way to a hanging. Heard that convicts hurled themselves from the third-floor tier rather than endure their stay, but truly, she didn't kill him. She shouldn't be here.

They'd hadn't even had the decency to put her in the cells next to the warden's residence that overlooked Centre Street.

Instead, they'd shoved her onto the top floor of the women's prison, like an ordinary criminal, her cell overlooking a vast inside courtyard, open to the view of the woman across the thirty-foot channel. Jinx sat on the metal bed in her five-foot cell, unmoving, hungry, shaking, watching a roach climb through a crack in the wall, back and forth, between her cell and her neighbor's. She watched the sunlight appear from the street outside, a fluid orange on the opaque window that ran floor to ceiling in the cell, the height of all three tiers. Bars crisscrossed it, cutting through the wan daylight.

They'd taken her reticule and given her instead an aluminum spoon, large bowl, and a cup. Her money they'd replaced with aluminum chips, used as currency, and on her first full day, a commissary man entered the floor, selling combs and writing paper. He also had sandwiches, but they smelled so rancid Jinx decided to continue her fast.

Surely someone would come for her.

Her counsel appeared early the second day. Mr. Loren, a tall, pinched man with no chin and hard eyes. He had her read a confession she didn't remember giving.

"Are you sure no one else could have committed this murder?"

She'd paused on the question long enough for him to ask it again.

"No. None that I can think of."

Bennett wouldn't kill his own brother, would he?

I'm going to kill him.

Bennett's words, softly, lethally spoken in her chamber, rattled through her again, and yet again. What if he'd gone downstairs, found Foster—

But he'd been standing in the foyer in his coat, had appeared genuinely horrified.

Repulsed at what she'd allowed her life to become.

I can't believe you didn't come to me. I would have given you a different life. A happier life.

Down the hallway, a woman hummed, a haunting melody that made Jinx put her hands over her ears. It drummed inside her, however, something mournful and raw. She scooted to the back of her bunk, pulled her legs to herself, wrapped her arms around her knees. She had refused to use the toilet in her cell, in view of all the world, until the urge became too much, and nothing would make her lay her head on the lice-infested wool blanket. But exhaustion ripped through her, her limbs on fire, her brain foggy, until she collapsed in slumber.

She hadn't killed her husband, had she? She braced her forehead on her knees. Why had no one come for her? Her mother, certainly, should have heard the news, should be fighting for her freedom. She, better than anyone, knew how cruel Foster could be.

Maybe it was best if the police didn't talk to her mother.

Oh…the news. She pressed a hand to her throat. Foster's murder would have made the papers.

She'd always longed to make the front pages, something beyond Page Six, but for some grand ball, perhaps, or a charity event she'd hosted.

She might be ill.

"Mrs. Worth, you have a visitor."

She looked up at the voice, the matron, a large woman who might have made an excellent housekeeper the way she communicated authority. Jinx got up, ran her hands over her skirt. It was about time someone came to get her. Finally. Perhaps they'd found the real killer.

She kept her head up as prisoners called to her, names that made her ears burn. Yes, well, they belonged here, not her.

They walked through the doors at the end of the cellblock, the steel grating through her, resounding in her spine, then she followed the matron down the hall to the Police Court entrance.

A guard looked her over, revulsion in his eyes.

She must look a wreck—she didn't even want to imagine what she must smell like, but— "Get your eyes off me," she snapped.

The matron opened an inner door and she stepped through, expecting to see the tall pensive form of Mr. Loren.

No. Bennett waited on a wooden chair, his hat between his fingers, lines drawn into his face. He looked up at her, something so raw in his beautiful eyes, it made her heart lurch.

Bennett rose as she walked over. "Are you well?" His voice, however, came from far away, as if he'd had to pull out a vellum card and read the words to know what to say.

"I'm fatigued and tired of this game the police are playing. I want to leave this awful place."

"Your counsel is working on getting your confession overturned—he said you hadn't signed it, that you had no recollection of your words."

"I confessed to nothing." Or had she? She shook her head, ran her fingers over her eyes. She needed a bath and a long rest. Then she might be able to unravel the last few days. Forget them even. "Did they find the murderer?"

Bennett drew in a breath, looked away.

"What is it?" She pressed a hand to her stomach. She should eat something, and soon.

"It's Jack," Bennett said quietly. "They're interrogating Jack for Foster's murder. They think it was he who went out the garden door."

"No"

"He told them that he saw his father push you, that he heard your argument—"

How much had Jack heard? She tried to unsnarl their conversation, but it all ran together. "But you were there—you said you fought with Foster."

"I did. But Jack must have been standing outside the door in the garden." His voice turned low. "Jinx, I heard him tell the police at the scene that he wanted his father dead."

Her world dropped from beneath her then, her knees simply surrendering, and she hit the floor hard, slapping her head against the brick wall.

"Jinx!"

She held her face in her hands, heard a moaning, and realized it came from herself. "No, no—"

She felt Bennett's hands on her back, as if to pull her into an embrace, but she pushed on his chest, away from him. "How could you let this happen? You know Jack couldn't have done this!"

He drew in a quick breath, searching her face. "What do you mean? He told me he hated Foster. And I wouldn't have believed that Foster had the capability to hurt people like he did, but you knew his cruelty. Why wouldn't his son be the same way?"

She slapped him. Hard, and it stung her hand. He recoiled, flinching.

"Get away from me. Just get away."

He stared at her, unmoving. He didn't even put his hand on the red bleeding into his cheek.

She drew in a trembling breath, couldn't look at him. "Jack didn't kill Foster. He could never kill anyone. Jack's not that kind of man."

"Is it so hard to believe that Foster's son could turn out just like him? Open your eyes, Jinx—"

"No, you open your eyes, Bennett Worth. Is it so hard for you to recognize your own son?" Her voice turned rich and dark. "That's why I know he could never kill a man—he *is* his father's son."

Only Bennett's breath, wavering as he searched her face for the truth, betrayed the impact of her words.

He closed his eyes, his face tight with emotion. "No. That's not true. You told me that he wasn't my child. You said—"

"I lied! I lied so you would have a life. You're right, Foster was unbearably cruel and he would have destroyed you. Destroyed me."

"Destroyed the life you'd built, you mean." Bennett backed away, his hand up. "I wanted you, Jinx. I sent you a note, told you I would wait. But you sent it back, torn into pieces."

"No—no, I never received your note. I did come, but…Lewis was there. He gave you…Oh." Her hand covered her mouth. "Foster found your note. *He's* the one who sent it back."

Bennett drew in a quick breath. Looked away. "I should have guessed."

"I feared for you," she said quietly.

"You feared for yourself, Jinx. Yes, Foster would have tried to destroy us, but perhaps we would have found a new life. Maybe you wouldn't have appeared every week on the society pages, perhaps you would have lived without an army of servants, but we would have been happy."

She looked away from him.

He ran his hand through his hair then met her eyes. "The shyster was going to leave you, Jinx. He had a plan to take everything, leave you penniless and marry some actress he was seeing. I met her Sunday afternoon at the Knickerbocker Theater. She—she attended with Foster."

"A blond, tall and willowy?"

He looked at her, frowned. "You knew about her?"

"Her name is Flora St. John. Foster didn't bother to hide it. Sometimes even brought her to the house. She's one of Ziegfeld's girls." Jinx had stayed in her room, the laughter from next door seeping through the walls. "Foster wanted to hurt me."

Bennett stared at her. "You knew and you didn't care? I thought you loved him."

She gave a harsh, ugly laugh. "Why would you ever think that?"

"Besides the fact that you didn't want me? How about the fact that you had a daughter with him? Unless—"

"Don't even say it. I've been faithful every day of my life." She held his gaze, daring Bennett to argue.

"Then why, if you didn't love him?"

"A woman's duty is to her husband. Even if she despises him. Even if he comes home drunk and invades her room. Even if she screams and fights him." She looked away then, refusing the tears. "Rosie was the only good thing to come from my marriage to Foster. She must never know the circumstances of her birth."

Bennett's face twitched with a sort of dark emotion. "I want to walk away from you, to hurt something or someone for the rage I feel, the frustration of knowing that everything I feared for the last seventeen years indeed came to pass. My child, the woman I love, trapped—by her own pride—in a marriage that destroyed her."

His voice changed, carried a ragged edge. "After leaving you in Newport, I tried to forget you. I tried to fall in love, to find a wife, but I couldn't dislodge you from my head, my heart. I dreamed of coming back to you, but every time I did, there you were, on Foster's arm. It ate me up from the inside, and I tried to stop caring.

She reached out to him, then, but he jerked away, his jaw hardening. "I told myself that you deserved your wretched life, that I was better off for not being around you, not letting you inside to destroy me."

His words were a knife, and she flinched. Indeed, she did deserve it. She'd created this world, clung to her empty life, her wretched marriage— her pride—and put herself in this prison.

Then he turned back to her, touched his hand to her face. His eyes glinted. "But, Jinx, I love you. I've never stopped hoping that you might come to me, that you might someday love me."

She caught her breath. Oh, she did love him. Had never stopped. She leaned into his touch, the words in her chest. "Bennett, I—"

"I went to Foster's office two days before I came to see you, and he told me how he was going to leave you, and like an idiot, I actually pleaded with him not to. I told him that you had helped him build his life, his position, his power, and that he should be the husband he'd promised to be. And then, he accused me of being in love with you."

She read his face, as probably did Foster, and saw the truth. "Oh Bennett."

"And then he said that he always knew you loved me too. That you hadn't been faithful to him that summer at Newport, that he knew Jack wasn't his. He looked too much like me, soft and bookish, not enough fire in him."

She called that gentle and patient, a man of honor.

But, of course Foster would have seen Bennett in Jack. She'd been a fool to think he wouldn't.

"That's why I came to you—I feared what he might do to you. I'd hoped that you would be glad to see me. I guess I had some sort of idea that, after all this, you might be willing to ignore the scandal and follow your heart."

"Yes, Bennett—"

"I've never stopped loving you, and because of that I'm going to fix this, Jinx. I'm going to fix this, and save our—my—son, and then you're going to be free."

He got up, and before she could reach out for him, he knocked on the door to the interrogation cell. "Let me out of here."

* * * * *

The house on Fifth Avenue still possessed the power to reduce Esme's resolve to ash, to turn her into a debutante, bidden by her parents to marry a man she despised. She stood on the steps after the taxi left them off, remembering Oliver's face as her father's footmen threw him into the night, her father's decree that she would marry Foster by the next night.

She had vowed never to return.

"Are you going to ring the bell?" Lilly said beside her. She had already lifted her hand twice, and Esme took a hold of it.

"Some things take some working up to," she said, smoothing her jacket. She pressed the bell. It tolled deep inside the house and she glanced at Lilly, who smiled up at her, more excitement than trepidation in her eyes. And why not? She hadn't left her home in the middle of the night, a fugitive from matrimony.

But Esme wasn't that woman anymore.

The door opened and she stared up at Pierce Stewart, Oliver's father, their butler. Nothing of recognition flickered in his eyes—not at first. Then, "Oh my, Miss Esme, you've returned."

And just like that, life filled her lungs. She hadn't realized she'd been holding her breath. "Hello, Pierce. Is my father in?"

He raised an eyebrow as he moved away from the door to allow her inside. She pushed Lilly in front of her, watching her daughter's reaction to the grand marble entrance, the arched ceilings, the parquet wood floor. Their entire first floor back in Montana might fit, although snugly, inside just the entrance hall. Sunlight fell in dusty streams to the floor like spotlights. "I'll inform him that you have arrived," he said and moved down the hall to the drawing room.

"Miss Esme, is that really you?"

She turned at the voice, so familiar, so forgotten. "Bette. I can't believe you're still here." Bette probably looked to her as she did to her former lady's maid, the padding to her figure, the beginning of lines upon her face. Her dark hair showed just the finest hint of white, but she appeared capable and with an air that bespoke her promotion to head of the female staff.

"Aye, ma'am. Your mother kept me on even after..." She swallowed. "I became the housekeeper of the Fifth Avenue chateau only a few years ago." Her gaze fell on Lilly, who had wandered away to examine a portrait of her grandparents hanging in the banquet hall.

"This is my daughter, Lillian Joy Hoyt."

Lillian turned at her name, gave a curtsey that could have knocked Esme over with a breath. So her daughter had managed to retain some of her instruction.

"Your father is ready to see you," Pierce said and stood aside.

She didn't know why she expected him unchanged, tall and strong, with those eyes that could bring someone to their knees, confess their sins. He'd had dark, barely salted hair when she'd left, and the last thing she remembered was his strong hand on her arm right before she'd escaped his office.

Now, those hands curled into themselves on his lap, his shoulders bowed as he slouched in a wheelchair on the hearth before the fire. He wore a blanket over his knees, and a strap around his chest kept him from pitching completely forward. He stared into the fire, unseeing.

August Price had shriveled into a broken, elderly man.

She glanced at Pierce, who gave her a tight, slim smile. She reached out and took Lilly's hand and entered the room.

"Father, it's Esme." No reaction as she slipped close to him, the ache inside almost devouring her. Why hadn't she returned sooner? Letting go of Lilly's hand, she crouched before the wheelchair. "I'm sorry I didn't come home sooner, Father. But I'm here now. And I've brought you a granddaughter." She glanced up at Lilly, who stared down at the old man with a sort of undisguised tragedy in her expression. Esme wanted to admonish her to wipe it away, but she considered that she too wore such a look.

Why had she let her pride steal her inheritance, a grandfather for her child?

Esme tried to remove the heartache from her voice. "I married a wonderfully kind man. You may have heard of him—Daughtry Hoyt. He attended a few social events with you years ago. He owned a copper mine in Montana and he loved me very much. He died trying to help some of his miners caught in a cave-in." Those words seemed closer suddenly, the grief, for a moment, fresh in her throat.

"You would have liked him. He was very proud of me." She swallowed, ran her gloved hand under her eye. "He gave me a daughter before he died—Lillian Joy. She's thirteen years old, and just like you. Stubborn and smart and beautiful." She eyed Lilly, who bit her bottom lip and turned away.

"I own the mine now, but I also own a number of newspapers. We have a daily and two weeklies." She put her hand on his on his lap, found it small and frail. "I'm a publisher, just like you."

Did his eyes flick over at her? She wanted to believe it, wanted to know that, too, he'd squeezed her hand. Perhaps he did. Yes, his hand twitched, and there—again, a squeeze.

Esme touched it to her forehead, kissed the back of it.

"Oh, Father, I'm sorry it took me so long—"

"Esme?"

She turned. Her mother stood in the doorway, her hand pressed to her mouth. "I can't believe it. You came home!" She seemed to collect herself then, or wanted to, but gave up and crossed the room, her face betraying her. "Esme."

Phoebe, in a skirt and high-necked shirtwaist and leg o'mutton sleeves, had lost weight also, her bones delicate beneath Esme's embrace. She smelled of powder and all the indulgences Esme had left behind. "I never thought I'd see you again." She blinked fast, swallowed. Forced a smile. "And this lovely lady is—"

"Your granddaughter, Lilly Hoyt."

"Lilly," Phoebe said, holding out her hand. Lilly took it, the perfect debutante, and bowed her head.

"Such wonderful manners. I can see you are your mother's daughter."

Oh, sure she was.

Phoebe glanced at her husband, sitting in the chair. His blanket had become dislodged, falling off his knee. She fixed it then turned her back on him, looping her arm around Esme. "You look so fetching, daughter. You've come back to stay, I hope?"

Esme watched as Lilly roamed the room, stopping to take in an oil of Esme, painted, obviously, from her debut photograph, although she remembered burning her copy. The portrait hung above her father's desk. She tried not to compare herself to the flawless perfection of a lady groomed for presentation into society.

"I don't know. Lilly needs..." A father. A firm hand. Culture. "Schooling."

Lilly glanced at her and scowled. Ah, there was the daughter Esme knew.

"Why didn't you cable me when Father had his stroke? Why did you wait until now to ask me to come home?"

Phoebe frowned at her. "I didn't cable you, Esme. I...should have, I know. But I—I had my reasons."

"She was probably afraid of me. Probably afraid that I would hurt you again," said a voice behind them.

Phoebe stiffened.

Esme stilled, her breath caught in her chest, her pulse swishing in her ears. She turned.

No.

He was an older, more confident version of himself: dark hair too long for his attire, a gray striped waistcoat, tie, a wool suit with matching trousers. A gold pocket watch hung from his belt loop to his vest pocket. All the same, she recognized the flicker of emotion, a longing she had never quite forgotten. Nor had she forgotten his brown eyes that now peered right through her, snatched out her heart, and left her bereft.

"Oliver."

Chapter 18

Oliver.

She stared at him, everything that had happened so long ago suddenly fresh and brutal. "I thought you were dead. You died in the fire. I—I don't understand." She glanced at her mother, who turned immediately away.

No wonder Phoebe didn't want to cable her, to ask her to come home. Oliver's words suddenly burrowed deep. "She knew you were still alive."

Oliver stepped into the room, glanced at Phoebe, at her father. "I wasn't even around for the fire. I was on the police beat. I came back early in the morning, and Colleen told me that you were there, and that she'd told you she thought I had died. I searched everywhere for you and finally came here. Your mother met me at the door...."

Phoebe pursed her lips into a tight bud of annoyance.

"She told me that you had married Foster Worth. By the time I discovered it was a lie, you were long gone."

Esme rounded on her mother. "You lied to him? But you sent me away to marry him. You knew I loved him, and you *lied* to him."

Phoebe's mouth tightened at the edges. "I never really intended for you to marry him, Esme. I thought your infatuation would run its course, that someday you'd return, realize your folly, and marry a more suitable match."

"And in the meantime, Jinx married my fiancé."

Phoebe's gaze hardened. "Someone needed to, and she was in love with him. I had hoped she would have a better chance at love than you and Foster." She turned away then, staring out the window.

"The paper today said that Jinx murdered him."

"Jinx did no such thing," Phoebe said quietly. "Not that the paper gives her any grace."

"It's news, Mrs. Price."

"It's my daughter, Mr. Stewart."

A muscle pulled in Oliver's jaw.

Esme frowned at him. "What's going on here? Why... Oliver, did you take my sister's picture, did you put it in the paper?"

He walked over to her father, knelt before him, adjusted the blanket, fallen again. "How are you doing today, Mr. Price?"

"So, what—are you my father's valet too?"

He stood. "I work for your father, yes."

She stared at him, a roar consuming her, not even sure where to start. Perhaps with— "If mother didn't cable me, then who did? I got a cable from the *New York Chronicle*. I thought it came from my father, but apparently he's no longer in charge. So, who would cable me from the *Chronicle*?"

"The publisher?" He offered quietly.

"He wasn't in when I went to the paper. I can only hope he's not running the Price legacy into the ground."

"I can assure you that he's not." He picked up a poker, turned, and readjusted the logs in the fire. Sparks spit into the flue.

"How do you know? Maybe he asked me to come back because the paper is in trouble. Maybe he needs a Price at the helm."

"I doubt that."

She frowned at him. "Excuse me?" She turned to Lilly. "Let's—"

"I'm the publisher, Esme."

He said it so quietly, in a voice she'd used too many times during mine labor negotiations to defuse anger.

Now, it left her nonplussed. "What?"

"I'm the publisher, and the current managing editor of the *Chronicle*."

She shook her head. "No—no. You were—"

"A stringer. A beat photographer. I know. But after you left, I hit the road too. Moved to Chicago and got a job as a stringer. Eventually, I worked my way back to New York and applied for a job at the *Chronicle*. I'm not sure why, but your father took an interest in me. He put me on the city desk as a writer then made me an editor. I moved up from there. I've been running the paper for two years."

Two years. "You're running the paper?"

He nodded. "And I cabled you when your sister was arrested. I thought... well, it was time for you to come home." For the first time, something like hurt pressed into his gaze. He looked away. "I thought your family might need you."

Her voice dropped to a whisper. "You knew where I was, all this time, and you never...you never came after me?"

"You didn't come home, Esme. And then, of course, you got married." His eyes flickered to Lilly, who glared at him.

"How did you know that?"

"There was an announcement of your husband's death in the *New York World*."

"Pulitzer picked up the accident?"

"Hoyt sat on the stock exchange for a couple years. The paper listed your name as his surviving kin." He said it without rancor, except for his eyes.

"I didn't know you were alive!"

Lilly had moved over next to her, now stared at her mother. Esme schooled her voice. "You could have written to me. Could have come out to see me."

His mouth set in a dark line and she read the truth on his face. Unless— unless he hadn't really loved her. Hadn't really meant his words, *Come back to me, I'll be waiting right here for you.*

"Well, I'm home now, and I'm taking over my father's office," she said, using her Montana voice.

He set the poker back in the mount. "I don't think so. I knew the emotional strain on your father during Jinx's trial would be tremendous, and

I thought you might want to be with him. But the *Chronicle* doesn't need your help."

She didn't recognize this man, the one who now picked out his pocket watch, read the time, returned it.

"Doesn't need my help? I am a Price. I am my father's heiress. I will take over the newspaper, and you have no say in it."

"Your father gave me power of attorney should he ever fall ill. I have every say in it." He moved toward the door. "And, I have to get back to work. I have a trial to cover."

Twenty years in the West had scrubbed all the decorum from Esme. She moved into his way, ignored his startled expression. "My sister's trial?"

He looked at Phoebe. "I just returned from court. She is supposed to appear in the Court of Special Session tomorrow morning, to see if they have enough evidence to hold her for the crime of murder."

He looked back at Esme, nothing of a smile on his face. Oh, she hated how, even now, she could find him so devastatingly handsome. And how, after twenty years, he could still make her heart leave her chest. He smelled good—a sort of mint upon his skin—and had freshly shaven. What had happened to the zealous photographer who had once kissed her under the lamplights in Central Park?

She managed to tamp down the emotion in her voice. "Jinx didn't do it. I know I haven't seen her for twenty years, but my sister could never murder someone, especially her husband."

"You don't know Foster Worth."

"But I do know my sister."

"The same one who stole your fiancé?"

I didn't love him. The words nearly leaked out. *I loved you.*

But maybe he hadn't loved her, not really. And certainly, from the way he looked at her now, a chill in his expression, he no longer dreamed of her return to his arms.

She backed away from him, glanced again at her father, still staring into the crackling fire. "I'm going to prove she didn't do it, Oliver, and when I do, the *Chronicle* is going to run a front-page article proclaiming her innocence. And then we'll see who becomes publisher of the *New York Chronicle*."

His smile vanished. "Welcome home, Esme Hoyt."

"Price," she snapped. "The name is Esme Price Hoyt."

* * * * *

How much had Jack heard of the quarrels that night in their home? Foster's accusation that Jack wasn't his son? Had he seen Foster threaten her?

Jinx sat in her cell, reeling back her conversation with Bennett.

But, Jinx, I love you. I've never stopped hoping that you might come to me, that you might someday love me.

She pressed her hands into her eyes, not caring how wretched she might look. *I loved you too, Bennett.* And Jack had been that reminder of the one brief moment when she'd felt loved back.

She'd been such a dupe to think that the glittering parties, the social power, her inheritance might be enough to balm the wounds Bennett's leaving inflicted.

I've never stopped loving you, and because of that I'm going to fix this, Jinx. I'm going to fix this, and save our—my—son, and then you're going to be free.

Probably he would dig into the Worth family fortune, make a contribution to the judge's larder.

But what if it didn't work? Worse, what if they still blamed Jack?

Please. She closed her eyes, not sure where to start, hearing what sounded more like a wail. *Please, God, save us.*

But why should the Almighty listen to her—she'd managed to tangle her life into a web of lies and betrayals. No, she was on her own.

Jinx lay on the bunk, finally giving in to exhaustion, not caring what climbed into her hair. She allowed herself a few spoonfuls of the chicken soup at lunchtime, and as the sun fell, her cell darkening with the shadows, she counted her breaths, the bricks in the walls, listened to the memory of Jack's laughter, Rosie's singing.

Feet upon the concrete. They stopped at her cell. "Visitor for you."

Jinx sat up, didn't bother to smooth her skirt, fix her hair. She shuffled down the hallway, back to the interrogation room.

A woman stood, her back to her, staring out onto Centre Street. Dressed in a belted suit coat, a skirt that hung just above her ankles, a smart, wide-brimmed hat, she held her dark gloves in her hand.

Jinx folded her hands over her chest and tried not to flinch when the bolt slid shut behind her. "Who are you?"

She turned, and words sloughed out of Jinx. She pressed her hand to her mouth, the other around her waist.

"Hello, Jinx."

She was so beautiful, even more than when she'd left; tall and graceful, her blond hair secured low on her neck, a gentleness about her smile Jinx had never seen before. "Esme."

They stared at each other a long, pulsed moment. Then Esme came and put her arms around her, pulled her close. "It's going to be okay."

Jinx wrapped her arms around her and sobbed.

Esme held her and said nothing.

Jinx knew that she had become loud, a soggy mess, a social misfit as she clung to her sister. But something about Esme's appearance, the smell of her, clean and fashionable, healthy and whole... "I missed you. I really missed you."

She hadn't realized how much until that moment. "I'm so sorry for what I did, for stealing Foster from you."

She felt Esme's hand on her hair. "I think you've suffered much more than I have."

Jinx drew away from her, but there was nothing of malice in Esme's expression. "He was an awful man." She looked away, her eyes soggy, and accepted her sister's handkerchief when she offered it. "I hated him. And frankly, yes, I wanted him dead." She wiped her face, turned back to her sister. "But I didn't kill him."

"I know you didn't."

Her words unknotted something in Jinx's chest, and for the first time in five days, she could breathe. Full and clean and— "You believe me?"

"Of course I do." Esme took her hand. "I'm your sister, right?"

Jinx could only nod.

"So, let's figure out who did."

Jinx nodded again.

"Which means you'll have to tell me what happened, Jinx."

Jinx drew in a breath, nodded.

"With words."

Jinx allowed a smile to press through her tears. "I'm not sure where to start."

Esme pulled out a chair, dropped a notebook on the rough-hewn table. "How about with a list of people who might want to hurt Foster?"

"Name anyone in New York City. He's a shrewd businessman, he has had affairs with the wives of politicians and judges, not to mention his harem of floozies down on Broadway."

Esme stared at her, probably shocked by the lack of venom in Jinx's voice. "He cheated on you?"

"Nearly from the day we married. I think he was angry that—that I wasn't you."

Esme blinked at that, drew in a breath. "I'm sorry either of us had to marry him."

"Did you ever get married?"

"Yes. I have a daughter."

"And your husband?"

"He died before she was born."

Jinx stared out the window, barred though it was, onto Centre Street, the street cars, the late afternoon foot traffic, a newsie on the corner, hawking his rag. "Oliver Stewart is publisher of the *Chronicle*."

"I know."

"Mother told me he was dead. He moved away, out west someplace. He showed back up about ten years ago, started working for Father."

"He wants to control the paper."

Jinx smiled. "But you're not going to let that happen, are you?"

A muscle pulled in Esme's jaw. She narrowed her eyes. "Tell me about these affairs—did Foster ever have a jealous husband come after him?"

"Not that I know of. But according to Bennett, he was going to leave me for Flora St. John. She's a Ziegfeld girl down at the New Amsterdam Theater."

"Bennett?"

Jinx drew in a breath. "Foster's brother. Probably you remember him— Bennett Worth?"

"Yes…he was the wild one, wasn't he?"

"I think Foster had him beat. Bennett is…underestimated."

Esme considered her. "You and Bennett are friends."

Jinx looked out the window again. "We were, once." *I guess I had some sort of idea that, after all this, you might be willing to ignore the scandal and follow your heart.* She stiffened. Looked at Esme. "Actually, that's not true. He's the father of my son, Jack."

Esme blinked at her. Put down her pen.

Opened her mouth. Finally. "Oh, Jinx."

She nodded. "I loved him, and I probably should have left Foster, but…"

"You couldn't live with the scandal."

"Yes. Or the fear. Foster was a despicable man."

"You mustn't tell a soul about Bennett, Jinx. It won't matter that Foster cheated on you with every woman in town. It's more evidence against you."

"I might as well move to Baltimore, or Philadelphia." Jinx smiled at Esme.

Esme smiled back. "Perhaps."

Jinx sighed. "I'm tired of living with lies. I'm tired of always trying so hard to please everyone. I've been living in the tombs long before this."

Esme's smile vanished. "I have to ask, Jinx. Do you think Bennett could have killed Foster? Perhaps out of jealousy?"

"No. Never. He—he didn't know Jack was his until today."

Esme glanced at her, her lips drawing to a thin line.

"I couldn't tell him. It would only make my staying with Foster more horrible. But the murderer had to be someone Foster knew, someone he trusted, because whoever it was shot him in the back of the head at close range. There was so much blood, Esme. So much."

"Shh...we'll find out who did this." Esme reached out for her, but the door opened.

Jinx turned. The matron stood before her.

"You're free to go, Mrs. Worth. They've caught the murderer."

Oh, yes, thank you—

"Bennett Worth has just confessed."

* * * * *

Esme had never been allowed to see vaudeville. She'd read about it, of course, in the occasional copy of the *Chronicle,* but as she stared at the playbill outside the theater, advertising the upcoming performances of the Follies and the late-night, rooftop *Midnight Frolic,* she considered she just might be in over her head.

Jinx looked so wrung out, it undid Esme just a little, her confidence deflating as she escorted Jinx home, wrangling them through the throng of reporters. She looked for Oliver but didn't see him.

A chill seeped under her coat in the mausoleum of a home Jinx had built, despite the French paintings, the tapestries, the renaissance style. While Lilly roamed the house on a tour with her cousin Rosie, Esme drew a hot bath for Jinx, tucked her into her bed afterwards, instructed Amelia to light a fire, and inspected Jinx's closet for something that might make herself appear younger.

Rosie might have a better chance at posing as a Ziegfeld girl than Esme did, but she managed to find a V-necked dress that swept age from her appearance. She added a peacock-blue cape with a gold brocade trim. If only she had shorter hair like Jinx's and Rosie's. Apparently the New York fashion meant she had to chop off her long hair.

She tucked her mane instead inside a turban embellished with a dahlia flower, from Rosie's wardrobe. She simply needed to get inside the dressing room at the theater, get close to Flora.

She counted on the prestige of netting a millionaire to get Flora bragging...and to the truth.

Now, Esme stood outside the theater, reading the playbill of the upcoming show opening in June. Bert Williams, Fanny Brice, Eddie Cantor, Will Rogers, and The Fairbanks Twins. Rosie's words as she helped her with her makeup returned to her. "Last year, Ziegfeld's girls danced on an electric mat that shot sparks from their shoes, wearing rose costumes. I heard that William Randolph Hearst sat in the same orchestra seat every night for eight weeks. Apparently he had a thing for Miss Davies, one of the girls."

Lilly, of course, watched Rosie with wide, hungry eyes.

"W. C. Fields was there, and this absolutely dashing cowboy—Will Rogers—who did tricks with his rope."

"A lariat," Lilly said quietly.

Rose looked at her, raised an eyebrow.

"The rope—it's called a lariat. I have one at home."

"Are you a cowgirl like Annie Oakley?" The way Rosie said it, it made Esme want to protect Lilly, but apparently her daughter needed no protecting.

"No. I'm a better shot than Annie Oakley."

Esme smiled even now, as she made her way down the alleyway to the side entrance. Indeed, Lilly was a much better shot.

Esme could hear the music as she opened the door.

A man sat at a table, arms folded.

"I'm sorry I'm late for rehearsal." She smiled at him, hoping the shadows were kind to her masquerade.

She began breathing again as she made her way down the corridor, backstage. The music floated from the stage, and costumes hung in racks outside rooms marked with the names of headliners. Their dressing rooms remained dark.

Technically, the Follies wouldn't open for six weeks.

Esme found the massive dressing room for the chorus girls and entered.

Apparently, they were on stage, because the room marked the disarray of pre-performance chaos. Makeup pots, burning lights, shoes, hosiery... a den of femininity.

She remembered the days when her life had been filled with the accoutrements of being a lady, of creating the mysterious allure seductive to men. She'd been a Ziegfeld girl of a different era.

Yet, for the same purpose.

She couldn't blame Flora too much for wanting a life of security, of prosperity.

Esme roamed the dressing tables for Flora's station then found a publicity photo framed near an office door. She searched the faces for Jinx's description. Tall, lanky, blond...

She found a face that stopped her cold. Nearly a younger version of herself, perhaps more shapely, but enough to convince her of Jinx's words. *I think he was angry that—that I wasn't you.*

Poor Jinx.

Esme trolled down the dressing tables, picking up mementoes and cards. She found cards addressed to Marion, Paulette, Irene, and Claire, but no Flora.

She sank down into a chair, studied herself. Picked up a pot of rouge, dabbed her pinky into it. Rubbed it on her cheek.

In the mirror, she saw a vase of flowers, wilted. She got up, moved over to the roses. American Beauty, the kind the boys would send her before a ball.

A vellum card lay tucked below the vase.

To my Flora, for the rest of our lifes.

She picked up the card, studied it. The handwriting was coarse, block letters, as if the author had no formal training.

And, he'd spelled "lives" incorrectly.

"Who are you? What are you doing in here?"

She turned, and a costumed woman stood at the door, entering fast. She wore a bathing hat of sorts, with a plume of red peacock feathers, a skintight V-neck dress, the arms fanned out in a flourish of lace around her elbows, with a tulle ballet skirt, white hosiery, and ballet shoes. Red lipstick and bright blue eyes made her look more garish than grand. She came close and yanked the card from Esme's hand.

"Who are you?"

Debate ate Esme's words. Hopeful dancer? Lost actress? She'd arrived with verve, but standing before discovery, it vanished. So much for her Nellie Bly moment. "Are you Flora St. John?"

"Who wants to know?"

She smiled then, honesty coming to her lips. "I'm a reporter with the *New York Chronicle,* and I want to make her famous."

For a moment, the lie sparkled in the girl's eyes. She seemed to glow, reaching up to pull off her hat. Long blond hair spilled down her back. "Yeah, okay. I'm Flora." She held out her hand. "Nice ta meetchya."

Esme placed her as a Bronx girl. "Esme. Price. I'm doing a piece on dancers who find true love on the stage, and someone gave me your name."

Flora glanced at the flowers, sadness in her eyes. "Who?"

"Does the name Foster Worth mean anything to you?"

She glanced at the card, tucked it back into the flowers. "Nope. I dunno what you're talkin' about. I think you'd better leave."

"My source said you attended the theater with Mr. Worth on the day of his murder."

Other chorus girls had begun to filter in, some sitting at their stations, others listening to their conversation.

"I don't wanna talk about Foster." Her eyes glossed.

Esme's voice gentled. "Do you have an idea of who might have killed him, Miss St. John?"

Flora looked up, blinking, then pressed her fingers under her eyes. "Nope."

"Flora, listen to me. This is just between us, but if you want, I can turn your name over to the police. Talk to me. Were you in love with Foster Worth?"

She flinched, and a memory seemed to scan through her eyes. Then, "I want you to leave. Right now."

"Flora, don't you want to tell your side of the story? It's going to come out—people might even think you had something to do with his murder."

"Stay away from me!"

Esme made the mistake of reaching out her arm, catching her. "Please— Flora. An innocent man might go to jail if you don't tell the truth."

Flora shook it off, rounded on her. "How do I know you're a reporter? You don't look like a reporter." She gestured to Esme's outfit. "You look more like one of those society ladies, like Foster's snooty wife."

Esme drew in a breath.

"Prove to me that you're with the *Chronicle*, and then, maybe, I'll tell you a story about Foster and who really wanted him dead."

Chapter 19

Her sins found her most often in the dead of the night, when Jinx heard nothing but the thrumming of her heart in her ears. Sometimes, in the soft padding of her room, upon her throne bed, with the tufted gold drapes at the headboard, the moonlight waxing through the windows onto the Parisian carpets, she remembered Bennett. Too easily she heard his murmurs, smelled his skin, her heart softening at the way he'd turned toward her that night nearly seventeen years ago, the way he'd taken her into his arms as if she belonged to him. That, perhaps, is what mocked her as she lay alone in her bed the months afterward, Jack growing inside her—the feeling that she'd belonged most to what she couldn't have, and in the years hence, the loneliness drove her from her bed to roam the house.

She had already stopped by Rosie's room, standing at the door, the moon caressing her daughter's form as she curled in her bed.

Jack, perhaps, had saved her from despising her life, but Rosie had given her back her contempt for Foster. Her daughter reminded Jinx that she owed Foster nothing.

Despite her penance, however, Jinx never truly felt redeemed. Her sins lay like a brick inside her chest, dusty and old, clinging to her memories.

Perhaps because she never truly desired forgiveness.

It seemed God's reckoning had finally come.

She stopped in Jack's room but found his bed empty. Wrapping her hand around his doorframe, she took a step inside. She'd decorated his bedroom in the sports memorabilia he loved—yachts and tennis, croquet and cricket. The room smelled like Jack, his sports clothes hanging over a pillow chair, his leather coat draped over his desk chair. A pile of books towered upon his bureau—Beadle's dime novels and Nick Carter detective stories. She'd seen him often as a child playing in the garden, conjuring up some sort of dime-novel scenario. Now, he and his friends listened to the radio accounts of the battles in Europe, replaying the battles in thick conversation.

Perhaps West Point hadn't been all Foster's idea. Thankfully, he was only sixteen, and still had a year of schooling before he made his decision. The war might end before then.

Jack had collected shells from Newport and piled them into a glass jar on his desk. She opened the jar, took a clam shell. She ran her thumb over the edges, smoothed by the ocean salt, the grit of the sand. She saw him at Newport, on the rocky Bailey's Beach, laughing as the surf teased his toes, his legs, the sun in his blue eyes.

No, she'd never wanted forgiveness for something that taught her how to love, to be loved.

She stared out his window to the lights on Fifth Avenue. This late, only a few motorcars passed. Certainly Jack wasn't still at the police station.

Not when Bennett had confessed. The thought became a fist in her chest. Bennett couldn't have killed Foster. He didn't have time, did he? He'd been retrieving his coat—Amelia walked in right after him. And Jinx had been only a few steps behind him.

Someone could have used the garden door to escape.

They believe Jack was standing outside, he heard Bennett and me arguing.

The shyster was going to leave you, Jinx. He had a plan to take everything, leave you penniless and marry some actress he was seeing. She dropped the shell into the container.

Bennett had confessed to protect Jack.

The truth reached up, wrapped hands around her neck, stole her breath. Bennett believed that Jack had killed Foster out of fury over his adultery, so Bennett had sacrificed himself for their son. She reached out for the bed, but it did little to catch her before her knees buckled. She saw Bennett hanging from the bridge of sighs at the Tombs, his body at the end of the rope, swaying in the wind. Because of *her* adultery.

She'd done this, created this lie, sentenced the man she loved to this fate.

Oh, she should have gone with Bennett. She let the possibilities seep through her. She would have sacrificed her life in New York, on the list of the 400, yes. But she would have lived without secrets. With peace, instead of sin, stalking her in the middle of the night.

She could nearly taste it—the sweet sense of redemption, the breath of peace filling her lungs. But as quickly as it came, it vanished, leaving only the memory of her sins behind, turning her to ash.

She drew up her legs, her breath shuddering out of her. How she hated living with secrets.

She couldn't lose Bennett. Not again.

"Mother?" Jack stood in the doorway, the moonlight on his face. He wore fatigue in his face, his derby in his hands. "Are you well?" He came into the room, extended his hand to help her off the floor.

She took his hands. In this light, he so resembled his father with his blond, unruly hair, those regal cheekbones, the wide shoulders. Oh, Jack. "Where have you been?"

He considered her a moment as she rose then set his Bible on the desk. "I was at the church."

The answer seemed to light an inferno inside her. "The church? Why?"

He looked at her, nonplussed. "Because I thought the priest could pray for us. For Father's soul, and for you in your time of grief."

She bit back what would have been a harsh, cruel laugh. Grieve for Foster?

"God won't help this family, Jack." She pushed past him to stand at the window. "We're beyond God's help."

"No one is beyond God's help. Did you not hear the priest on Sunday?"

Yes, indeed, she had. *The face of the Lord is against them that do evil, to cut off the remembrance of them from the earth.*

But Jack touched her arm. "The righteous cry, and the Lord heareth, and delivereth them out of all their troubles."

She looked up at him, his face, the eyes that seemed so terribly believing, and feared for his lost innocence.

"I am anything but righteous, son." She wasn't sure where the words came from, or how she managed to allow them out, but they spilled free and she turned, pressed her hand on the cold window.

"Mother, you are one of the most righteous women I know. You attend church regularly, give of your time and money to charity work, you never make a social faux pas. Everyone loves you—you are invited to all the social events of the season, men beg to dance with you, women want to emulate you. You are blessed with power, and wealth and fame. How could God not hear your petitions for justice for Father's murder?"

She drew in a breath. Were those blessings? She didn't know anymore. She once believed that she had deserved them. Now, they seemed to clog her throat, suffocate her. Oh, to be like Esme, to have run away, found herself on the other side of the world.

Oh, God, what had she done? Jinx pressed her hand to her mouth, her eyes on Jack, suddenly hearing then the rest of the priest's Sunday reading. *The Lord is nigh unto them that are of a broken heart; and saveth such as be of a contrite spirit.*

She didn't deserve God to listen to her...but what if He still would? What if He'd hear the weeping of her heart?

She turned back to the window, staring out at the stars, so carelessly flung through the sky. Or deliberately placed?

She'd created a life she thought she wanted. But perhaps that had been the problem. Maybe blessing had nothing to do with wealth, but knowing that God ordained it, provided, protected.

Forgave.

Perhaps it was better to be poor—because then, if she were rescued, she'd know she hadn't done it herself. Indeed, if she'd allowed God to choose her life, she might truly know that she hadn't created it, but that God loved her. Wasn't that the essence of being blessed?

Jack moved away from her. "I hope Uncle Bennett hangs."

His tone caught her breath. "No, Jack. That's not right. He didn't kill Foster."

"Then who did? I knew you couldn't have—although you had every right to." His eyes grew dark. "They accused me of it, and truthfully, I sat there in the station, knowing I'd harbored that thought in my heart. I heard the shot, but I was putting the motorcar away after bringing Rosie home from the Fishes'. It wasn't until I heard Amelia's scream that I ran through the garden and saw you, there, with Uncle Bennett." He didn't look at her then.

"You did think I did it."

He ran the heel of his hand across his cheek. "I hated him for what he did to you."

The words shook through her. *Hated him.* And then he turned, his eyes gentle. "I did wonder. But then I saw your face, saw your horror. No, you didn't do it."

But she wanted to, and that truth only added to the weight in her chest.

"Uncle Bennett didn't shoot him either."

"Then who did, Mother? He confessed. He's being arraigned tomorrow. The police have their murderer."

"No, they don't!"

Jack looked as if she'd slapped him. "Then what was Uncle Bennett doing here, in our house? He never comes here—and Father hated him."

"Your father's words about his brother were lies. Your uncle Bennett is an honorable man." Her voice betrayed her, however, the tremor in it. "I know he didn't kill your father."

Jack just stared at her.

She turned away from the window, pressing her cold palm against the warmth of her other.

"What are you not telling me, Mother?"

She shook her head.

He reached for her hand, but she brushed him aside. "Go to bed, Jack. Please, just go to bed."

"You can't fix this, Mother. No amount of money will buy Uncle Bennett's innocence. He's going to pay for his crime."

She turned at the coldness in his voice, shaken. He stood there, bathed in the moonlight, anger flushing out of him. Oh, to be so young, to think you know so much. Her voice gentled. "You are a good boy—no, man, Jack. You deserved better than Foster as your father."

Then she turned and she walked out of the room, pulling the door shut behind her. Her hands shook.

She made her way down the hall, down the stairs, out onto the terrace. The springtime air still carried the bite of winter, raising gooseflesh under her silk wrap. The tulips and irises had just begun to peek from the earth, silvery under the moon.

You can't fix this, Mother.

No. But maybe God could. Maybe—maybe He would listen to a bereft and parched soul.

She raised her eyes, debating. What, really, did she have to lose? So this was, then, what it meant to be poor, to have nothing, to have to reach out for help. "O God, I know I got myself into this mess...but I'm not leaving until You bless me." She wrapped her arms around herself, shivered. "Because the truth is, I need help. Your help." She ground her teeth then, letting her tears sting, relishing them as they broke her free, rattled her teeth, sent her to her knees before the wrought-iron chairs in her garden. "Please, God. Please forgive me."

She felt it then, the smallest niggle of heat inside. Whether produced from hope, or just her words flung out among the stars, or whether it might be something greater, for the first time she considered that riches might come from the inside.

* * * * *

"Esme, are you kidding me?"

Esme hated that she'd expected a warmer reception from Oliver.

She pressed the receiver to her ear to hear over the scratch of the phone line. As she sat in the booth in the darkness across from the theater, the wind scooted old paper down the muddy road. "I wouldn't be calling you if I didn't need you, believe me. Flora knows something, I feel it inside, but she won't talk to me unless she believes I'm truly a reporter from the *Chronicle*."

"Which you're not."

"Oliver, be serious."

"I'm entirely serious, Esme. You are not employed by this paper—"

"I could own the paper!"

"But you don't. Yet. Maybe never. And until then—"

"Oliver." It was the way she said it—it surprised her too—an emotion in her voice that bespoke their past, the pieces of her heart she'd long ago given him that must have made him pause.

"Esme, I'm just putting tonight's edition to bed."

"Hold the press for me, Oliver. Bennett Worth has confessed to a crime he didn't commit. Wouldn't that make front-page news?"

He said nothing.

She leaned her head against the phone box. Across the street, light streamed out of the open door where the guard waited for her return.

"Where are you exactly?"

"At the New Amsterdam Theater."

"Just stay put. I'll be there as soon as I can."

"Thank you—" But he'd already hung up.

She stood on the sidewalk, her wrap tight around her, shivering, waiting for the lights of his cab. The night he'd saved her from the bum in Hell's Kitchen revived inside her. He'd been her hero then, her young heart so easily wooed.

But he hadn't loved her enough to send her a telegram. To tell her he was alive. She needed to keep that centered in her brain.

Oliver didn't love her. Anymore. Perhaps, ever, really.

Besides, she knew what love was, what it felt like. *Thank you, Daughtry.*

A Studebaker sedan pulled up to the curb and Oliver climbed out the driver's side.

"Is this your car?"

"It helps to have my own transportation," he said. He'd been working—she saw it in the way his hair was mussed under his fedora, the fact that he fixed his tie as he walked toward her. His eyes caught her, ran over her in her dress.

"You don't look much like a reporter."

"I'm in disguise."

He raised an eyebrow. "Undercover, huh? Like Nellie Bly?"

Was that a smile? "Thank you for coming."

"Let's get this lie over with." He held out his elbow, however, and she took it as they walked down Forty-second and into the side entrance.

Oliver presented his card—the guard looked it over, allowed them entrance. She had to smile at the way he tucked it back into his jacket, not looking at her.

They found the chorus girls mostly dressed—in chiffon dressing gowns, some with trench coats and day suits, on their way home. Flora sat in the corner, changed and in a low-waisted dress, wearing a turban and a boa. She smoked a cigarette, staring at her flowers.

"Flora, this is Oliver Stewart. He's the managing editor of the *New York Chronicle.*" Esme liked how his introduction rolled off her lips, a strange swell of pride at all Oliver had accomplished. She looked at him and smiled, letting it show in her eyes.

He glanced at her then shook Flora's hand. He handed her his card. "My reporter here said that you had a story to tell us about Foster Worth?"

"Uh-huh." She blew out a stream of smoke. "I'm going to make the front pages, right?"

"We'll see." Oliver folded his arms. "Do you know who killed Foster Worth?"

"Naw." She picked up a flower. "I dunno."

Esme stilled. "You said—"

"Yeah. Well, maybe I got an idea." The rose had wilted, but she held it to her nose.

"Who are the flowers from, Flora?"

She sighed. "My secret admirer. He sends me flowers sometimes, after the shows, so that I'll know he was in the audience. They still smell, even for a few days after they die."

"You don't know his name?"

"He never signs it."

"You've never met him?"

She let a harsh laugh escape. "Why would I? I had Foster." But her voice dipped on the last word.

"You're lying, Flora. Who is this guy?" Oliver's voice dropped, and the danger in it made Esme glance at him.

Flora pursed her lips then shook her head. "I can't say. He's a dangerous man. Even more than Foster, maybe. He worked for him."

Esme glanced at Oliver. "How?"

"You know." She dropped the flower in the trash bin. "Did his dirty work. The kind that made people fear Foster. The kind that breaks strikes and makes people pay on time." She picked up the entire vase, dropped it in the trash. "The kind that settles scores."

"Did Foster know about your affair?" Esme asked.

"Maybe. Foster came by one night, after the show, and saw the flowers." She looked away. "He got real mad." She gave a wry smile. "That's how I knew he loved me, you know. He'd get mad and he'd—well, it weren't no big thing, and he was always so sorry and sweet afterward. I knew he'd never get so mad at me if he didn't care."

And Jinx had spent her life with this man. Esme wanted to weep. No wonder her sister appeared skittish, wounded.

"Did your admirer know about Foster? Did he know that Foster hurt you?"

She lifted a shoulder. "Yeah. He got real mad too. But not at me."

"Do you love him, this admirer?"

"How could I ever love him? He's not in my set." But the way she said it, a lilt in all the wrong places, it felt like a lie. Like something Esme might have said about Oliver. She didn't look at him.

"But maybe he thought you did?" Oliver said, his voice strange.

Flora lifted a shoulder. "I dunno. I got these flowers the day after Foster was murdered."

"Did you know that Foster was planning on running away with you?"

She looked up at Esme, studied her, her eyes slowly filling. She ran her hand across her cheek. "Naw, he didn't tell me that. But sometimes he talked about leaving his wife. Said he'd been tricked into marrying her. Said that she'd cheated on him, that his son wasn't his."

Esme kept her expression even. "People will say anything to justify their actions."

"We saw his brother at the theater, though, and he acted real strange. Foster said that he was going to make them pay for what they'd done. I didn't know who he was talking about. I asked him but..." She curled her hand around her arm. "He didn't like me asking questions about his life."

Make who pay?

Bennett?

Jinx?

She glanced at Oliver.

"When does your show open, Flora? I'll be sure to send a photographer, see if we can't put your picture in the paper."

"Really?" She looked up at Oliver, her eyes bright. "We open June 12."

"Thank you." He reached down, took her hand. "You've been ever so helpful."

She blushed at his attention, and, well, Esme would have also.

The night air scurried under her wrap, sent a shiver through her as they stepped out into the alley.

"Are you cold?"

She shrugged. "I'm still trying to put together her story. What if Bennett is telling the truth about Foster planning on leaving Jinx? And what if this secret admirer heard him, decided to stop him? The card did indicate that they would spend the rest of their lives together."

"But what about Foster's threat? Do you think he might have been waiting for Bennett with those dueling pistols, maybe for an old-fashioned duel?" Oliver reached down and took her hand as they reached the street. The moon shone upon it now, turning it to platinum.

His hand warmed hers, and more. Something so protective, so sweet about it, made her mind do loops.

"Or, what if Jack did hear them arguing? What if Foster turned on Jack—"

"Or Jack turned on him? You never can tell what a man will do when he finds out he's been lied to." Oliver glanced at her, and she drew in her breath.

They reached the car. "Can I give you a lift home?"

She wanted to reach up, touch his face, to ease the hurt from it. "If I had known you were alive, I would have never left," she said softly. "I never stopped missing you, even when the grieving wore off."

He drew in an unsteady breath, considering her a long moment. And then the hardness dropped away from his face, his emotions suddenly in his eyes, his voice. "I came back to New York because I hoped that someday you would too."

Oh. She swallowed, her throat tight. Oh, Oliver.

But he'd already stepped close. "Esme, I've missed you so much. I couldn't believe you'd left me—it felt as if your father had won. And worse, as if my heart had been torn from my chest. I walked around with a gaping hole inside me." His voice fell, his eyes in hers. "It's never been healed."

And then—perhaps she asked, perhaps she mumbled his name, for sure she raised herself up on her toes as he bent to kiss her. Not a gentle, exploring kiss either, but a kiss abated for twenty years, something of urgency and hunger, longing and hope. A kiss that he deepened as he wound his hand around her neck, as she dug hers into the lapels of his jacket, then inside, to palm his chest. His arms went around her and she molded to him, relishing the taste of him. He had matured, no longer the tentative, shy boy. Oliver had become a man, confident, possessive, even bold. He kissed like that man she knew—no, hoped—he would become.

And she kissed him like a woman who'd known two worlds, one of decorum, the other of survival. He tasted of coffee, smelled of the night air and a husky masculine tang.

Oliver.

He pulled away from her, nuzzling her neck, kissing her cheek, then pressing his forehead to hers. "You've changed."

She smiled. "I have changed."

"I love you, Esme. Oh, I never stopped. I looked for you every day, around every corner, hoping. Believing that someday you'd come back to me. And I'd be right here, waiting, just like I promised." He kissed her again, then, gentler, lingering. Finally, he pulled away. "Forgive me for not coming after you? For letting you leave and only listening to my wounded heart?"

She ran her gloved hand to his sandpaper cheek. Oh, she'd loved these whiskers, the way his beard darkened after a long day. "You believed in me, Oliver, and that's what I took with me to Montana."

He pressed his forehead to hers again. "We have an article to get to press."

* * * * *

Jinx had spent her life wheedling into places that forbade her entrance. Hadn't she married Foster Worth and edged the Worth and Price families into the elite station of Mrs. Astor's 400? Hadn't she trumpeted into Newport society, outwitting Alva Belmont at her own motor carriage event, catapulting her own motoring ball into the venue of must-attend events?

Yet, Jinx had to admit to a curl of heat in her stomach as she stepped out of her Rolls Royce onto the sidewalk outside the Halls of Justice—the Tombs, where Bennett sat in his pre-trial hearing on the second floor in the Court of Special Sessions. Too easily she conjured the stink she'd managed to scrub from her skin, the haunting song from her block mates. Too easily she heard the indictments as she instructed her driver to stay, and climbed the stairs into the building.

Please, bless me, Lord.

She walked down the marble-floored hallway, past the pictures of court justices, a copy of the Ten Commandments, the closed beechwood doors of the Police Court session, to the second floor.

She'd pulled out a new dress for the day, a V-necked Carmeuse day dress in a deep green, edged in orange trim and braids. It would make the papers...if her appearance didn't manage it. She wouldn't wear black quite yet. Perhaps never. The shorter hem showed her flesh-colored silk stockings and black and green silk-heeled shoes.

Although, yes, she'd had her lady's maid secure her new under-bodice corset just a bit tighter. It kept her posture straighter, her insides from whirring as she marched up the second-story steps.

An officer stood guard outside the Court of Special Sessions. She drew in her breath, walked past him, put her hand on the door.

"Excuse me, ma'am, but this is a closed session."

She stopped, looked up at him the way she might one of her footman. "I'm sure it is. But not to me." She turned back to the door.

"Ma'am—"

But she pushed open the door and entered the courtroom.

She'd seen it in her head for the past four hours, as she edited her words, bathed, ate her breakfast, attired herself, and prepared for the scandal that would follow this morning's truth, so she expected the murmurs, the stir at her entrance.

The judge looked up from the bench as she marched down the aisle. Sturdy yet small, the judge wore a speckling of white amidst his graying hair. He narrowed his eyes at her. "This is a closed session."

"Not to me," Jinx said again.

Bennett and Mr. Loren, the Worth family lawyer, sat at the defendant's table. A prosecutor stood at the other table.

She glanced at Bennett, who stared at her as if she had entered the courtroom in her bathing costume. His eyes widened, although his handsome face bore a grizzled shadow. His suit appeared rumpled, and she had no doubt he smelled like something that crawled out from behind the alley. She shot him a slim smile then turned back to the judge.

"I have something to say."

"I'm sorry, but we're not calling witnesses," said the prosecutor.

"You don't have to call me, I'm already here." She'd finally reached the gateway at the end of the aisle. "Your honor, Bennett Worth lied."

The judge stared at her. She heard her name hissed out of Bennett but she ignored him. She could barely hear him above the whoosh of her heartbeat anyway.

"He lied in his confession about killing Foster Worth."

"Jinx!" He didn't bother to hiss this time.

She put out her hand like she would to one of her servants.

"Why would Mr. Worth lie about such a heinous crime, Mrs. Worth?" The judge leaned forward.

"Your honor, this witness was held in suspicion of her husband's murder—" the prosecutor started.

"Which I didn't do either. Because"—she took a breath—"I was with

Mr. Worth. And he—he was with me. So, see, neither of us could have killed Foster."

The judge glanced at Bennett, who had cupped his hand over his eyes.

"Is this true, Mr. Bennett?"

He looked up at Jinx, frustration in his eyes. She could nearly see him doing the math—if he denied her words, then suspicion would fall back upon her. His shoulders rose, fell. "Yes. Right before Foster was shot, I was in Mrs. Worth's chamber."

The judge raised an eyebrow, looked back at Jinx.

She smiled. "We were talking." But, just because she'd come here to be scandalous, to allay any hint of deceit, to deflect the attention from Bennett's guilt and onto the flurry of a scandal, she added an exaggerated wink.

She might have imagined it, but the judge seemed to redden.

"About what?" This from the prosecutor who had come out from behind his bench. He reminded her of Foster, dark eyes, intimidating. She drew in a breath.

"About our son."

Beside her, Bennett laid his head on the table, onto his folded arms.

The judge's voice turned low. "Your son?"

Behind her, she heard the door open, close, as if one of the reporters might have rushed out to make the morning papers. So, just so they got it correct, she drew in a long breath. "Yes. Jonathon August Worth is Bennett's son, not Foster's."

Bennett raised his head and his eyes were flames burning into her skin.

"Did Foster know of your indiscretion?"

She shook her head. "It was our secret. Until Sunday night. Then, Foster invited Bennett to our home. According to Bennett, Foster was going to leave me for a dancer he'd met in the Follies. Bennett came to my chamber to inquire after my well-being. And discuss our son."

She delivered that last line without a hiccup. But she'd practiced it so many times, it seemed nearly natural.

They had discussed Jack, just not exactly at that time. But without the immensity of the secret, of the potential scandal, Jinx guessed the judge would never believe her story. Indeed, the truth seemed, once voiced in the wood-paneled chambers of Special Sessions, to be suddenly bold, even indictable. She took another step toward the bench. "So, you see, Your Honor, when Bennett discovered that Jack might be a suspect, he panicked and confessed to a crime of which he is innocent. He didn't want our son to go to jail for a crime he also did not commit."

Through her periphery, she saw Bennett stare at her, wide-eyed, shaking his head.

The judge looked at Bennett then back to Jinx. She managed a smile, managed to hold her chin up, despite the heat on her face. Perhaps that would work in her favor. Perhaps, as people remembered this moment, they'd remember that Jinx may have been a fallen woman, but she crashed with dignity.

"Have you seen today's paper, Mrs. Worth?" The judge held up the *New York Chronicle*. Even from her vantage point, she could read the top headline: ACTRESS ALLEGES AFFAIR WITH MURDER VICTIM.

Jinx stared at the headline, little explosions bursting in her head, her chest. "No," she said, although her voice suggested otherwise. "Is it about Foster?"

"And a little missy down at the Ziegfeld Follies. It seems your husband was equally...adulterous."

She tried not to flinch at that word, but her chin dipped, just a little.

The judge stared at the article while her heart thundered in her chest. Her hands sweat inside her gloves and she needed more breath than her corset allowed.

"The article suggests a motive from someone in Mr. Foster Worth's employ; that she had a secret admirer who had planned revenge for an assault on the woman." He looked up at Jinx, who had stilled.

So, she wasn't the only one whom Foster bullied.

"Do you know anything about this?"

Jinx pressed her open palm over her corset, ducked her head. Bennett had his hands in a clench on the table, his eyes closed.

"In light of this new information, I don't believe Mr. Worth's confession, nor am I reasonably convinced the prosecution has enough evidence to bind Mr. Worth over for indictment by the grand jury." He looked at Bennett while Jinx swallowed her heart back into her chest. "You are free to go."

She turned, caught in Bennett's expression what appeared to be confusion, even frustration as he looked at her then past her.

"Mother."

She stiffened, turned.

Jack stood in the aisle, his shoulders rising and falling, stricken.

Rosie stood behind him, her mouth in a grim, tight line. She shook her head.

Oh no. Jinx wanted to weep at the terrible expression on Jack's face.

"You don't understand, Jack. I…" Oh, how could she not make this worse? She couldn't tell him that she'd snuck into Foster's bed, that she didn't realize it was Bennett. She glanced at Bennett.

Because that, she knew long ago, wasn't the truth, either.

No more secrets. She walked up to him, lowered her voice just for him. "I love Bennett. I always have. And he is your father."

With those words, she could breathe. The suddenness of it shook her. No longer the coil of agony in her chest, tighter each year as Jack grew, as she read about Bennett's trips to New York. With the truth, it simply sprang free. Fresh air, into her lungs, her soul.

She turned to Bennett, who had followed her up the aisle.

He wore a devastating, breathtaking smile, and nodded.

"My entire life is a lie." Jack's voice emerged low, dangerous.

Jinx turned back to him. "Jack, listen to me—"

"Stay away from me. Stay away." He shrugged out of his sister's grip and fled the courtroom.

She met her daughter's eyes.

Rosie shook her head. "I'll go after him."

Jinx watched her go, a different kind of pain in her chest.

Then Bennett was there, turning her into his embrace. He caught her face in his hands, stared down at her with something of disbelief. "Oh Jinx, you do know how to land on the front page, don't you?"

She couldn't respond before he kissed her, right there in the courtroom, his lips sweet, his touch so gentle she wanted to cry.

That, too, made the papers.

Chapter 20

Esme woke to the rumble of the elevated train outside the window of her father's former *Chronicle* office. It seemed to roar through the room, shaking her out of the sweet, exhausted darkness and into a shaft of bright sunlight that blinded her, made her shield her eyes with her hands. She peeked out between her fingers.

Oliver stood staring out the window, his wide back to her, his shirtsleeves rolled up past his elbows, his black hair a wreck after hours of inserting into the *Chronicle* the front-page article on Flora. The sun streamed past him, over the wide mahogany desk, onto the parquet floor, and he resembled a caesar surveying his world. My, he had broad shoulders, sinewed forearms, his body lean and strong. Indeed, he'd grown into a man during her absence.

"Did I fall asleep? The last thing I remember, the presses were running."

"I couldn't tell if it was the sound of the presses or your snoring that was louder." Oliver turned, his face dark with whiskers, tease in his eyes.

Esme peeled herself up from his leather sofa, her cheek sweaty and lined. She ran her fingers through her hair, shaking it out.

Oliver watched with a smile that made her warm to her bones. "I lived for the day I might see you in the morning."

She gave him a look then smoothed out her suit. "My daughter will be worried about me."

His smile dimmed. "I forgot you had married. And that you had a daughter."

"You would have liked Daughtry Hoyt. He was a good man. He reminded me of you. But now, you remind me of him."

"I'm not sure—"

"He was the son of a Crow woman and a miner who became a gentleman. But he died trying to save the miners who worked for him. Believe me, it's a compliment."

He narrowed his eyes then finally nodded. "Your daughter is lovely, Esme."

"She has her father's features, dark and dangerous. She grew up in the West, knows how to shoot a gun, can herd buffalo, and I will just bet that Abel, our hired man, taught her to chew tobacco. So, you can save my feelings. She's not the deb I was, nor will she ever be."

Oliver came over to her and lifted her chin with his hand. "No one will ever be the deb you were, Esme. But if you'll recall, that didn't exactly work in my favor. I much prefer this woman who had to parse every word, bossed around my linotype machinists, fed paper into the presses, and passed out bundles to the newsies. That's the woman I knew you were, that's the woman I fell in love with." He pressed a sweet kiss to her lips, and it awoke something still asleep inside her. She wrapped her arms around his neck, wove her fingers into his dark, silky hair. Let herself surrender to his touch.

Oliver.

He drew back. "I want to show you something." He got up, took her hands, and drew her to the window. Below, the city had already awakened, fruit and bread vendors in the square, pigeons creating a scandal between their feet. Traffic—horse-drawn trolleys, motorcars, pedestrians—crossed Chronicle Square. Around them, taller buildings loomed. And, on the corners, newsies peddled the *Chronicle*.

"I love to watch them, to see people buy the paper, read the front-page articles." He slipped his hand into hers, warm and strong. "Your article."

"Our article," she said.

He glanced at her, raised an eyebrow, then picked up the paper from his desk. "Your article." He handed it to her.

She read the byline on the top of the article. "Where's your name?"

"It's your article. I wanted you to have your own byline. You deserve it."

She read the article through. "I wish we'd been able to pry the name of Flora's suitor out of her."

"I suspect she'll be having that very chat with the police by lunchtime. My court reporter called. The charges against Bennett were just dismissed."

Esme ran her hand over the article, the feel of the paper so familiar. Newsprint came off on her hand. She set the paper on his desk, turned to watch the square. "I have to admit, I thought that someday this would be my view, my office. I thought I deserved it because I was a Price. But this office has to be earned, not bequeathed."

"Are you saying you don't deserve your inheritance?"

"I ran away. So, no." She looked up at him. "I went to Montana thinking God wouldn't bless me because I'd despised all the other things He'd given me. But He blessed me anyway, despite my mistakes." She tried a smile. "I figured out when Daughtry died that blessing wasn't about being rich or powerful. It was about knowing that through all of it, rich or poor, I could trust in God's love for me. Being poor in spirit is about needing God, and it's when I needed Him that He poured out His riches into my life. My daughter. My town…" You. She wanted to say it, but she wasn't sure what lay beyond this moment, this day.

She turned back to the window. "I just wish my father would have believed in me, known that I grew into a woman who loved newspapers, just like he did."

"He did believe in you," Oliver said, frowning. "He kept everything you ever wrote."

She stared at him, and must have worn her bewilderment.

He gave a laugh, something that sounded more like disbelief. "Of course." He took her hand. "Come with me."

He walked her through the lobby—clearly not caring that his receptionist watched them with censure on her face as they exited his office, Esme in her rumpled clothes, he in his shirtsleeves, and walked her down past the editor's offices to the library. Racks and racks of archived newspapers lined the shelves, their dates written on placards on the shelves below. Oliver pulled her through the room to the back, to another set of shelves. He pointed to a placard.

The *Copper Valley Times.*

She let go of his hand, lifted out a newspaper. One of her first, she recognized it as one she'd sent to her father. She ran her hand across the flimsy paper, eight pages of poorly written news. "I sent this to him."

Oliver nodded. "And then, one day, you stopped. He told me about how he waited for the paper every week, how he closed his door, read it cover to cover when he received it, how he saw you between the lines, growing into a businesswoman, a pioneer. He was so proud of you, Esme."

She blinked back the burning in her eyes. Swallowed. Slid the paper back into its place. "But these…" She read the dates on the next stack. "I didn't send him these."

"He ordered these. He didn't want you to know, so he had them sent to Chicago, and his correspondent there forwarded them to the *Chronicle.*"

She remembered that, the post office box in Chicago; she had thought it might be the subscription of one of the former miners. "Why didn't he want me to know?" But she could answer that for herself; she didn't need Oliver's wince, the way he tried to find a clever truth.

"His pride. I know it too well," she said quietly. She moved her finger down the row. It seemed he'd collected every paper she'd ever published. She pressed her fingers under her eyes, caught the wetness there.

"Now you have newsprint on your face," Oliver said, turning her. He took out his handkerchief, held her chin as he wiped it off.

She caught his wrists. "Oliver…I know that this paper doesn't belong to me anymore. And I'm so proud of all you've become here. But…do you think I could have a job? A real job, as a reporter?"

She couldn't read his expression—amusement, disbelief?—and she suddenly wanted to steal the words back. What was she doing? She had her own life, her own paper, her own mine back in Montana. She didn't really want to stay here, resume her life…

Except, yes, she did. Standing in the *Chronicle* office, with the bustle of the street below and the elevated train rumbling by, the current of the city had rippled through her, the dormant passion fresh, young, burning to live inside her.

She wanted to stay here, introduce Lilly to her legacy. Fall in love all over again with Oliver. She saw them skating in Central Park and attending the opera, or even one of the Ziegfeld Follies, saw them writing articles late into the night, stopping when he looked at her with those dark eyes that could unravel her thoughts....

Like now.

"Esme," he said quietly, "I can't give you a job."

Oh, she tried not to flinch, tried not to let the betrayal show on her countenance. She gathered up the society woman inside and took a breath. "I understand."

She nodded, moving past him, toward the door. "You're right, of course. I have a good life in Montana, and people there that depend on me, and—"

"Esme!"

She felt his hand on her arm, turning her. In the murky light of the library, he suddenly appeared the young, angry man she'd remembered that day when she'd visited him in the tenements, shocked, even frustrated at her appearance. "Esme, I can't give you a job, because you're the heiress. This paper is yours."

She blinked at him, frowned. "But you said—"

"I thought I could make you go away. I thought you'd give up, and frankly, I couldn't take letting you into my life only to break me again. But here you are, with newsprint on your face and your hair down to your waist, asking me for a job, and I—I'm a scoundrel if I don't tell you that making you publisher is exactly what your father wanted."

Her mouth opened, and she might have uttered a sound, but she had nothing comprehensible.

Oliver stepped closer to her. "Esme, this paper belongs to you. It's your inheritance. I was wrong not to go after you, but I thought you didn't want it."

Her voice dropped to a whisper. "I want it. And…I want you to run it with me."

She closed the gap between them, ran her hands up behind him, hooked them onto his shoulders. "Run this paper with me, Oliver. It belongs to you too."

He drew in a long breath. "Would you still marry your footman, do you think?"

She tucked herself into his arms, drew in the smell of him at his neck. "It'll make the headlines," she said. Then she kissed him beneath the dust and shadows of the *Chronicle*, right above the cloakroom, where they began.

* * * * *

"Roll up the carpet, Amelia, and add it to the fire."

Jinx stood at the doorway to Foster's den, the hearth roaring, spitting out ash as it devoured Foster's things, the pictures of his motorcars and the *Jinx*, a stash of playbills she'd found in his desk drawer, even his tuxedo, which she'd found in a closet in his den, the stink of him in it, a woman's kiss at the collar.

She'd dispose of him, incinerate him from her life.

Start again, clean.

The doors to the garden hung open, the smell of the room drifting into the spring breeze. She'd arrived home after dropping Bennett at the Waldorf-Astoria and set about creating a life that lived outside society's whims.

She would have burned the dueling pistols, but they'd disappeared after her arrest, probably in police custody.

"And the picture, ma'am?" Amelia gestured to the oil of Jinx and Foster, the one Jinx had commissioned early in her marriage when she believed in a happy ending.

Perhaps she still believed in a happy ending. Just not one of her own making. "Burn that also."

"Jinx!"

The voice turned her on her silk heel.

Her mother stalked up behind her, dressed in the latest fashion— a V-necked blue silk dress, cinched tight at the waist, her face betraying the horror that Jinx knew she should probably feel. "What on earth are you doing?"

"I'm cleaning house, Mother." Jinx turned back to the room. "I'm starting over."

"With nothing!" Phoebe grabbed her arm, turning her, too roughly. "I was in the middle of my morning tea when Elizabeth Fish called me and informed me of your public declarations of"—she chiseled her voice to low—" your indiscretion with Foster's brother."

Jinx jerked her arm away. She'd had enough of people intimidating her. "You needn't whisper, Mother. Bennett and I are getting married, today perhaps, and by this evening, I will be a scarlet woman no longer."

"Come to your senses, Jinx! No woman benefits in society by admitting cuckolding her husband. You will be cut, uninvited, your family ignored in society. You need to retract your statement, tell them you were under duress. Perhaps even take an extended trip to Europe at some sanatorium. Maybe then you will be accepted back next season."

"I couldn't care less about society, Mother. Haven't you noticed? There's a war on. No one cares about debutantes or gala balls or the opening of the opera. My life—your life—is worth nothing but what the *New York Chronicle* declares. I'm tired of trying to end up on the social pages."

"The social pages are what built your life."

"No, I built this mess, Mother. Me. And you, thank you very much."

Phoebe recoiled, and for a moment Jinx wanted to yank back her words. Her mother seemed to shrink, the lines on her face suddenly crevassed and brutal. She still wore hair rats, still cinched her corset so tight that her internals probably had begun to lose their moorings. Jinx didn't want to end her days like Caroline Astor, dementia requiring her to rearrange the dinner settings of imaginary guests long into the night.

"I did nothing of the sort," Phoebe finally said, her voice but a haunting whisper.

"Oh, Mother, be honest. You lied so I could marry Foster—"

"I did that for you."

"You did that for *you*. Because it was all you had—society. But see, I have more. I have Bennett, and Jack, and Rosie. Despite everything, God has blessed me, and I'm not letting go of that."

"Don't talk to me of God's blessings. You are an adulteress."

She didn't let the epitaph bruise. "But maybe God blesses even the sinners."

Her mother stared at her, a muscle pulling in her jaw, her eyes fierce. "I very much doubt that."

Jinx turned away. "I did too. But that's where I think we're wrong. I think God's blessing might have everything to do with Him and His riches, and nothing to do with whether we deserve it." She walked into the room, where Amelia and her staff were removing the painting. She reached out for it and then met Amelia's eyes. On the count of three, they heaved it into the fire. The frame broke, the canvas curling in the heat.

She turned back to her mother. "I don't want society's blessing—I want God's. And this time, I'm going to be strong in the belief that God loves me. Not rich, socially competent Jinx, but possibly poor Mrs. Bennett Worth. Although Bennett has surely made his own way these past years."

Phoebe now pressed her hand to her mouth, shaking. "You have destroyed our family."

"I think you and Father took care of that long before I came along."

Phoebe blanched. "You will have nothing. I will make sure of it."

"Then I will take care of her." Bennett came up behind her mother, his blue eyes on Jinx, her hero in a gray sack suit, vest, a black tie, obviously cleaned up from his stay in the Tombs. Something had resurrected in him when Jinx declared to the court reporters that she loved him, and washed clean the shame upon his countenance. She saw in him a man tasting redemption.

Now, he brushed past Phoebe. "If she'll still have me."

Jinx pressed her hand to his chest. "Find me a judge."

He laughed and kissed her cheek. "Bossy Jinx, always in charge." He looked around the room. "I approve of your changes. What will you do with the room now?"

"I have no idea," Jinx said, and looped her arms around Bennett's neck. He met her gaze. Oh, he had eyes she'd spend the rest of her life finding herself inside.

Phoebe came near the fire in the hearth, her gaze upon the burning portrait. Her eyes glistened.

"Jinx." Bennett took her hands. "I don't want you staying here tonight. I talked with the police detectives—they seem to think that it might not be safe. Whoever killed Foster might come back, finish with Rosie and Jack."

"Don't be absurd, Bennett. I have my staff here to protect me. No one will hurt Rosie, or Jack."

"Mother."

Jinx looked up. Rosie stood in the doorway, her eyes red. She looked at Bennett without warmth, back to her mother. "Jack's not coming back."

Jinx stilled. "What?"

"I went after him, but…he's enlisting."

Jinx's breath hiccuped from her. "What, no, he's only sixteen.…" She looked at Bennett.

"I'll find him, Jinx. I'll stop him." Bennett kissed her hands. "I won't let our son go to war."

"Oh, Bennett, thank you."

He turned to go then stopped. "Jinx, get behind me." He reached out his hand behind him, grabbed hers.

She glanced at her mother, who had paled.

Jinx stiffened, looked around Bennett.

Foster's valet stood a foot from Bennett, one of Foster's dueling pistols pointed at his chest. Rosie had moved away from him, toward her grandmother.

Bennett raised his hands. "Now, Lewis, I don't know what you believe happened, but Jinx was telling the truth when she said I didn't kill my brother."

Perhaps the valet had come to collect a sort of severance. Jinx started to step out from behind Bennett, but he pulled her back. "Stay put," he hissed.

Fine. She wasn't tall enough to lean over his shoulder, so she peeked out. "Listen, Lewis, if you want money, I'm sure we can work out something—"

"Shut up."

She stiffened at his tone. And a ripple went through her when he stepped forward and pressed the dueling pistol hard to Bennett's chest.

Then, to her horror, Lewis reached out, grabbed her by the arm, and yanked her forward.

She cried out and Bennett leaped for her, but Lewis flung her to the floor and slammed his beefy fist into Bennett's face.

Bennett spun, banged onto Foster's desk, and hit the floor.

By the time Bennett popped back up, Lewis had her by the hair. He dragged Jinx to her feet. She clawed at his hands, pain needling through her body. "Please, Lewis—"

"I told you to shut up. You talked enough today." He wound his arm around her neck, cutting off her breath, pressed the gun to her chest.

Bennett held up his hands, his chest rising, falling, so much panic in his eyes she wanted to cry. "Please," he said. "Please don't hurt her. I'll do whatever you want."

Lewis dragged her over to the desk. Pushed her into Foster's chair. "Open the safe."

"What safe?"

He pressed the gun to her head. "Press the lever under the desk drawer."

She felt under the desk, found an indentation. Pressed it.

The front side panel of Foster's desk popped open. Inside were the deeds to their home, his yacht, his motorcars, and a stack of stock certificates, T-bills, and bonds.

Foster's net worth.

She took them out, spread them upon the desk. "I didn't know about these."

Lewis grabbed them all, shoved them into his suit pocket. "Get up."

She managed to stand and he pushed her over to the fireplace, next to her mother and Rosie. Bennett, he made kneel.

"Me and Flora had a plan. We were going to go out West, start a new life. She was going to be a showgirl, maybe I'd buy a little hotel. Have people working for me for a change." He kicked Bennett, hard, in the face, and he fell back, onto the stone hearth.

"Bennett!" Jinx made a leap for him, but Lewis grabbed her, tossed her into her mother. Phoebe locked her arms around Rosie.

Lewis's eyes narrowed at Phoebe. "Foster wasn't always like this, stealing other men's women. Not until he married your daughter. Not until she turned him away—"

"That's not true! Foster never loved me. He wanted Esme, not me."

"And he would have had her too, if—"

Someone slammed into him, from behind, tackling him hard onto the floor. The dueling pistol skittered out of his hand. He roared and pushed his assailant off. The man tumbled back, and only then did Jinx recognize him.

Oliver.

He swung at Lewis, but the man had the girth of a bear and his punch lifted Oliver off his feet, dropped him hard.

Esme had run at Jinx, now grabbed her hand to pull her away. Jinx shook free and lunged for Rosie.

Her daughter wore a wild-eyed look and shrank into the corner. Slapped at Jinx's hand.

"Rosie!"

Oliver rounded on Lewis, took another shot in the jaw, but held his ground and launched himself at Lewis, tackling him back into a Louis XVI chair. It splintered under their weight.

A shot shredded the sound of Lewis slamming Oliver to the floor.

Lilly stood at the open door, the other dueling pistol pointed at the ceiling. "Get off him." She pointed the pistol at Lewis. "Trust me, where I come from, they taught me how to use this." But her voice shook.

Lewis got up and a smile slid up his face, something sickly. "But they didn't teach you how many bullets are in a dueling pistol, did they, little girl?" He took a step toward her.

Lilly glanced at her mother, all thirteen years in her eyes as Lewis closed in.

Jinx wanted to leap too when Lewis reached her, but Esme was already there, tackling her daughter, yanking her from Lewis's grip, even as he grabbed the useless pistol and tossed it away.

Jinx turned, searched the floor for the other one.

Bennett sprawled on the marble hearth, blood pooling under his head. No—oh, God, please— She ran to him as her mother began to cry. "Please, leave us alone!"

Rosie stayed locked in the corner.

Jinx reached Bennett and pushed her hands under his head, searching for the wound. "Bennett, wake up, please, Bennett."

She put his head on her lap, not sure where the blood came from, and looked up.

Her heart caught in her throat. Esme stood in front of Lilly, wearing the look she'd seen the day she'd stood up to their father, the day she'd run away to be with Oliver.

Lewis had produced a knife and flicked it at her. He nicked it into her chest, near her heart. A bead of blood rose, trickled into her dress.

Oliver didn't move, caught five feet away. Jinx couldn't bear the agony on his face.

"You," Esme said softly, not a hint of tremor in her voice. "I recognize you. You were there the day Oliver's apartment burned." Her voice lowered to a wisp that sounded less of fear and more of fury. "You—you set the fire, didn't you? You thought Oliver was there and tried to kill him."

Lewis stiffened. "He was supposed to be there. I saw him go in. Saw his light flicker on."

"People died." Her breath seemed to be leaking out.

Lewis advanced, and Esme cried out.

"Shut up."

"No." She choked out. "It was you. You killed Foster too. You learned it from him—eliminate the man in the way. Oliver. Foster—"

"Shut up!" He grasped her throat, his fingers digging into her flesh.

Esme clawed at his fingers. "But what you don't know is that Flora would have never married you. You weren't good enough for her."

Her mother had crept behind him, and Jinx wanted to shout when she saw that she'd scavenged a leg from the destroyed chair. No, Mother—

"The police are probably wringing the truth out of Flora right now. She's probably singing your name all over the tombs—"

"Shut up!"

Phoebe slammed the leg into Lewis's head. He howled and rounded on her, but she launched herself at Esme, Phoebe's arms shielding her.

Lewis roared and tackled the both of them.

Lilly screamed as Oliver dove at the mass.

"Under me, Jinx—" Bennett came to life beneath her. He pulled out the pistol he'd fallen on, still loaded, and shoved it into her hands.

Jinx hit her feet just as Lewis straddled Oliver, both hands at his neck. Oliver clawed at him, fighting for his breath.

She would thank Foster for the one good thing he'd forced upon her.

Skeet shooting lessons.

Jinx aimed and hit Lewis square in the chest. He tumbled back, off Oliver, and hit the parquet floor with a thud.

Blood blossomed out of his chest.

Esme was weeping. Jinx stared at her in horror as Esme bent over Phoebe, rocking back and forth, her hands covered in blood. "No, please, Mother…"

Jinx dropped the gun. Stumbled over to her mother. Esme pressed her hand to the stab wound in her mother's chest, blood pouring between her fingers.

Jinx fell to her knees. "Mother, why did you do that?"

Behind her, she heard Amelia yelling, Lilly weeping. Rosie had stumbled over, now cupped her hands over her mouth, shaking. Bennett pressed a hand to the cut on the back of his head, knelt behind her.

Phoebe took Jinx's hand, touched her other to Esme's. She looked at her daughters. "I love you. Both." She nodded then, a whisper of a smile upon her face. "I love you both."

"Mother, don't you die on me. Not yet," Esme said, her voice tight. "Hold on."

Oliver had taken off his shirt, now pressed it against Phoebe's wound, but she'd started to fade. Her gaze became distant, her breaths shallow.

Oh, God, please, no…

But as Esme wept into her bosom, Phoebe's blood stained the parquet floor. Jinx gripped her cold hand she slipped away.

Jinx finally leaned down and pressed a kiss to her mother's pale cheek. "I know, Mother. I know."

Epilogue

"Jinx, it's too cold for you to be standing out here like this."

She expected his admonitions, of course, but didn't move as Bennett came up behind her and put his hands on her shoulders.

"You can't see every ship off. You don't even know if Jack's on it."

Jinx refused to let his words sting. He didn't mean them to be cruel, but—

"What if he is? What if he's one of those doughboys climbing the gang-plank, looking back to see if there's a familiar face in the crowd, loving him, praying for him as he goes into battle? I need to be here, Ben, just in case."

His hands tightened on her shoulders. "You're shivering."

"I'm fine. They're nearly finished anyway, the last have already boarded." She'd gotten as close as she could to Pier 88 and the four-stack troop ship as the three thousand-plus soldiers filed on. She hadn't really expected to see their son. But perhaps he'd see her.

Know that she missed him so desperately she could hardly breathe with the sorrow.

The November wind had long ago slipped under her mink coat, turned her legs to ice. Still, the baby in her womb kept her warm, flopping around even at five months so that he had the ability to turn her seasick.

"I'm sorry I didn't find him." Bennett said it every time, so often that she knew misery burned through him also. He'd never helped his son grow up.

Maybe never would.

Jinx squeezed his hand, unable to find the words.

So much they'd lost that day. Jack. Mother.

So much she'd also gained. Bennett. Esme and Lilly.

Freedom.

She hadn't even cared about the scandal, or her plummet from society's register. She let her seat at the opera go, put her home up for sale. She and Rosie and Bennett moved into an apartment at 927 Fifth Avenue, at the new Warren and Wetmore building.

Bennett managed to maneuver Foster's stocks into Jinx's name, despite the suspicion surrounding his death.

Flora St. John headlined at the Follies all summer long.

And Oliver and Esme finally married in a ceremony that Jinx attended as the matron of honor. She waited at the altar of Trinity Episcopal Church and smiled at her sister as she wheeled their father up the aisle.

He'd looked up twice during the service, and once, even smiled.

The gangplank began to draw in, the soldiers standing at the rail. Jinx scanned their too-young faces, most of them too far away for her to make out.

"Did you see him?" Esme joined her at the rail, her hands gloved, her long hair cut short now. "I'm sorry I'm late—we had a problem with one of the presses."

"Did you get the paper out?"

"On time." She pressed her hand upon Jinx's. "I hope you don't mind. Lilly and Rosie wanted to come."

Jinx nodded, turned, and watched as the girls exited Oliver's Studebaker. Rosie had cut her hair even shorter since Jack's disappearance. Lilly, however, still wore hers long, in two dark brown braids, the Crow in her. Still, they looked like sisters, in their sable coats down past their knees, their cloche hats. Behind them, the New York skyline caught the morning sun in the windows. A thousand shiny eyes watching their boys leave for war.

Oliver exited behind them, his face grim as he watched them walk toward the rail. "Oliver should forgive himself for Mother's death," Jinx said. "It wasn't his fault."

Esme tightened her hold on Jinx's hand. "He has a servant's heart. He can't get past the fact that his father spent his life taking care of us and yet he failed."

"He's a good man, Esme."

Lilly and Rosie joined them. Rosie stood beside Jinx, not looking at her. Someday, perhaps, Rosie would forgive her mother.

Maybe when Jinx forgave herself. Maybe it was enough, for now, knowing that God had forgiven her. In fact, only that held her together and convinced her that someday, yes, she'd see Jack again.

No one spoke as the lines were cast off, the departure horn sounding, a sad wail reverberating through the harbor, right down to her bones. Her eyes filled. "It's the not knowing that's the hardest." She leaned back against Bennett's chest. "All I do is pray that the war will end, that he'll come home."

"'O taste and see that the Lord is good: blessed is the man that trusteth in Him,'" Esme said.

Jinx drew in her words, relished them, allowed them to nurture her. *Blessed is the man that trusteth in Him.*

She watched as the troop ship slipped away from the pier. "Come back to me, Jack. I'm not going anywhere. I'll be waiting right here for you."

Author's Note

What if you could buy anything you wanted, at any time? What if you had servants to wait on your every desire...had numerous glorious homes, clothing, and jewelry...and could take extended vacations on a whim? Would you be happy? Or is there something deeper about life that money cannot buy?

In our pursuit of happiness here in America, sometimes I wonder if we've forgotten what true happiness is. Could it be something simpler? What would we give to attain it?

This question drove me as I researched the extravagance of the Gilded Age of America. During a time when most workers averaged five hundred dollars a year in salary, there thrived a portion of society—the elite Mrs. Astor's 400—who had such breathtaking wealth that they would have dinner parties costing in excess of $250,000 (and employ half the city doing so). This elite set—the Carnegies and Astors and Vanderbilts and Rockerfellers and Roosevelts and JP Morgans—ran our economy and adhered to a set of society rules that rivaled that of the royal courts of England.

But under all the glitter and gold simmered stories of adultery, murder, embezzlement, and unrest. People who weren't satisfied. People who thirsted for more out of a life that had already given them "everything."

I believe it's because they—like all of us—were searching for love. They simply didn't realize they couldn't buy it.

Into this backdrop, to explore this world, I set Jinx and Esme. Patterned after the story of Jacob and Esau, I wanted to create two daughters of wealth and power and portray the way each handled the deep longings of her heart.

I also wanted to explore what it meant to be truly blessed. Is it possible to be blessed in poverty? In wealth?

I believe it is. It's just a matter of stepping back and understanding the security, the belonging, the richness of being a child of God. Of being an Heiress of the Kingdom.

My life is deeply enriched—blessed!—by those who believed in me and helped me write this story. My deepest gratitude goes to Carlton Garborg, who believed in me enough to challenge me to write an "epic series." This is for you, big C. And Jason Rovenstine, whose enthusiasm is absolutely catchy. I am so blessed to work with Susan Downs on these novels—my former writing partner, dear friend, wise acquisitions editor. And of course, this book would have never been written without my writing therapist Rachel Hauck on the other end of the phone. (She always has the answer to: "What do I write next?") Ellen Tarver smoothed out the story so that it flowed, and Nancy Toback made this manuscript shine. What a team!

My gratitude also goes out to Bill and Lisa Pomroy, for their willingness to sit for hours as I drilled them with questions about copper mining. What a gift to me they were (I mean, really, I wasn't actually expecting an answer when I asked, "Do you know anyone who has been inside a mine?" It's just like God to provide someone nearby who answers, "I've worked in mines for twenty-five years." Wow.)

To my children David, Sarah, Peter, and Noah, who make me rich every day—even when we lived in a garage without heat or running water. You bless me when you call me Mom.

And finally, I'm so grateful to be married to a man who always makes me feel that, indeed, I am an heiress. I love you, Andrew.

Thank you again for reading! I welcome your thoughts on this story at www.SusanMayWarren.com. And look for the continuing adventures of the Price and Worth families in the next installment: *Baroness*.

Susie May

Reader Questions

1. Esme is expected to marry a man whom her parents choose, but she loves someone else. Do you think her parents were being cruel to arrange her marriage? Why or why not? What would you have done for your daughter if you lived in that era?

2. Jinx is frustrated by her sister's lack of understanding of society and believes she doesn't take her responsibilities seriously. Have you ever stood on the sidelines, watching someone behave in a way that you disagree with? Has their behavior affected your life in a significant way? Did you do something about it? Why or Why not?

3. Esme wants to prove to her father that she can write—so she first does it secretly through the letters of Anonymous Witness and then finally tells him the truth. Have you ever wanted to "prove" yourself to someone? Did you do it anonymously? What would you have done if you were Esme?

4. Does Jinx marry for love or for her family? Do you think she is right in what she does? At the end of the first section, did you believe that Jinx and Foster would have a happy marriage?

5. Jinx loses three babies to miscarriage early in the story, and her marriage is in jeopardy. Do you think this is the real cause of Foster's estrangement to her? Why do you think Foster treats her the way he does?

6. Jinx carries a terrible secret—which blossoms into a sin that she must then cover up. Was she right to stay with Foster, or should she have left him for Bennett?

7. Esme leaves her family behind and starts a new life in Montana, armed with only her jewelry. Have you ever struck out on your own to start something? Would you have had the courage to do what Esme did?

8. Esme is caught between two men with two different views of "union" life. Would you have been for or against the union back then? Now?

9. Jinx is accused of murdering Foster. Did you suspect someone else? Who? Were you surprised to discover the identity of the new Chronicle publisher?

10. Jinx and Esme both struggle with the word, "Blessing." What understanding of the word do they come to? What do you think will happen next in the Price/Worth family story?

About the Author

 SUSAN MAY WARREN is the best-selling author of more than thirty novels whose compelling plots and unforgettable characters have earned her acclaim from readers and reviewers alike. She is a winner of the ACFW Carol Award, the RITA Award, and the Inspirational Readers Choice Award and a nominee for the Christy Award. She loves to write and to help other writers find their voices through her work with My Book Therapy (www.mybooktherapy.com), a writing craft and coaching community she founded.

Susan and her husband of more than twenty years have four children. Former missionaries to Russia, they now live in a small Minnesota town on the shore of beautiful Lake Superior, where they are active in their local church. Find her online at www.susanmaywarren.com.